ALL SYSTEMS DOWN

BA ANDERSON

Consigliere Publishing

DEDICATION

This work of fiction is dedicated to Pat Donohue, my lifelong friend. He appears as the inspiration for one character, and he was one of the first people to read this in its entirety. He passed away June 24, 2016.

ACKNOWLEDGMENTS

I would like to acknowledge the assistance of my family. MJ, whose help, encouragement, and editing advice made this project more than just a lark. Dennis, who encouraged me and made me believe maybe I could write. Randi, for her reading and editing suggestions. Colleen, while too dangerous as an editor, inspired me by her dogged pursuit of writing. Finally I was most inspired by seeing the results of lazy writing in television and movies.

PROLOGUE

By the spring of 2020 the world had undergone years of calamity, disasters, and screw-ups -- some mother nature, some human generated. Coastal cities began depopulating as sea levels rose; global food shortages generated political instability. The food shortages were born of compounding catastrophes: pesticide overuse caused Colony Collapse Disorder in honey bees, drought caused by global warming, and soil salinization. Small countries in Africa were warring over lack of growing space. Food supplies remained weak and the world was perpetually on the brink of starvation, at least in the poorer parts. Food riots were becoming commonplace in many countries, including members of the G-20.

There had been political unrest, rebellions, and wars. Wars in the Middle East had been frequent, bloody, and indecisive. To many people's surprise Israel did not get directly involved, not overtly anyway. The unrest drove up oil costs, making a few people very wealthy. The instability worked to the advantage of all the oil producing countries.

There had been natural disasters too. Massive solar storms caused long blackout periods in Europe. This had caused the fragile European economy to accelerate the tailspin it had already started into after Brexit. The Eurozone had since disintegrated.

In Asia, there had been a massive earthquake creating

another tsunami, destroying most of Japan's microprocessor chip production capacity. China had stepped up to fill the gap for a few years, but the Western governments, very leery about buying Chinese-made microchips, eventually bought the chips only to discover secret backdoors. This caused a worldwide microchip shortage, which meant everything from fridges, to cars, to critical infrastructure did not get repaired in a timely fashion. The whole world was suffering, yet the wealth of the 1% increased until they controlled 70% of the worlds wealth.

The one calamity which out-shone all the others, The Chinese-Russian war in 2016, became a world wide disaster even though the fighting never went beyond their borders and no other countries got directly involved. It had become a 'limited' nuclear war – limited because neither side nuked the other's population bases. But Electromagnetic Pulse attacks had been used. This caused Chinese tech production to shut down. With Japan's production already suffering, this meant much more to the world than no more iPads or cell phones. Frequent disruptions for every modern economy were commonplace. Everything from banking to vehicle registrations was affected.

The global shortage had become so serious it once again became profitable to build production facilities in North America. By 2020 those were just starting to come online. The Sino-Russian war had ended without a treaty or any settlement, the fighting just seemed to stop. It was like when two bar brawlers were too tired to continue but they still hated each other, and neither would admit defeat. Their little war brought the world economy into the largest contraction in history. Manufacturing capacity in Pakistan and India also suffered. In short,the whole world's microelectronic production capacity had been reduced to less than half in one year. This left the world very fragile.

ONE

"No arts; no letters; no society; and which is worst of all, continual fear and danger of violent death; and the life of man solitary, poor, nasty, brutish, and short."

- Thomas Hobbes, Leviathan

"Hey Rosie, come on in." Jim Alderson invited his former student in to his windowless office. Rosie, a student with a difficult family life who had moved on to high school last year, came to visit him at the end of the school day.

"Hey Alderson, I am really pissed at the school," she said in her slightly manic manner.

Noting her increased energy, edgy attitude, and animated speech, Alderson knew something was again going wrong in her life. A year of daily visits to his office had allowed Alderson to get to know her very well. Just keeping her in school and attempting to function, or motivated just to arrive had been a daily routine in that last year. Getting to know some students very well was one of the advantages of his counseling role at the school.

Although it was a busy time for Alderson, former students often visited in May. They were starting exams in

1

high school, regular classes were finishing, giving them extra time off from school. Alderson needed the distraction from planning for the next year, a mundane, tedious, but complicated task. It was an opportunity to rest his eyes and clear his head. Times for the school were tough, making planning a more difficult task. The government had cut resources again, meaning fewer teachers for the same number of students. Regardless, he always had time for Rosie.

Rosie's animated demeanor told Alderson something was going on with her, some life crisis. She came to him, one of the few adults she trusted, for advice. This would probably be a long visit.

Rosie bee-lined to the cabinet door, a habit she had from the past year, looking for the coconut macaroons she knew he kept there, turning back to him with a macaroon in hand. "Hey Alderson I know you might be mad at me. I haven't really been attending classes. I have been doing fuck-all at school." She started the conversation. The pretty, pale-skinned, 16 year old looked at Alderson with that defiant look Alderson knew well.

She is looking for a reaction. Another test, students like her had to test to see if the relationship would break, or if he would judge her, criticize her, or lecture her like everyone else did.

"Rosie you know I am not mad at you, but I'd like to help you find a better way. You know I want you to do well in school. I'm guessing things are mmm... not working at home."

"Not working! Why don't you just say they're shit. Once I get away from home I'll focus better, I'll get back into school. My mother is being a cunt." She looked at Alderson smiling, seeking confirmation.

Alderson opened his mouth to speak when his office went dark. His computer screen flashed white then faded to black, there were popping sounds from the library next door, and sudden quiet, the only light filtered in from the library windows to his open inner door.

"Ah! That scared me," exclaimed Rosie.

Alderson looked around, his eyes adjusting to the semi-darkness. "Damn another power outage. Probably lost the report I was working on. This outage looks like a big one, it popped the lights in the library. Some kind of surge." Jim thought for a minute, his laptop battery should still work in a power outage. It had a power bar with a fuse so it should have been safe from power surges. Before he drew the next conclusion, Rosie interrupted his thoughts.

"Is this one of those "imp" thingys you told me about last year, like what happened to the Chinese and Russians?" she asked, her lower lip quavering. "Those are really bad aren't they?"

Alderson remembered the conversation with Rosie which had freaked her out. He had explained to her how an EMP, Electromagnetic Pulse, could end the world as they knew it. Jim could see her looking to him for a quick explanation, looking to him for hope. She normally had a slight smile with the petulant look of a someone who always gets her way but now, eyes widening, she gulped – the smile gone, escalating terror visible on her face.

Power blackouts had become commonplace in the last few years. Distinguishing between a regular power outage and an EMP should be simple; they just had to go outside and observe. Alderson stood up, hugged her and said, "Things will be okay, but let's go take a look." Opening his office door, Alderson scanned the dark hallway, no emergency lights; phones in the school being dead would be normal; the laptop and emergency lights should have survived, this was not looking good.

He thrust his hand into a desk drawer and grabbed the flashlight he had stored there, and flicked it on. It worked.

Rosie stayed close as he walked into the main hall toward the front door. There was a bobbing light from behind them, turning he saw Angela, a young Phys Ed teacher coming toward them. Her shoulder-length blonde hair, impeccable figure, and gentle personality made her a heartthrob for all the teen boys, and the cynosure of male eyes.

"Hey Mr. Alderson, it looks like another power outage," Angela called to him.

"Yeah, I'm going to have a look outside and see what's going on," he called down the hall.

"I'll be in the library," she called back. It was an hour after school, all students were gone, only a few staff remained.

A follower of history and a closet paranoid, Alderson knew enough about EMP to know what would happen, however he could not fathom why it would happen now. The wars were over, the whole world was staggering and just starting to recover, there weren't any ongoing disputes with major powers, so he did not, could not, believe an EMP would happen now. He hoped it was a giant solar storm, or a power station blew up, or massive lightning strike, even a terrorist attack on the power grid, something repairable, a continent-wide EMP would be much more devastating.

Taking a few steps outside, Alderson and Rosie looked around. Rosie pointed, "Look, Alderson, that car is stopped in the middle of the road!" she said with clipped, higher pitched voice. "Oh my god, it *is* one of those EMP things isn't it?" Grabbing his arm, moving closer, he felt her fingernails digging into his flesh. She squeezed hard, her breathing was ragged, he could sense her impending panic.

Normally a confident, even brash girl, she was on the edge. Alderson was normally a very even-keel person, now his mind raced with a million possibilities, all bad, all apocalyptic. Rosie had once asked Alderson about 2012 and why many people had believed the Mayans' prophecy about the end of the world. He had the given her his theories about the end of the world, he just never believed anything would really happen, at least not in his lifetime.

"I know it's scary Rosie, but let's get more info, find out how bad things are," Alderson said in a quiet, controlled voice. "It might not be so bad, could have been sunspots or something else." He, breathed deeply and tried to appear calm, suppressing his own spiking fears.

Then it hit him – quiet. Abnormal quiet, a quiet never heard in a large metropolitan area. Absent was the hustle and bustle of the big city; absent were the sounds planes, trains, and automobiles make. Only people, bird, and dog sounds remained. Coronal Mass Ejections, giant solar storms, would not stop the cars in their tracks, only an EMP would, at least as far as Alderson knew. "We should walk a bit and see what is happening on 26th," he said, getting them both moving.

Holding his arm Rosie whispered, "I'm really scared Alderson, what's going to happen?" She held close to him.

Alderson knew she liked being with him, he always listened, never judged her, even when she got into drugs, hung out with sketchy street kids, or skipped school. But now, he thought, she is looking to me for security. Security in this future would be difficult. He hoped he wouldn't let her down.

"If this is the end of the world, I'm glad I'm with you."

"I know Rosie, I'm glad you're here and not somewhere more dangerous. Let's walk to the train line and get a better view of what's happening," he replied, trying not to let his own fear show. Walking along it became clear, more dead cars, people outside their cars talking with each other, some trying to make cell phones work, most just looking stunned, anxious, verging on panic stricken. Some even actively worked on their cars in a vain attempt to make them run.

"If it is an EMP, would planes still fly?" Rosie said pointing up. Seeing planes overhead was common as the school was located on a flight path for the airport.

He looked where she pointed and saw a silent large-bodied aircraft much lower than it should be. "Oh fuck, oh god, Rosie it's going to crash!"

Looking at him, shocked, she had never heard him swear before, but they had never been near a plane coming down overhead before either. Alderson was going into stomach-churning panic. "We have to call the police, fire trucks, ambulance, or something," she squeaked out.

Screams rose as other people watched the plane in its silent, surreal descent toward a crowded roadway. The plane must have been on approach to land, now it was losing altitude way too fast, it would not make it to the runway.

Rosie started to run toward where it would hit.

"No!" Alderson yelled as he grabbed her wrist, "Come with me."

"Maybe we can help, I have to see," she yelled, pulling hard.

"There will be a fireball and if it hits the road there will be cars burning and exploding too."

Rosie looked at him in horror.

"It's too dangerous, we can't help without equipment. Stay with me Rosie, back to the school!" She looked ready to cry. "Run!" he yelled, more to get her unstuck than from fear of damage from the plane.

They ran toward the school a hundred yards and then slowed to a quick walk. Rosie stopped and grabbed Alderson, saying "Are they going to kill us all, will they nuke us like what happened to the Russians and Chinese?" The usually strong, confident, girl blinked her eyes rapidly, holding back tears. "What the fuck, Alderson, I don't want to die!"

"You won't be dying, I don't think we will get nuked. But I don't know why this happened Rosie. I do know I need to get some things from the school. I'll help you get home, I'll get you there safe." His mind raced, things would not be lawless yet, the law should hold a few days, because people would *choose* to respect the law. Police would have little ability to control problems with limited mobility and communications. Whether anyone else knew it as yet, Alderson knew each person would be a law unto themselves in short order. A city of a million people would be thrust into a state of nature.

Rosie cried, "No, I want to stay with you, my mother is a useless cunt."

Rosie was right about her mother, Alderson knew her mother well enough to know she would not grasp the magnitude of this situation, she would be no help to Rosie. Her mother would want to control Rosie, not deal with the immediate survival problems. A pretty girl like Rosie would be a target as soon as lowlifes realized there was no law, no cameras, and small chance they would face consequences. She would be vulnerable. Rosie viewed herself as a tough street kid but she wasn't tough enough for this reality, nobody was. Survival meant being part of a smart group.

"Rosie, you should be going home, your mom is your legal guardian." Alderson attempted to officially do the right thing, even though he knew it was not the best thing. He knew it would be weeks at best for order to be restored, probably years, but he was trying to follow protocol, just in case.

Standing there, paralyzed in thought, wavering between doing what he was supposed to do and the right thing, Alderson resolved to take Rosie with him. There would be a lot of dying before order was restored, Alderson wasn't going to be a casualty -- and he wasn't going to let Rosie be one either. A loud boom snapped him back to the present. They both looked north. Billowing oily black smoke leapt and roiled above the homes, a conflagration erupting where the plane had come down. People on the street screamed and pointed, some ran toward it.

"No fucking way, I'm staying with you!" Rosie ordered emphatically.

"Okay", Alderson agreed, voicing where he had already

gone mentally. "Okay, I'll keep you safe as much as I can," knowing it was the better choice for Rosie anyway.

Alderson's mind raced as they walked back. Finding out the extent of the damage caused by the EMP would be very difficult, it could be as small as several hundred kilometres radius, or as large as several thousand. Services could be back in a month or two, but if it affected most of the populous parts of North America, it could be years to be returned to a semblance of normal. Acting as though it were the worst case scenario was just prudent, Alderson figured. The government and police never coming back was the most likely result, at least not as they had been known. The police would protect those up the food chain, maintaining government is their first mandate; general order would devolve to the lowest common denominator in a few days, or weeks at the most. Having a community that worked together would be key.

At the school they found two teachers out front and two grade seven students who had been playing outside standing chatting.

Alderson directed them, "Hey everyone, let's go into the library."

"Mr. Alderson should we come in?" asked Di, a student, "We were just hanging around."

"Yes, I think everyone should come in." he directed. Light filtered in through the library windows. "Blake and Angela can you round up anyone else in the building and bring them here?" he asked. Frowns of worry and wrinkled brows showed the stress developing in everyone, no one questioned Alderson. Flashlights in hand, they nodded and went off through the school. Once they were all together, there were five teachers, two current grade seven students

9

and one former student.

"Cat, you live quite close to the school, don't you? Are your parents at home?" Alderson asked.

"Yeah, just a block away. I think they're home."

"Then you should go to them, they'll be worried. Can Di go with you?" he asked.

Cat grimaced. "My mom doesn't like Di so it probably isn't a good idea."

"Okay then, you should go home." Alderson felt bad sending her home because he was sure he knew how bad things were going to get, but this was best, her parents were good and would worry about her. "We will make sure Di is safe," he added.

Cat gathered her things skipped out the door. "Bye Di, see you tomorrow."

"Bye Cat," Alderson and Angela called out. Alderson didn't want to crush Cat with what was likely to be coming. He believed there would be no more school. "Di, where do you live?" he asked.

"In Whitehorn by the LRT tracks," the little blonde waif replied, unknowing about the possible fate of houses in that area. "Did something bad happen?"

Whitehorn was the next district north, with the LRT, rapid transit train station just north of a shopping centre. A fifteen-minute walk, but also where the plane had gone down. Alderson didn't know if she read the lurch in his stomach or she was just frightened, because she began to whimper.

Angela took her close and held on to her.

"Okay everyone, I am pretty sure this isn't just a power outage, this is way worse. I believe it is an Electromagnetic Pulse or EMP. Like what happened in China and Russia during the war. A power blackout does not cause planes to crash or cars to stop, and that's just what happened. It also means someone launched an attack. This might not have even been intended for Canada but EMP doesn't stop at borders. What I do know is we are in a pile of shit right now. Oops, sorry Di."

"If I am right this means our cars won't work even though they weren't turned on. We will be walking home across the city. There will be risk every step of the way. Blake, Charlene, I know you two live close to each other and you want to get to your families. We need to prepare for a hike across the city. We should break open the vending machines and fridges and take what food we need. We will be traveling for hours to get home. Going to the foods lab and the shop to collect things for weapons would also be wise. Take what back packs you can find and load them."

"Weapons, really Jim? Do you think people will be like that right away?" Blake asked.

"Jim, shouldn't we just wait for power to come back or the authorities to make some announcements?" Jolene, a young, single teacher interrupted. "Surely we won't need weapons?"

"I think this is a major EMP attack, authorities might not even be able to make announcements before things get much worse. You won't be able to call for help regardless of what happens. You will only be as safe as you make yourself. Unlike sunspots, EMP destroys much more than just the power grid, it fries microelectronics in anything that was exposed with power in it. All the cars, trains, and planes have stopped moving outside. Phones are dead. The power surge from an EMP can even travel through buried cables. Weapons are a precaution, I don't think you'll have to fight your way home."

He looked around. "Does anybody's cell work? Sunspots usually won't affect the electronics in buildings except by power surge. If I am right, and I think I am, we are in for long term pain."

Everyone checked their cell phones, Blake blurted out, "Mine is working, but I can't get a signal, including the wireless." Alderson's still worked as well.

"Where were you and your cell phone when the power went out?" Jim queried.

"I was in the main office."

"That's why, the office is a cell signal dead zone which likely protected it against the EMP. Take it to the window and see if you get a signal."

Blake did, still no signal, he just shook his head.

"I suggest you take the battery out, just in case and you may be able to use the apps later, but I suspect it will be a long time before it will be usable as a phone. If any of you are as scared as I am, we need to take action."

Everyone sat stunned. "Angela and Jolene you live in the same general area I live in, we should travel together. I have some critical supplies in my SUV, and by the way, we should check our cars see if they work." Alderson acted like a general enacting a battle plan. Alderson's only advantage was he had thought about events like this for years and he kept a pile of survival supplies in his vehicle.

"Jim, why should we check our cars, you said all the traffic was stopped outside?" Jolene asked.

"Well there's a chance I'm wrong and things which were turned off would not be as affected, or being close to the school's walls might have made a difference, it's worth a check."

He continued, "Blake and Charlene I know you live a long ways but if you need to escape the city out once you get there, I will set up at Bowness park or near the river there for a few days. It's a good location, close to the edge of the city and with the river right there gives water, sewage disposal and transport. If I can't stay there I will leave a spray painted message which will start with NNS (for Naheed Nenshi School)."

Jolene spoke up for everyone and asked, "Jim why do you seem to be so far ahead in thinking about this? It sounds like you planned ahead for this."

"Well it might be just because I am a bit paranoid and have often thought about it. But I never imagined it would really happen. Just because I'm paranoid doesn't mean the world isn't out to get us," he quipped. "Look, I don't want to be an alarmist, but you should be alarmed. This is seriously bad news. This is likely to be the worst disaster you'll ever face. In short order the city will not be liveable. Within a day sewage and water may fail to flow. If we're lucky the city has emergency generators which weren't damaged but don't bet the farm on it. Nobody here knows how bad it will be, maybe the Russians or Chinese could tell us but I lost their phone number, so we can't ask. There will be law and order only until the nasty types figure out there will be no response from police. Don't trust anyone without reason."

"Jim do you really think this will be that big a disaster? I mean, blackouts are common and something like sunspots would take a week or two to get back on track. This is all sounding a little extreme and it sounds like you're a little too paranoid." Blake voiced questions everyone had.

"Did you hear that explosion a few minutes ago?" Alderson asked.

"Yeah, what was it?" Charlene queried.

"When we went outside and walked north, there was a wide-bodied jet on what looked like landing approach, but it was way too low and had no engine noise. I am quite sure it was the plane crashing you heard." Alderson added, "If you go outside and listen now it's what you don't hear that's the problem, not a single siren. I will admit I could be wrong, the government could have a plan to get the city functioning. But if I'm right, every minute we wait will make things harder for us."

"Jim you are scaring us a little," Charlene added with a nervous chuckle, looking around at the others. Blake looked a little skeptical, Angela and Jolene had wide-eyed, near panicked looks.

"Look, all the signs suggest an EMP. What we know about EMP is the more electronics we use, the worse it will be for us. However, I can tell you it missed being as damaging as some predicted. Some cell phones are still working. It may be more things and back-ups are working than I think, but transportation will be a problem and without it a big city like

Calgary will start starving. Even if we had power systems, it would take weeks just to remove the dead cars." Jim was worried that every minute wasted increased their risk.

Angela asked, "How will we contact our friends and family?"

"That'll be very difficult Angela, and I don't have a good answer," Jim added in a sombre voice. "Look, on our way we will stop at the hospital and see if the emergency generator is on. If it's working this may not be a worst case scenario. If it is no go, we're be in bad shape. But even if there are working generators, infrastructure components may be damaged so power delivery may be sporadic at best." At this point Rosie, Jolene, and Angela were in tears.

"I'm so sc-scared," Rosie quavered.

Jolene sobbed, "What about my babies?" She referred to her dogs, a German Shepherd and a Rottweiler.

"Jolene, we need to get your dogs, but it means making the trek across the city," he said, which seemed to brighten her up, "It will take us hours to get there."

"Get what food and water you need for a long hike," Alderson said as he started gathering food and drink from the school stores, hoping the action would get people's minds off the disaster moving into the here and now. The others followed and filled some packs.

In thirty minutes they were as ready as they were going to be. The air was poor in the school and the smell of burning petroleum started to come in.

They all tested their vehicles, Angela trying hers first:

"My car is completely dead and it's brand new." All the vehicles tested dead.

"Collect any gear which could be useful including tire irons, and if there is a hydraulic jack take it," Alderson said as he loaded his survival gear into a backpack. Jolene pulled out a jack and some tools and had a large bag with her. "What do you have in the bag?" Alderson asked.

"Oh just my usual stuff, books, marking, you know." Looking at Alderson and the others a look of despair came over her face and she sighed, shoulders slumped. "I guess I should just leave that stuff." She tossed the bag in the car, then she emptied the bag, and kept it with her. She locked the car behind her.

Distributing the gear among them, they then began walking across the field between two schools. Had the situation been different it would have been a nice walk in the awakening springtime. Mid-May in Calgary is when things truly begin to leaf out and grow, birds were singing, bees buzzing, the occasional cat watching or dog barking; it appeared so normal, but it was surreal in the context of the end of the world. There were people milling about, talking, crying, pointing at the flames and smoke, frantically waving their arms; all were very tense.

Waving at some students and their families, Alderson felt bad about not taking them, or stopping to explain, but managing a large group would be too much and what he knew was just speculation at this point. He hoped their families were competent to survive, or at least as competent anyone else in this situation. He knew that if this went on for months many would die. *If I were at home I would not be moving so hastily, I understand their lack of action. I am sure most people believe things are going to get better,"* he thought. Alderson was a little less blasé, his reputation of being a bit paranoid was now an asset. Being paranoid looked like a good strategy.

His wife would be thinking about the ramifications more than most people, just because she lived with him. She might wait for him but not knowing how long it would be before he got home, he hoped she might take action quickly. Learning to shoot and handle guns might just pay off for her now, too.

"Di, you will have to show us where you live," Angela asked her.

The girl looked north and a little west, her face grimacing a touch. She pointed at the column of fire and smoke from the plane crash, "Near there."

On the main road, the scene was something from a disaster movie. The overpass to the LRT station was smashed, nearby houses aflame, grass scorched around several houses, people yelling, running in and out of the burning buildings. Cars on the road were burning, one had already exploded, others would likely go off too.

Di began to run, then stopped, "My house is burning, help me. My parents! Help! Mr. Alderson, Miss Knight please help me!" Frenzied, panicking, she began running toward the burning houses.

Taking a few quick steps, Alderson caught her by the arm. "No Di, it's dangerous, I'll help them if I can. You stay here. Which one is it?" he asked, holding her head to look at him, distracting her from the scene.

"That one, the blue one!" she cried.

"Angela keep her here and give me the axe." He took the axe and a mask, which didn't work so well over his long goatee, he was wishing now he had shaved off his beard. Stripping off his nylon shell, moving forward toward the house, he readied the axe to break the doors. He had a fire extinguisher, but it was too small to use on this fire.

Approaching from the front, he saw something sticking out the back that caught his attention. It might have been part of a car, he couldn't tell, but if it was only the back of the house that was burning, there might be hope. The front door was locked. Turning around, he mule-kicked it, driving with all his force. He heard wood splintering, the door gave in. "Anyone in here!" he screamed as his eyes teared up with smoke.

Moving through the main floor as best he could, he moved toward the stairs facing the intense heat, sweat already pouring off him, yelling as he went. A loud crash upstairs told him he didn't have long. Half way up, a smoldering corpse lay, the stench of burning flesh in the air, the victim looking like he had burning fuel on him when he ran toward the stairs. The walls were aflame with a roiling blaze crawling higher, forcing Alderson back. *What a way to go,* Alderson thought as he coughed the acrid, oily fumes from his lungs despite the mask.

Running down, he found the access to the basement and spied another body partly under a collapsed rear wall. He recognized Di's mother. He grabbed her hands and started pulling, she wouldn't budge. Coughing and gasping for good air, he hacked at the wall stud which held her in place. Then, tossing his axe behind him out the door, he grabbed her arms and heaved, dragging her outside, not even knowing if she was alive.

Stripping the mask off and gasping for air, Alderson checked the woman for a pulse. None. Breathing, none. Checking the body for wounds, he saw it, a large wood spike through her inner thigh, her pants blood-soaked. She had bled out from her femoral artery long before he arrived. Seeing Di and Angela running towards him, Alderson stood up. He snatched Di into the air in a tight embrace, "Hold on Di. Don't look at her," he said in vain, knowing he couldn't soften the blow.

Squirming loose, the tiny girl ran to her mother's corpse. Already sobbing, she probably knew when she saw Alderson dragging her mom out. "Where's my dad? Where is he?" she yelled through her sobs.

Alderson bent over and held the slight twelve year-old close to him, "Di, did anyone else live with you? "

"Just my big brother but he is away right now. D-did you see my D-dad?" she asked between sobs.

"I don't think your Dad made it either Di, I'm so sorry. I saw a man on the stairs, it must have been him, I'm sorry Di," Alderson held her while she cried.

Angela joined them and held Di close.

"I think we have to move from here," Angela said. "The fire seems to be spreading."

Looking up, Alderson nodded to Angela. "Yes, let's move."

"Di, we have to move now, stay with us," Angela said.

Crying inconsolably, Di took Angela's hand and started

walking.

Neighbours, who had been trying to stop the grass fires, came over. "What happened Di?" an East Indian woman asked. Di just cried and pointed at her mother, unable to get words out.

Jolene answered for her, "Her parents were killed in that fire. We'll take care of her for now. We're teachers from her school. Her only other family was out of town."

"This is terrible, we can take care of her. Why are there no fire trucks? We could not call, our phone does not work," the woman offered in a thick accent.

Looking up between sobs, Di answered, "It's okay Mrs. Patel, I,I, I'll stay with my teachers for now."

"There will be an emergency centre at the school or the hospital we hope?" Mrs. Patel asked.

Alderson glanced back at the corpse, a shiver ran through his body. Alderson hated dead bodies, dead things of any kind, dealing with a dead mouse was traumatic for him. He worked to regain composure. "I hope so too Mrs. Patel, but we will look after Di for now." Secretly he was not betting on any real government response. Canada did not have enough military to deal with anything like this. Calgary had some limited reserve and militia units, but no major equipment or anything. Looking around, he realized the axe he had tossed out the door would soon burn, flames were engulfing the whole house now. He ran back to grab it, but intense heat forced him to retreat. He could get another axe.

As they walked away, Rosie took up Di's other hand, it was a tender side of Rosie which Alderson liked.

"Okay Jim, which way do you think we should go?" asked Jolene.

"My vote is south to the Canadian Tire, there's useful stuff there, maybe bikes." Canadian Tire was a store that sold everything except groceries.

"Will they be open still?" Angela asked.

"I have to explain something and this will not sound good," Alderson answered. "I think to survive we are going to have to steal, and maybe threaten, to get things. Some stores will still accept cash, if they're fools, but if places do not accept cash we may have to just take what we need. We need bikes to get us home. I doubt we have enough cash between us. I don't want to start thieving from other survivors, they need their stuff to live. Companies are different, it won't hurt anyone personally to take stuff from there. I have only $100 in cash, not enough to buy everything but I will try to negotiate," he said.

Bewildered, the others just nodded their assent, not really believing it would get that bad, and started walking south past the throngs of dazed people, many moving toward the fires. Alderson felt bad about leaving the fires but with no water or equipment there was little that could be done.

As they passed the hospital, diesel exhaust smoke could be seen coming out of the roof. This was a good sign; the emergency generator worked. Pointing it out first, Rosie asked, "That's good isn't it? You said if the hospital had power it was a good sign, we should go in and see if they have information."

"You're right Rosie. Let's do that," Alderson answered.

People were streaming in, nurses, doctors and staff, some dragging supplies like bottled water, others yelling instructions; the hospital was a scene of disarray, chaos in every direction. Patients waited in the halls or outside. However, it was not as bad as it could have been -- there was power, and they were able to care for the worst-off patients. After waiting ten minutes at the info booth, Jolene asked the volunteer at the desk, "Does anyone have any information about this disaster?"

The old woman eyes drooping, leaning on the desktop, looked at Jolene and said, "We are pretty sure it's an EMP. We are getting the emergency communication gear up and running but so far we've heard nothing. We will create a message board and post information out front when we have some. Right now we are using power for critical operations so we won't be printing anything on computers." Just then, she got a call on the in-house phone system, listened a bit then hung up. She took out sheets of paper and started writing a poster.

Expect Delays with All Emergency Services.

Emergency power 2 hours/day starting tomorrow.

Curfew from 9 pm to 9 am.

Non-emergency personnel must return home.

Await further communications from authorities.

Alderson thought to himself, that's good response but the police will not be able to control much. There are 2000 cops for 1.2 million people, no transport and poor communications, lawlessness will begin soon. The apparent organization was a hopeful sign, but it would still be a while before things could come close to normalizing.

"I doubt they will get power up and running that fast, even if the power stations produce, there are likely downed wires. Those will take a while to fix. As we travel we should look for old, old cars, pre 1980, or perhaps underground garages. I am guessing maybe cars stored in those places might still work." Alderson was musing, but speaking out loud.

"How will we get those cars?" asked Rosie.

"I guess we will ask nicely or Mr. Alderson will use his disarming charm," Angela quipped. They all snorted a little.

Alderson had been told that people often found him intimidating. They cited his facial expression, powerful build, or bald head and goatee. Nobody ever figured him for a teacher, let alone a counsellor type. Angela could have been making a double entendre, she knew he had the skills to disarm people physically, since he was well trained in martial arts.

"Hey Alderson," interjected Rosie, "You know Carrie is working at the mall today?"

"Really? I guess I should go see her. The rest of you keep going to Canadian Tire. I will meet you out front of the store."

"Hey dude, she's my friend, I'm coming with you," Rosie said.

"Okay then, let's go talk to her." This meant a slight detour but he needed to do it. Carrie was another young, attractive, former student. She was a very nice person with a very good heart. Like most teens she made some bad choices at times, but she needed to know what he knew about the new world order.

Outside the mall doors, in a crowd of people smoking -- mostly employees from inside -- they found Carrie, smoking and chatting with the others.

Seeing Alderson and Rosie approach, Carrie dropped her cigarette and ran over to them with a big smile. "Alderson!" she said as she hugged him. "Rosie!" she exclaimed hugging Rosie and kissing her.

"Carrie, I am so glad we found you," he said, returning her infectious smile. She always smiled, even when things were going bad for her. "Carrie, lets go talk a bit. Something big has happened."

"You have to listen to him Carrie, this is some bad shit, he knows." Rosie added.

"Carrie, this is not just a simple power outage, I think you should leave here. It'll be hard to work with no power anyway. This thing is serious, you should head home while it is safe. Where is your dad? Is he at work or at home?"

Carrie looked at Rosie, then back to Alderson her perpetual smile fading, biting her lip. "He is visiting my aunt in Lethbridge, do you think something bad happened to him?"

"I doubt it Carrie, but this event probably happened there and everywhere south of Calgary too. It could be a long time before you are reunited unless you're going to walk there or he's going to walk here. You should come with us," Alderson suggested.

"How did you end up with Alderson?" Carrie asked, looking at Rosie.

"I was visiting him at the school when this shit happened."

"Cool, I'm with you. I should go tell my boss, I am going to see if he can give me my pay in cash too."

"Good idea Carrie, cash has only a couple days before it is useless, unless they get things working again," Alderson agreed.

Skipping off and up the stairs into the mall, she returned ten minutes later, "He would only give me half, about 400 bucks."

Alderson grinned "That makes you the richest member right now Carrie, but we may need to pool cash to get everyone through."

"No prob, I know you are good for it," she grinned.

At the Canadian Tire store they found the others watching. They could see a manager standing just inside the doors turning people away. Most of his employees were outside. The mechanics were busy trying to get some cars running in the parking lot.

Alderson took off his pack and cut it along the bottom left side where he could slide the machete upside down into the pack, keeping the machete mostly concealed, yet ready to be drawn. The others looked at him quizzically.

"The element of surprise can be critical," he answered the questioning looks. "I will talk with the manager and see if

I can get in. Wait and watch. If I have to use serious persuasion you might want to wait to follow me. I know this is not good, but we have to do it. This manager won't lose out if a few things are taken."

The pack slung on his left shoulder, Alderson approached the manager. Alderson canted his body to keep the machete handle behind him and out of sight. "Hey, I want to buy some bikes, can I get in?" Alderson asked.

The manager was a large guy, six foot one maybe 230, built like a marshmallow with the figure of a pear, mid thirties. "No we're closed, no power, can't do any transactions." He held what looked like an AR, or assault rifle. Alderson, being a shooter, spotted the markings telling him it was an Airsoft gun, not a real firearm.

"What's with the paintball, you going to a nerd shoot?" Alderson asked.

"It's not paintball, Airsoft, it hurts more," the big guy replied.

"Sure but it just hurts, doesn't stop anyone." Alderson added, "What are you so worried about, are you the owner?"

The manager shifted his feet and looked away, "Pff, no just the third in charge, but we are still -- no light or cash registers, it would be unsafe to let you in"

"No biggie I have light" Alderson showed him a flashlight. "Hey dude I have some cash, I would even leave a credit card for what I buy with ID if you like." Alderson had a feeling this guy might be intractable. That might force Alderson to make a threat, a path he preferred not to tread, yet.

"No, we're closed, please leave."

Reading the manager's name tag, Alderson kept talking, moving closer and trying to take a conspiratorial tone. "Hey Kareem, do you realize how serious this outage is? This is not just a power failure. Power failures don't kill cars. This," he said, waving his hand to the parking lot, "is what happens after a nuke. It's called an EMP. Somebody dropped a nuke near us. I know about this, I was in military intelligence. It's gonna be months before power is on. Look, you and I both need to take what we can get, and bug out. This is no joke." Alderson looked Kareem in the eye, using what he hoped was his steeliest look, adding the lie about his background for credibility. "If you are not the owner, don't worry, they're insured."

The manager blanched, starting to sweat, colour draining from his face. "Are you serious? I have heard about EMP, but how could it happen here, who would do it?"

Alderson could see Kareem begin to shake a little, his breathing ragged as he gulped twice.

Relieved he was making headway, Alderson breathed, thinking he might be able to talk his way into some goods. "I don't know who might have done it, that doesn't even concern me, what concerns me is how I, and those with me, are going to survive. Everyone who stays in the city for any time is going to be in for a pile of ugly. Look dude, work with me, you can join our plan or make your own escape, get out and warn your friends, your employees," Alderson said.

Alderson imagined Kareem's internal dialogue as he stared at Alderson in disbelief,"*Fuck me, if I go with this guy and loot the store I am fucked for my job, but if he's right there is no job left.*" Alderson watched Kareem agonize and chew his lip, it was a terrible decision for him.

"Okay but I will take the credit card just in case I might still need a job in the near future," he croaked out, his voice hoarse and dry.

Alderson waved the others in and took out his AMEX Platinum, and handed it to Kareem. Alderson turned and gave directions: "Okay everyone, first, find a suitable bike and helmet, good packs, sleeping bags, cold weather ones, some tents, and all kinds of survival gear. Don't worry about food we will get that as we go. Tire pumps for the bikes and extra tubes and patch kits"

Kareem, looking stunned by the rapidity with which Alderson got things going, stood there watching. To any observer Alderson looked like he had a well-thought out plan. It smacked of military precision, but Alderson was going on gut instinct alone, choosing action over panic.

Kareem, watching Alderson, got drawn into the dour efficiency and interjected, "I am going to get my girlfriend I will be back in fifteen minutes, don't leave without me, please. I don't know what to do, but I am going to go with you." He grabbed a bike and bolted out but he stopped long enough to tell the employees, to go home and get what they needed.

Alderson, loading bike panniers with knives, machetes, and ammunition, moved like a man driven. He grabbed an Airsoft pistol, the realistic look would provide some intimidation factor. The others, tentative about looting, hesitated, needing Alderson to reassure them it would all be paid for by his credit card when systems returned. "You just have to write things down," he said to them, knowing it would be meaningless.

Kareem returned, a stunning, petite, dark-haired girl with him on his bike. She looked to be in her twenties. "This is Arya," Kareem introduced her. "Sweetheart, get the stuff he's saying." He grinned, seeing the Airsoft gun, "It might not fool you, but it will fool some people."

"Roger that," Alderson agreed.

The small group gathered their gear, and mounted up ready to ride. "By the way, I do have a plan if you are joining," Alderson started as they rode, introducing the others as they moved, describing the outline of his plan, and giving his opinion that it would be years of recovery, or maybe years before recovery could even start.

TWO

Officer Larry Mancha was on routine patrol when he received a call to attend a shoplifting incident at the Best Buy. It would be another typical call, some young well-to-do punk stealing things just because he could. He would talk with the store about pressing charges, the kid's parents would be some sort of professionals, they would come in and talk the store out of pressing charges. The call would kill an hour and a half. In Mancha's mind the young offenders needed much harsher consequences and punishments. He was no longer allowed to even take the kid for a ride and show him why shoplifting hurt, cameras in the squad cars put paid to that. He should make Sergeant soon and he could get more control of things. Sadly most cops were becoming bleeding heart liberals, too many liked to mollycoddle the little brats, just like everyone else.

Mancha demanded respect, he did not let punks get away with disrespect. He would transfer to a tougher district when he could. There things were rougher; if you broke a few heads it wouldn't be noticed as much.

He was cruising along at 80 km/h, pondering this, when

suddenly his engine quit, and the steering got tough. "*What the fuck!*" he thought. Then he noticed all the cars were slowing to a stop around him, many trying without success to pull off to the side. He coasted a bit then he noticed the car in front was stopping faster, but no brake lights. Stomping hard on the brakes, very stiff with no power assist, no collision avoidance, stomping the brakes he would stop just before hitting the Mercedes in front of him. In 30 seconds every car on the road had stopped, some bumped into others, creating many minor fender benders.

Putting the car in park, he tried to restart the car to no effect. Radio dead, cell phone dead, computer dead, the only working electrics he could see were the brake lights on some cars, but only some.

He got out of the car, 24 degrees Celsius was warm, but not sweltering, unless you had body armor on. Outside the car you could still smell diesel and exhaust, but it was so strangely quiet with no road noise, on a major road – just the animated yelling, talking, and slamming of doors.

Immediately people came up to him asking what happened, or asking him to call a tow truck because their phones were dead, most appearing stunned to realize he was in the same boat as they were.

The enormity of the event stunned him too, at first, standing and listening to so many people. "Please calm down," he heard himself saying a number of times. People were as confused as he was. Remembering a course they had on emergency preparedness, Officer Mancha recalled there were instructions for this event. He hadn't paid enough attention, concerning himself with real policing, working the street, now he wished he had seen the relevance of that course. He imagined that he should head for the district office. Having come to that, he turned only to find a crowd gathering around him. Others opened the hoods of their cars and stared in disbelief or tried vainly to tinker with their car engines.

"Help me please. My child is sick I have to get him to the hospital!" a desperate woman pleaded with him. The rest of the crowd talked animatedly among themselves. Mancha followed the woman to her car. She pulled a feverish little boy, about four, out of the car. "Well ma'am I think you should put him in the stroller and start walking. I don't think the cars are going anywhere right now." Helping her get the kid in the stroller, he watched as she then began walking quickly pushing the stroller, sobbing as she went.

Trying to make his way toward the district office, he was inundated with more questions. Finally, losing it, he screamed at the crowd, "Shut the fuck up, I don't know any more than any of you, I can't do anything for you. Now I **order** all of you to go home and leave me the fuck alone, that's a police order!"

A wiry guy, with a scruffy beard, tattoos, and greasy hair called out, just loud enough to be heard, "When you need them, the pigs are useless." Mancha stormed over to the guy who was leaning against his dead truck. "Turn around and put your hands on the truck," Mancha ordered.

"What for, you can't arrest me. Go fuck yourself."

Pulling his Asp baton, snapping it open, Mancha stepped up, baton at the ready. He would enjoy giving this asshole some pain before he got to district office, bonus no cameras.

"You wouldn't dare, there are witnesses, you have no cause." The belligerent guy challenged him, stepping forward.

"Refusing a police order in an emergency," Mancha growled as he struck the guy's thigh. The guy folded but remained on his feet, howling in pain.

Righting himself, the tough guy took a step in and punched Mancha in the stomach.

The body armor dulled the blow, Mancha showed little effect and struck again, precisely on target, hitting the nerve a few inches above the knee. The guy crumpled to the ground this time, holding his leg, screaming. Mancha kicked him in the stomach with the police issue steel-toed shoes. People who were staring gape-mouthed at the violence, began to move away nervous and fearful.

Handcuffing the guy, Mancha marched him, still limping, to the police cruiser and cuffed him to the cage in the back. Taking his second pair of cuffs Mancha got out again, people still looking at him as he pounded his asp baton on the ground to retract it. He yelled again, "I order you all to go home, this is a state of emergency. You are ordered home."

They guy in the car started yelling, "You can't leave me here, that's illegal!"

"Do you need another lesson in what's legal?" Mancha said, looking back but continuing to leave. There would be rampant looting soon and he would have to deal with it; he thought as he walked, he might need some back up. He headed to the nearby mall to see if there were any working facilities, any communications.

Once he got inside, he had do deal with the same inane questions. He wondered if people thought being a cop meant you had magic powers. They could see everything was fucked, why did they think one cop would have the answers? He found a restaurant with people coming out.

He spent an hour talking with people at the restaurant, hoping at some point land lines might be restored. The restaurant staff provided him some free food and drink, such as they could with nothing working. Free food he shouldn't have accepted, but "*why not*" he thought.

All kinds of crazy theories were floated about what happened everything from the Russians are coming, to space alien attack. He didn't know what the truth was but he felt a little better having had some food now. "*Go back to the car to release the idiot,*" he thought, in case things got better and someone had seen. He arrived at his car to find the perp was gone, the cuffs still attached to the wheel and somewhat bloody with one hanging open. The guy had figured out how to pick the locks.

He was once again having to contend with more questions and badgering from civilians. He ordered them to push cars to the side, telling them it was for emergency access, when all he wanted was to keep them out of his way and give them something to do. Some complied, others just left. It was one way to take care of the stupid questions. Trying his radio again and swearing, then tossing it on the seat, he left.

As he turned toward the residential area to make his way toward the district office, he saw a guy with what looked like a shield strapped to him, obviously trying to steal a bike at a corner house. Larry Mancha was in a foul mood and he needed an outlet. Drawing his weapon, he yelled at the idiot: "Police! Stop and put down your weapons, now! Move away from the bike."

- - - - - -

Sitting at home watching an Indy car race on TV, Aidan distracted himself from his problems. There had been no work for a few days, due to the sluggish economy. The action on TV had finished so he took a walk over to the convenience store at the gas station. Having a cigarette as he walked, he suddenly he noticed the silence. "Weird," he thought, "no cars in the middle of the day."

Seeing Centre Street, it was more than weird. He saw cars, all stopped, and people getting out of their vehicles. People were pointing to the southeast sky. He looked where they pointed and saw a reddy-orange glow, high up, above the clouds, but the sun was southwest at this time. It was almost like two suns, but the new one was fading quickly. "This can't be good," he thought. "But if it were a nuke and you weren't blinded by it you're okay." It looked far away. Walking out to the street, some people were getting out of their disabled cars, wondering what was going on. Continuing his errand, he went into the convenience store.

"Hey Abdul, how's it goin'?" he asked the clerk.

"Aidan, I'm doing good, except our power just went out. How about you?" the clerk asked. Aidan proceeded to load up on water, better foods, and a couple packs of smokes, all totaled about fifty dollars' worth. "I hope you have cash Mr. Aidan, without power I cannot do debit or even credit," Abdul added as he saw Aidan collecting things. "I cannot run my cash register, everything seems to have died at once. I will have to use paper," Abdul said.

Thinking to himself, "This is looking really bad, might be time to bug out,"Aidan looked around. Abdul completed the adding and showed him the paper, Aidan paid in cash. "Thanks buddy, you know this power outage doesn't look good. All the cars outside are dead too," he added as he headed for the door, his brain racing about what to do next. Abdul followed him out the door.

"Holy shit really? That's very bad, this happened when I was in Pakistan several years ago, the Chinese-Russian wars, you know. The EMP that hit the north," Abdul said.

Aidan had got to know Abdul well over the last two years, being a frequent customer. Abdul had told him the story before about how he and his daughter, now 16, had been visiting Pakistan when an EMP hit there. Abdul had been in the south and was not affected, but got the news coverage the next day. He was a Canadian citizen and so was able to get back to Canada. His wife was not so lucky, she was with family in an the far north, in a city affected when the Russians launched a multiple EMP attack on China. He decided after a week he had to leave for the sake of his young daughter. They left with the last Canadians getting out. He had described it as the hardest decision he had ever made. He was culturally Canadian, his family was from Lebanon, his wife was from Islamabad.

"Hey dude, if you're right you should lock up and go get Nyela. Fuck the store for now," Aidan said as they stood and watched the scene.

"You are right Aidan, I will," Abdul said with conviction.

He had left his wife in Pakistan for his daughter, he wasn't about to stop protecting her now.

"I am going to go find Alice," Aidan said, leaving the store. Alice was working at the hospital pharmacy, they should have emergency power. She would be off in one hour and he was supposed to pick her up. Making a quick bug out bag, then walking to the hospital, seemed like a plan to him. He would head up to Jim's place; Jim had guns.

Knowing this situation was going to be bad, Aidan made a mental list as he walked: he would take the kukri, the katana and his bow, maybe his shield, a pack with as much survival gear as he had. He could not wear the armor or carry it so it was something he would have to come back for. Not having a well-developed plan, he focused on just a few things.

This could be the start of a war and he did not want to be in the city when that shit happened. Maybe it did not affect vehicles which were not turned on, he hoped.

Absent-mindedly he turned on the tap for some water, when it just trickled out, it hit him -- no power meant no water, meant no sewage, big problems. Alice worked at the largest hospital in the city, so if emergency information were going to be available anywhere it would be there. He started collecting his gear, stopping to write Alice a note so she would know where he had gone if she got home before he found her.

Aidan was lean, wiry, 5'8" and in good condition but after walking for 20 minutes with all his gear, he thought *"Being in good shape for 50 is not the same as being 25!"* A bike would greatly ease his travel. Being close to the university should make that easy.

He took to the back alleys, thinking bikes might be more visible. Being close to the university also meant many of the people living here were students who rode to school. When he got got on to the main drag the magnitude of the calamity struck him. In the intersection, he saw people wandering about, going all directions. There were only the sounds of people, and birds. Hours after the EMP, people were still stunned. One woman sat on the roadside with a young child, maybe 5 or 6. She looked beaten and tired; she sat and just sobbed. Aidan, walked up and sat down beside her. The woman was maybe 30 years-old, well dressed, and pretty. She was wearing a nice perfume that had lost some strength after hours of sweating, her summer sundress was soaked and stained with sweat. She sat rubbing her feet, her high-heeled shoes on the ground beside her.

"It's okay mommy, don't cry." The little girl looked at Aidan as he sat down. "Who are you?" she asked innocently.

"I'm Aidan, who are you?" he said back in a pleasant voice.

The little girl replied, "Jeanie. Are you like a knight or something, why do you have a sword and shield?"

He pulled his pack around and took out a two bottles of water and some chocolate bars he had bought. He handed them to the Jeanie and her mother. "Nope, not a knight, I don't have a horse," he replied grinning at her. The mother looked up and smiled broadly, "Thank you so much, my feet hurt so much and we have such a long way to go."

"Where are you going to?" Aidan asked genially.

"I live in the Marda Loop area, we were coming from the

doctor's office. Do you know how bad this is? What happened to all the cars?" she asked, pleading.

"It's bad, things won't be normal for a long time I think."

"Why aren't the police doing anything? I have to get home to my husband, he is so sick right now with a bad flu," she sobbed, breaking down again.

"I don't know about the cops, but I know if you are going to make it, you are going to need to find new shoes. You should go back to the mall and see if there is a shoe store there," Aidan advised. He stood up and looked around again, "Hey there is a cop car over there, did you ask him what to do or for help?"

"That cop has lost it worse than anyone else. When I went past he had his gun in his hand and was ordering people to push cars out of the way. Some people ignored him. He got angry and kicked the sides of a car, and yelled," she said dejectedly.

Jeanie added, "The policeman is very bad, he used bad words, he scared me."

Looking around, Aidan spotted a bike. "I see a bike over there I am going to try to liberate, if I get it I will see if I can find some for you, it might be the only way to get home for you," he suggested.

"Oh please don't steal something for me, that would be wrong," she replied.

Cocking an eyebrow at her, he said, "Lady you need to look around you, the world has gone to shit and it is a long walk home."

"I have to have faith God will help me!" she said with conviction.

"Looks like God did a good job this time, good luck getting home, but I would suggest doing something rather than waiting for God." Aidan, shaking his head, went back across the street and looked at the bike. Old and not in great shape, the tires were okay, the lock was a cheap inline combo, six position four number, easy to crack, just trying every combo. He opted for easier, breaking the chain with his pliers. He heard shouting behind him but ignored it – until he heard, "Drop your weapons! Move away from the bike.".

THREE

Being able to cycle and move quickly took a little subsurface panic away from Alderson. The rest of this little group thought he was so calm, cool, and collected, yet under the surface he was ready to break down and cry, crawl away, and curl up in a ball. A sense of immediate purpose was the only thing keeping panic at bay. Riding, moving quickly past dead cars and long lines of people, allowed some planning and thinking time. These people needed to know his short term plan, even his plan for getting home. "Hey everyone, I have a little bit of a plan, I will lay it out and you tell me what you think," Alderson started as he lead the group onto a bicycle path which would take them over Calgary's largest freeway. Deerfoot Trail was a road choked with traffic during any rush hour, gridlock was now a permanent feature. The cycle bridge avoided the panicked masses and dead vehicles. The roads they cycled on to get there were side streets with the occasional dead vehicle in the middle, easy to avoid.

"First, as we ride I need everyone to keep their eyes sharp and shout out if you see any of the following: any person or group of people who look like they could be a threat, you know carrying weapons, looking threatening, watching us too closely, or blocking our path. I need those riding at the rear, including you Di, to sometimes check behind us." He was also giving the traumatized girl a task to focus on. "Make sure you call out if you see anything suspicious. If we don't see it, we can't be ready for it. Awareness is the very first component of survival!"

"Second, if you see very old cars let me know, some might still run. It is too early to break into garages to see if any cars work, but if you see any on the road or an underground parking area, let me know."

"Do you think we will see any working cars Jim?" Jolene asked. "There are some apartment blocks with parking under the building on the way along 16th Ave near 10th street," she added.

"I don't know, conventional wisdom would say no, but I have some hopes. I would say it would depend on the type of the building above and the whether the vehicle could be seen from where the blast occurred. However some say the EMP waves travel through the ground and so could affect anything," Jim responded. "It's always worth checking it out. Unfortunately, I don't have a good criminal or mechanical past so I don't know how to hot-wire a car."

"What is 'hot-wire' Mr. Alderson?" asked Di. "Isn't that some travel company?"

Kareem, Jolene and Jim all gave a slight snort, "No, it is a way to start and steal a car without a key," Kareem chimed in, then added, "Didn't they teach you that in the special forces?"

A few heads turned, looking at Alderson quizzically.

Alderson, looking around, decided he had to be straight up. "Ah yeah, about that Kareem, I was never in the military, but it doesn't mean I don't know about EMP. I used it as a ploy so I wouldn't have to get into a fight with you, sorry about that," he said, turning a little red.

Ayra piped up, "Kareem you said he was a Green Beret or something?" She sounded more chiding of Kareem than concerned Alderson wasn't the real McCoy special forces type. "By the way Carrie calls you Mr. Alderson you might be a teacher?" she added perceptively.

The others laughed a little. "Guilty as charged," Alderson answered. "But what I have is a lot of pre-thinking about how this EMP would be. I am not an 'in the woods' survivalist. But I am more mentally prepared than most people."

"I have a good general idea of what to expect, however no one can completely predict what will happen, because we don't have enough info. So let me continue with the plan. Just ask your questions so we can work out the bugs. Just remember, like the saying goes, 'A battle plan never survives contact with the enemy.'"

"I do not expect we will see a lot of violence today or maybe even the next two days. Sure there will be some, we are in a big city. For a couple of days most people will respect the law. Most people will wait for the government response. So will I, but I will also be preparing for the worst."

"Hey Jim, I get you are a smart guy," Karen jumped in, "but if you have thought of this so have the *real* military types. We should expect them to establish some response shouldn't we?"

"Yeah, it's true the military will have a response but there are a couple of factors to consider. One: Calgary has no regular military units. We have reserve units, but they have no way to call up the members, with communications out. I would assume they have standing orders to report in this kind of situation, but they will be a day at least gathering the troops. All totaled I suspect the militia units amount to a thousand, maybe two." Alderson continued, "Police have about 2000, but the thing they are lacking right now is command and control, and mobility."

"So what do we do until they get things fixed?" Angela asked.

Not wanting to scare people with his most dire predictions, Alderson continued laying out his immediate plan."In the short term we have to consider a couple of important necessities: water and sewage. Neither will function without power. So here is what I propose in the short term. I suggest we hole-up at Bowness Park. The reason is easy access to water. I have a microbiological water filter which will be good for a few days, and we can dig a pit latrine for sewage."

Arya spoke up, "You seem to have had time to think about this. Will water from the Bow be safe? How good is the filter and can it clean enough water?"

"To answer you simply, I'm a bit paranoid so I *have* thought about it. Water will be safe if treated. The filter will be good for over 1000 litres until we can obtain a new filter cartridge. We will need camping gear, we can easily obtain propane for cooking, I even have two tanks at home right now, which is on the way to the park." Alderson stopped talking for a minute to see if there were any responses.

"This plan is good for the next week or so depending on how things fall out. If the authorities get things going, good, if not we have to start planning for phase two."

Rosie piped up, "Just how long do you think this will go on for? Just how long do you expect me to live in a tent?"

"Ah Rosie, well we have no say over that. The sad fact is the houses will all be intact, but without sewage and water, how can you live in them? It might be a long hump to the water. Digging outhouses in the backyard is bad if a million people do it."

"Ewww, outhouses are gross!" Rosie shuddered.

"I have to agree with you," Jolene added.

"Yup they are gross, but sewage backup in a basement is grosser if you ask me," Alderson responded.

They had arrived at the bridge to cross over Deerfoot Trail. Kareem and Arya in the lead, came to a stop. "Wow it's crowded on this bridge!" Kareem noted. "I think we should dismount and walk the bikes." Everyone followed his lead. Alderson eyed the thronging crowd, looking for suspicious types. Moving east, the crowd was slowly coming toward them. Checking his machete and hunting knife, making sure they were easily accessible, Alderson proceeded. He decided this crowd was just weary workers making their way home on foot. As they crossed the bridge, jostling around the hot, tired crowds of people, Arya stopped and pointed toward the downtown area: "Hey, something big is on fire downtown."

Taking the cheap mini binoculars out of his pack, adjusting them, then scanning the downtown, Alderson blurted, "Holy shit I think it might be the Bow building!" Calgary's largest office tower had been completed only a few years before the beginning of the calamities. From this vantage point, everyone was in awe of the surreal and unnerving landscape of dead vehicles for miles in both directions on Deerfoot Trail, people milling about like ants. But there was no vehicular movement on the six-lane highway.

"Can I see?" Arya asked, "Wow, the last company I worked for moved its offices there. Hey do you know what happened?" she asked a weary looking passerby wearing a disheveled suit with his tie half-off.

He stopped, eyeing the group, glancing at the visible knives Kareem and Jim wore. "Ahh no I don't think anyone knows, some are saying it's some kind of attack," he answered.

"No, I meant at the Bow building," Arya clarified.

"Oh, I heard a helicopter crashed and started a fire on the roof when it all happened. Someone said other planes have crashed too," the stranger replied.

In a subdued, somber voice, Jolene added, "Yeah we know at least one crashed just north of the Lougheed Hospital on 36th street, started some bad fires." Di began sniffling again. Carrie moved over to Di, stood by her, putting a hand on her shoulder, then hugging her.

The office worker looked to Jolene, then to Di, then asked Jolene, "Where at on 36th, do you know?"

"Right at the Whitehorn LRT station," she replied.

The stranger went pale and looked crestfallen, "Oh shit, look will someone sell me a bike, I will pay $500 right now." The group looking at Alderson, their *de facto*, not by choice, leader.

"I'm really sorry, but I don't think we can do that we are trying to escape this shit storm; we have a long way to go." Alderson replied for the group. "But I would bet someone alone and going your direction might take you up on the offer."

"Yeah, shit, ok." The man dropped his briefcase and moved off at a jog, weaving amongst the crowd on the bridge.

Leading everyone, Kareem started the group moving again. They followed along in single file without saying a word till they had crossed the bridge.

Crossing the bridge first, Kareem and Arya waited, Alderson yelled from the back, "Go north Kareem, there is something I want to check out on the way."

Mounting up, Kareem started the troop moving north along the golf course. Groups of evening golfers were on the course, it was a surreal sight, the world falling apart, yet guys blithely playing a game. Carts had stopped, the beer girl wasn't coming, but they played on. Alderson, looking at the golf course, imagined it might yet become a refugee camp, open space and a small creek nearby.

"Hey look, there are moving things, a digger thing," Rosie called and pointed. Seeing a front end loader on the road moving dead cars aside, a few working buses in the bus barns, these were the first signs civilization was not going to completely crumble. There was still viable transport here. The buses, housed in steel barns, were protected from the EMP. They watched as buses pushed buses on the south side out, giving a clue as to the direction of the original blast. It had, as Alderson had suspected, come from the south. Over the US, maybe Idaho or Nevada, but could be a half of the USA. They would be both be more fucked, because it was higher intensity closer to the blast, and better off because their military was better prepared for an EMP.

Arya, watching thoughtfully for a few minutes, suggested, "I think we should go and ask what the city's plan is, what information they have. They might be in contact with the authorities." The others nodded their assent.

Arya rode into the yard, when a mechanic yelled out, "Hey you can't ride in here, you'll get hurt!"

"Where's the office? We're looking for information," she called back, moving to the edge where it was safer. The mechanic just pointed, putting his hearing protection back on. They cycled around the perimetre inside the fence until they could see the front office with a number of people outside, one guy giving directions.

They rode up to the throng. The guy in charge came over with a scowl and stated angrily, "You will have to leave. You are in restricted area and we are in a crisis."

"Hey we would be happy to leave," Angela stated in her polite, demure way, "but we need information, like where we should go? What is expected to happen? Are you in contact with the police?"

The manager tersely replied, "Just leave, I don't care where you go. We have had no contact with anyone yet, but we have a disaster plan and we will follow it. Leave or I will have Protective Services remove you." There were two uniformed, uncomfortable looking officers with him. This was Canada, they were armed with pepper spray, handcuffs, and batons and one of them had already shucked off his body armor, deciding the heat was more of a threat at this point.

"Look buddy, we were just trying to be good citizens and do what our government needs us to do, but there has been no word or information," Alderson chimed in with an irritated tone in his voice.

Another employee spoke up, "Ahh sorry, we have no information. We're just trying to clear main roads starting here. It seems we have some of the only working equipment. Computers inside got fried, but buses in the north half didn't and some of our yard equipment is ok. I would say go home and try to connect at a fire hall -- they have emergency communications set up, we don't. Sorry." Tensions deflated a little. Feeling a little more hopeful, they rode off.

"Well those buses and heavy equipment are operating, that's a good sign, it means we can hope emergency generators will start up and the city might be okay. But it will be a while before the dead vehicles will be removed," Alderson said in a brighter tone.

"Does this mean we will be able to live in homes with running water and toilets?" Carrie asked.

Alderson looked at her trying to smile a little. "I hope so, but until I see more progress I am staying with my plan, it is up to each of you if you want to stay with me or go home.

This is not something you want to fall behind the curve on."

"I'm totally with you Alderson," Rosie piped up. Carrie nodded, Kareem and Arya did too.

Jolene, chewing her lip, was almost crying, "Will we be able to get my dogs today? I don't want to leave them alone overnight."

"Jim, I think I am with you today and then we will see after that. Is that okay?" Angela asked.

"Angela, that's definitely okay. Jolene, I guarantee we will go get them, I would never ask any person to leave their children behind, and pets are children in my world," Alderson added. "On the way I want to stop and see if I can pick up some friends. These people will be very valuable to us and they are both just a couple of klicks south of us."

Riding on with little talking, they stopped for those who wanted to use a toilet at a gas station. The attendant at the gas station asked, "What has happened? What is the meaning of this disaster? My boss would be unhappy if I leave but I can do nothing here."

Kareem answered, "Hayder, my man, this is a shit storm of epic proportions, if you listen to Jim here, you should pack up and get the fuck out of Dodge and take what you can carry."

"Hey Alderson, the toilet worked, taps didn't really, is that a good sign?" Carrie asked.

Alderson raised his eyebrows, frowning a little. "Sorry Carrie, that's a bad sign, most toilets are good for one flush once the water is off. The water off means no power in the pumping stations."

Hayder looking somewhat panicked said, "But my boss, he will be angry and I will lose my visa, I have to complete the exam to be mechanic here. I have to stay."

Alderson looked at Hayder, examining the grease-stained overalls. Mechanics would be valuable people in a post-apocalyptic world, regardless of where they hailed from. "You do what you have to Hayder, but if your boss doesn't show and you need to leave, you do it. Do you have family here?"

"No family sir, I am a temporary worker wanting to be a licensed mechanic, but my boss makes me work here not at his shop."

"If you have to leave Hayder, make your way to Bowness Park. Do you know it?" Alderson asked.

"No sir, I do not know of this place."

Alderson looked around and found a dusty ten year-old printed map. GPS gadgets were no use now. He took it out, unfolded it, took a pen and drew a path to Bowness park and circled it. "If I am right and this is going to be very bad, we will have need of a good mechanic, and such things as visas won't matter at all, they don't matter to me. If not there, look for us on the other side of the river." He circled the other spot as well.

Everyone mounted up and began riding again. They had ridden a block when Alderson had a thought. "Keep riding till you get to 12th. If I haven't caught up by then just wait for me. I won't be long"

He turned and rode back to Hayder. "Hey Hayder, do you have bolt cutters here?"

"Yes, sir I do," Hayder answered.

"Good, I will buy them from you," Alderson said.

"Oh sir, they are not for sale my boss says," Hayder answered ringing his hands.

"Look, I will give you fifty bucks and if your boss complains tell him I threatened you with this knife," Alderson added, pointing to the knife on his belt but not taking it out.

"Very well sir, you shall have them."

Alderson handed him the fifty. "Thanks. We will likely see you in a couple of days."

Hayder waved and smiled.

Alderson, pedaling hard to catch up, came up behind Di, as she lagged behind. "Boo!" he said. Shrieking, she almost wiped out. Everyone else looked back, a few chuckled.

"Sorry Di, but someone has to keep checking the six, checking behind. We don't want any nasty surprises," Alderson said.

Rosie quipped, "I didn't think you were *that* nasty," being the smart-ass she was.

Just performing the task of riding, everyone was more relaxed, a double-edged sword: relaxed people felt better, but their awareness was also relaxed. Figuring that today even the scum were just surviving, Alderson let it slide. They crossed

16th Avenue, a major highway through the city, now just a large graveyard for modern transportation. There was one old truck working, trying to clear a pathway. There was some heavy equipment nearby, which had been working on one of the vacant lots, it wasn't moving. The workers had all gone.

Weaving through the pile of cars, they made their way across the road. People stared enviously at their bikes, the only mechanical things moving; most people had to walk. The pillar of smoke from the Bow Building, black and oily, hung in the air, dominating the southern view. Unusual for Calgary, the air was still, the smoke would make it hard to breath soon enough. Pulling his bike up to an older four-plex, Alderson asked everyone to wait.

He walked around the back, pounding on the door and windows, calling out. No response. Taking paper from his pack, Alderson wrote a note. "Marc, city worker party you told me about 2006, everyone busted, meet me there. Jim." Tacking it to the door, Marc would know what he meant and where to meet him. Marc was probably walking home from work, he of all people would understand what happened and what the implications were. It was Marc who had first told Jim about what EMP was. Marc, a US military intelligence veteran and historian who had eventually deserted to Canada, was very knowledgeable about all things military and some survival issues. He would add to the group's skills and knowledge.

"Okay, that was a bust, Marc isn't here but I left him a note. He will be a very valuable guy when he joins us, and he will join us. But I warn everyone, he is a little odd," Alderson explained as he remounted and began riding west again.

Aidan was the next one to try, also a very useful guy. He lived closer to work and would have been able to walk home by now. Alderson took them up the road to Aidan's place. On arriving, he noticed Aidan's black truck was there -- either he didn't take it to work, or he wasn't at work but home when the nail got pounded.

Alderson got no answer at the door, so he went to the front balcony. "Hey, someone give me a hand." Jolene came over, others decided to take a rest on the lawn for a few minutes. She locked her hands so he could get a boost to pull himself up on the balcony.

"If he's not here, why are you breaking in?" she asked.

Alderson pulled himself onto the balcony. "Well I need to know if he has left because of the disaster or he hasn't been home yet, I'll be able to tell." Pulling the half-broken balcony door, he tried to reach in and get the piece of wood blocking it, but it jammed. Finding a wire on the barbeque for holding a grease cup, straightening it out and putting a hook on one end, he reached in and hooked the wood up, allowing him to push the door open. Inside it was clear Aidan had left prepared. His swords were gone, his bow was gone, and when Alderson looked his shield was gone but not armor. He looked on the table and found a note.

"Alice I will meet you at the hospital, I will take 24th all the way to Crowchild. Love Aidan"

Alderson added to the note, "Come to my place, or Bowness Park- Jim."

Leaving the way he came in, Alderson went over the balcony. Kareem asked, "So did he leave after or before the event?"

"After," Alderson replied.

"How would you know?" Kareem questioned.

"Well I have known Aidan my whole life, but the easy way to tell was he took his sword, his bow, and his shield," Alderson explained. "No other reason to take those."

"Sword, shield, and bow, is he some weirdo?" asked Angela.

"He laughed. "Yeah, the same kind as me, but better skilled with those weapons. He can even make some weapons. We used to belong to the Society for Creative Anachronism, a bunch of medieval weirdos who like to dress in armor and beat people with sticks."

"Oh I remember you telling me about that." Rosie added, "Sounded fun to watch but a bit freakish."

"Kind of like a Renaissance Faire?" Angela asked.

"Yup somewhat like that," Alderson said.

"So we are looking for a guy with a sword and shield and a bow?" Arya asked.

"Yes a large round shield, modern bow, likely in a case, and a katana," Alderson said, "and depending on the time he should be walking along 24th Avenue to Crowchild Trail." He understood why Aidan would take this route, it was direct and would make him very visible to Alice.

They rode along, scanning everyone that could

potentially be Aidan. Coming up to an intersection they heard yelling, "Drop your weapons and move away from the bike!'

Hearing no other voices, rounding the corner, they saw a cop, his gun drawn, pointing at someone. Alderson heard Carrie gasp. Looking past a bush beside the corner house, where the cops gun was pointing, he knew why she gasped: she had recognized the person the gun was pointing at.

Beside Aidan was a bike, across his back a big round shield, on his hip a katana, the bow case was laying on the ground. The bike was locked with a chain, Aidan had pliers in his hands; it was clear he was trying to steal the bike.

Thinking quickly, moving to the lead, Alderson said so only the group could hear it, "Back off and wait". Dropping his pack and riding forward, Alderson got within three metres of the cop. Aidan, with his hands in the air, looking like he wanted to find an escape route, was about fifteen metres from the cop, the cop aiming at his head. It would be a tough shot, especially if Aidan moved. Alderson, dismounting on the fly, let the loaded bike drop with a thud. The cop was of average build, young, maybe 25, dark skinned, with a nearly-shaved head. About ten centimetres taller than Alderson, the cop had the look of someone pissed off at the world, a sneering angry look, filled with disdain for everyone. The cop glanced over his shoulder as Alderson approached his gun side. Alderson said, as calmly as possible, "What seems to be the problem officer?"

Responding with anger and near panic in his voice, the cop said, "This guy is looting during a disaster, he could be shot for that! Police business, back off!" He sounded unhinged, ready to go. Aidan side-stepped a little away, making the cop focus more on him. "You move again and I will shoot you!" he yelled, his voice breaking.

"Come on officer, he didn't kill anyone. Canada has no death penalty, even for looting," Alderson said, hearing the panic rising even in his own voice, now just one step away from the cop. The cop spun on him, finger already in the trigger guard, gun high. Alderson, moving just fast enough, stepped in blocking the cops right hand, with his right hand. Alderson's years of jujitsu training took over despite his being rusty. The gun was not yet aimed, but the cop having his finger on the trigger, combined with Alderson's aggressive block, made the gun go off.

The blast ringing in his ears, Alderson's adrenaline spiked. His right hand slid down the cop's forearm and hand, grabbing the slide of the gun and pushing it slightly back, just enough to prevent the gun from being able to fire again. The police issue sidearm was a Glock, internal hammer, so he could not grab the hammer, Alderson had to hold the slide and hope nobody was in the line of fire. His left hand grabbed the cop's right wrist, driving the barrel of the gun hard and fast for the cops ribs, twisting the wrist inside, not the best gun removal technique, but the one available right now.

Trying to use what he had been trained to do in retention techniques, the cop pulled back. Alderson was faster, pushing through, stripping the gun from the cop's hand.

Lurching away, avoiding Alderson's swing at his head with the gun, the cop stepped back. Changing his grip, repositioning for shooting, Alderson aimed the gun, the cop went for his taser on the cross draw.

Alderson didn't want to shoot the cop, he lunged in, driving an elbow into the cop's midsection. Alderson's power and size knocked the cop back, off his feet. The body armour absorbed most of the blow, the cop cleared the taser, and pulled the trigger. Catching Alderson in the midsection, the cop squeezed the trigger three times, trying to discharge the shock, but no effect. Alderson took aim on the cops head, saying, "Taser's dead. Roll on to your belly! Now!"

The cop started to roll, then said, "The safety is on," hoping to distract Alderson.

Firing a shot into the ground a few feet from the cop Alderson barked, "I've shot a Glock before." A gasp and shriek from someone in his group behind him. The cop complied immediately. The whole tableau had taken 3 seconds from the time the cop spun to the time he fired the taser.

Kneeling on the cop's back, Alderson took the cop's own handcuffs out. "Put your hands behind your back," he commanded. Handcuffing the cop, he got up and pulled the taser darts out. Aidan came toward him from one direction, the others rolled forward on their bikes, all in stunned silence.

"Jim, that's a cop you assaulted and you took his gun!" A stunned Angela stated the obvious.

"Yeah, an out-of-control cop threatening to shoot someone for stealing a bike," he agreed.

"We could get in a lot of trouble," she added.

"Okay, if things get back to normal turn me in," Alderson said.

"You could have killed him," she stated.

Alderson answered, "Yes, but clearly I didn't want to, or I would have. I do know how to shoot and I do know how to kill someone without a gun. Look, I don't want to frighten you but if the authorities do not get it together in 72 hours, shit like this will happen everywhere. I didn't want to do this but I wasn't going to let him kill my friend, or anyone else, for a stolen bike. We are likely to have to steal more than an old bike before this disaster is done. I'll stand up to a judge and say so if I have to. I still might go to jail for doing the right thing. It wouldn't be the first time that happened to someone."

"Dude you're scary, but I have known that for years," Aidan said, half-jokingly.

Kareem and Arya stood gobsmacked and not sure what to do. Carrie and Rosie rode up. Rosie grinned like the Cheshire Cat, "Wow you kicked ass on the piggy."

Alderson rounded on her, "Rosie that is not what it is about. I did what I had to, to protect a person, it isn't about kicking ass."

"But Alderson you have to admit you were pretty fucking sweet in that fight," Carrie added. Alderson looked around at the group, motioning for them to move away from the cop. He introduced Aidan, "Everyone, this is Aidan, we have been friends since the dawn of time." He went around, giving Aidan each of their names.

Aidan said, "Thanks for the rescue, how did you find me?"

Jim answered, "I broke into your house and read the note. I assume Alice is working at the hospital?"

Aidan nodded, "But now what do we do with the cop?" he asked looking around, seeing there were some people who had witnessed this.

Alderson put the Glock in the back of the waistband of his pants and reached down, grabbing the cuffs and lifting the cop up. "Aidan get the bike you were trying to get. Officer Mancha, I don't think you can be trusted with the power vested in you," Alderson said as he searched and found the officer's ID. He took it and put it in his pockets. He took the officer's pepper spray, extra ammo, and gun belt even though it was too small for him. He threw it to Aidan. "This might fit you," he said. He ditched the dead radio, but took the keys for the handcuffs.

"Well here is my thinking, I know you are all shocked by what I just did. I understand, if you want to bugger off and turn me in now, go for it. I won't be there when they get around to looking. Just be sure and tell them the whole story. If you stick with me you risk being labeled an accessory, terrorist, gangster, or whatever," Jim said, looking around.

Jolene, looking shocked and bewildered, moved up and said, "You look as good as any other authority right now, I'm with you Jim."

Aidan looked up and said, "You know I'm with you, but I have to get to Alice and see what she is doing in the giant world shit storm."

Alderson explained his plan to Aidan, taking care that Mancha couldn't hear him. "We're going to collect a few people and head to Bowness park, easy access to water and the edge of the city. At least for a few days and see what happens. Right now I need to go with Jolene to get her dogs. So for the short term here's what I'm asking. Go first to the hospital and meet up with Alice. If you need another bike, take my bolt cutters. Aidan, you take my bike, it's heavily loaded with ammo but you will be on the flat. Head to my place, lead everyone there, and connect up with Jenna, I will be along later. There's enough food and space to sleep for the night, we also have water. I have to head up to Citadel with Jolene, all uphill. I will try to collect Alex on the way."

Di, who had been staring blankly, piped up, "I don't want to go with him."

"Di you will be with everyone else including Ms. Knight. You will be fine," Alderson consoled her. "But before we go, officer Mancha needs to show us where his car is."

Mancha snorted, "Fuck you."

"Fine." Alderson started to undress the cop.

"What are you doing?" Mancha screeched.

"If you don't cooperate, I will leave you buck naked," Alderson said in a cheery voice. Rosie and Carrie laughed.

"Okay fine, it is on Crowchild near halfway between here and Brentwood. It doesn't work anyway," Mancha said, seething but resigning himself to the situation.

"I know that," Alderson said as he handed Aidan the Glock. "Just in case," he added.

"Jolene, I want to collect another useful friend en route.

Good luck everyone." He mounted the bike and started riding toward Brentwood with Jolene following. The others started making their way to the hospital. Finding the police car, he used the keys and found what he was looking for, a first aid kit and a shotgun with two boxes of double-ought buckshot. Riding side by side, they chatted about life before the EMP. Jolene talked about how she came to have the two dogs, and her aspirations for life.

FOUR

"It is better to be feared than loved,
if you cannot be both."
- Niccolo Machiavelli, The Prince

As the rest prepared to ride off, some chattering excitedly, Aidan was still in a daze from what just happened, but he willed himself to act and started talking. "Hey everyone, I'm guessing Jim must have told you something about me. Don't believe too much of it, but let's get ourselves going." Riding across Crowchild Trail, Aidan looked for the woman and child he had talked with before. Not seeing them, he wondered where they might have gotten to in such a short time – he doubted God had picked her up and flown her home. The gunshots had probably frightened her, a number of people scattered after those.

"He told us we were looking for a guy carrying a bow, a sword, and a shield. Those were true!" Arya said. "And he told us you were in some Society for Creative Anarchism and about making weapons and armor and fighting with swords. I hope we are not going back to the middle ages though. They had terrible sanitation," she added wryly as she rode up beside

Aidan, looking at him as they rode.

"I think our sanitation is about to go all to shit," Kareem added. The others snickered or groaned at the obvious pun.

Riding on, making idle chit chat, it took ten minutes to get within a block of the Foothills Hospital. Throngs of people were outside, one person standing on a make-shift raised platform was speaking to the crowd. Others were milling about, some purposefully engaged. On the north side there were dozens of people on their bikes, clearly people were learning that you could get information here. Two military-type vehicles were there clearing other vehicles. A military helicopter came in to the landing pad. This was the best sign so far that maybe there would be some sunshine after the giant shit storm. It was hope.

"I'm going into the hospital, I need to find my girlfriend. I need someone to take my stuff, I think they might not be too happy with me bringing this gear inside," Aidan said. "I might be a while, it looks a little crazy." He handed the shield to Kareem, it was unlikely anyone else could make any use of it. He handed the sword and kukri to Arya, and the bow and pack to Carrie.

Walking toward the hospital, he was able to hear the person speaking from the platform. The middle-aged man was wearing a white hardhat with a logo on it. He called out to the crowd, "There will be emergency power starting tomorrow. It will rotate throughout the city in two hour blocks. Not all areas will get power where the lines are damaged. We have only a few available repair trucks and limited materials. We hope to get sewer and water running but all water should be considered contaminated until further notice."

He was interrupted by calls from the crowd asking how to boil water with no electricity. The official waited for quiet.

"Work with your neighbours to boil drinking water or use bleach, two drops per litre. We have some brochures available at the information tent." He pointed to a small festival tent with two confused-looking individuals trying to organize. "We are asking that anyone with a working vehicle, particularly trucks, meet at McMahon Stadium as soon as possible. Your city and neighbours need your support. Needless to say all events, schools, and non-essential worksites are hereby closed. There will be a curfew in effect starting tomorrow from 9 pm to 9 am. That is all for now." At the end of his talk there were instantly hundreds of hands going up and questions, none of which he answered. He left, disappearing into one of the buildings.

When Aidan got to the doors, he was stopped by a security guard. "Emergency triage is over there," the guard said, pointing.

Aidan replied, "My girlfriend is working in the hospital and I need to get her a message."

"Oh," the guard replied, "just write down your message and give it to the information booth, only emergency communications are operating. They will get her the message, but all shifts are doubled, we are hoping the next shift can make their way here."

Aidan wrote out the note saying he would be at Jim's and he hoped she knew where it was. He drew a crude map and hoped it was good enough. If she worked double she would be at the hospital past midnight and would not likely leave until daylight.

He walked out to the others, who had moved close enough to hear the speaker. When he arrived they were all smiling. "Hey, it looks like this won't last long, they expect to have emergency power up tomorrow, sewer and water should come on then?" Kareem was saying.

"But most transportation will be down for a while. It will mean walking or riding for a a long time, months probably." Arya added, "Why do you think Jim thinks it will be so much worse?"

"You will have to ask him, but I wouldn't count on things being fixed as easily as they say, that would be their best case, 'Don't let the populace panic' scenario," Aidan said. "I think preparing for the worst and playing wait and see for a few days is the best bet, but each of you do what you think is best."

Di, sitting down with a thump, began to cry. Carrie and Rosie moved over to her, consoling and hugging her. Angela spoke in a low voice to Aidan, "She lost both her parents today and has no family we know of nearby. It's going to be tough, and when the services are back Child and Family Services will have to take control of her. But how do we even contact them right now?"

"Well that sucks, so is Jim taking care of her, or you?" Aidan asked

"Well I guess we will do it collectively for now," she replied.

Aidan, addressing the group, said "Okay everyone, we are a half hour from Jim's place. He has a barbecue which will still work and I am sure he has gallons of good water, so let's get on the bikes and start moving out."

"Hey, I thought the plan was Bowness Park?" Kareem asked.

"He lives just up the hill from there. I think he wanted to stay at home tonight, collect gear, then start the schlepping tomorrow. He will meet us at his place. He has a shit-pot full of guns and ammo so it will be safe."

They started riding, Aidan guiding them along a back road through the university, to avoid the large numbers of dead vehicles on main roads and any groups of people.

- - - - -

Officer Mancha was humiliated, livid, fuming. He had his gun taken from him and then was treated like shit, by a fat old man. No one, not one bystander, came to his aid and he was a goddamn cop. Could society fall apart so fast? People always feared crime so much, but were not willing to help a cop in distress. There must have been ten people who saw what happened but did nothing. If society was so fucked they couldn't help him, then fuck society. Making his way to the car, hands still cuffed, he found the extra cuff key and unlocked himself.

He would remember that cocksucker, what did they call him, Alderson. He would hunt him down and teach him a lesson. Hell if things didn't get fixed he would fucking blow his head off and piss in the hole. If things did get fixed that fucker would go to jail. What were the odds that he was buddies with the looter. All that kung fu, ninja shit was useless when you're pepper sprayed then and hit with a baton. Alderson would just cry like a schoolgirl. Mancha seethed, working himself into an even more foul mood as he walked along. He would teach that terrorist a lesson if it was the last thing he ever did. Alderson he would remember, a fat fuck with a bald head and a stupid looking goatee. He would love ripping the goatee off his face.

Mancha walked on for an hour, seething anger all the way. No belt, no weapons, he didn't even feel like a cop now. That fucker Alderson had taken the shotgun from the trunk of the cruiser. He needed to secure a weapon. As he approached the main road near the District Office, he spotted two young punks in face paint and clown gear, Juggalos, wanna-be gang members who listened to some awful noise that some called music. Recognizing the make-up from a distance, he knew these two punks. Smiley and Jiggles were their 'family' names. It was the term Juggalos used to refer to their nicknames, claiming to be all one big family. These were not major bad-asses, just bad-ass-wannabes. Pulling himself behind a tree, Mancha waited until they were close. Stepping out, he surprised the pair, "Hey Smiley, What are you doing?"

"Uhh, uhh well our car stopped so we were walking home, *sir*," Smiley answered, emphasizing the 'sir', not wanting to provoke a cop, knowing Mancha had a bad temper and reputation in the area, particularly when people didn't give him respect. Jiggles, the more timid one, said nothing.

"Let me see what you are carrying in the pack, Jiggles," Mancha ordered, thinking it might be something that could be used to coerce these guys to help him.

With uncharacteristic verve Jiggles blurted, "No way man, you can't just search us."

"Look you little asshole there is a state of local emergency, I can do whatever I want. This is martial law," Mancha said getting angry. Reaching out and snatching the pack straps, Mancha grabbed the pack as Jiggles stepped and pulled back. Mancha snapped out a jab into the bewildered Jiggles' face. Dropping like a sack of rice, Jiggles flopped to the ground. Mancha deftly stripped the pack off as the kid fell. "Don't move!" he growled at the stunned-looking Smiley. Unzipping the pack and dumping it, Mancha grinned as several small bags of weed, maybe three grams each, labelled "$30", fell to the ground. "Ho, what do we have here, drug traffickers, well, well," Mancha gloated. Before the event he had wanted to grab these two but they often eluded him, he liked busting no-account punks, that was his job. Dropping the pack, grabbing Smiley by the neck, he kicked out a leg and sent Smiley to the ground.

"Okay you little fucks, this can be a trafficking charge as well as disrupting order during an emergency. Those could even be supporting terrorism charges. But here is what we are going to do. You are going to take me back to your place now, I don't need any warrant, this constitutes 'probable cause'," Mancha said with glee in his voice, waving a bag of weed. Jiggles was groaning and coming to.

"Okay man, but what has happened why are all the cars dead?" Smiley asked in a whiny way.

"Just shut up and take me to your place." He had the two walk in front. As they got close he asked, "Is there anyone else at home?"

"No man, look dude how can we help you, please don't do this to us we didn't hurt no one," Smiley bargained. Mancha, not answering, just shoved the punk forward.

Arriving at their basement suite, Mancha could smell the stale weed even from the outside. Inside, the place was a pigpen, smelling of rotten food, stale weed and beer. Unwashed dishes littered counters and tables, unwashed clothes lay in corners, the carpet was filthy. His eyes, scanning the scene, snapped to a safe in the middle of the room. That was out of place. These guys were working for someone bigger. The safe was too fancy, and required too much forethought, for these two punks.

The two of them were high, they hadn't noticed his missing belt and gun. Mancha ordered them to kneel facing a wall but with enough space for him to walk in front. "Which of you two bright lights knows the combo for this safe?" Neither of them responded. He booted Smiley in the gut and made the punk puke. "Next one is in your balls," he said, placing his steel-toed boot in Smiley's groin then drawing it back, making ready to kick.

Smiley winced, shaking, his face a grimace of terror. He knew there were supposed to be rules but all those seemed to be gone. "Okay man I know the combo, three left to 26, two right to 21, then to 56, but you need the key in my pocket." Mancha searched his pocket from behind and got the key. He proceeded to open the lock. He expected to find a lot of cash but he found about $500 and a very nice Kimber 1911 .45 cal handgun with 3 magazines and a box of ammo. "Hey boys, I think maybe you have committed some weapons offenses unless you can show me a gun license."

"It's not ours," Smiley said

"Doesn't matter, you had control of it. Tsk tsk, that'll add to your trafficking sentence. Trafficking with a weapon dangerous to the public peace, possession of a restricted firearm, possession of a firearm without a license," Mancha said, loading the gun, then jacking a round into the chamber and snapping the safety on.

Looking over his shoulder, not sure if the slide being

racked meant he was going to be shot, Smiley saw Mancha tuck the gun in his waistband. His eyes widened in revelation, "Hey man where's *your* gun?"

Mancha's countenance darkened, "You shut the fuck up or I will shoot you with this gun. Who are you fucks working for?"

Jiggles, who had completed high school but had little common sense said, "Don't you mean, For whom are you fucks working?" then sniggered to himself.

That earned him a kick in the back, driving him face-first on the filthy carpet. "Okay you little shit, who is supplying you," he said, grabbing Jiggles by the hair and pulling his hand back, cocking his hand for a punch.

"Pinky, Pinky Finnegan, the HA's" Jiggles blurted out, trying to avoid further abuse.

Dropping Jiggles' hair, letting him do another face plant, Mancha stood up. "Well, well, well. I think you two just became useful," Mancha said, thinking these two could be his ticket to a promotion. He just needed enough info to execute a warrant on the Hades Animals and get in there with the Tac and Drug teams and he would look like a friggin' hero. "I am imagining you guys don't want to go to jail, for a long stay. Am I right about that?"

"No sir, we don't," Smiley answered.

"Then you two will keep working for Pinky and you will feed me the info I need. Have you been in the club house? Did Pinky give you this directly?" Mancha questioned.

"No way man, you have to be at least a probie to get in

there, we just deal for them. They supply, we deal. It was a guy said he was working for Pinky, and we should act like what he said was comin' from Pinky," Smiley answered.

"Okay dumb shits," Mancha said walking to the fridge where he found some beer and a bag of Ex. He collected a beer and the bag and packed it up. "We're moving out to the station for now."

The uphill climb took 40 minutes, only to find a sign on the door ordering all officers to report to either McMahon, or the Emergency Operations Centre. *Fuck that*, thought Mancha, *tomorrow*. Deciding he could rest here, he broke the front glass door and went in. Finding the sergeant's keys, he opened an interview room and locked the two punks inside. Mancha crashed on the couch in the briefing room.

Six hours later, Mancha woke. It could have been six hours or six minutes, he really couldn't tell because the clocks weren't working, but it was dark now. It seemed like the city was going to shit in a hurry. Wandering through the quiet precinct offices, he found a snack and drink machine, not functioning of course. He would have to break in. Eating junk food and drinking, he pondered different scenarios. The emergency protocols demanded he report in, but fuck, he knew the few cops and military the city had could not keep shit together.

Reality of this apocalypse was setting in. He was better off to go and carve out his own kingdom. His bitch of an ex-wife lived much closer than he did, she wouldn't let him in the house, but it was his house damn it. Remembering how she forced him out, he also remembered she had gone away for a month, she wasn't even likely to be back. Of course he had to deal with the two shitheads, let them rot in a room or use them? Fuck it he thought, *I'll just go back to sleep.* Sleeping another four hours till dawn gave him some light in the office.

More rummaging through the office, he found a drawer with extra pairs of handcuffs and handcuff zip-ties. He got his stuff from his locker, but the arms locker had been emptied. There was duty belt, holster, flashlights, and a couple of canisters of pepper spray. Retrieving the punks and making them work for him was his immediate plan. He would go to his place, his place that his bitch-wife forced him out of, and collect some gear he knew was there. Punks would be his pack mules. Opening the interview room, a foetid stench of stale shit mule-kicked him in the gut. "Fuck, you guys are disgusting," he said.

"Hey man you left us here without a shitter, what was I to do?" Smiley whined at him.

"I ain't walking around with you smelling like shit. Go to the locker room and find something and clean yourself," he said with a sneer.

"Is there any food or water *sir?*" Jiggles asked, exaggerating the 'sir'.

"Yeah, junk food and water. But if you try to run I will shoot your ass," Mancha crowed patting the .45 now in a holster. He showed Smiley the locker room and told him to find some clothes but not a uniform. Leading them to the lunch room, they found more snacks, ate then prepared to move out. That consisted of Mancha cuffing the two.

"Hey officer, where are you taking us? We didn't do much, just selling some weed. It seems like a big hassle for you to take us with you. You have the evidence, if you wanted you could come and charge us when things are back to normal," Smiley started talking, looking for a way out.

"You guys aren't too smart are you? There really won't be a 'normal' again for a very long time. I have other uses for you. Do you have any idea what all this shit means?" he paused. "We are all royally fucked for a long time. We are going to have to live differently, like roughing it. You punks are now my lackeys, you're working for me," Mancha said.

Looking at each other, then at Mancha, the kids seemed stunned to silence, their faces masks of horror, not able to envision what that would be like. Smiley opened his mouth like he wanted to protest, looked in Mancha's eyes, and clamped his mouth shut.

In Mancha's old neighbourhood, some of his former neighbours were milling about chatting. All eyes turned to them as Mancha marched the punks forward. Some came over to him and talked and asked questions about the crisis. He gave them nothing. "Fend for yourself," was his only reply.

He still looked like the cop he had been, some people still had some nominal respect for authority. Most of the neighbours would not come near him, there had been lots of rows with his wife and they all took the gossipy bitch's side. As he started to break into the house the bitch next door came up to him nattering, "Larry you are not supposed to be here, there's a restraining order, you know that."

"Fuck you cunt, things have changed. Fuck off or I will arrest you too," he said, rounding on her with a glare and his hand resting on the .45 on his hip. She retreated inside her house. Having no keys, he just kicked the door in, it wasn't the first time he had done that. Pushing the Juggalos through the door and into the living room he bellowed, "Sit down and don't move." He went to the basement and collected camping gear and his shotgun. The shotgun was in a hidden in a secret place, which his bitch-wife had never known about. When she had the locks changed it was sudden, he never mentioned the shotgun because it was illegal, a bad thing for a cop to have. It had no serial number and he did not have a civilian license, so he could not own a civilian gun. He stuffed some packs with necessary gear and gave the two packs to the punks, be damned if he was going carry the weight.

When they were loading up, another neighbour came knocking at the door. "Larry, Larry are you in there?"

"Fuck off!" Larry answered, turning to look at the door, seeing Mike Racine standing there with a shotgun held in both hands but not aiming.

"Larry we don't want you here, you're not supposed to be here, you're violating the restraining order, that could be bad for your job," Mike said in a somewhat threatening manner.

Larry laughed, "You think I give two shits about the job, look around you the world is fucked and you don't even get it, the cum-swilling cunt isn't even here. I should stay just to piss you off. You may try to look tough with your shotgun but you have no balls, you would never shoot me," Larry sneered at him.

Mike raised the gun and aimed at Larry's head, putting his finger on the trigger, "Shall we see, just give me a good reason," Mike said between clenched teeth.

"Whoa man, okay, I wasn't going to stay, I was leaving anyway, I just came to get some of my shit she never gave me. My friends are just going to put the packs on and we are out of here." Mike kept the shotgun aimed. After taking their cuffs off, Larry helped put the packs on Smiley and Jiggles. The packs would serve to retard attempts to escape. Then he put them in front of him and started toward the door, Mike backing off to his own yard but keeping the gun aimed. By this point there was a crowd of neighbours watching in the cul-de-sac.

Once out of shotgun range, Mike lowered the gun. His wife and daughter were on the step of his house watching.

Larry yelled back at him, "Hey Mike, is your little retard a hot little fuck yet, I'm sure you must have tried her or I can come back and help you break her in." They rounded a corner, but even at that range he was sure he could feel Mike turn six shades of purple. Mike's daughter was a very beautiful, but mentally-handicapped, 14 year-old. Mike and his wife were extremely protective of her, and leading activists for the disabled, they absolutely hated the word "retard".

Larry laughed at the feeling of having tweaked Mike.

"Hey Larry, I'm glad we're friends now. Your neighbours don't like you much do they?" Smiley said.

That was a mistake. From behind Larry slammed into the pack Smiley was carrying, knocking him to the ground. Smiley scratched his face hitting the dirt. "I am not your friend, I am your fucking overlord, and don't talk about my neighbours unless you are telling me you killed them or fucked their daughters or wives!" Mancha yelled at Smiley. Jiggles stood with a stunned, horrified look on his face. "And if you do fuck that little retard you could get promoted in my kingdom"

"Sorry man, sorry, I got it, I work for you, sorry it won't happen again," Smiley groveled, struggling as he got up.

"Where are we going sir?" Jiggles asked.

"Hmmm well, we need to get transport and for that we will need to watch the roads. We also need to recruit some more people or you two will have to do all the work, cause I have to supervise your lazy asses," Mancha said. "I think we should set up camp on the hill and we can watch the roads and the city from there and that way goods will come to us."

Hiking up Nose Hill, the highest point in the city, to a place where it overlooked a major roadway and provided easy access to necessary items, took a while. Several hours more consisted of Larry directing the two to set up a camp with a couple of lean-to's, latrine, and cooking area. Mancha just directed the other two, he liked the feeling of being in charge, maybe he could make the best out of the disaster. If it went on for long, which he was sure it would, there would be dozens of lordlings with little fiefdoms, he would be one. He could grow an empire of his own in this fucked world. Setting up a situation where he had enough reliable people working for him would take a little time. His first two choices were not yet reliable, but they would be eventually. Not bright but they feared him. He needed reliable, loyal people or malleable enough to get them to buy into the system. Loyalty or Death would be his motto.

Directing the punks to build the camp to his satisfaction encouraged Larry; being boss while others feared you and worked for you, this was a good thing. Tossing the guys a bag of weed when they finished, doling out the pay, a good feeling of power, and it should keep them happy for a while. Looking at Mancha the cop suspiciously at first, they began smoking up, getting high, and just laying around the camp. Mancha's lean-to was separate, for security. Mancha napped while the others vegged out. The former Juggalos feared Mancha, he knew it, he was sure they would not run, they were afraid of the situation and seemed to think he would help them through it.

- - - - - -

Kevin "Papa Bear" O'Reilly was chairing the weekly business meeting of the Infernal Cherubim Motorcycle Devotees Corporation. It was the corporation Papa Bear had created to do legit business for the local Hades Animals Motorcycle Club. They also discussed Club business as the two organizations were one and the same, except the corporation was incorporated and the government had not deemed it a "criminal" organization, which was largely due to the political consultants Papa Bear had hired to smooth the way. The meeting was held in the club's Bowness motorcycle repair shop, a steel Quonset building, and one of their legit businesses.

Without an external antenna, signals could not be sent into or out of the Quonset, which made it safe from police surveillance. Papa Bear strictly enforced the "nothing illegal happens at a legit business (except broad money laundering)" rule. Finishing the meeting of the corporation and moving on to club business was the usual agenda. This had just started when the lights went out and a few of the high intensity lights exploded. Everyone jumped, assuming the cops were raiding them. It was pitch black inside, by design there were no windows to let signals through. A few guys took out their lighters and made enough light to find the flashlights. Even the emergency lights did not come on as they were supposed to.

Papa Bear read the mood of his guys, they were spooked yet ready for action. He required all weapons be checked and locked at the door. "Okay Pinky, arm up who brought their weapons." Pinky Finnegan was their sergeant-at-arms, nicknamed Pinky because when he spent any time in the sun he turned bright pink. Pinky, a tough guy, had done a stint in the military, including a tour in Afghanistan -- even trying out for JTF2, Canada's super elite Special Ops commandos. He hadn't made it because he was considered a loose cannon, after that he was cashiered from the military for being "psychologically unstable". It wasn't Post Traumatic Stress Disorder like lots of combat vets got, it was that he was considered too uncontrollable and violent. He got out of the military and found another calling, being a biker with a real nasty reputation, only exceeded by that of his boss Papa Bear. Being sergeant-at-arms, he was also the *de facto* 2-IC, second in command, for the club.

By flashlight and lighter, the bikers armed up and moved to the front doors. They saw nothing, no guys in black with night vision, no doors blowing open, nothing. Just silence. Slowly opening the door, looking outside, nothing. No cops, no blockade, just the usual scene. Just a power outage.

"Okay guys, seems like we will have to take business outside for now," Papa Bear announced. Outside, it hit them almost immediately, the strangeness of the silence -- no cars, no sounds from the highway.

Pinky, looking around, stepped out into the street, came back and spoke to O'Reilly. "Hey Papa, this is looking like bad news," Pinky said. "This is no ordinary power blackout. Could be an EMP. Remember how I insisted we stockpile all that food and gear in the bunker?"

"Yeah, this is what you were thinking of?"

"Yes, it was. I'm pretty sure, lets look around. The world around us is in shit now, if we move quickly we can take advantage of it. The authorities will be fucked for a while, particularly the cops, they will need military help and there is precious little of that here," Pinky added.

"Okay Pinky, I'll bite what do we do?"

"One, check to see what bikes and vehicles are working, things inside the shop should be okay but let's check." Opening the bay doors using a chain hoist, they began checking, starting up the bikes, they were all fine. Vehicles outside were not so lucky, except an old, classic muscle car one of the guys had driven today. Parking the bikes inside to avoid attention was the standard meeting day practice.

"Next we need to arm up, go back to the bunker and get some more firepower. We should not be facing any effective opposition from the law right now, they'll be off-balance. After we arm up, two things: recruit workers, and control the food supply, which for the short term is the Safeway and the other smaller grocery stores down here."

O'Reilly nodded and gave orders. "Gamgee, get your prospects, associates and hang-arounds, arm up and go with Little John. Take the Safeway, kick anyone in there out and we will bring you radios later. Chief, get your nut monkeys here, get a generator going both at the bunker and here. Squawker, Boots, Jonesy, you guys are in charge of recruiting and getting people to work for us. Don't whack the civilians yet, when they are desperate they will come to us. If Pinky knows what he is talking about this is long term and we will build our kingdom here."

"Hey boss, you wanting me to arm hang-arounds?" Gamgee asked.

"Mmmm, depends how much you trust them, your call, but let everyone know the rolls are wide open and we could be offering patches to those who prove themselves in this event," Papa Bear announced. There was a murmur in the crowd, the group was always cautious about letting new members in but they would need more hands if they were going to run a bigger operation. In most cases they would just increase the number of associates but this situation demanded some incentive, give people the chance to climb to the top and they will work for you. For all others, they needed to fear you.

Rumbling up to the Safeway, two hours after the EMP, Gamgee and his crew surveyed the scene. Unfortunately a police car was parked out front, half on the sidewalk as cops like to park. Staff milled about outside, a manager talking with them, it looked like everyone was waiting for the lights to come on. In the abnormal quiet everyone noticed the sound of the working bikes, watching in awe as the gang rolled into the parking lot.

The cop looked nervously around at the bikes. He uncuffed a shoplifter, freeing him, then focussed his attention on the bikers. Alone, the cop stared at the full-patch 81's and associates, all well armed, not even hiding the guns. Easing his way to the back of the car, the cop moved carefully, not sure of the intentions of the bikers.

Their actions clarified things. Unslinging a shotgun and raising it, his prospect following suit, Gamgee yelled, "Put your hands in the air, cop!"

Diving behind the cover of the car, the cop tried to open

his trunk, the electronic clicker failing, leaving him down behind a car with no backup. Drawing his gun , then popping up, he took two quick shots, missing with both. The two shotgun blasts aimed at him didn't miss, a red spray showered from behind his skull as he took a couple of buckshot pellets to the head, and crumpled to the ground. He was the first, but not last, local casualty of violence loosed on the world by the EMP. Bystanders and store staff took flight, a prospect collected the cop's gear, the bikers took control of the store. They had proven there were no limits for them. Mission accomplished.

At the bunker Papa Bear was busily sending out guys to gather the troops, Pinky arming the reliable. There were thirteen patch members locally, but were another thirteen in Edmonton and some in Red Deer. Each Patch had one prospect and up to six associates and any number of hangers-on. All totaled he had fifty reliable people that could be called on and another fifty that could be used. It was a good start. There was an assault rifle, and a shotgun for every Patch, all having their own handguns. Some associates even had legal firearms, but that pretty much ended when an associate became a prospect, law enforcement did not take kindly to gun owners becoming bikers. Sending his prospect and a senior associate north to make contact with others, Papa Bear was going to build his empire locally and rely on a larger network for support.

Only a short time after Gamgee went out, one of his associates returned to report that they had taken the Safeway, but Gamgee had killed a cop in the process. If Pinky was right, no problem, it just established their control creating marketable fear. If the Government re-established control, Gamgee would have to leave, too many witnesses.

Insisting they control Bowness Park, or some point where they could encamp people and draw water, Pinky outlined his plans. Pinky continued describing how they would need to establish some kind of water treatment. Papa Bear, being more cautious and thoughtful than Pinky, decided they would wait a couple of days and see the reaction of authorities. That would give the civilians time to get out, making it less of a fight for them, and there was lots else to do.

They gained supporters easily. The club provided food to those in need, they had once helped put out a fire, and were publicly good guys. Papa Bear remembered the experience of the Yakuza during an earthquake in Japan, they were first in with relief and support, they became local heroes, they made the government look inept. People don't care if you are a criminal if you are helping them, they care about the help and they'll be grateful for it. At the store they doled out drugs and food to those who needed it, for now.

"Look guys, there are a lot of potential recruits for us in Spy Hill and Remand. We already know a number of them. I think we break them outta stir," Papa Bear said, looking around at he senior team. Breaking people out of the jail would be an operation, but he was sure it would help. "Okay, I want reliable people not just whacked out junkies. I don't want users, I want the one who will be smart," he added.

"But we should free everybody, give the cops lots to chase around after," Pinky interjected.

"On the mark Pinky, cops will be so busy they won't be able to affect our operation until it is too late and we are established. This job is priority one."

"Papa, I think we wait a couple of days." Pinky edged in.

"Given 48 hours and no relief or contact, the guards and cops there will collapse when we sneeze on them. But I say we send a couple of associates to surveil the place and let us know the situation."

"Right, I have a couple in mind for gathering info," Lug, a short, very stocky patch added. "I was going to send them out for intel anyway."

Monkey, the mechanic in charge of the shop, came into the meeting. "Hey, Papa Bear, I have reports of two helicopters. Military type, over by Foothills."

"I don't like to see the military getting their shit together," Papa said, sitting back and thinking.

"Those will be tied up with dealing with a million people, Papa Bear, I wouldn't sweat it. I'm sure they expect the jail to hold fast for 72 hours. We just have to move inside that time frame," Pinky said, dismissing the concerns.

The team worked on a plan. People, even armed guards, rarely want to fuck with ten bikers at any time -- they certainly were unlikely to in the middle of a crisis where they had no real access to backup. They would move at dawn the next day. The tall radio mast at the jail was a concern, if the jail had communications to city officials it could be riskier, and there were some working vehicles. The whole plan was a hit-and-run raid: get in, get out, less than one hour. A .50 cal rifle that could punch a hole through the front doors, even the walls, would rattle the guards and hopefully get a quick surrender.

"You guys cannot seek revenge on any bulls you might know. It might spark the authorities to expend resources on dealing with us. If it is just a jail break of minor criminals, well, they have bigger fish to fry right now," Papa Bear ordered at the end of the planning.

While the club was well-armed and dangerous, they were still no match for even a small military unit, or a concerted effort by the police, numbers alone were against them. A simple break-out was all they needed.

FIVE

"Never let your sense of morals get in the way of doing what's right."
- Isaac Asimov, Foundation

Jolene and Jim turned off, riding north and eastward, taking them near another school. Seeing a loud, boisterous crowd, they cautiously approached, trying to understand what was happening. A young guy sat on an old trail bike, a running 1970's-era Husqvarna, occasionally revving its engine, arguing with an older balding guy. There were several adults arguing about what to do. "You know, there may be quite a few working bikes, or ATVs. They are simple and don't have the fancy electronics that screwed us all. Old vehicles and simple ones are more robust and more repairable too."

As they approached the group, from the other side of the road, the older, balding guy yelled, "Hey, you two -- come here!" in an authoritative voice, a voice that had the sound of someone who is usually obeyed.

Jim nodded to Jolene, then whispered to her, "I'll see what he wants. Stay back a pace. Hold my pack, it has the machete in it if you need it." He pointed to where the handle protruded. He rode over to the group. "Hey, how's it goin'?" he said casually, but the shotgun was near at hand.

"What's happened, do you have any news? We are trying to decide where to send junior here. I say he should go to the store and get some goods, this dufus," pointing at a taller grey-haired guy, "says he should go to the cops and find out what's going on."

"Oh well, by now most of the stores will be locked up as it has been more than two hours without power. The cops are a good idea to get information. We saw some city transit buses operating a while ago, they were trying to clear the roads near Spring Gardens so they could get out," Alderson supplied.

Jolene added from ten feet back, "We found out at the Lougheed that there would be some power restored tomorrow."

"The Lougheed, you guys have travelled a long ways today," a younger man commented.

The loud one was wearing a knife and had some sort of handgun under his windbreaker. Alderson made a mental note, so laws about concealed weapons were already being ignored. Of course, Jim was openly carrying a loaded shotgun, also a legal violation. "I would say get the info then you can decide what else to do, but thats just my opinion. Later dude, we have to get going, we have a ways to go before dark and the city is supposed to be under curfew at 9:00 pm," Jim said.

"What, how do you know that?" the old guy asked.

"They were posting it at the Lougheed, I wouldn't worry though, I don't think even the cops know about it yet," Jim added as he started riding away.

When he reached Jolene, he said, "We should travel the alleys and see what we can find on our way."

"And do some more theft?" she asked with a touch of

fear. She seemed nervous about that idea.

"It may be theft, but it is survival, and survival takes precedence over property in my view. One ATV could save lives," Alderson responded. "It would make a lot of things easier to even have one ATV." They rode along some alleyways, finding nothing of immediate benefit.

"They are probably all in garages," Jolene commented as they approached Alex's house.

"Yeah, I know where I can liberate some, but that will have to be for another day." Alderson pointed, "Alex lives in that building, I'll see if he's there. He's another teacher. But he is well-armed and has good survival skills."

Alderson went into to the building and pounded on Alex's door, "Alex you in there, it's Jim." A few minutes later he heard movement.

Alex opened the door. "I just went to bed, I see there is still no power. I got home about half an hour ago, I was dead tired from the walk home. I should have been getting used to riding the bike."

"You're right. Alex I am pretty sure this is an EMP attack; I don't know how bad it is going to get but I do know it will get worse before it gets better. Alex, by the way, this is Jolene, she teaches with me at Nenshi," Alderson explained. "I have a bit of a plan, I think you should join us and give me your thoughts."

"What's your plan?" Alex asked rubbing sleep from his eyes.

"Well the short-term plan is to collect some people and things and hole-up at Bowness park. The city has no control. I figure BP because it has easy access to water and we can dig a pit for sanitation. You and I both have water filters so we should be okay for water safety. There are fire pits and we can get propane or white gas stoves. It is also close to the edge of the city if we want to bug out. Access to the river can be good transport, at least if we want to go downstream," Alderson said.

"Okay but how will you get propane or white gas? How long do you think this will last? I did see a couple of vehicles running," Alex queried.

"Well I don't know but if power isn't restored, water and sewage become the first concern, but that is not news to you. I figure at Bowness Park we can make forays to see if the authorities have got their shit together, if not we can bug out. In the meantime we build a bug-out cache," Alderson responded.

"How did you get here by the way? If you had walked from your work you wouldn't be here yet."

Alderson continued, "We have bikes, my legs are very stiff, and we are nowhere near done yet. We need to go to Citadel to pick up Jolene's dogs. I have Aidan on the way to my place with the rest of the collection I gathered. I will tell you all about it. We have been through fire, robbery, and assault." Jolene sniggered at the last statement knowing that it was really the group doing the robbery and Alderson doing the assault, all with good reason of course.

"You with us?" Alderson asked.

Alex said, "I don't know, I'm really tired, I could catch up with you tomorrow."

"I would hope you would come with us now because things are so unpredictable, I would hate to get separated. We will be making some forays back to get gear. I am thinking of snagging some ATVs, at either Bow Cycle or Bass Pro tomorrow."

"Okay give me twenty minutes to get stuff. Are you able

to take any extra gear?"

"If you have packs and slings on your rifles then, yes," Alderson agreed.

Alex spent the twenty minutes packing bags and putting on his sword, he decided against the armor but hid it under the bed, just in case. He grabbed a shot gun, a .22, and his scoped Mosin Nagant 7.62 x39 Russian sniper rifle, and some ammo for them. In his pack he added a hand grain mill. Alex had always been a collector of survival gear, without being a back woods, black rifle, government-is-out-to-get-you survivalist. He did have some very useful resources they would have to come back for if this didn't get fixed in the short term.

"Well I am relieved to see someone else is thinking about a plan," Alex said, as he packed up to start moving. "This thing could be really big, and life could get -- as Hobbes said – nasty, brutish and short. On the silver lining side, at least there is finally some quiet in the world," he added with a smirk. Alex often complained about the constant noise of the modern world.

They began riding north. This would take them a good 200 metres up in elevation and several kilometres away. This trek afforded them a panoramic view of the city. Coming back would be slow because of the dogs, but all downhill.

SIX

The uneventful ride to Jolene's place ended with the enthusiastic greeting her very happy dogs gave her. They growled a little at Jim and Alex but settled quickly with some food, water and freedom from the house. Letting the dogs run, Jolene gathered all the gear, food, and water she could carry.

She noticed Jim eyeing a neighbour's truck loaded with an ATV. Jolene spoke up. "It is my neighbour's, it would be wrong to steal it. He will need it too," she said in a pleading voice.

"You're right," Alderson replied, recognizing there was still a strong need in people to maintain the facade of a civil society. "I don't want to start robbing people, taking from big businesses is different, nobody's relying on those things for their own survival. But it is good to note and if he doesn't return in a few days, it might be necessary. Someone should make use of it if it works."

It was a down hill roll all the way home, Jolene rolled slowly so the dogs could keep up, Jim and Alex rolled a little ahead.

"Hey if we go on top of that hill we can see most of the

city," Alex said as they were coasting down. The detour would provide some good intel but not really cost them any time.

"Let's do it," Jim replied. He and Alex climbed the hill on foot, Jolene rested at the bottom with her dogs.

Surveying the city with binoculars, the lack of vehicular movement was shocking, the quiet, unnerving, yet natural – only wind in the trees and bird noises to be heard. Alex peered toward downtown. "Big fire down there, that must be the Bow building you were talking about." He noted, "Some more fires in the far south I think." Then he pointed, "Helicopter, it looks military, at Foothills maybe. Some things are working." There were still groups of people, trudging homeward, the foot commute. "You are right Jim, this doesn't look good."

After the survey they made their way down the hill and remounted their bikes. "We saw a chopper by the Foothills Hospital, so some things are working, but much more will have to function if a city of a million is going to survive," Alderson explained to Jolene.

They rolled the rest of the way to Alderson's place, the big dogs loping along beside the bikes. They arrived about as the sun was setting in the late spring evening, to what would have seemed like a party at any other time, yet a party with no music, in the world of unnatural quiet. More like a camping event, but unlike anything any of them had ever experienced.

SEVEN

What might have been 7:00 pm if clocks had been working, saw Aidan and the others arrive at Jim's place. Jim lived in a townhouse with a great view of the mountains and easy access out of the city. Very few cars lined the parking lot, a sign of something amiss. Aidan went up and knocked on the door several times, no answer, the blinds in the front were closed, this was a bit unusual, but these were risky times. He then dragged his fingernails down the door, he knew if Jim was in there it would irritate him. Then he decided to yell. "Hey Jenna, it's Aidan, are you in there?" Then in his usual joking manner he added, "If you don't answer I will huff and I will puff and I will blow the door in." He heard some foot steps and the door opening.

"Aidan, I didn't expect to see you here," she said holding a single shot shotgun in her hand. Not the best gun Jim had here but the easiest to load for her. "Is Jim with you?"

"No, sorry Jenna, just a tail of people he left with me, I will try to introduce them but I only just met them," Aidan answered.

"But you have seen him then?" she asked

"Yes, and that is a bit of a story, but he can tell you more about it when he gets here," Aidan said as Jenna invited people in.

"Just wait I will get some chairs, sorry the place is messy, I wasn't really expecting company," she said while she opened the blinds.

"No problem, the whole world is a mess right now. A messy house is the least of our worries," Arya said in a very sweet, calming voice.

She brought in some folding chairs. "We have some bottled water in the cooler, and with the power out we have some stuff in the freezer we should probably cook to eat, usually Jim does that stuff. I know we are good on propane because he just got some a few days ago," Jenna said. "Please tell me who all these people are and where Jim is."

Angela started "Hi I'm Angela, I work with Jim at the school, those two are Carrie and Rosie, they were students at the school last year and this is Di, she is one of our current students." Di was clinging close to Angela, she had been uncharacteristically quiet since the death of her parents. The other two girls waved and said "Hi".

"I am Arya and this is my boyfriend Kareem. Kareem met Mr. Alderson at Canadian Tire where Kareem worked. That is a whole story one of them will have to tell you, it seems Jim should have been an actor," Arya said, the whole time maintaining a very calming, charming smile.

"I'm Aidan, I think you know me," he said grinning. "We may have Alice joining us later, she was working and all I could do was send a note and hope it gets to her."

"Oh, it must be very difficult at the hospital right now," Jenna nodded.

"Well they have emergency power and there was some bureaucrat telling everyone that there would be emergency power, water, and sewage restored tomorrow," Aidan quipped.

"Well I am guessing this was an EMP attack, Jim has talked about that a lot and what things might look like. I sure hope he is wrong about how bad it is, I hate having to use outhouses, they're disgusting," Jenna added.

All of the women except Di murmured their agreement.

"You think that is bad you should see how they do things in Pakistan, even before the wars," Kareem told her.

"I think that's right and it *is* an EMP, but maybe not as bad as the worst predictions. Jim was going to get Alex and then go with another teacher up the hill to retrieve her dogs, I would think he will be another hour, it's a long uphill ride." Aidan went on, "If you point me to the food I'll get started with the grilling."

"I moved some things into coolers in the basement so those might keep a few days, but in the freezer up here there's some meat that will have to get cooked."

"Jenna, does Jim have any five-gallon buckets? We are going to need something for a crapper and I don't think using the toilet will be a good idea, and we definitely should not use drinkable water to flush it," Aidan added.

"I think we are supposed to get some thunderstorms tomorrow, maybe we can collect water?" Arya spoke up.

"Yeah, that's a good idea," Kareem added.

Aidan and Arya began cooking, Arya was impressed by the array of spices available and offered to help make the meal taste Indian. They cooked way more than 10 people could eat, but cooked meat would keep better than raw.

As they were cooking some neighbours started dropping by, some just arriving home after walking back from work. There was lots of chitchat about what had happened and what people were seeing. There was lots of talk about the burning Bow building, a sixty-story skyscraper can burn a long time, some were concerned it would collapse like the Twin Towers of 9/11. Most people believed the government would have critical systems up and running in a couple of days. Many believed that even cars would get repaired and moving within a month, two at the most. Aidan and Jenna were not so optimistic, Jim would be even less so.

The skeptics among them knew important politicians would be living well in fairly short order, but for the average Joe, this was going to be hell, nobody really knew which level of hell, or how much punishment they would have to endure.

"Hello everybody!" A call came over the fence. The group just starting to eat looked over the fence to see Jim, Alex, and Jolene ride up the back with Grimm and Jager loping along beside. As soon as they got inside the fence people were giving the dogs scraps and water, that was the longest walk they had in a long time.

Jenna moved quickly to Jim and hugged him and kissed him, "Thank god you're okay. I've been so worried. Is this it, the apocalypse you have always wanted?" she said chidingly.

"Hey, Jim! We're eating your food and drinking your

wine, there might even be some left for you," Aidan greeted him.

Alderson looked around, "That was the plan. Hey where's Alice?"

"They were on double shift at the hospital so I had to leave her a note. The bureaucrats there say there will be running water and sewage tomorrow and power restored," Aidan replied, a hint of skepticism in his voice.

"That's great, if it turns out to be true, it will only take us months to a couple of years to function properly again." Alderson added, "I will prepare and see."

"Jim, you're such an optimist," Jenna said sarcastically.

There was fifteen minutes of greetings and exchanging stories and information about what people knew or what they had seen. The whole story of the trek from the northeast was told. Aidan and Kareem talked animatedly to Jenna about Alderson's take down of the crazed cop.

"I really thought that cop was going to shoot Aidan for stealing an old bike. I had to act." Jim pleaded, "You know how trigger-happy cops have become these days. I guess it's a good thing Aidan isn't black or the cop might have just shot him."

The young ladies, Rosie, Carrie, and Di, were asking to have some of the wine. Jolene answered first saying, "I'm not your parent, you better ask Jim."

Angela answered, "You shouldn't, it is against the law."

To which Jim piped up, "If being charged with

contributing to the delinquency of a minor is the worst thing that happens to me after today, I will call myself very lucky. Just don't make yourselves sick we have a long difficult days and more ahead of us. I would say 'knock yourself out', but you might take it literally – but sure, have a drink I don't care."

Trying to be sophisticated about it, they all had some, but they were kids. Typical for teens, it was clear Di did not like wine, the other two claimed to like it.

After the eating, chatting, and drinking seemed to subside, Alderson suggested, "Hey everyone, we should get to sleep we have some real planning and thinking to do tomorrow. We'll need two to inflate the double airbed which we can set up in the living room, a third can sleep on the couch. Arya, Kareem and someone else can have the spare bedroom, Aidan the computer room. We can also take two in the floor space of the master bedroom." Feeling hopeful and more relaxed, they retired from the day civilization's coffin was nailed shut -- Jim had dubbed it Nail Day – hoping the next day would dawn brighter. Everyone had the feeling things could not get worse so they had to get better.

- - - - - -

Larry Mancha knew he needed to start gathering people and goods to himself. This was going to make him a chief, a king, or a lord of his own domain, but he had to organize, then find a spot near supplies. He had Smiley and Jiggles to get supplies and they were doing well, but he would need more. Watching the road that day he noted a group of four of guys, armed with bats and knives, pushing an East Indian guy and his daughters along, harassing and threatening them with the weapons. All were heavily laden with packs. Larry and

Smiley got ahead of them and took cover. "You wait and follow my lead," he told Smiley.

As they got close he could hear the tall guy swearing at the East Indian guy, "You fuckin' Paki, you shouldn't even be here, you are going to take us to your place or we will beat you and your little slut twins bloody. You will give us the cash you have been stealing from this country."

One of the other guys was grabbing and fondling the young, barely-pubescent girl's backside. That was a guy who believed the rules were gone.

Seeing that the guy had a shotgun that was slung, but was using the bat to poke and prod the captives, Mancha realized these could be allies. Those who knew authority came from the barrel of a gun, or the thud of a club. Waiting till they passed, Mancha popped up, gun drawn, "Police! Any of you move, I will blow your brains out. Now very carefully place all weapons on the ground and put your hands up."

He was almost surprised by the complete compliance. Walking up with Smiley following him closely, he took the shotgun and holstered the 1911 Kimber. "Now all of you on your knees!"

Turning, the East Indian man ran toward him saying "Oh thank god, thank you so much you have saved us." However when he was a step away, Mancha, using the butt of the gun, cracked him hard under the chin and knocked him to the ground. One of the girls screamed. The other guys looked on in shock.

"I guess he didn't understand English, I said everyone on their knees!" Mancha yelled, checking to see the shotgun was loaded then leveling it at the group.

The girls, who had been slow to comply, quickly went to the ground crying. Larry walked to each member of the crew he had just captured and put the shotgun against their noses in turn with his finger on the trigger, saying, "Which is the worst scum? What do you think Smiley?" Two of them pissed themselves. Mancha laughed.

"Okay you lot get on your feet. Help this Worthless Oriental Gentleman to get up." He snickered as he said that, only the East Indian man knew what he meant. He then handcuffed all of the assailants. "Smiley, lead us home," he ordered.

As they trudged up the hill, the East Indian man said, "Where are you taking us? Should we not go to the police station?"

"Shut the fuck up or I will hit you again and leave you for the coyotes to eat," Larry said belligerently.

In the camp and he ordered them to all sit on the ground. He then started to talk to the assailants. "So why did you have this good gentleman captive?"

"Well, we figured his kind take money from people here and they always have lots and we need some money to survive 'cause our bank machine ain't workin'," the tall one, called Rick, said.

Larry walked over and clouted Rick in the head. "Are you fucking stupid? What do you want money for? Money is worthless. It died yesterday. Did he have anything else of value?"

"I don't know, he wouldn't take us to his place yet."

"You want him to take you to his place? Well watch this. Hey mister..." he left a gap.

"Dhaliwal, Sir," the man inserted.

"Mr. Dhaliwal, you will take us to your place correct?" Larry asked.

"Why should I want to do that Sir? I do not think we need to go there, I am beginning to doubt your authenticity as a police officer," Mr. Dhaliwal replied.

"Oh really, well if I wasn't a cop I would be inclined to let one of these guys here fuck your daughters if you didn't do what they wanted, but because I am a good cop, I won't let them do that if you do what I want," Larry said with venom in his voice.

"No! You could not do such a thing. It would be wrong, they are but little girls!" Dhaliwal said in horror. "But you may go to my place there is only my wife there. We have little."

"See how compliant he is?" Mancha said. "But what would we want there when we already have what is most valuable." he looked leeringly at the two innocent girls. He took Rick aside a while and started talking with him. When they came back Rick was uncuffed.

"Guys I think we should work for Officer Mancha, he has a good plan." His virtually silent followers heartily agreed. Larry tossed Rick the keys and then said "Unlock them, then cuff the old man."

Dhaliwal was in shock and dumbfounded by this betrayal of authority. He could not react. Rick asked, "What about the girls?"

"Well go get some chain and cables at the Canadian Tire to leash them up good. After that, if you do your work well, then you have fun," Mancha said matter-of-factly.

Whooping like he had won a lottery, Rick smiled. He would like the new world order.

EIGHT

*"At his best, man is the noblest of all animals;
separated from law and justice he is the worst."
- Aristotle*

The first morning after Nail Day saw everyone sleeping to at least 7:00 am even though it was light much earlier. Everyone was dog-tired from the tribulations of the previous day. Among the first to wake, Jim found the piss bucket and relieved himself. He took his cheap mini binoculars and started looking around. He saw little movement. He walked around the complex, just a few people starting their day but no vehicles moving, it was the same nightmare he went to bed with last night. When he got back to his unit Aidan and Rosie were awake.

"Must have coffeeeeee!" Aidan chanted, looking at Alderson bleary-eyed.

"You will have to boil some water for that," Alderson said pointing to the burner on the barbecue.

Rosie looked at him and said, "I can't believe people are going to see me like this. How will I ever fix my hair or take my make-up off."

"Girl, those are least of your worries right now," Aidan supplied. "First we survive, then you worry about hair."

"Easy for a guy to say," she said, looking pouty and moving to the washroom. At about that time they heard a rattling and banging noise, it sounded like water coming back into pipes.

Alderson went to a tap and turned it on, air and sputtering came out, a sign there was pressure. He heard the toilets start filling with water. "Hey they got it turned on!" he said excitedly. Then he tried the electricity, no such luck there. This meant the pumping stations had emergency power and water was flowing. Gas would be a bigger problem, they couldn't just restart that without risking explosions. They would have to send teams door to door through the city to ensure houses were ready for the gas, that would take weeks to months. That was okay, this was progress. He hoped the sewage lift stations had their emergency power, otherwise there would be sewage backup for sure.

Jim came back upstairs and said, "No gas yet but that may take a while."

A number of the household woke with the sound of the pressure returning in the pipes. Aidan told them the good news, "Hey everyone we can take a proper shit and have a drink of water."

"Well I am not sure about the drink yet, we maybe should boil water for drinking at this point, we don't know if the water treatment plant is operating properly yet," Alderson warned. "But hell, I will take water and sewage as a good sign."

Everyone was very happy, the buckets could be emptied, cleaned, and they could use a proper flush toilet. They could boil water on the camp stove for warm baths. Everyone was feeling like it was a party and a camp out rather than the biggest disaster to ever befall humanity.

Breakfast was made of the leftovers and some foods that hadn't been cooked last night. After that everyone met to discuss and plan. "Well, what are you thinking?" asked Kareem, looking at Alderson. "It seems the authorities are getting their shit together, sewer and water, and even gas should come back soon, it shouldn't be too long before we get power back, ya think?"

Jim looked around thoughtfully, most people were nodding their heads in agreement. "Well, I agree these are good signs, and if anyone wants to go back to their homes I would say you should do so, but here are a few things to consider."

"First, the damage to sewer, water and gas distribution was only lack of electricity. I suspect that most of these facilities had some kind of back-up generator within the buildings so all they had to do was turn the jennies on, maybe repair a few basic circuits and things go again. Power to homes is different. The E3 wave, or third wave of an EMP, is only damaging to very long transmission lines, it's the one that kills things that are plugged in that were not killed by the E1 pulse. The E1 kills micro-electronics. The E3 is similar to the geomagnetic storms that brought down power in Russia and China, just before their war went nuclear, or for those of us old enough, the storm that brought down the Quebec power grid in '89. So they may get power stations running again but that doesn't mean we will get the power," Alderson lectured.

"Okay, so we won't have power for a while, but that doesn't mean we won't be okay for a while. It's summer, we don't need furnaces, and it is light till late. We can use propane to cook," Angela added.

"No power means no refrigeration, means no access to anything that needs to be kept cold for a while," Aidan chimed in. "We could go up to the Safeway and see if they are open and selling goods, but I would bet it is a cash only world right now."

"There is potentially an even bigger problem, if this is as widespread as I imagine it to be, that is, if this was done by a nation-state. Then only one sufficient-sized nuke over Kansas is good enough to fuck 98% of the population of North America, this would mean all transport other than military is screwed and from what I have seen at most 1% is still available. No transport means no incoming food. If train controls are down, nothing coming in that way either, and things will get very bad in a couple of weeks. That gives a city the size of Calgary about a month before there is insufficient food to survive."

Jolene joined in, "Jim you make it sound so dire, so hopeless, what are you suggesting?"

"I am not even going to suggest what each of you should do, but I will lay out what I will do," Alderson started.

Rosie broke in, "Alderson I will stick with you but I sure hope you are wrong, I don't like the buckets at all." It was typical of her to think of the comforts of life, not the bigger implications. She could talk about injustices and bad things governments do, but when it came to the ramifications of something like this she was focused on what it was doing to her now, not in a week. But how many people out there were thinking of the next week, month, or year?

Alderson continued laying out his plan again. "Okay, but that may be the reality. Here is what I will do. First, I will collect material and food and some means of transport that works. That is going to mean bikes and motorcycles and ATVs. I will stay here unless water stops again, at which point I will move base camp to Bowness Park."

"Why Bowness Park, it is in a valley and we can't see what is going on. Wouldn't higher be better?" Arya asked. She seemed almost excited by the prospect.

"Water," Alderson said. "The park meets several criteria, not all, but most importantly it has easy access to water and egress from the city."

"Won't it be easier to get food in the city?" Carrie asked.

"For now, yes, but in a month the situation will start to become critical and we will have to find another plan. In a month there will also start to be bigger issues of uncontrolled looting, lack of medication, violence. What I know of human nature says the nasty elements will be likely ahead of the curve. They will be the first to understand, a lack of law enforcement will mean each person is a law unto themselves. They didn't respect the law before, but they feared it. Now that fear will be gone," Alderson lectured.

"What we have to create is a collective of people capable of working together, but they have to be willing to protect themselves and to do what is necessary to survive. You have to remember that there will be no effective police response until they have transport and communication, Calgary is more than 35 kilometres end to end. There are only 2000 cops for over 800 square kilometres, that is less than three cops per square kilometre. Divide that by three for sleeping time. Then imagine how lack of communication will hamper their operations."

"The safest plan is collect shit and wait and see," Aidan agreed. "If we don't need it we will all be happier, but we will be much sadder if we don't do it when we should have."

"Okay, if we are with you, where do we start?" Carrie asked.

"That's a good question, our short term plan," Alderson said. "There is a Co-op, Safeway, and Canadian Tire all within a short ride."

"Are we just going to start the looting early?" asked Jolene, sounding down-trodden and worried again. She had never been anything but law-abiding and she was not sure it was necessary to start with robbery and looting yet. She was very confused. Things did look dire, she knew Jim was right, food had to be brought to the city – it wasn't produced here. There were a million people and they would soon start run low and panic, but surely people would work together.

A rhythmic thrumming sound from outside galvanized a few to run out. They could see helicopters coming in low, doors were opening in the complex, others were coming out, everyone wanted to know what was happening. A military Chinook helicopter, flying slow over the community started broadcasting: "Due to damage on power lines there will be no power available today. All citizens should remain at home. Leave home only when directed to do so or in emergencies. Only those traveling to home will be permitted to travel." This message was repeated on a loop as the helicopter made an S-pattern going from outside the city to the core. It used as its limit the escarpment that was just north of the river, when everyone went to the edge of the escarpment they could see at least 3 other helicopters doing the same thing. People standing on the path along the escarpment started cheering, believing things were getting better.

"Great, they're wasting resources, telling us they have it all under control. That is the government's first priority: look like you have control. It doesn't matter if you do," Aidan commented, sneering.

Kareem said, looking at Arya, "I think we will try to get back home today." He was thinking that the helicopters themselves were a good sign and as soon as the power came on he would be expected to be back to work. He would need communication and bank connections or the store could not operate. He assumed Arya would agree with him.

"I don't know, sweetie," Arya said, sounding doubtful. "I think the plan Aidan and Jim have is safer, at least until we know. Being with people in a crisis is safer than being alone." She was looking at Aidan when she said it. Everyone in the room noticed her look at Aidan while she was talking.

"You heard the choppers, they will get things fixed," Kareem argued.

"I hope they will too," Arya said. "But I'm not convinced Jim is wrong."

"Hey Arya, I'm not convinced I'm right. I'm just being cautious, some would say paranoid," Alderson put in, feeling they were be about to be in the middle of a lovers' quarrel. Arya seemed to be the more spontaneous and willing to take a risks of the two of them.

"Just because you're paranoid doesn't mean the world isn't going to shit," Aidan added.

Alex, who had been listening the whole time, spoke up. "There is going to be a very long time where things are difficult. People are not going to be able to show up for work, people can't call for help, food will be difficult. If we wait too long we won't be able to plant food for the winter. One of the problems in our area is most farms are industrial -- they either ranch or practice monoculture farming, usually cereal or oil grains. Very hard to harvest by hand. Best to plan and work now rather than wish we had later. I am with Jim and Aidan."

Jolene added, "You guys sound crazy paranoid to me, but this is a crazy state we're in, I'm with you guys."

"Carrie, your dad was in the Hat wasn't he?" Angela asked.

Carrie nodded, then added, "I'm staying with Alderson."

Rosie added, "I'd rather be here if the world wasn't fucked, I am sure not going to my mother and her stupid husband in this situation."

"Kareem, I don't want to convince you against your will, we may do some things which are illegal. You have to know that going in, it's up to you," Jim concluded.

Kareem decided to stay with the group mostly because Arya was adamant she wanted to stay at least for now. Figuring to hit the Co-op and Canadian Tire first, Alderson had cash in the house, pooling all they had it amounted to $3500, that would give them some spending power if anything was open.

Jim, Aidan, Alex, and Carrie would make the foray to the store and bring shopping carts back through the less-used routes. They hoped the choppers were still covering the city. The choppers started at the west end and moved east. The group would bring a shotgun and two handguns, illegal to carry in public, but these were unprecedented events and security was the first concern. Alderson made sure the guns were concealed.

Riding along, they saw very few people out and about, most were obeying the curfew. Their previous foray to Canadian Tire had netted enough sleeping bags and camp gear, but more propane, additional stoves, white gas, lanterns, walkie-talkies, solar panels, and small windmills were all a priority items, as well as food, water and medications.

"My future plans say we should make a long ride to Bass Pro ASAP," Alderson suggested as they rode. "They have a lot of guns and gear, including reloading supplies."

"I expect the RC's will go there too or military," Alex said. "Bass Pro will also have ATVs and those might just work."

"Worth a shot," Aidan added.

There were a number of people milling about the Co-op, it was clear that even the security lights were not working. Some were discussing breaking in as they rode up. One woman was sitting sobbing by the front door. Aidan and Jim parked near her. "What's wrong, can we help?" Alderson asked.

She looked up, red-eyed, "M-m-my girl is diabetic and I left the prescription too long, she will d-die without it and without p-power we can't keep it cold," she sobbed.

"Look, you come in with us and get what you need, and I will show you how to keep it cold," Alderson said.

Alderson stood up and looked at the crowd. "This woman's daughter needs critical medication, does anyone have a problem with saving the girl?" No one spoke but there was a murmur in the crowd. "Then let's open the store."

People watched gape-mouthed as Alderson took out duct tape and covered the door, then hitting it several times with a crowbar, smashed the glass. The tape mostly held the glass and he and Aidan moved it aside and unlocked the door. The woman followed but didn't even have a light so Aidan gave her his flashlight.

At the pharmacy, they had to work to break the lock on the cage. Aidan climbed over the counter and opened that door. Flashlight bouncing, the woman entered and went directly to the fridge, still slightly below room temperature. She grabbed all the insulin she could get.

Alderson started grabbing antibiotics, analgesics, condoms, asthma puffers and first aid supplies. While he was doing this Alex and Carrie were getting the food, they grabbed a bunch of meat that could be cooked today and staples of flour, salt, rice, pasta, fresh vegetables -- this might be the last chance for those.

Filling two shopping carts they moved out. Other people continued "shopping". The woman walked with them, pushing her own cart, following them to the Canadian Tire. No people were hanging around here. Using the same method they broke in again..

Alderson found an electric cooler for the woman, the kind that plugs into a cigarette lighter. He added a battery booster, and a solar panel. Alderson showed her how this could be hooked up to keep things cold. Thanking and kissing him she started pushing her cart home. She travelled with them for a few blocks. Aidan started talking with her about surviving this disaster, telling her that if things did not get better to meet them at Bowness park in a few days.

Crossing the main road, on the last stretch home, they were approached by five young men -- big, fit, and rough -looking guys. "Hey, where did you get that stuff, you guys are looters!"

The biggest and roughest of them said, "You best give us that stuff or we will turn you in," looking back at his buddies for a laugh.

Jim and Aidan stared at him, Aidan said, "You should go home, you can't win this." Carrie's face went into a mask of panic. She did not want to see a fight, violence scared the hell out of her.

The tough wannabe said, "What! You guys are too old and fat to stop us." Alex pulled his jacket back to unveil a holstered 9mm CZ, Alderson did the same to show his Sig P226.

"Those aren't real, Airsoft, you were looting the Canadian Tire," the kid said.

Aidan pulled the shotgun out of the cart and pumped it once, ejecting a shell for effect.

"Real enough for you?" Aidan asked.

Seeing the bore of the shotgun, the toughs backed away. Everyone stood a few minutes watching what looked like spoiled rich football boys retreating. When they were about twenty yards, one kid called back, "You are going to pay for this, the cops will be on you."

Carrie started to shake and cry, "I thought someone was going to get killed." She grabbed Alderson.

"It's okay Carrie, most people make smarter decisions and leave when they know they are beaten," Alderson said. Continuing home, Alderson checked behind making sure those trouble-makers were not following.

"Did Alice show up?" Aidan asked when they returned home. Everyone shook their heads. "I have to go back to the hospital or home to find out where she is."

"Okay I'll go with you," Jim offered.

"No, you need to be here to organize and plan the next step, but I have to go to her. She should have been here last night," Aidan said, visibly disturbed that she had not shown up yet. Alice was very young and pretty, and trying to make the trek here alone at night would be somewhat risky when things were normal. Right now they were effectively in a state of lawlessness, even if most of the population did not know it. People just tacitly agreed to obey the law, for now, just because they always had.

Arya, who had been listening added, "You should not go alone, I will go with you. I don't think I will be going on the trip to Bass Pro." She smiled that disarming smile. Seeming barely phased by all the events, even somewhat excited by it, Arya was handling things well.

Arya's smile and closeness to Aidan seemed flirtatious. Kareem was her boyfriend but did not seem phased by her behaviour. She respected Kareem but maybe Aidan just seemed more exciting to her.

Kareem was a good honest guy who didn't buy into all the patriarchal, repressive ideas of his culture. He, in fact, had pretty much abandoned that culture when he committed the great crime of apostasy. It was a very bad thing in Muslim culture, not as bad for a Westernized Ismaili, but still there were members of the community who would not talk to him once they found out he had nothing to do with the religion any more.

Arya respected him for that. However, he just did not possess that edgy aura of danger and excitement that Aidan portrayed.

"Okay if you really want to," Aidan agreed. Why not, Arya was a hot young East Indian girl, it would be good to have company with him. Alice was not the jealous type, besides he was going out to find her.

Unpacking the shopping carts, repacking the food staples for transport later, everyone pitched in to get the work done. Fresh food needing cooking was set out for immediate use. The walkie-talkies were taken out and checked for power on the rechargeable batteries, three-quarter power meant they did not have to be charged for now. Setting up solar panels to charge battery boosters was easy, but no one knew how long it would take to charge. Hopefully, two could charge while they used one.

"Take these and some water and food with you -- be prepared, like a boy scout," Alderson said, taking a CZ 85 handgun, opening the slide and pointing it at the ground, then handing it to Aidan along with a holster, two loaded magazines, and a walkie-talkie. "When you are out there you should scan the channels with this button just to see what you can find out," Alderson instructed pointing to the scan button. "But if you want to transmit, we will be on channel 30-06, easy to remember. Let's make your call sign Ferrari. I will be Juju, home here will be Viewpoint, Carrie will be Blue for her eyes, Rosie Red for her hair, Kareem will be Abdul," Alderson smiled, "for basketball. Alex will be Comrade."

Aidan grinned, he was a racing fanatic -- well he had been before the pulse.

Kissing Arya goodbye, Kareem saw them off. Jenna was standing behind shaking her head. She said quietly to Alderson, "I think Arya has designs on Aidan."

He looked at her and said, "She might, but that's his problem, not mine. I don't get involved in friends' love lives."

"I don't like it." Jenna added, "I am not sure about her."

Alderson also had a hand-cranked flashlight with emergency radio two-way built in. Working the radio Alderson got the same broadcast that the helicopters had been spewing, nothing useful at this point. But it did tell him they had the emergency broadcast network running. Nothing about that told him he should stand down his plan of action. Trusting the government was not in his nature, that was learned of many years of being told things were improving while he saw an increased level of systemic failures around him. There were always superficial explanations: "A freighter was sunk," "Labour strife in (fill in the blank)," or "A natural disaster" were the usual run of explanations for poor planning and allowing corporations to run rampant.

Some people got extremely wealthy, while the majority had their standard of living eroded. This was such a consistent truth, it had to be by design. It was not random chance. If you were in the top "one percent", it took a lot to erode your position; if you were in the majority, very little chaos created anxiety, fear, and the erosion of your lifestyle. He wondered how well prepared the extremely wealthy were for this calamity. Nope, he would keep going with his plan, and he might just look in on the local scions of wealth and class.

NINE

"Hell is truth seen too late."

- Thomas Hobbes, Leviathan

Lazily driving his cutting machine, Marc was thinking about the upcoming weekend when the machine just stopped. It was half an hour from his shift ending, if it needed repair or fuel his foreman would not get that done till after the day was over. Getting out to check the fuel level, Marc quickly understood there was more going on than his cutting machine failing, cars on the nearby road were stopping. Taking off his ear muffs, the weird silence immediately struck him. Bird noises, people's voices, and a few bangs as moving cars hit stopped ones were the only sounds. Absorbing the incomprehensible scene, Marc checked his cell phone, dead, he knew what that meant. His military background and study of military history told him it must be an EMP.

"Aw fuck, a year from retirement and someone has to let off some EMP nuke," he said out loud, as if cursing the gods. He sat down, sweat dripping down his face, the smell of oil from his machine and freshly cut grass around him, and waited. Looking at the sky, he fully expected nukes to follow in the next thirty minutes, he would just sit there and take it, if a nuke was coming you didn't want to survive it. Surviving a nuke meant you would just die slowly, painfully, better to go

116

quickly, vaporized in a flash of heat.

The nukes didn't come. Marc fell asleep in the shade of his vehicle, waking up some indeterminate time later. The EMP left Marc far from home, walking was the only option -- probably 15 km after a day of work, he didn't look forward to it. He dragged his feet as he slogged homeward, despondent. Suicide was a viable option.

The only question was how? Drugs, jumping, or guns? He didn't have guns, finding the right drugs would mean looting a pharmacy, jumping required the least work. Most of his life he knew if there was a disaster he had some skills to survive, having some woodcraft, military experience, and volumes of history in his head to help him, but doing it alone just didn't make it worthwhile. If this had happened earlier in his life he would have found will to survive and even thrive, but at his age, alone and depressed, why bother? He would go home tonight, then figure out how to die most painlessly the next day. He couldn't suck exhaust fumes as a painless way out, no working vehicles. Someone had taken a shitty, fucked up world, and found a way to make it worse. The idiots who ran this shitshow had just exceeded their own failure.

He arrived first at the city parking lot. Just on a chance Marc tried his old truck, quite dead. Some people had thought cars might not be affected in an EMP but clearly they were wrong. The skin of most cars was connected to the ground wires and so directed current through the vital components. Collecting his lunch bag and his large plastic insulated coffee schooner, he set out for the long walk.

After going a couple of hundred metres, rethinking the situation, trudging back to the truck and rummaging in the back, he found a tire iron and baseball bat. He took them knowing that some protection was going to be necessary in this new world. He was a big, tall guy. He hoped his size would be intimidating, but keeping a weapon for insurance was just prudent. He tucked the tire iron in his belt, slung the lunch bag and mug on the bat and put it over his shoulder like a bindlestiff, and restarted the trek.

Tired, thirsty, hot and sore after hours of walking at the end of a work day, he arrived at home to finding a cryptic note pinned to the door. Finding no roomies at home, he barely gave a thought to what happened to them. The cryptic note was from Jimbo. Jim was going to set up a base at Bowness park. Probably a reasonably good interim place, close to home for Jimbo, but another ten km walk for Marc. "Not today," he decided for either choice, going to Jim or pulling the plug. Finding some juice and food in the fridge, he ate and drank, then crashed for the night.

He woke in a panic, his alarm didn't go off – he was late for work. Noticing nothing worked, it all came back, and it wasn't a dream. Looking outside he estimated it was likely around 7 am, harder to tell on a cloudy day, but he had a feel for it. He sat on the couch thinking. Was it worth it to meet up with Jimbo? Jimbo, good friend for a long while, was a fairly competent guy to have, particularly in a fight. The question remained. Was survival worth the effort? Life was going to be rough. Marc's age didn't help, being nearly 60. Jimbo had left that note, he could be a help to Jimbo. Wondering what kinds of people Jimbo might have collected made Marc curious.

Deciding living was just as easy as pulling the plug for now, Marc would meet up with Jim, he'd put that much effort into surviving the upcoming hell. He could always end it later if things got too bad. Lighting up the barbecue on the balcony, he cooked meats he had in the fridge and ate what he could. Using a cold pack from the freezer that had not thawed yet, he packed what foods and water he could in a lunch kit, putting that inside a backpack, surrounding it with clothes for insulation then adding his survival gear.

The large diver's knife he put on his belt, concealed under a loose shirt. He took the bat again, better range and less lethal than a knife for another long walk. His path took him along the highway jammed with dead vehicles. Anything that hadn't died in the EMP had moved to another location he imagined. A working vehicle was gold now.

Slogging along, keeping his eyes open for useful survival items, and watching to see what people were up to took the monotony out of the trip. The giant edifice to corporate power and greed that dominated the downtown skyline, the Bow building, was burning from the top down.

Marc chuckled. All the oil barons, lawyers, bankers, and corporate heads would now be just as insignificant and meaningless as he had been. The black smoke and oily pall was their power burning. This new world demanded action, not artificial self-importance, and talk. He hated the wealth and power that the oil companies and other rich bastards flaunted while the population starved. Some were still in their towers and penthouse suites waiting for rescue, waiting for the authorities to turn things on, he imagined, laughing to himself. What a great equalizer, a great democratizer, this EMP would be. If anything helped to lighten his mood, it was the vision of power crumbling.

Along the highway, he saw dead cars and closed businesses. He saw groups of people, confused, stunned, some angry and suspicious. He was curious about what people were thinking. He approached one mixed group. Sidling up, he listened.

Agitated speculation about what happened ran through the crowd, some talked about EMP, but none really understood what it might mean, some speculated about who had done it, several talked about the government contingency plans. Clearly nobody knew anything for certain. One guy turned to him and said, "Hey man, what chu tink man? Who fucked us up?" The short, stocky guy had a swarthy, wind-burned look of a Latin American, probably a refugee from several years ago.

"Well, could be Russians, Chinese, Arabs, or even the Americans," Marc started.

"What chu fuckin' crazy man, the 'Mericans is our friends man. Why would they do dat man?" The guy bellowed, talking with his hands, getting irritated.

"Well, for a very long time they have had battle plans that involved nuking themselves to prevent an enemy from getting things, just like the scorched earth policy of the Russians in World War II. Or it could have been a rogue, or a test gone bad. We really can't know yet," Marc continued amiably.

"Chu some kind of commie man, chu don' know nothin'!" the other man said, getting angry.

Another bystander joined in, "That's bullshit, I was in the forces, there is so much integration, the Americans would not have done this to us. If they wanted control they could have had it. I think it was Haji terrorists. The government and military have lots of contingencies, they will have things fixed in a couple of days, at least power and shit." He was young, maybe 25. Probably did a tour in the militia, but had no knowledge of secret plans of the military.

Marc knew much more than they did, he had seen plans when he had a high security clearance, although that was a very long time ago. Looking at the crowd he decided it was better not to argue.

"Hey guys, I was just saying things I had heard, I don't know what's true or not, but I have to be on my way. Good luck," he finished, and began to leave.

A uniformed cop walked up and sternly asked, "What's going on here?"

"Not'in copper, we was jus talking, is that a crime *sir?*" the Latin man answered, emphasizing the last word to show he did not respect the law or cops, but was sounding like he did.

The six-foot-two, 100 kilogram cop glared icily and said, "This city is under martial law, there is no travel except critical personnel and those making their way home. People should not be gathering." The Latin man got less bellicose and backed off.

"Okay sir, I'm goin' home now," he said as he started leaving.

The cop eyeballed the rest of them, then looked specifically at Marc. "You, where are you going?" he asked aggressively.

Marc, who was never a good liar and had trouble making up a story on the spot, answered too honestly: "I'm going to a friend's place in the Varsity area."

The cop put his hand on his gun and said, "What did you not understand about 'No travel except to home'? Show me some ID. You look like you're armed like an anarchist with that bat, I don't think you're going to play a game of ball. Put it on the ground." Keeping his eye on Marc, he said, "The rest of you fuck off and go home, do not let me catch you gathering again or you will be taken in."

Marc had kept his wallet, now he wasn't sure why, he did have a hundred bucks, which maybe someone would accept, but his bank card was useless now. He took out his wallet and gave the cop his driver's license.

"Marc Antundersson it says you live on 12th. If I do not find you there in one hour you will be arrested and locked up," the cop threatened.

Marc complied, turning around. As he started walking, he noticed the cop going toward the downtown. Turning a corner Marc doubled back into the alleyway. If the cop went to his place in an hour, he would be an hour away. He wasn't going to go there and wait, for what? Help from the government? That was a joke at anytime, now it was outright hysterical.

Marching on, assiduously avoiding contact with people, Marc eventually arrived at the Foothills Hospital. He surveyed the scene of activity. It was clear that this was a centre of government activity: helicopters, ground vehicles, military, and police. Some things were working, but it was a scene of chaos. Watching from a distance, he knew he should stay away, it would be too easy to be drawn into the fray. He detoured through residential neighbourhoods, taking alleys and treed roads where it was harder to be seen by air. Marc was sure they would not waste resources to try and make sure everyone was following whatever edict the local dictator had issued, but he wanted to minimize his contact with any authorities, that was always the safest.

His path would take him near a major shopping mall, scouting it out for possible loot would be a worthwhile exercise. Large scale looting probably hadn't started. If he could get in it would give him an opportunity to get his choice of gear.

Continuing to avoid contact with others, he made his way to the mall with its sea of dead cars. He spotted occasional groups of people looting cars, or just recovering their own goods. Strangely, there were people waiting at the store, an orderly crowd, but no one had broken in. "Only in Canada," he chuckled to himself. In the States if the power went out for an hour in some places, there was looting. It had already been at least 18 hours.

Circling the mall to get the lay of the land, it was clear people were not waiting on the side away from the grocery store. Taking a chance, using the handle of his knife, he shattered a glass door, hoping he would not attract attention. Looking for observers, seeing none, he slipped in, kicking the broken glass aside with his steel-toed boots.

He made his way to the Sport Chek. More of a trendy sports apparel store, it would not have the best survival gear but it would have a bike, clothes, panniers for the bike and a few other items. In the darkened mall, not even the emergency lights were functioning. On the inside he had to break another glass door. Inside, Marc found the gear. He was somewhat surprised no one else had broke in to take anything; clearly the gravity of the situation had not struck most people yet.

Seeing the bobbing flashlight of some poor security guard far down the mall, Marc quickly made his way back out. The guard may have yelled at him but he paid no heed. Coasting down the hill to Bowness made the ride quick. Rolling through the community, he found a centre of activity near the Hades Animals hangout, a barricaded Quonset with visible guards. Those guards concerned him, making him move faster.

The ride through the old town saw only occasional people and little activity. Approaching the large park area he noted a number of people trekking away from it, carrying an assortment of items in unsuitable ways, likely people who had been trapped at the park and waited to leave. Inside the wooded park, cruising around the paved oval, going to the amusement area, he found only a group of kids fooling around, some locals walking their dogs – no Jimbo setting up camp. The kids had built some kind of lean-to in the forested area by the river. He hoped they knew you should not drink the water untreated.

That worried him, something could have befallen Jim before he got home, certainly it was becoming a world of new dangers and tenuous law at best. Jim had left the note yesterday, even walking Jimbo should have been here long ago. Marc spent an hour, even asked the kids if they had seen a bald-headed guy with a goatee come in, but no luck. He made sure they knew not to drink the untreated water. Jimbo's place wasn't too far from the park just all uphill. Perhaps Jenna would be there and she might have news. What else did he have to do? He began the climb up the escarpment, walking his new bike. He was too old and out of shape to try and power the bike up the steep hill.

There was a knocking on the front door, "Shave and a Haircut, Two Bits" – that could only mean Marc. Marc was an old, but odd, friend. A very lecherous guy, his leering attentions and unwelcome advances made many women uncomfortable. Alderson let him in. Marc would be undeniably useful. Marc's experience in the US army, life experiences in the wilderness, and extensive knowledge on all things military would prove useful in the new world order. While he had combat experience, he was not in any way a fighter – big and intimidating, but not aggressive or skilled in hand to hand combat. "Hey Marc. Glad to see you. Sorry we didn't get to the park yet," Alderson said.

"Yeah, I went through there. Some people were camped, others are leaving today," Marc said. "So the Apocalypse has finally arrived with a vengeance."

Everyone gathered around and Jim introduced them all. Marc, true to form, leered over-long, staring at Angela and Jolene, his eyes fixating on Jolene's breasts. Lowering his voice, he smiled unctuously. "I am very pleased to meet you," he intoned to the voluptuous Jolene, voluptuousness was always Marc's weak point. When introduced to Carrie, another well-endowed female, Alderson made sure to note that she was a recent student, making her too young for Marc.

As Jimbo introduced him to this interesting crew including some young hotties, Marc's brain raced; in a normal situation these women, mostly young, pretty, with successful careers, would not give him the time of day, but this might become a different situation. He might just end up being the last available man on earth, or at least in this survival group. In his mind the young teacher Jolene was particularly hot, big breasts, blue eyes, blonde hair, nice smile – also known as the perfect woman for Marc.

Jim had these people following his direction even though it didn't seem like he was issuing orders, for some reason he had garnered their respect. The teachers, kids, and even Aidan he could understand; if they knew Jim well, they would know he was a good thinker in many areas. Marc didn't quite understand how he got Kareem onside after knowing him less than 24 hours, but he was here and seemed to be on-board. They would soon see that Jim didn't necessarily have the military background and historical background to be the leader for the long term. In the long term, Marc imagined, he might need to be the group leader, then the girls would see him differently, he might have his pick. In fact this disaster could be a boon, providing all kinds of desperate women for him to choose from.

"So this looks like the end of the world as we know it. Probably an EMP, an EMP is a an Electromagnetic Pulse created by a nuclear weapon." Marc started on a lecture, "It destroys electronics and electrical systems..."

Alderson, sensing the impending lecture, cut him off, "I have explained all of that to everyone here, they're mostly up to speed."

"So things could get really bad, there will likely be a failure of the sewer and water systems, and no food will come into the city..." Marc restarted, until Alderson cut him off again.

"We've had a good discussion of possibilities and probabilities. Let me bring you up to speed on what we know. We have gathered some goods and some information," Alderson started, trying to shut down Marc's professorial lecturing, which annoyed people or put them to sleep.

He filled Marc in on the government broadcasts, what they heard at the hospital, what they had done so far, and finally, the next plans. Alderson was telling Marc about the small incident with the cop when Carrie chimed in.

"You should have seen Alderson, I thought he was going to get shot one second, then next second the cop is on the ground with Alderson pointing the cops own gun at him. He is seriously bad-ass, then he shot and just missed the cop, but he missed him on purpose."

Alderson wanted to shut down this talk of his dubious exploit, so he switched topic and began to discuss the next plan. "Let's get Marc some food then discuss next moves"

"What I see as the next job is an important and risky one. We need to make a foray to Bass Pro. It is a long ride and will be risky because the guns there will attract others. It will be at least a twenty-k ride but I hope it will be easier coming back if we can find some ATVs that are working. I think we need to get four people resting and ready for tonight. Who will go with me?" Alderson asked the group.

Kareem, Marc, and Alex volunteered. That would leave just females behind, he was not sure he liked that idea. But hopefully Aidan would be back by then. "We also need someone to volunteer to keep watch on the roof, but you can switch off that duty. And two people to watch at the overpass on Crowchild Trail."

"Rosie and I will watch on the overpass, I ain't going on the roof, I'm afraid of heights," Carrie volunteered. She and Rosie could sit and gossip the time away.

Angela suggested, "Why don't you and I take the roof Di? It'll be good." Di agreed half-heartedly, she was very subdued today, the horrors of yesterday were just starting to sink in.

"You need to report back regularly so everyone knows what's happening, okay?" Alderson said to the assembled group.

"Jenna and Jolene man the crank radio. For now the four of us will try to get rested so we are ready for the evening."

" *'Man'* it? We can't *'man'* it, we're not men!" Jenna grinned.

"Okay then 'staff' it, just don't get an infection, I don't know which antibiotic is good for a 'staph' infection," Alderson joked, and several people groaned.

The girls rode out to the overpass, Alderson having made sure they were armed with knives and the Airsoft guns. He told them to let people get somewhat close then shoot them in the face if necessary, but getting on the bikes and pedaling fast was still their best defence. The guns looked real, especially from a distance, but they were't lethal. He was not really ready to arm them with firearms, they had no training, no history with guns. Jim made sure they took chairs, water, and snacks.

They arrived at their observation post and quickly tried out the Airsoft guns, firing pellets at anything they thought they could hit, challenging each other.

Reporting back to base, the girls identified only people on bikes or walking along the roadways, some looting the vehicles, no real threats. There were a couple of motorcycles, but no one was clearing the roadway. It was still too soon for the government to be that organized. The EMP had happened at rush hour, leaving thousands of dead vehicles. Later that day, the girls reported seeing a helicopter far to the south, the only sign of likely government action.

"You seem to be planning and thinking just like gamers," Marc said approvingly.

"Do you want some food, we are going to cook up the fresh we got from the store. I also have an electric cooler working because we have solar panels up there," Alderson said.

They talked and planned what they needed for some time. Alderson, concerned he had not heard back from

Aidan, got on the radio to the girls watching the main road, "Blue this is Viewpoint, have you heard from Ferrari?"

"We did about an hour ago, he said Alice wasn't at the hospital, he was going home for now," Carrie responded.

"Roger that. Blue, Ratel (Jenna), and Green (Jolene) will replace you soon," Alderson said, "so you can get proper food."

Jenna and Jolene rolled out to replace them when the sun was in the last third of the sky. Alderson gave Jenna the single-shot shotgun, just in case. A short time after, they radioed in, "Viewpoint this is Ratel. We heard from Ferrari, he is returning in about one hour, has not found Alice." Jenna worried about what had happened to Alice, she was also concerned that Arya seemed to be getting too close with Aidan. In general, she didn't trust men, her opinion was if they could fool around they would.

The team was preparing the for the next forage run when Aidan and Arya returned. His face was drawn with concern. "I don't know where she is, she hasn't been to my place, and the hospital said she left at 4 am. I looked at some nearby friends' places, they weren't there either. At the hospital the cops ordered us to go home, so I did, then I left again," Aidan stated.

"Then they gave us this," Arya said handing Alderson a piece of paper. It was a poster saying. LOOTING IS ILLEGAL. LOOTERS WILL BE ARRESTED AND DETAINED. EMERGENCY SUPPLIES CAN BE OBTAINED AT MCMAHON STADIUM, THE SADDLEDOME, AND THE LOUGHEED HOSPITAL.

"That's fucking awesome," Alderson said, "What will the rest of the city do? I don't think they can maintain control. I still intend to go ahead with my plan. So Aidan are you going to stay here, I don't want to take everyone with me. Can you watch the fort?" Aidan was competent and Jenna would help

128

him.

"Sure if that is what you want, I can do that," Aidan said "I am burnt out from all the riding today, not used to it." He looked depressed and worried, having Arya with him had allowed him to worry less when he was waiting and riding, but now that was over and he was settling in to worry some more. Alice might just have gone to a co-worker's place and she might go work another shift tomorrow. He would have to be patient, even though that was not in his nature.

TEN

The team going to loot made ready about an hour before dark. Alderson, feeling the effects of the long ride and all the adrenaline of the previous day, willed himself to prepare. He quipped, "Yeah, I think the EMP was just a government plot to fight obesity, greatest fitness plan ever! In about an hour bring in the solar panels, and call the watchers in. It will be too dark to bother watching. We probably won't return until after really late in the morning. Keep a radio going till we lose contact."

They rode out, taking the ring road to the giant shopping mall. It would be at least a twenty-five kilometre ride, with some significant hills. They took two shotguns and two handguns and some water and snacks, wrecking tools, bolt cutters, and empty packs.

At every high point they tried radio contact, but they lost radio by the time they had gone ten kilometres, too many intervening hills. With the sun setting, the temperature was dropping. Calgary, with its thousand metre elevation, had cool nights even in the hottest days of summer, and this was only spring -- the temperature could easily drop to freezing. This evening had some cloud cover which would keep the temperature from dropping too low.

As it got darker, the ride became more surreal. The lack of city lights, the lack of city sounds, only the sounds of animals, mostly coyotes, and wind, made this unreal to the group of born city dwellers. Their own breathing, pedaling, insects, frogs, and those coyotes, were all that kept them company on the long ride. They saw cattle, "grasshoppers" or pump jacks, silent and unmoving, silhouetted by the faint glow on the horizon, or the occasional fire at a farmstead. This province was known for cattle, and oil, Texas North, some called it, but it was silent now, dying. Seeing the fields, knowing they had been planted, Alderson pondered how they would get harvested. He imagined crews of people with old fashioned scythes cutting the wheat, agriculture was going to be every person's work soon.

"Chopper!" Kareem called, pointing south. They had travelled about half-way.

Alderson and Alex looked around for a hiding place. All that was available were dead cars. "Behind the transport!" Marc called and pointed to a big rig. They made their way to a transport that had been headed east on the road.

"I hope they don't have thermal imaging," Marc said, "or we could be fucked already."

"Maybe right under the truck is safest," Kareem suggested. They all crawled under and watched the chopper from behind the tires. It was doing a search pattern with a large spotlight several kilometres south. The team waited anxiously, lying under the transport, not wanting to give their position away. They talked in the hushed tones of conspirators, even though there was no one for kilometres to hear them.

To Kareem this felt so surreal, a day ago he was second assistant manager at a Canadian Tire store, no brilliant career, but decent enough, but today he was a makeshift commando going with some guy he barely knew to rob a sporting goods store, now hiding from the only authority there was. He felt

131

like he should go screaming to the chopper 'Help us', but seeing the kilometres of dead vehicles he was beginning to sense the magnitude of the situation. He knew a couple of choppers could not do much for a million people. He wondered how other parts of the country or even the world were doing. If Alderson was right, North America was screwed. He was numb, just following others, he didn't know what to think. His beautiful Arya seemed a little too comfortable with the whole "End of the World" idea, she was always adventurous and resilient, that was just another part of her attraction. To him it remained so unreal, so impossible, it had to be a very, very long, very bad dream.

The chopper circled, the circle spiraling out, clearly searching, the spotlight illuminating some neighbourhood. Alderson looked at his watch, an old simple watch with no chip, it had been close to an hour that chopper searched. It flew further south not seeming to have found its prey.

The crew pulled themselves out from under the transport.

"I say we see what this was carrying!" Alderson said with a bit too much verve. He got out the bolt cutters and cut the lock at the back. The door swung open after being unlatched only to reveal bagged top soil and peat moss, not very useful right now. They loaded up and continued on their way, all the stiffer for having rested for a full hour.

"Guys I don't want to travel up the QE 2, it is a bit too open for my liking." The main north-south highway would be jammed with dead cars and likely camped people. "I know another route, but we will be on gravel for a couple of K." He lead the team on the route that would only cross the big highway.

On the overpass, Alderson stopped. "Let's have a long look first." He took out binoculars and looked then handed them to Kareem.

"Hey there is some light at Bass Pro," Kareem whispered, even though there was no one other than the crew for a thousand metres or more.

"We should turn off the bike lights," Alex stated. "They'll give us away from a long ways off. I think we should drop the bikes at the north side of the mall."

"Kareem, you seem to have the best night vision so you take point," Alderson directed. Kareem led off and the others followed being as quiet as possible. They hid their bikes among the dead cars at the north side of the dead mega-mall and crept slowly around toward the Bass Pro. It would be the number one target for looting so nobody would be surprised if someone had beaten them to it.

A hundred metres from the front door Kareem spotted a guy sitting there in a chair, wearing a camouflage jacket, and halted. Everyone watched for a while. The guy had a long gun, likely a shotgun, across his lap. His head lolled forward, it looked like he was sleeping. Marc made hand signals indicating to look around for others. The front door to the store appeared smashed. They could see no other guard. Alderson took a bead on the guard and then signaled to Alex to do the same. Alderson then holstered his gun and took out his knife, he was going to try and get close. He had to travel over landscaping rock. It would make a noise, but he had to risk it. If he went slow and careful the noise might not seem unnatural. The crunching and crackling of gravel, the only noise in the still night, rattled Alderson's nerves. But the lookout's head remained slumped forward, still asleep. He had a scruffy beard and baseball cap with the Stampeders' horse logo on it and camo clothing, but he wasn't military.

Once behind the guard Alderson sheathed his knife and noticed the guard's hand was not on the gun. Alderson whipped his right arm around the guys neck and clapped his left over his mouth. He twisted hard to his right pulling the guy out of the chair and face down on the ground in a second. The gun and chair clattered to the side making a cacophony to break the still night. Alderson remained on the guard's back with his arm locked in. If he had to he would put the guy unconscious with *hadaka jime,* the naked strangle, but he really wanted to talk to the guy and get info. The guard murmured and tried to fight, but found it hard to move with a tightening boa constrictor around his neck and with the weight of an anaconda on his back. Alderson whispered in his ear, "If you yell I will snap your neck." Alderson was bluffing but the guard didn't know it. This was actually a very hard position in which to snap someone's neck. Marc had moved to aim his shotgun inside the door in case anyone else showed. The guy tried to nod his head, Alderson understood the intent and removed his hand from the guy's mouth.

"Don't kill me, please don't kill me, I-I'll give you w-w-what ever you need," the guard pleaded. Alderson noticed a spreading wetness on the pavement, the guy had pissed himself, understandable being woken up face down with someone choking and sitting on you.

"How many inside?" Alderson whispered.

"None, j-just me." The guy tried to lie.

Alderson squeezed his arms shut a little for 2 seconds, long enough for the guard to know he would soon be out. "That was me not believing you," Alderson snarled in his ear.

"Okay, okay, there are five of us, everyone is on the second level where the camping gear is, they have guns you know." Marc had retrieved the shotgun and handed it to Alex who was keeping his pistol at the ready but willingly took the shotgun and put the handgun away.

Alderson released the guard and told him, "Go over to the bushes, nice and careful." Once there Alderson began, "Look we don't want to hurt you guys, but we are going to get what we need, you are fools if you think you can hold this. The military will be here soon, I am kind of surprised they didn't get here already and they are locking up looters you know. Here is what I propose, you get your buddies to come forward and we will take what we can carry and fuck off."

"Yeah but we were going to make people trade for this stuff, we own it now," the guard complained in a whiny voice.

Alderson cuffed him in the head, "Fuckin' idiot, you will have nothing if the military gets here, we're not trading we're taking, just like you. The difference is we are taking what we can and then moving out. Now here is what you will do, you will step inside the door and yell to them that you see a chopper approaching and headlights on the highway, then come back outside the door to look. If you deviate from my script I will put two in your back. If everything goes well you will get to take what you can when we leave." Alderson stepped back and drew his Sig. "You understand what you have to do?" Alderson stepped back, aiming at the hapless guard. The guard nodded.

He did as he was instructed, he had to yell several times to get a response. Once finished, Alderson told him to run, pointing south. He did. The others came out just as clueless, they each had a rifle or shotgun in hand, but none at the ready. They stepped out of the door and Alderson yelled, "Drop your weapons or we will shoot!" They looked around at three shotguns and a handgun, and to a man their guns hit the ground. They were directed by muzzle point to the parking lot. But there were only four of them. "Where is the other one?" Alderson yelled.

"He's inside still, just at the doors," one said, his voice quavering.

Alderson yelled inside, "Come out with your hands high, unarmed or we shoot your buddies then come for you. And in this world you will need your buddies." Alderson fired past one of them into the remaining glass, the violent crack of the shot and shattering of the glass echoed through the night for miles around. "The next one is a buddy of yours."

A shotgun came sliding out. Then a guy came out hands on his head. "Grab the para-cord and tie them up," Alderson said to Kareem as he kept aim on them with Alex and Marc.

"You got it," Kareem replied, "Are you sure you are not ex-military? You sure act and plan like it."

"I'm not, but he is," Alderson said nodding toward Marc.

Alderson explained how it would work, they would collect all they could carry out and then when they left, this group was free to do what they wanted. Alderson added, "I suggest you guys do the same before the military shows up, you lot are no match for them" .

It took more than two hours to get the gear and find four ATVs, and securely attach the stuff. They obtained some key survival gear and a dozen rifles, .22, .308, .223 calibre, the most common and useful. They grabbed shotguns and handguns too. They loaded some ammo onto each ATV, but Alderson and Marc insisted on more primers, powder, and bullets. They were thinking about the long term. There was ammo closer to home at the Canadian Tire. All of the ATVs at Bass Pro seemed to work except the most expensive types. They grabbed crossbows, bows, and all the high-tech arrows they could find, these were all weapons for the long term. Preparing to leave meant having to drain some cars of fuel as the ATVs were not gassed up. That was made easier by the presence of a hand pump liberated from the marine section of the store. The ATVs being packed high, going back meant leaving their bikes, they could get more of those at home too. The gear they collected was the very best in the store, including binoculars that would have cost Alderson a month's wages, night vision monoculars and very expensive night vision scopes, but leaving expensive GPS units, they weren't going anywhere they could get lost. Simple compasses had more longer term viability anyway.

Finally roaring out of the lot, the engine noise echoing and rattling the night, silenced the twittering of early birds.

With only an hour of dark remaining, they moved quickly toward home. Their progress back was much quicker until Kareem roared ahead, pointing and yelling "Chopper, south!" They had hoods to hood the lights of the ATVs, but hiding would still be wise. They killed their engines as they pulled in beside the same transport they had hidden under on their way out. Taking out a scoped, but not zeroed, rifle and resting it on back of the transport, Marc sighted the chopper.

"There is one guy in the door, armed, looks military," Marc reported, "circling again." Waiting till dawn for chopper to leave, Alderson tried the radio, but no luck. Everyone was probably sleeping, and they were situated in a depression again. When they could no longer see the chopper, they moved again breaking the stillness of the early morning. Their engines, the only sound of mankind's industry, could be heard for miles.

"Hey everyone, cut your engines and let's do a neutral roll down this hill, it will make us less noticeable in the quiet," Alderson suggested as they crested the hill, dodging dead cars. They would have to restart on the flat.

Arriving in the early daylight hours they parked the ATVs in the condo common area where they could be hidden from arial view, covering them with tarps and branches to break-up their silhouette. No one was up yet when they came in. Jolene and Di woke as the crew came in, others arose over the next couple of hours. Marc told the story of the take-down at the Bass Pro, and how they saw the chopper hovering a couple of times.

"I wonder what that was about?" Jolene asked.

"Well, any choppers are a sign of the government." Marc added, "It is the first step toward them exerting control where they can."

Breakfast was prepared on the propane grill and everyone ate, making small talk and seeming hopeful. "I'm going to look for Alice again," Aidan said as he ate.

"Do you want someone to go with you?" Jenna asked.

"Nah. Should be fine. It just worries me I haven't heard from her yet."

"Okay, but take a radio."

As the gathering ate Jim suggested, "We need to get some jennies. Canadian Tire or Wal-Mart, maybe Costco are the easy pickin's for that, or even Rona."

"A couple would be helpful, we could keep food cold at least," Kareem joined in. "Do you think the forklifts at the stores would be working?"

"Hmmm, I don't know, if they were inside or if they are simple enough, they might be working," Alderson said. "We will need to get organized and see what is happening. First plan of action, set some watches, get info. Info will be a valuable resource." They arranged watches with those who had just awakened. Those who had just returned turned in to sleep, perchance to dream. For most of them it was a fitful sleep, dreams fueled by the adrenalized events of what they had been through.

ELEVEN

It was only six hours later when most of the raiding team awoke. Finding sewer and water working, the others started the day with buoyant sense of hope. Power and transport remained an issue, but hope was in the air.

"I really think we should head home, I think in a day or two things will start getting fixed," Kareem pleaded with Arya. She looked at him, looked around at Alderson and Marc, but she said nothing.

"It is your choice Kareem, you know what my views are, and you know where we plan to be if things get worse again," Alderson said neutrally.

"Hey man, if you feel that is what you want, but think about how difficult things are going to be during the recovery with no transport," Marc interjected.

"Kareem, love, I know you are afraid and, I know your law-abiding sense has been shattered by what you have seen and been part of, but really I think Jim and Marc are right. I would say, there is strength in numbers and these people seem to have a good sense of how to prepare, so why don't we wait just a couple of days."

Looking at Arya, Kareem, concern in his eyes, looked down, "Okay sweetheart, we can wait a bit."

"Do you think they have cell service yet?" Rosie asked, "I'd like to check Facebook and Tumblr."

To test it Alderson got his phone, that had been shielded enough in the initial EMP that it still worked, but it only gave the "No Service" and even the GPS was not functioning.

Arya looked over at his phone. "No cell service yet." she added.

The discussion of what to do next went on for what seemed hours. Jim pushed for a plan of action for the next day. The basic day plan called for some watchers to go high up the hill and survey the city. "I'll go," Marc volunteered. He would be a good choice because of his military background he was likely to focus on important features.

"Kareem, would you go with him? You have good night vision, younger eyes," Jim asked. "I want you two to go at dark because that will give you clear signs of electricity working or fires burning. I will need a couple for radio relay."

"I could set up on the overpass, it should provide a good point for relay and viewing," Alex added. Angela and Rosie volunteered to join him in that duty.

"I am going to say anyone who knows how to handle a gun should carry one, but while you're out try to train the others during the dead times," Jim said, not wanting any firearm accidents.

Again there was almost a party atmosphere, people sipping drinks and chatting amiably about a variety of topics, when Jolene yelled that there was incoming on the radio from

Ferrari. They all went to listen.

"Go ahead Ferrari, this is Viewpoint," Alderson transmitted. He gave the radio a few cranks just to ensure it had the juice to be heard well.

"Jim, is that you?" a distraught Aidan said.

"I'm here, go ahead."

"She's dead Jim, they said she died in a house fire," he said sobbing. "I don't think they gave her my message." He continued, "I-I'm coming back now".

"Okay brother, we'll be waiting for you, over," Jim said somberly.

They waited about an hour before Aidan came riding slowly up. "Aidan, I'm so sorry, man I wish we had just waited for her, I'm so sorry," Alderson said quietly as he held his longtime friend. Arya and Jenna joined them, offering their support.

"They said she must have gone to another staff member's place after her double shift last night. That person lived just a block from a fire hall and close to the hospital, but there was a fire in the night. Fire fighters tried to fight it but they had only garden hoses, they were too late." He sobbed as he told the story. "They said she likely died before the fire got to her, her friend from work died too and two kids." With that he sat down with his head in his hands, after a bit he looked up. "Have you got anything strong to drink?" he asked.

Alderson brought him some rum, knowing that was Aidan's preferred drink. Aidan shot about half of the drink back. He looked at Alderson and said, tears in his eyes, "Is this how it's going to be, people near you dying, a wasting away of everything we know?"

"I don't know Aidan, but I do know we can work with each other to make things better for us, I am really sorry we didn't have someone wait for her. I really thought we would see her this morning," Alderson said, consoling Aidan.

"Yeah, me too, I thought she was just waiting till daylight, I thought she might even get here when I was out looking for her, I should have waited." Aidan drank the rest of the rum. "I don't know what to do man, I just don't know."

"For now have another drink," Arya said as she poured more rum for him.

He accepted that an took another shot. Di went over to him and held his hand saying, "I don't know you much Aidan, but I know how you feel, my mom and dad died in a fire right after it happened, and no one could save them, it feels terrible. I want to help you." By this point everyone in the room was sobbing. Aidan drank some more, Di staying with him. She instinctively didn't say much but just sat with him.

He drank a fair bit then stretched out on the couch, Di just sat on the floor beside him, they both sobbed a while.

Alderson and the others moved into the back yard. They started to talk after a few minutes of quiet. "This brings us to another point," Alderson said. "We need a 24/7 watch seeing things like detectors and whatnot might be inoperable and because of electrical issues. If power does come on the likelihood of a fire is greater in the short term. We need two people on watch to ensure they stay awake."

"Aidan and Di need some time to grieve, we should leave them out of it today," Jenna said.

"We can for now," Alderson agreed.

"Hey Jim!" Alderson heard someone different calling his

name. It was Percy the condo association president.

"Hey Percy," he said as he opened the gate inviting Percy in. "These are friends of mine staying here for now." He then introduced the ones in the back yard.

"Jim are those quads out in the common area yours? Do they work?" Percy asked.

"Hmm, well we are using them and they do work," Jim replied.

"You know you can't park them there, they need to go in the parking lot and you can't have people up on the roof either, insurance rules," Percy added nervously.

Jim laughed so hard he sprayed the wine that was in his mouth all over, "Are you living in a different reality than me? Than the rest of us? Have you noticed what has happened?"

"Those are rules. They are right in our bylaws, you have to respect them!" Percy blurted.

"You pompous, self-righteous, officious moron, what kind of a delusion are you living in? Do you think this will all just be better tomorrow? You think the insurance company will even exist in a month? Go ahead and try to contact their offices."

"Well just because there is a disaster doesn't mean the rules don't apply, there will be consequences if you don't follow the rules," Percy said, reddening and looking nervous.

"Percy you idiot, you could not control late night loud parties when you could pick up a phone and call the police. Do you imagine in this disaster I give two shits or a flying fuck about you and your rules?" Alderson said in an intimidating manner. "Consequences, fuck you idiot, we are all going to face consequences if we are not prepared."

Carrie and Rosie were sniggering. "Go Alderson!" Carrie

said.

"Well if you were paying attention you would know the authorities said we would be getting power back soon," Percy said, trying to not shake.

"Sure they will, and then what? No transportation, do you have any idea what happened, why nothing electronic works?" Alderson was laughing at him again. Stunned, Percy just stood there, looking for words. "You're a moron Percy, if you touch anything here or bother anyone else, you will deal with me and you won't like it," Alderson said, having had enough of Percy.

Rosie piped up, "He will seriously kick your ass. He's very bad-ass." She was thinking it was quite exciting watching Alderson work.

"You can't threaten me, there are witnesses here, I will have you arrested," Percy said, almost crying.

"That's not a real threat," Alderson said. Leaning in close to Percy he whispered, "If I broke you, and threw your body in a ditch, there would be no cops to find you for a long time. That's a threat." The others could not hear what Alderson said but the could sense the chill in his voice, and they could see Percy go white, turn and leave. "Presidents sometimes get deposed," Alderson said aloud with a grin. "He's an officious knob, he can fuck himself. If he interferes with us I will beat his office-boy ass," he added.

Rosie smiled, fist pumped the air and said, "Yeah Alderson, you are a bad-ass!"

A few moments later another neighbour, a very large Native guy whom Alderson could only ever remember as White Eagle came over with his wife. "Hey Jim, what did Percy want?"

"Pffft, he was telling me we can't put people on the roof

or park the ATVs here, I told him to fuck himself," Alderson answered.

"You think this thing is serious?" White Eagle asked.

"I believe it has the potential to be extremely serious, maybe the most serious disaster in human history, how serious it is right now, nobody really knows. My opinion, it will get much worse before anything gets better. What I do know is that I am going to prepare for the worst and hope I'm wrong. And I am not going to let a bureaucrat wannabe like Percy stop me. He's really an idiot if he thinks he can stop me," Alderson said, trying to gauge White Eagle.

"Preparing sounds prudent, but I have no idea what could have happened to make cars stop like they did," White Eagle said.

"Well I believe that it was an Electromagnetic Pulse from a nuclear weapon," Alderson started.

Marc jumped into the conversation. "That doesn't mean we got nuked. It could have happened a 1000 miles away and it would have been high in the atmosphere. Nobody would have even died in the blast."

"Really, you think we are at some kind of war?" White Eagle asked.

"Well, it wasn't likely even meant so much for Canada, except that we are an American ally, but the effects don't obey political boundaries," Alderson replied.

"How are you preparing for the worst? What do you think the worst will be Jim?" White Eagle queried.

Alderson answered, aware that White Eagle's wife looked very worried. "Collecting survival gear and looking for a way out of the city eventually. My long-term depends on what the authorities do. As for what the worst is, you don't want to know, it's real scary. Let's just say I'm planning to live in a mostly pre-industrial era."

"Where will you go?" asked White Eagle

"Well as long as things look good, and water and sewage still run, I will stay and collect gear. When those stop I will set up at Bowness Park for a while until the city is too unsafe." Alderson added, "You could join us. But I will be honest with you, what we do while preparing may be technically illegal, but it's survival."

Looking concerned, White Eagle paused then answered, "Thanks for your honesty and your offer Jim, I think we want to wait and see but we won't get in your way. But you know Jim, you white people just take property way too seriously anyway." He completed that with a big grin.

They shook hands and White Eagle and his wife went back to their place where they appeared to be smoking meat in the backyard, also a violation of the condo rules technically, but no one cared.

The collective went back to discussing and planning, but in a more sombre mood. They would send out the two groups of watchers, giving them several hours before dark to set up then to watch the night for signs of electricity or other activity.

"I will head over to COP and try to get to the top of the ski jump," Alderson said. "It would be an incredible view point and I should have direct radio communication back because of the line of sight. I'll have a great view of the city, including the hospital where there is power and activity."

Kareem and Marc would go up the hill to the north, while Alex, Angela, and Rosie would watch from the pedestrian overpass on the main road giving them a broad view of that route.

Kareem and Marc left first, heading up the hill that dominated the city's north side. At it highest point the ice-age glacial till was 200 metres above the downtown, overlooking almost all of the city that was not hidden behind other landforms.

Preparing to head out after the large group left, Alderson would take a bike. As he was about to leave Jolene said, "I'd like to go with you."

"Uh, we need some to stay back at base," Alderson replied, not wanting to have to worry about how someone else was doing things.

"Look Jim, I have lots of hiking, biking and camping experience, I think I have done it all more recently than you have."

"Okay, I really have no special skills for this just paranoia and shooting skills," he said loading his Sig P226 and snapping it into a Kydex holster, then slinging a a short-barreled pump 12 gauge shotgun. He packed some water, food, as well as some very fancy binoculars and the radio. Leaving Aidan, Di, Jenna, Carrie, and Arya at home, he hoped there would be no trouble; while he would normally trust Aidan with his life, Aidan was not in great shape to handle anything right now. Jenna knew how to shoot but she didn't really like to. He kissed Jenna goodbye and noted the sour, slightly unhappy look on her face. He imagined that she might be jealous of Jolene. Jolene was young and vivacious, but he had years of trust with Jenna.

Alderson and Jolene rolled down the road to the bottom of the hill that took them over the river to Bowness Park. Alderson stopped part-way, dismounting from his bike and putting it on the kickstand. "Hold up Jolene, we need to give it the eyeball first." He took out the binoculars and scanned the bridge and the park on the other side.

"See anything?" she asked. "Wait, what's that over

there?" she was pointing in the park area. "It ... it looks like a lean-to or something."

He was impressed by her sharp eyes, "Good reason to have someone young along," he muttered to himself. He focused the binoculars on the identified area, she was right, there was a lean-to in the park and some movement in the trees, he could identify about four people. The park had one road entrance and several ways in on foot. As well, there were some well-to-do people who had property that backed on to the park down an embankment, but those people would not be living in the park. There were multiple ways for people on foot to get in there. Jolene leaned in close to him.

"It's a bit chilly," she said. He handed her the binoculars. She scanned a while then said, "Looks like five people, two girls, three guys, very young. Perhaps rather close with each other." She smiled and winked.

"Let's go meet them once we get down, I don't see any issues on the bridge or on this side. We will have to take a trip down to the dam one day, that could become an issue if there are no controls," Alderson said, thinking for the first time what would happen if there were no controls on the dams in the city or further upstream. He assumed they must have manual overrides and emergency power, at least he hoped so, and somebody manning those controls. The big spring runoff from the mountains would not hit its peak for another month, that could be bad if significant rains also followed.

Rolling down the hill to the open park gates, they rode in. The small recreation lagoon that housed some canoes and paddle boats was there but locked up. It was normally a busy place any time the weather was nice, but it was late and no one had transportation. The parking lot, half full with abandoned dead cars, seemed too quiet. It was clear some people had camped out one night (which was nominally against the law) and then left. The pair followed the loop around to the north side near the river, crossing over the track for the kiddy train. Alderson pondered how they might make use of those tracks if they could make the train work. Dismounting, they walked quietly along the path feeling the cool night breeze off the river, seeing the last rays of a beautiful sunset on the water, taking in the beauty of the natural world, the natural world they now had to find a way to live with rather than conquer.

Jolene put a hand on Alderson's chest freezing him in place, putting a finger to her lips. Alderson followed her lead. She appeared to be listening intently. Pointing to the right and squinting in the long shadows of early evening, she looked for something. He could not make out what she was pointing at. The two-way radio went off, shattering the quiet of the early evening. "Juju this is Viewpoint, do you read." He had left the radio on and that had compromised their safety, he still had a lot to learn. Jolene ducked down suddenly and he heard movement in the bushes, he made himself low too. The movement did not come toward them but moved toward the river.

Alderson pointed at her eyes then around in a 360 indicating that she should keep watch all around. He took the radio, that cat was out of the bag now. "Viewpoint this is Juju, we are not on location yet. Over."

"Juju we have info from Comrade. He's telling us he has activity south, vehicular, maybe military, on Crowchild, looks like clearing he says. He has not heard from Sarge yet. Over." It was Carrie speaking on the other end, doing a good job, he thought.

"Roger that, is all quiet at Viewpoint? Over." Alderson said.

"Yes sir Juju, all is good." Carrie replied forgetting to say 'over'.

"We will come back in a few, over and out for now." Alderson said. He whispered to Jolene to get her flashlight ready. Working their way through the trees, using the twilight, they moved quietly to the river, almost falling into the campsite. No one was there. Their heads swiveled, scanning the deepening dark in the shadows of the trees.

"They are likely afraid, with you looking scary, sounding all military," Jolene joked. "Didn't Marc say there were some kids down here?" Alderson examined the campsite, finding blankets and sleeping bags inside the lean-to. Garbage bags had been used to water-proof it, but there were minimal supplies, and a slight odor of burnt, stale weed. Alderson called out, "We don't mean to cause you any problems, just come and talk to us. If you don't come out we will throw your stuff in the river."

Jolene gently slapped his arm and whispered harshly to him, "You won't do that!"

"Shhhh!" Alderson put his finger to his lips.

He waited a few moments, then a dirty face appeared by the trees a few metres away. It was a young male maybe fifteen years old, probably Filipino. "What do you want from us?" he said. Alderson could see he was holding a stone in his hand.

"Hey you don't need the rock, we just want to talk to you," Alderson said, sitting on a nearby stump too look less threatening, being very careful to be sure his gun remained concealed.

Nervously the kid asked, "Are you some kind of cop?" He was shifting his eyes between Alderson and Jolene, who was smiling in a very disarming way.

"No, we are much worse than cops, we're a couple of teachers," Alderson joked. "Don't worry though, we cancelled school for a couple of days."

Jolene laughed and the kid looked a little more relaxed.

"Hey, kid you may be very smart seeing you have holed up in the ideal place," Alderson said. "Why don't you tell me the story about why you are here. Don't worry I won't tell anyone. Hi, I'm Jim," he added with a wink, holding out his hand.

The kid dropped the rock, stepped forward and shook Alderson's hand. "Well," the kid started nervously, "I'm, errr, Moses. Well, like, my friends and I came here the other day on the bus and then there was no bus to get home, no phone to phone home, and like not even any cops or anyone nearby. We got scared, and all the people here with cars, their cars quit working except a couple bikers." Alderson noted that for future reference.

"Hey Moses, I understand it was scary, it was for everyone, why don't you invite your four friends to join us. You are very safe with us," Jolene added. She was good for calming and disarming people, she was petite, pretty and smiled a lot, and when the kid looked at her he definitely didn't see a threat.

Moses looked around, still a little nervous, but then said, "I think it's okay everyone you can come out. But how did you know there was four of us?"

"We watched you from far away with binoculars," Alderson admitted. The other four came out. One much younger boy, maybe eleven or twelve, who looked like Moses. Then a blonde girl who went right up to Moses and put her arm around him, well-advanced for her years. Then another Asian boy and girl. "So tell me where are you from in the city that you didn't walk home already?" Jim questioned.

Moses was obviously the *de facto* leader, much like Alderson himself, yet Moses probably was unaware of how much power he really had with his friends.

"We live in Forest Lawn, it is a long way and we don't really know the route on foot. So we thought we could make a lean-to and camp until help came," Moses began.

"Really, all the way from Forest Lawn, that's a long way. We came all the way from Rundle on the day of the problem, but we had bikes," Alderson said. "So if you were here on that day at that time you had to have left quite early before the school day was finished?" Alderson queried the boy.

"Umm yeah, we had a PD day off," Moses stammered and looked sheepish.

"Moses, Moses, we're teachers, I am pretty sure Catholic schools did not have a PD day, and I *know* public schools didn't, and something tells me you are not private school kids. It is okay, I don't care why you came, I just want you to be honest with me," Alderson reassured him.

Moses was likely blushing, but this was camouflaged by the shadows in the setting sun. This was not really a kid used to lying. "Well okay, we skipped to come to the park. We were meeting someone here."

"Yeah I imagine you knew someone who had some good weed, doesn't matter now, that's not important. The five of you have been sleeping in that lean-to for two days in three sleeping bags," Alderson said. Raising his eyebrows he added, "I really hope you have been using some protection because you really don't want a pregnancy with the way the things are now. By the way, where did you get sleeping bags?"

One of the girls gasped in embarrassment and hid her face, Moses and the other older boy gulped and looked sheepish. "Um, well there was a car of people, looked like tourists, who walked out and left their stuff," the youngest boy said, earning a sharp silencing look from the older teens.

"Look," Alderson went on, "I can help you get back to your families at some point, but it might be better if your families come to you because you are in one of the best spots to be in, next to Fish Creek park. We will help you with that at some point. But for now I need your help and we will help you."

"How do you need our help?" Moses asked, confused.

"Well, I want to move my group to this park in the near future and you can watch it for me and tell me what happens. We will also provide you with food later tonight when we come back this way," Jim said as he rummaged in his pack and pulled out the extra radio and the little mini binoculars. While he was doing this the tall Asian girl gave a little gasp and everyone looked at her.

Pointing at Alderson's waist, she said, "He has a gun."

"Yes, I do, these are going to be some dangerous times, don't worry that is only for dangerous situations, you guys are not dangerous. It's a legal gun," Alderson said, ignoring the fact that carrying it was not legal.

The young boy who looked like Moses asked, "Will you give us a gun?"

Alderson answered, "No, you guys are too young and I won't give anyone a gun until I know they are safe with it."

"He won't even give me a gun yet," Jolene added, "And he knows me."

"When you use the radio you must use a call sign, hmmm let me see, yours will be Red Sea." Alderson said grinning. Moses just rolled his eyes. "My call sign is Juju, and our base is Viewpoint. Always start messages with who you are calling, then your call sign and end your message with 'Over'." Alderson took out his other radio and keyed the mike, "Viewpoint this is Juju do you copy. Over." He waited a few moments and repeated the message.

"We copy Juju, this is Viewpoint," said Jenna.

"Viewpoint, we are adding Red Sea to our net, Red Sea

will report from base 2. Will explain later. Over."

"Okay, Juju we understand..." Jenna said questioningly.

"That's how you do it, we want you to report at least 3 times a day and anytime someone comes to the park, or anytime you see something that might be important," Alderson said. "And later I will want to hear your whole story. But we will be leaving on our specific mission right now. Keep the radio off until you need it so you save the battery."

"Okay Mr. … err … Jim, when will you be back?" Moses asked.

"Probably four or five hours, but I don't know if or when we will move to the park. But we will keep in contact." With that, Alderson and Jolene started moving out, found their bikes and started riding.

Jolene started talking as they started the steep climb up the ski hill. "Was it a good idea to leave them there? Do you think they'll be safe? They are so young and doing things they shouldn't."

Alderson smiled at her as he reached the limit of where he could pedal, and dismounted. "Well they managed on their own and we will give them some help, but they have tasted the forbidden fruit, it's not like telling them to stop will work, when we come back we'll find them some condoms and hope that works for them. By their reactions, I don't think they were virgins before."

The ski jump tower provided a spectacular panoramic view of the city in darkness and silence – the darkness only broken by a few small lights and some fires, the silence broken more by a distant coyote than any sounds of human endeavour. The few highlights of light in the city stood out against the black backdrop. The hospital, the stadium, individuals who had generators, fire in outdoor pits, all these they could see. Three raging fires on this side of the city, were more than fire pits, burning buildings, burning with no effective response possible, no fire protection services. Alderson handed Jolene the binoculars, she scanned the city, looking for things he might have missed. She stopped and noted that there was a line of vehicle lights on the main highway by the hospital, she counted maybe 20 vehicles. Alderson looked again. "There is some heavy equipment, looks like they're moving dead vehicles."

They had observed the operation for a long time when Jolene commented, "Look, the those helicopters seem to be spreading out through the city." They were black helicopters, not in the colours of the Canadian military.

The radio broke the silence ten minutes later, "Viewpoint, Comrade, this is is Sarge, do you copy. Over." Alderson heard Marc on the radio, realizing they must have good line of site.

"This is Viewpoint we copy," came Arya's voice.

"This is Juju, I copy too Sarge," Alderson squawked in. They did not hear a response from Comrade, that worried Alderson.

"Roger that, we have a situation. I have one helo, several ground units in a neighbourhood, they appear to be rousting the locals. I have heard gunfire, possibly 5.56 and some single shots of louder gunfire. Cannot determine action. Approximate distance 2500 metres to arial target, advise. Over." Marc detailed the scene, terse, pertinent, and valuable.

"Roger that Sarge, this is Juju, I advise hold and unless you know you will be compromised. We believe we observe your arial and others. Viewpoint go to listen only, stay alert. Comrade do you copy?" Alderson said wondering where Alex and the girls were.

"Juju, we copy your half, we do not have the visual.

What do you want us to do, we cannot relay. Comrade out."
It was Alex talking.

"Comrade if it's clear, move to the overpass view on main again. Otherwise hold until further notice. Over."

"Wilco first. Over, Comrade out," Alex answered.

Jolene was a little freaked out by what she had heard. "Jim, what do you think the shooting was about? Do you know where this was happening?" she asked, moving close to him on the platform.

"I'm not sure. I think maybe in the Brentwood or Charleswood area, too close to home," he said. "I don't like those developments. I think we should scan closer to home and see what might be important for our next move.

The two of them began to scan, starting with Bowness, close in and moving toward their base. That neighbourhood had been its own town sixty years earlier, and had a reputation as being a bit rougher for a west side neighbourhood. There was a well-known Hades Animals clubhouse in the area and many backyard mechanics, but there were also multimillion dollar homes along the river.

Alderson scanned, looking for activity, and found almost every house along the river and many others had backyard fires or barbecues going. This provided meagre light to surveil at night. Alderson found activity at the biker clubhouse. It was close to the firehall which had no activity. Functioning motorcycles moved around, the only moving lights in the area. The older Harley Davidsons bikers preferred were robust enough to live through the EMP. As he watched Alderson was aware the bikers had electricity. The glare of flood lights surrounded their clubhouse.

The night time surveillance helped them easily identify where there was power and vehicles. There were many near the hospital but precious few elsewhere. He scanned the areas closer to his own location. He tried to identify other points of interest but the lack of light was too limiting.

He knew where the local food and drug stores were. They would be quite lootable. "Hey Jolene, I know some places down there we could to get some goods from, also I would say we should check out the neighbourhood and see if unaffected vehicles might be found."

"Are you going to do some more robbery?" she asked with a wry smile, "I never thought you for such a criminal. I sure hope we don't get caught after this is all over."

"Ahh yes, a misspent youth. Unfortunately I never learned how to steal a car," he admitted. "Let's go down and check it out. After I check out what's up with Marc." He keyed the mic on the radio, "Sarge, this is Juju, can you give a sit rep. Over."

Two static blasts on the radio, he took that as silent keys to say he could not respond. That bothered him but he did not know where Sarge was. "Let's go," he said getting up and moving to the stairs.

TWELVE

Marc chatted with Kareem as they lay watching. Kareem, a nominal Muslim, had been born here in Calgary. He had been working for six years for Canadian Tire and had become a shift manager. Marc worried a little about the Muslim background. Recent history made people question strong Islamic beliefs. However, Kareem talked more like an agnostic than any kind of true believer. Mark imagined that he would have a hard time being with Jim and his group if he was devout of any flavour. Jim was an extreme, possibly radical, atheist. He disdained religion, and especially those who devoutly believed in any god, in the face of science. Marc too had no use for religion or the religious, but Jim was that much more vehement about his dislike of religion.

"So what do you do for fun Kareem?" Marc asked.

"Well other than the usual, TV and movies, I like paintball and Airsoft. I wouldn't say I am that good at it though. I always die."

"Well a basic understanding of target acquisition, shooting, and moving in cover, might be useful. I haven't fired a gun more than a couple of times in the last 20 years, and I'm not so young, you might be a better shot than I am."

"Well I've never fired a handgun with real recoil, so who knows?" Kareem said.

When their conversation moved to women, Marc could tell Kareem was deeply infatuated with Arya, drawn to her adventurous, risk-taking nature.

Marc selected their position in a copse of trees, on the south side of the hill, in a small depression between hills, knowing was not ideal for breadth of view but had excellent cover. Understanding the tedium of long-term surveillance, and how a soldier's focus and alertness can lag, Marc suggested they switch duties every two hours, or anytime either felt tiredness taking over. The watch was only for the night. They were looking for problems, power, and people.

Several hours into their surveillance they watched choppers lifting off from the Foothills Hospital area, their lights a beacon in the twilight unhindered by city lights. The soft thrumming of the rotors could be heard even at this distance due to the strange quiet of the failing city. Kareem had called it to Marc's attention when the choppers came closer into view. The helicopters moved toward them. They watched as two of the choppers descended on a nearby neighbourhood, while a set of headlights weaved their way past dead vehicles into the same area. Putting the earpiece in the radio, Marc quietly reported what they were seeing. Only a moment later one chopper turned their way, ominously pointing exactly their direction, shining searchlights over their position, as if looking for them. The radio crackled again, Jim's voice coming over the earpiece, but all Marc dared as a response was to key the mic twice, hoping that the message was understood. If that helo had thermal imaging they could be compromised. The spotlight was disconcerting as it scanned the trees around, but it didn't linger, allowing Marc and Kareem to breathe again. Marc had taken the precaution of covering them in foliage, a poor man's ghillie suit. Movement at this time was out of the question.

The helicopter searching the area for twenty minutes kept tensions high, till Kareem spotted a bigger problem, putting his hand on Marc's and pointing. Three grunts coming up the hill toward them.. The soldiers were heavily laden with large square packs that looked like they contained some technical equipment. The soldiers, by-passing their position, headed toward a high point where they started unpacking the gear. Marc and Kareem heard them cursing, their voices indistinct but carrying across the still night air.

Marc and Kareem chanced movement so they could watch as the grunts sat up a tripod and a large dish. They hooked a laptop to the dish which began rotating to and fro in a sixty degree arc. The soldiers searched the neighbourhood areas of the northwest, but were not scanning any of the hill itself as best Marc could surmise.

One soldier repeatedly spoke into a mic and the dish swiveled. They looked out where the dish pointed and saw a helicopter hovering, using its spotlight to illuminate an area. On the ground they saw old style military vehicles, deuce-and-a-half type troop carriers, very old reserve vehicles. The helicopter used a loudspeaker, breaking the night quiet, but too far with too many echoes to be understood close by.

"Kareem," Marc uttered in a low voice, even knowing they could not be heard at this range, "we need to start making our way back, I think it is too dangerous to use the radio at this point, we'll take the long way." The long route meant going over the other side of the hill and then back through residential areas. "There will be a risk of exposure to the helo when we crest the hill. If we are lucky we will be able to make a break for the far side when the helo is occupied."

An hour of picking their way through the trees brought them to the top of the hill. Looking back when they came out of the trees, no helicopter was visible. Resting first, then making for the hill crest as quickly as they could, left the two large men gasping for air at the top. Once they achieved the back side of the hill Marc attempted radio contact again.

"Viewpoint this is Sarge, do you copy. Over." He waited a minute and tried again, no response.

Kareem scanned the sky using the binoculars, seeing only one helicopter far away in the south. Following the hilltop pathway to the roadway lead them out of the natural area and into one of the highest elevation communities in the city, still facing a long walk home.

Residential areas provided more more cover from helicopters and troops than main roads, but lengthened their path, and left them more exposed to locals who might be desperate. "I would rather be seen by the locals than the helos," Marc stated. "The government tends to get very draconian in times of war or emergencies and every petty tyrant with a thirst for power gets their drink, given half a chance. Those petty tyrants and militia boys on a power trip are as scary as the EMP." Marc disliked the powers that be, and in this world there would be no restrictions on them, no one would protect the rights of the citizens. "Besides, we're armed and most locals aren't," he added, checking the gun on his hip.

As they got closer they tried the radio again. He knew Viewpoint would be listening only, but he hoped he could raise Comrade or Juju again. "Comrade this is Sarge, do you copy? Over."

"Sarge, Comrade here, where are you at? Over." Alex was talking.

"We are returning to base the long way. Will report on return. More than an hour to base," Marc said.

"Copy that, will relay if Viewpoint did not copy," Alex said.

Wending their way back through residential neighbourhoods and green spaces, most with little activity in the early morning hours, seemed like any stroll in the city – if it weren't for the lack of city noise, and the pitch dark.

Without warning Marc felt himself lurching forward, his radio flying to the ground as he was putting his hands out to stop his fall. They had been walking through a park in a residential neighbourhood and all appeared quiet, a few dogs barking, when he was hit from behind and driven to the ground. Hitting the ground he felt a weight on him, and a dull pain in his back; he heard Kareem yelling "Don't hurt me!"

Marc started struggling to get turned over. As he did he saw someone standing over him with a baseball bat. It was a young kid, couldn't have been more than twenty years old. Another kid was climbing off of him.

"Don't move or I'll crack the shit out of your skull old man," the standing kid was saying. Marc looked around in the dark and saw two other young males with aluminum bats menacing Kareem. Kareem's eyes were wide open, quavering in his voice, he looked in near panic. One of the youths was shining a bright flashlight in their faces.

Marc felt a pain in his side where he had hit the ground and then he realized it was the 1911 handgun that Jimbo had given him, concealed in an inside-the-waistband holster. It would be a very tough draw from this position. He waited to see what would happen next.

"Get on your knees, faggots," the beefy kid standing in front of Marc said. The kid was blonde haired, muscular, a lot of acne, and a lot of anger, "*Likely a juicer*," Marc thought., getting to his knees slowly trying to make sure the gun stayed concealed. It hurt to be in this position. Kareem got to his knees just as slowly.

"Faggots, don't you know it is illegal for you queers to be moving around at night? Give us your packs, cocksuckers," the blonde leader demanded. The packs were light as they had not been on a scavenging mission. Marc tossed his to the right side of the blond punk.

"Hey look guys, they *are* cock-sucking faggots or they would not have done it when we told them to." The leader sneered at them, snickering at his own juvenile humour. "We're going to have some fun, I'll bet cocksuckers this old are really good at it, lots of practice. You geezers are going to blow us, then you are going to work for us." He stepped forward and started unzipping his pants. The punk next to him started doing the same.

"Hey I'll bet Arabs are real cocksuckers, my dad was in Fagistan and said they were nasty shit," the dark-haired, shorter one in front of Kareem said.

"I won't, you can kill me first!" Kareem yelled as he punched straight out at the guys groin.

The kid doubled up moaning, yelling, half crying, all bewildered, "He hit me!" The kid behind Kareem swung into Kareem's head with the bat, knocking Kareem over. The punk then put the bat around Kareem's neck and pulled him back up to his knees, keeping the bat there to show he could choke him anytime with it. "Now you will choke one way or the other, either with this bat or with Dylan's big cock," he said.

"Isn't that how you got on the team Sammy?" The blonde kid said, sneering at the other.

"Yeah well we *all* did our duty for the team didn't we. You included," the other responded.

The blonde kid stepping forward toward Kareem unzipped his pants, pulled his penis out and bellowed at Kareem, "Work it sand nigger!"

Kareem, refused to open his mouth. The kid behind pulled the bat tighter, Kareem gagging and gasping as the blonde leader backhanded him across the face. Seeing this Marc was stuck in indecision, calculating whether he could make the draw, click the safety off and shoot before he being hit by the guy behind him. He tried to remember if he had put a round in the chamber. He hoped he had.

"I could just fuck you in the ass *then* make you swallow my jism if you don't blow me now," the kid said. The look of fear and revulsion on Kareem's face transformed to panic and rage.

Marc was mobilized by the fear that if he didn't act now either he or Kareem, or both, would end up dead. He would go down fighting. Slipping his hand to his back without knowing where the kid behind him was looking was a risk he had to take. Drawing smoothly, targeting quickly, he snapped the safety off and squeezed the trigger. The shot broke the relative stillness of the early morning with the reverberating boom. All eyes went first to Marc, then quickly to Dylan who was yelling and falling. In a kind of a panic-fire Marc hadn't aimed well but he had hit Dylan in the leg or butt. As if in a slow-motion video, Marc, trying to stand, stumbled, watched the one with the bat swing again at Kareem's head. Hearing the sickening crack of metal on skull, Marc turned aiming the gun at the club-wielding punk. Seeing the gun, the punk ran into darkness, dropping the bat as he fled. Marc, gun in a single hand, fired again, with no satisfying result. He slowly rose on stiff legs. Dylan, howling on the ground, drew his attention. Dylan was a bully and Marc, remembering the stings, the victimization of his childhood, loathed bullies, hated them with a vengeance. He aimed the 1911 carefully at Dylan's head.

Dylan was sniveling, "No don't shoot, please don't shoot, I'll suck your cock, I will." Marc aimed coldly at the kid' s head.

Crack!

A shot pierced the night air. It wasn't Marc. It was the boom of a rifle. Marc felt the shock wave pass by, a near miss. He ducked and turned to see who was firing at him. He surveyed the area, looking for figures in the dark, Dylan still mewling on the ground.

Silhouetted against flickers of flashlights he found someone across the park aiming a rifle at him, and a second shooter with that one. One guy was working the bolt for the next shot, Marc fired the handgun again, making the other shooter flinch and move rather than shooting. Even missing, the shot bought Marc time to move. He saw his pack with the radio attached and grabbed it and ran for the trees, moving side to side as he did, just to be a harder target. Hearing another shot, he found cover in the trees and looked back. He could hear yelling and saw the other person moving out with a gun. Moving deliberately in a semi-crouch, gun at the ready, the new addition had a tactical bearing. Marc knew he had to move. It meant leaving Kareem.

- - - - - -

Alex had been snoozing when Rosie woke him, "Mmmm Alex, we heard something like gun shots maybe, off in that direction." She was pointing northwest. He noted she had a very pretty smile to wake up to even if they were living in a nightmare.

"Have you heard from anyone, Viewpoint, Juju, Sarge?" he asked groggily.

"Not yet, would you like some ice tea?" she asked thoughtfully.

"Thanks," he said, taking the thermos of drink and taking a swig. "Excuse me a moment." Walking off the overpass, out of sight of the two women, he took a quick piss, thinking that Angela was about as awake as he was, that is not at all. He came back scanning the area with binoculars, looking for signs of what was happening. He noted there was some helicopter activity again but he could not tell where they were going. "Keep listening, your hearing is better than mine," he said to Rosie. He leaned over Angela and shook her again, she was dozing again. "There were gunshots. You need to be awake in case we have to leave."

"Okay, are we done? I would like to be back in bed now," Angela said, shaking sleep from herself.

- - - - - -

Running from the park, pushing through gates, and cutting through yards, Marc ran. He was not mapping his way out, but using instinct and understanding to guide him out, downhill and south, were his directions. Getting to an alley and finding a temporary hiding spot, he called in, "Viewpoint, Juju, this is Sarge, I'm in trouble. Over"

"Sarge? This is Comrade, where are you? Over." Alex radioed.

"Yeah it's Sarge, I am being chased by armed guys, lost Kareem, he may be dead. Don't know where I am yet," Marc replied between breaths.

"Can you see Crowchild or Sarcee, Sarge?" Alex called back.

"No but I think I am heading toward Crowchild," Marc responded.

Alex took the rifle out. It had one of the fancy night vision scopes they had collected from Bass Pro, he turned that on. Alex was not normally one for relying on tech, but knowing it would be valuable in the dim light, he picked up the rifle and scanned at minimum power. The scope was not zeroed, so an accurate shot would not be possible, but it should still provide cover if needed. Alex handed the radio to Rosie. "Rosie, radio Sarge to look for a sound-barrier wall and follow it until there is a break. That should bring him to one of the main roads," Alex instructed.

"Sarge, this is Red, Comrade says to find a sound-barrier wall and follow it till you find a break, that should bring you to a main road, he has you covered. Red Over." "Oh-oh, Alex, I hear helicopters," she said looking around.

Alex looked around from his scanning and saw there were several coming down the trail in their direction. This could not be good. He went back to scanning, then he saw Marc stumbling out of an opening in the sound barrier. "Tell Sarge to go straight south, I have him covered. Then tell him radios off," Alex said authoritatively. Alex worried that "they" were tracking radio transmissions. Rosie relayed the message.

He watched as Marc crossed the main road then two rifle-carrying guys came out of the same opening. Alex fired, he wasn't trying to hit them, the range was over 500 metres with an unzeroed scope so chances would have been slim. He did hit the wall near them and that drove them back behind cover. "Time to bug out and get to cover.", he said urgently as he grabbed gear and started moving. Luckily the choppers seemed to be moving fairly slowly. The three of them ran over the bridge into the residential district and started to wend their way back to base.

Marc got across the highway and heard a shot, hoping it was Alex shooting and not the other guys, he didn't stop to look, he just kept moving. On the other side was a small forest of trees that had been planted by the city, it was orderly and nicely groomed, it would be good cover .

Not wanting to draw these guys back to base, he knew going to ground would be the best policy. Marc found a place and dug in, covering himself in mulch and dead leaves. As he lay there, watching and waiting, he thought, "*If they killed Kareem that would be bad, but if he was still alive that group would be coming for us, after they beat the location out of him. Either way this was a bad gang. Good news, we're better armed, thanks to the Bass Pro raid.*" He heard the sound of a chopper, it seemed to be searching the area he had the come from, finally setting down in that neighbourhood. He continued to wait and watch. It lifted off , then sharply angled away, moving at high-speed. As it left Marc could see someone searching out the side door with binoculars.

Making their way, meandering through a residential area for cover, Alex, Angela and Rosie heard a chopper approaching. Angela found a garage with an open side door. "Guys," she whispered loudly, "in here, it's open!" Inside they chanced a dim pocket light. Alex hissed seeing an old truck in pristine, rebuilt condition, realizing this could be a critical find. The restored truck was a vintage showpiece; probably only driven out to the annual 'Show and Shine' for collectors. It was a lovely blue 1956 Chevy truck, a short box vehicle. Durable, very useful and certainly untouched by the EMP. He needed to know if anyone was home, an owner present would complicate the issue.

"That truck is very baller," Rosie said. "Do you think it'll work?"

"It should," Alex whispered, not wanting to be loud. "It should be too old to be touched by the EMP." Looking around it was clear that there was normally another vehicle parked there that was not present, that was likely one that got fried in the EMP.

They waited a good while, Alex peering into the night every few minutes. He finally said, "I think we're good to go now," motioning to everyone.

"Aren't we going to take that truck? I mean if it works we need it right?" Rosie questioned as they started to go.

"We can't just start stealing it but maybe we could get the owners to join us," Angela suggested.

"Let's just check it out, see if someone is home, shall we?" Alex added. As they left he peered in the bottom floor windows with a flashlight. No sign of anyone here currently. Alex checked the mailbox in front. It looked like there was several days worth, that would suggest no one was home at the time. Even in times of crisis people follow routines if they can, people would likely have checked their mailbox out of habit.

"Really guys, we wouldn't have to walk everywhere," Rosie insisted.

"No, we can't yet, we need to know more," Angela argued.

Alex nodded in agreement. "If we must, we will get it later."

Rosie grumbled quietly as they carefully picked their way back to base. The base was serious and armed when they arrived. Jim had radioed to go to radio silence and they had heard Marc was in trouble everyone was in a state of apprehended panic.

"I heard Marc say someone had taken and maybe hurt Kareem?" Carrie asked Alex. "What should we do? I didn't know what to say to Arya."

"I think, for now, all we can do is wait for Marc, and more info," Aidan suggested. "If he doesn't show by daylight we can try to go to his last known position. But right now we need intel. Jim and Jolene are more problematic, we don't know their last position."

THIRTEEN

"Political power grows out of the barrel of a gun."

- Mao Zedong

The third day after the Event, Papa Bear O'Reilly decided, was the day he was going to personally scout his domain. Pinky and he would determine where to set control checkpoints. He wondered why there was a lack of people joining their cause at this point, surely people could see they were the only protection, certainly young hotties should see that. Maybe he had to make the point more obvious. Desperation makes whores, soon everyone would be desperate. The more vulnerable and weak -- the more desperate and cheaper the whore. Years of pimping and drug running taught him that simple truth. His power would grow out of their desperation. This was the way of the world.

They started surveying the eastern limits of the three bridges, he would need to control these eventually, but the main highway would draw attention, so not yet. A checkpoint at the two eastern bridges and the train tracks would give him some control. He would also need to control the northern bridge, the foot bridge and one other road and that should give him an effectively controlled area with a lot of river on one side and an escarpment and major highway on the other. It would take a while for people to accept the control. It would be easiest for him to let the resistant ones that might be problems leave. But girls, they belonged to him. They were a valuable commodity at any time. In this world real commodities mean trade for real goods. Whores were a gift that kept on giving. There were a lot of growth possibilities for the club in the post-apocalyptic world. His team would do what he wanted; he was the one with vision. Pinky had ruthlessness and foresight. Together they would be much more than an enterprising gang. But Papa Bear was visionary, a ruler, a king, no longer just an outlaw criminal.

Pinky's prospect, the Mouth, was taking notes as they surveyed. Pinky had an idea of the possibilities, he had been the one to get Papa Bear prepared for this event. He knew about the possibility in the first place. While surveying the area, people often approached them, always respectfully, usually looking for information. This gave Papa Bear the chance to win some recruits.

Papa Bear would win those he could, crush those he couldn't, cow the rest. People were looking to how everyone could work as a community, that was fine, but Papa Bear would be issuing the orders. He paid close attention to everyone, when they left he had Mouth make some notes, particularly if he thought they might have weapons since those people would have to be recruited or eliminated. There were a fair number of hunters living in the area and he needed to know who they were.

Eventually they came to the northwest side and Bowness park. The club often had parties here, there were quite a number of dead cars located in the park. Papa Bear had Mouth make note of them to ensure they drained the gas and collected any parts that might be useful. They toured on foot just to prevent anyone from knowing they were coming.

"It looks kind of empty, we should go. Mouth arrange to get some guys set up here, this will be a useful water source,"

Papa Bear directed.

"Hey wait Boss," Mouth whispered holding his finger up in a gesture for quiet. They all listened.

"Oh baby you're so hot, suck it," a young male voice was saying. They heard sounds coming from the trees, a girl giggling, the slurping, sucking sounds of a guys dick being sucked, and the moans of a young guy. This struck a cord with Papa Bear, they sounded young, he liked them that way. His usual girl had just turned eighteen but had not been found yet, but she was just a plaything, he could have others, it was his choice. He motioned to the others to approach quietly. They spotted a lean-to and heard the sound of sex coming from inside, but now it sounded like there were more voices, little high-pitched moans of another young girl. It sounded like a group grope.

"Hey I don't know about you Pinky, but I think I will be wanting some of that," he whispered. Pinky nodded and licked his lips. There were at least two. For effect Papa Bear O'Reilly drew his gun and stepped around the front to see a small Asian girl blowing a teen boy, another couple of kids watching, the other boy with his hand inside the other girl's shirt groping her. None of them could have been more than sixteen but clearly they had some experience. The whole scene turned Papa Bear on.

"Whoa, what do we have here?" Papa Bear called out. "Illicit young sex in a public place, I believe that would make you sex offenders in the eyes of the law." The teens stopped and looked at the bikers. The boy went limper than overcooked spaghetti. They all acted as if they had been caught by their parents. "I think you had better come out here and tell us why you are breaking the law like that."

The boy pulled up his pants, the girl started to cry and beg, "Please don't hurt us, please we weren't causing you any problems please," she whimpered.

They went out into one of the grassy areas of the park. "Ohhh, are you afraid of my little gun here?" Papa Bear said waving it around. "That's not the gun to be afraid of my little girl, my real gun is here." He grabbed his crotch and pulled. The girl cried. "Hey there little sweety, have you done this a lot, you looked like a pro. I suppose they teach you Chinese girls that young. Did your mommy show you how she does it to your daddy? Maybe you have even done daddy. Well your beau there and your daddy won't be the size of Papa Bear."

Ivy hung her head and covered her face in horror at the things that were being said. The boy she was blowing was looking around like he was going to try something. "Hey there young buck, don't get stupid, you three go over there and Mr. Mouth is going to watch you while I help give your girl here some lessons.   You are now living in Papa Bear's kingdom."

Pinky said leeringly, "If you do something stupid your girl will have something to really cry about, I'm sure you don't want that." Pinky grabbed the girl in case she was going to be un-cooperative, he made sure the boss was going to get what he wanted.

"Please don't hurt him, I'll do what you want, really I will," she said hoping to save Moses. Moses was crying with the frustration of powerlessness.

- - - - - -

Jim and Jolene wandered down into the residential neighbourhood. It was still a couple of hours before the sky would lighten, but they needed to be somewhat stealthy to make their mission successful. Finding forty year-old vehicles would be a challenge. They started cruising the alleyways in the older parts, checking garages. They came to one with an old school bus that had been converted to a camper vehicle, this would be ideal but neither of them had any idea on how old the vehicle was. He noted it and started to case the house. He didn't get very far before they heard the barking of a big dog in the yard. It was very protective German Shepherd. "I should have brought my female," Jolene whispered, "she might have distracted him." Alderson pointed to some trees in an adjacent yard and they went in there for cover, from there Alderson threw rocks at the fence to get a reaction from the dog to try to get a reaction from the house. Eventually a weedy, aging blonde guy yelled at the dog from the window. It shut up and settled down. Alderson noted that the guy was likely a backyard mechanic with good skills and maybe they could recruit him. He made a note.

They continued and looked at probably fifty more garages, many with vehicles that could work if the garage provided enough protection. Unfortunately the wood-framed, asphalt-shingled garages probably did not provide that protection. Then he came upon the prize he had sighted from the ski jump, a sixteen-foot high garage with aluminum roofing as well as siding, things inside this could be protected. Sadly there were no windows into the garage. The yard had a ten-foot high chain-linked fence with barbed wire on top. Inside the yard they saw a speed boat with a cover over it. There was money here. Alderson cased this one carefully, he noted no light or activity. The garage had a chimney for heating and another one for exhaust, which indicated there might be a generator; that could mean a very good garage inside or just a weed grow-op. The generator was not running which again could mean one of two things, ran out of gas or it was not operating. This one was worth waiting until a little later in the day. He also noticed the doors and locks seem more heavily built on this place. There was even a large antenna, and security cameras, not working he imagined – even with power the EMP should have destroyed them.

"We should watch this one until at least well into the light," he said quietly, "it has some good potential." They decided to lay down in a nearby park and nap now with the light coming and the day warming. It looked like it could be very warm that day later, for now they huddled together to keep warm against the night chill for a while longer.

Alderson dozed off and dreamt that he was in a fight with a cop and the cop kept laughing and shrugging off the blows he landed, he could not throw or lock, the cop was immune to everything Alderson tried. Then in the middle of the dream he was shaken awake by Jolene. "Jim, Jim, wake up you're fighting something!" He woke and shook his head. "Besides, there are several working motorcycles showing up," she added.

Alderson had to shake his head to wake himself, he looked around to orient himself and spotted the house as he was remembering where he was and what this new world order was. Those weren't just motorcycles Jolene was pointing at, they were "Property of the Hades Animals" Harleys. Three grizzled bikers, typical to their type -- large, bearded, loud and obnoxious – rolled up. The throaty heartbeat of the Harley Davidson was unmistakable. The old-style and inefficient engines still worked, making a mockery of all the high-tech, electronically controlled bikes out there today, most of which could not be started now. These Harleys still used a kickstart, *"pretty friggin' reliable."* Alderson thought.

"Jolene we have to slowly sneak away, we are in serious danger," Alderson said quietly as he started to roll up and grab his pack.

"Why? We're not bothering them, we can just pretend to be a couple in the park," she said with a grin.

"Jolene, these guys had no respect for the law before this disaster. They see a hot girl like you and they will seek to obtain you, and you will have nothing to say about it," Alderson said with serious intent. "Jolene, this is no joke, you can be certain they're armed." They got up and quietly made their way in the opposite direction. They seemed to have escaped and headed toward the small strip mall. They quickly went into the drug store that had already been broken into. It had a big sign stating they did not stock narcotics, Alderson knew they likely had a few in a safe but that wasn't what he was here for. Inside it was a shambles, someone had not only looted some stuff but wrecked a lot of things. Alderson grabbed a couple of good first aid kits, some rubbing alcohol, and several boxes of condoms. He went to see if there were more antibiotics to be had, he managed to get several boxes of Azythromycin, a powerful antibiotic. He also found the book that describes drugs and their uses. Very useful when the was no internet. They loaded up and got on their bikes when the radio went live.

"Red Sea, this is Red Sea, Mr. Juju do you hear me?" one of the kids was saying. Alderson couldn't tell which of the boys.

"I copy you Red Sea, go ahead. Over," Alderson said.

The kid came back on sounding breathless, "Juju there are bikers here they have Moses and the others."

"Keep yourself hidden. I'm coming. Over." Alderson replied. "Jolene those kids are in trouble, you to ride for home, get help if possible, tell them to come armed, you are the better rider and can get there faster than me. I am going to see what I can do," he said as they started riding toward the park.

"You will be in danger by yourself," she said trailing after him, "I'll stay with you."

"I'm not being mean but you will put us both in more danger if I have to worry about you," Alderson said. "Get me Marc, Alex, or Aidan, they have shooting experience."

She reluctantly agreed and continued across the bridge on her own.

Scrambling down the embankment Jim began working his way into the park from the river side rather than the road where the bikers would have come in. As he got closer to the kids' encampment, he heard a girl crying and screaming submerged in the coarse language and laughter of much older males. He caught a glimpse of a couple of Harleys. He could hear Moses was begging, asking them to let Ivy go, the other boy and another girl were just crying. He could see Moses, his brother, and one girl sitting on the ground facing his direction. Jim moved forward, hoping that if the kids saw him they would not betray his presence. Two bikers were molesting the other girl. One had her with his arm around her neck as he groped her naked breasts, the other was in front of her kissing her other breast and rubbing his hand on her naked vagina. That one had his pants around his knees and his dick out.

"This little bitch needs to clean me before I will fuck her. Bring her down Pinky. She likes cock, but she needs to taste a real man," the big hairy biker with his pants half-down said. Then to her he said, "You will get lots of man spunk today, in all of your tight teen holes." Pinky and the other biker who had his handgun trained on the other kids laughed.

Alderson raised his shotgun thinking to himself, "*Ten yards to target, spread may have pellets miss, behind the target, 3 sitting, shouldn't hit them.*" The girl's screaming and crying intensified as she was forced to the ground. Jim acted, using the cover of her screams to take a few quick steps toward the biker guard. He jammed the barrel of his shotgun in the back of the bikers head. "Drop your gun. NOW!" he bellowed. "If anyone moves for a gun, he dies," Alderson added, adrenaline coursing through his veins.

It seemed like the biker was taking a long time to drop the gun, a shiny short-barreled Ruger GP-100 .357. All noise except sobbing from the girl stopped, and everyone looked at Jim.

"What am I hearing! What the fuck!" Papa Bear said as he turned toward where he heard the impossible sound of someone ordering him. He was flabbergasted to see there was indeed an asshole with a gun on Mouth.

"If you guys go for a weapon I will blow his brains out, and I will still have a shotgun and you will be still naked," Jim said.

Pinky, his arm still around Ivy's neck, yelled out, "You're gonna hit her if you shoot me," shifting enough so he was behind the girl.

Rather than answer the biker Jim stepped in delivering a vicious butt-stroke to the back of the Mouth's head, sending the gun tumbling out of his hand as the Mouth stumbled, falling forward in an unconscious face-plant. Alderson moved the shotgun, training it on the now limp-dicked biker in front of the girl.

Seeing a shotgun and two handguns five feet from the would-be sex scene, the leader eyeing them, Alderson growled, "Go ahead punk make my day," quoting the old Eastwood movie. "Tell your flunky to let her go, NOW and put your hands in the air." The biker nodded at Pinky who let the girl go.

"Now here's how things will go," Alderson said as he took a step to the side of the downed biker, "you two will walk ten steps forward, away from those pieces, and park your asses on the ground." They complied. "Ivy, move over there." Jim said using his head to direct her. She ran grabbing her torn clothes, trying to cover her exposed breasts and vagina.

"You know you are messing with the Hades Animals," Papa Bear said, trying to discomfit Alderson.

"I just see a couple of scared punks," Alderson responded, infuriating Papa Bear, "but maybe I should just kill you and throw your lice-ridden, maggot-breeding bodies in the river." He pulled the shotgun in tight for effect. "Moses you pick up that .357 and get some rope or string." Moses scampered to grab the gun.

The missing kid came back into view, "Man, Juju dude, you are awesome, you dropped that fucker good!"

Alderson bared his pistol so the bikers could see it and walked closer to the two conscious bikers to make sure they couldn't lunge up for the guns. "Okay kids grab those guns, DO NOT point them at anyone and do not put your finger on those triggers. Get some rope, string whatever."

They rummaged around for a while and came up with shoe laces, that would have to do. "Okay on your bellies," Alderson ordered the bikers.

"Hey man, at least let me pull up my pants," the leader said.

"Absolutely not, if you like having them down in public so much then live with the consequences. I hope your dick gets sunburnt," Alderson answered, smirking. "Now on your fucking belly. Put your hands behind your backs." Pinky complied but the leader was too big to get his hands together. "Moses get over here, hold this shotgun on that prick and if he moves shoot him, but keep your finger off the trigger till he moves," he ordered.

Jim went to the prostrate Pinky, kneeled on his neck enough to control him, slipped the shoe lace in a slipknot over one wrist, then pulled the other wrist close and tied the two together. Going to Papa Bear, Alderson directed Moses to cover Pinky while he kneeled on Papa Bear's neck.

"You're fucking dead, you're a dead motherfucker. Fucking dead!" the biker screamed.

Alderson put more pressure on his neck. He began following the same procedure, but was unable to get the hands together. He had to leave a bit of distance between them. Using the biker's knife, Jim cut the guy's pants in half. He took the shotgun back from back from Moses. "Okay you two," he said indicating the other girl and Moses' brother, "take these shoe laces and make a slipknot. Put the slipknot

179

over his cock and balls then tie the other end to each his wrists." Alderson was laughing.

"How are we going to do that?" the girl asked incredulously.

Alderson said with a smirk,"You are going to reach under him and grab his package and put the knot around it, then pull it tight and tie it to his wrists from between his legs. Then if he tries to hard to get his hands free he will pull his limp dick off."

"Ewww, you want me to touch him....there?" the girl squealed.

"Well, it is better than letting him touch you," Jim retorted.

"You fucking faggot, I'm going to fuck you with a knife while you swallow my cock, you cum-swilling, ass-eating, diseased cunt!" Papa Bear screamed, starting to struggle. Walking up to him, Alderson put his foot on the biker's neck and applied pressure.

"What's your name my lovely bitch?" Alderson asked the biker, letting up a little on his neck. There was no answer forthcoming. "Aww, my little bitch doesn't want to answer." He pushed the shotgun on the side of his mouth. "The next time you taste this tool it will have your shit on it. What's your name, Bitch?"

"I'm Papa Bear and you better not forget it; if you don't kill me you are a fucking idiot."

"Mr. Alderson, shouldn't we just kill him?" Ivy asked between sobs.

"Not today Ivy, not today," Jim replied quietly.

The others followed the directions trying to touch his genitals only gingerly while connecting them to each wrist.

While Alderson had been directing with some amusement, a sudden yelling from the other kid drew his attention. Startled, Alderson turned, "Aww shit, I forgot the other prick," he blurted out. The unconscious biker had woken up and grabbed the kid, holding a knife to the kid's throat from behind.

Alderson slung the shotgun and drew his Sig. "I'll kill the kid, I will, drop your gun!" the half-stunned biker demanded.

"Nope, won't happen, if you hurt the kid you will eat two to the body and one to the head, before the kid falls from your arms. I guarantee I can make the shot." Alderson's adrenaline spiked again, he was not really as confident as he sounded. Breathing carefully and deliberately suppressing the adrenaline rush, he readied to take the shot if he must.

The biker, pushing the frightened kid toward Jim, dodged around the kid, lunging for Alderson. Jim dodged the attack and lost the shot. A girl screamed. The biker took a quick, vicious forehand swing at Alderson's head with the knife. Alderson blocked instinctively with both hands, stepping in and locking the arm; to gain control of the knife he had to drop the gun. He clamped the knife hand against his body, sliding his hands toward the wrist to control it, simultaneously stomping on the guys instep, causing the biker to scream in pain. Alderson spun back out before he got clocked in the head, while controlling the wrist in a lock, twisting it hard. Holding on with his right hand, striking the bikers knife hand with his left, they traced a spinning arc into the grass, Alderson twisted more, bringing the wrist toward him. Then using his left forearm to apply pressure to the biker's elbow while pulling back a step, he forced the biker's face down on the rocky ground. Finally he dropped a hard knee on the elbow to be rewarded with a snapping, popping sound of the elbow leaving the security of its joint. That was followed a moment later by a yell of anguish from the biker. Alderson released him, the biker rolled, cradling his nearly-disconnected elbow. Alderson cringed, remembering the pain from a similar past injury.

Alderson took a step back and took a deep breath, feeling his whole body trembling with adrenaline, he looked around, searching for the knife and the gun. The five kids, staring slack jawed, stood looking at the scene of what had just happened, stunned and unable to move. Alderson collected his gun, and two revolvers off the bikers, relieving two of them from the kids. Some bikers preferred revolvers because they didn't leave casings to be found by the police.

He took the stunned teens aside, "Just let yourselves calm down a bit, you've been through a lot," he stated. He kept an eye on the bikers, he didn't want to have another fight. Even in this short time, he could see the sun burning Pinky. The one with the broken arm was sitting cradling his elbow, moaning in agony. Alderson had separated him from the rest because he was not tied up. Pinky was sitting up but Papa Bear was not moving, afraid to pull his balls off. The kids started chattering, asking questions. Alderson answered what he could.

"I'll answer the rest of your questions later, for now I have to call in." He needed to let the base know all was good. He would have to bring the kids home with him for now and figure out how they would be getting them home, or getting a message to their parents, later.

Alderson, creeping exhaustion taking over, realized he was going to need sleep. Not having had more than a couple hours of sleep in the last twenty-four, and being in an intense fight, both were beginning to take their toll. "Viewpoint this is Juju, will report, you stay on silence. Have taken care of problems on Base 2 for now. Still considering how to proceed. Will be leaving soonest. Over." Alderson had a feeling that being on air was not the best policy but he needed to let them know.

He provided instructions to the kids on the use of the shotguns. The bikers had kindly provided a nice double-barrel, sawed off, clearly illegal but good for a "room broom". Alderson showed them how to use the firearms and impressed upon them the four laws of gun safety. "I want you to watch the entrance from a distance and make sure no one comes in. I need to search around to see what is happening. I need to know if it is safe to leave. I should be back in fifteen minutes. Someone stay on the radio."

Alderson walked back to his bike then cycled up the road far enough that he could see incoming activity. He came back to find Adam, the youngest, on guard, but the others not present. As they walked toward the lean-tos there was a loud boom that brought Alderson running to see Joanne on her ass in the water holding a shotgun, and Daman standing laughing beside her.

"Jesus fucking Christ, this is not a toy!" Alderson yelled as he snatched up the shotgun, cleared it, pointing it into the river. He looked at Daman, who still seemed to think it was funny and said, "You fucking fool, you are lucky to be alive, when she fell she could have squeezed off the second shot and taken your head off. I was right when I first thought you lot were too immature to handle firearms."

Alderson could hear Pinky laughing and Papa Bear saying something unintelligible but angry. Time to move on. "Everyone, I need to meet with you in two minutes. Here." He was not disguising his anger. He gathered the gear he had dropped when he ran.

He got back and started emptying junk food and condoms and other supplies he had collected for the kids. "Okay you lot, here's the deal, I am not sure what to do with you, leave you here to hold the fort or take you with me. I think you could be in serious danger staying here. These guys were not the only Angels around and others will likely come looking for them. But I am not sure I can trust you lot to avoid trouble."

"We could do better I promise you Mr. Jim, give us a chance and you will see," Moses pleaded.

"I thought you were going to help us get home." Ivy sniffled, "I want to go home." A murmur from the others indicated that they wanted to get home too.

"I can do that, but not this second. You guys need to come to my place but I am going forward alone. You will have to catch up." He checked to make sure he was out of earshot of the the bikers. "I will explain how to get there, But I need one of you to take this shotgun and keep it hidden. It is still against the law for you to have it, if there's any law left in this land." He looked around at them and saw he had their attention. "Look, if you have to shoot a shotgun, especially this one, you either have to be my size or lean into it like you are pushing a car. I will help you find your parents but first I have to get back home. When you get to my place you will get proper food. You must not speak of the directions after I tell you. If you get lost use the radio and someone will find you." He explained the simplest way to get to his place. "Hey do any of you know how to ride a motorcycle?" They all just shook their heads, too bad, he could only take one of the bikes. After they split up he went over to the bikes to see what he could find. He found a box of each calibre of ammo, with a few missing. He found knives and weed and some pills which were most likely ecstasy, he pitched those on the ground so the bikers could see and ground them underfoot. He took the five bags of weed he found and gave one to the kids.

"Hey thanks, Mr. A., that's cool, a teacher giving us weed," Damon said.

"Only get high when you are perfectly safe and have nothing to do. If you are coming to my place you had better understand, you will have to follow orders." He added, "and that's the first one, do NOT get high on the road!"

He picked the least chopped bike, a Softtail with blue and gold. It had been many years since he had ridden a motorcycle and he hoped he could remember the controls. He took wires from the other two so they could not be easily started. Giving the kids knives he had liberated from the bikers, he said, "These are tools, they are only good as weapons in the hands of the trained," but his intent was to give them a slightly increased threat level. Looking at the kids he could see Ivy was a wreck, flinching when others came near her. She was trying to put on a brave face, but she was in shock. Her clothes were torn and revealing, she could present a risk to the others, both from not being able to respond and because she appeared an easy target for the next criminal.

He walked over to the injured biker and gave him a bottle of tylenol with codeine for the pain. He then used the bikers own shoelaces to tie him to a tree. "You are a stupid motherfucker leaving Papa Bear alive, he will find you. Especially if you take his bike, man," the biker said.

Yelling out loud, Alderson called to Papa Bear, "Your friend here thinks I should cap your ass." Then to Mouth, Alderson answered, "Whatever, if he comes looking I will feed him his own balls with fucking ass sauce and he will beg me for more." Alderson hoped he sounded tougher than he felt.

Unsure of how Ivy would react, Alderson presented a plan. "Ivy, I think you should travel with me, it will be safer for all of you. I know that it's a scary idea to leave your friends but it will be only for a hour at most. I am just worried that with your clothes torn you will be a target."

To his great surprise she ran over and hugged him without saying a word. He handed her a helmet, "I have to warn you it has been a long time since I drove a motorcycle but we will be going slow. See the rest of you at base, remember the rules!" He drove off , the throaty thrum of the Harley throbbing underneath him, with Ivy holding him so tight he had to focus on breathing. Once they were across the river and going up, she relaxed a little.

Jim's hiking boots were poorly suited to riding a

motorcycle, making finding the gears difficult. When he had nearly arrived, cruising up the hill toward home, he stopped the bike to listen, he was sure he could hear what sounded like choppers. Unable to see from where he was, he increased his speed, he would be able to get a better view from the rooftop. Seeing two figures on the roof as he approached, likely Aidan and Di, Alderson revved the bike to draw attention.

Aidan yelled, "Nice bike dude," then squinted and called down to him, "holy fuck man, some not very nice guys are gonna to be looking for you." Aidan headed for the ladder to come down from the roof.

Di stopped Aidan as he was about to descend, pointing toward the south and saying something.

"Helos, two or three of them coming this way," Aidan yelled, going back on the roof.

Alderson introduced Ivy as he went through the house and then, taking Jenna aside he told her, "She was almost raped by bikers, she and the Red Sea group were living in Bowness park. The rest of the group should be here within an hour or so. Can you and Angela talk to her please? I need to see about these choppers."

Alderson made for the roof with Alex just ahead of him. Once at the top, Aidan started bringing him up to speed on Marc and Kareem as best he could. They watched three choppers coming along Crowchild, all in a line, very military-like. They turned a bit north as Alex said "I wonder if they are going to the area where we last saw Marc near."

Jim thought for a minute, "I need to contact Marc and risk the radio, we need info." He grabbed the mic on the base station radio, cranked it a few times then, "Sarge this is Viewpoint. If you are okay key two, need assistance key three, need to hold key one." He released the mic and waited.

Within thirty seconds there were two keys and "I'm good coming in, Sarge out."

Everyone went back to watching the choppers. One hovered over a residential district to the north, then a number of military types dressed in black fast-roped out of one chopper. Then the radio came on. "Citizens using two-way radios are ordered by the conditions of the State of Local Emergency to report to either McMahon stadium, Max Bell arena or to the Emergency Operations Centre command camp. You must also immediately stop using all electronic communications." The broadcast was extremely powerful.

"The government is trying to make sure there can be no opposition," Alex said. "They're getting ready to put people in internment camps, you watch. Next they will round up anyone they know has a gun license. I think it might be time to bug out. Jim I need to get stuff from my house, do you think I should take one of the ATVs? I have some armour, a long bow, and some other useful items."

"That's a good plan but we should make a looting plan to make the best use of the time," Jim said.

"We found a likely truck too, fifties era showpiece not far from here. The people were away on vacation, I think," Alex told him. They continued watching the choppers. Two helicopters turned and moved directly toward them. Everyone went low. Jim was still watching with the binoculars when everyone noticed the sky get very bright, like a second sun. There was a collective "Oh my god," then, "Oh shit." Everyone gaped at the shrinking orange orb in the sky. It was most likely hundreds of miles away, high in the atmosphere. But the effect was immediate. The helicopters that had been tilted forward for moving fast started falling quickly out of the sky. The auto-rotation safety systems did not require power, but the choppers were just starting to move forward, not moving fast enough to perform an auto-rotation landing. These were going down hard, it didn't look good. It was a macabre, surreal tableau as the sound of choppers disappeared, followed by a few seconds of quiet, soldiers jumping just before the unseen impact. Then the impact, the first chopper did not seem to explode and may have landed safely, the next two were not so lucky. After impact, an explosion and fire, they were a couple of kilometres away but seeing the oily black smoke rising only took a minute. Everyone watched in stunned silence until a small voice was heard.

"Aidan look, over there!" Di said grabbing his arm, pointing in the direction of the hospital. Everyone on the roof turned and looked, watching another helicopter going down. It seemed to be much higher in altitude, the auto-rotate appearing to engage in the heavy-lift chopper with an attached container.

Alderson thought, his mind racing, 'Someone did another EMP, someone really wanted to glue our coffin shut after nailing it. Who the fuck wants to kill most of North America slowly. It would have been nicer to have nuked the cities directly. Would the city be able to recover critical services? Had there been any military response and did this kill it? Would power ever be restored? How many people would die first?' One thing seemed certain, living in a city was not likely viable at all. Time to finalize the bug-out plan.

As everyone stood in quiet shock, Marc came up, looking at the roof and calling up. "Hi guys, I think we just got it again, another EMP. I think the radio is dead. That would make us just another shade of fucked."

Alderson grabbed the mic and keyed it, it was indeed dead. "Yeah we need to get some plans going." Climbing down the ladder he said, "Come on, time to rethink."

Everyone came together in the backyard. It started with Marc relaying his story of how Kareem was taken and how Marc had escaped.

Then Jim jumped in. "I can only speculate what this

means for the recovery and when I speculate it's very bad. I need everyone's input and thinking."

"What about Kareem, we can't just leave him," Arya said.

"We can try to go back for him," Marc said. "With more people we should be okay. I think I can remember where he was, I think they are armed with hunting rifles and shotguns.

"We have to do that, but at the same time we have to start dealing with the fact we may be in worse shape now than we were. We have to move to a site that will allow us to get water close by, that means the river. So one way or the other we have to move camp there and prepare to move out of the city," Alex added.

"Do you think this is worse than the first one?" Angela asked. "They got water back the first time, why can't they do it again? They probably didn't damage the damaged systems any more than they already were."

Jim shrugged his shoulders, everyone else was equally unsure. "I guess we have to work with what we know. Water and sewer will go out again, we should get whatever water we can right now with residual pressure. Fill up everything we have."

"The other problem is all the vehicles that survived the first time but were vulnerable, they were probably taken out this time." People started moving, finding every container in the house and working with every tap, people completed the emergency task. They were able to fill the bathtub, many 18-litre bottles, pop bottles, wine bottles. It took about an hour and they didn't seem to lose pressure. They were able to use the toilet as well, but a strict "don't flush the pee" rule was implemented. This was still a short-term, single problem solution. Their problems were much bigger.

FOURTEEN

"Men ought either to be well treated or crushed, because they can avenge themselves of lighter injuries, of more serious ones they cannot; therefore the injury that is to be done to a man ought to be of such a kind that one does not stand in fear of revenge."

- The Prince, Niccolo Machiavelli

After the flurry of activity a glum quiet settled about the whole place. Marc started the conversation, "We have a series of things we need to do to improve our survival position. We have to find out what we have that still works. We have to find out what became of Kareem. We have to figure out where we are going, both long and short term and we have to start soon I think. Kareem is a risk, they could beat our location out of him."

Alderson added,"Let me say, from the beginning my plan has been to move to Bowness Park and stockpile, get equipment, then move out. I think Bowness Park has been compromised at this point, however we need to be situated near the river, not a couple of hundred metres and up a hill from the river. You're right Marc, we need some people to

190

find out what happened to Kareem, but we don't have a lot of people with fighting capability. We also need to do another raid on food and supplies stores, just to add to our list."

"What say we have a couple scout a site on this side of the river and then get everyone there, while others look for Kareem?" Aidan suggested. "But the first order is take stock of what works."

"Let's find out what works," Jim agreed. A roar and rumble told everyone the Harley still worked; unmuffled, loud engine noise said the ATVs still worked.

"All the radios are fried, but the solar panels may still work," someone hollered. Those four ATVs were what they needed to transport goods and they seemed to be mostly EMP-proof.

"We need to get organized and get to work," Alex said.

"Is someone going try to rescue Kareem, please, I am so worried. From what Marc said he could be in serious trouble. I-- I convinced him to join with you guys, now he's missing," Arya said pleading, looking at at the group, tears welling in her eyes.

"She's right, we have to try to find him," Aidan added to general murmurs of agreement. "I think we need to do it carefully with some recon. It could, or it will, get rough and ugly."

"Aidan, you and I should do this, I have my martial arts and shooting, you can handle yourself too. I need Marc and maybe Rosie to go on a scavenge run to get more supplies."

"Kareem is my boyfriend, I want to come with you," Arya implored. Jim agreed reluctantly. After some discussion it was decided that Marc and Rosie would take two ATVs and make a run to Canadian Tire and a food store. A list of goods to collect was drawn up. Alex would take Jolene and Angela and make a scouting hike down the hill and find a good spot for a few days.

Jim, Aidan, and Arya would head out first to find Kareem. Alderson debriefed Marc carefully to estimate where to go. They did not want Marc to come as he might be recognized. "Marc, if you guys find working radios leave one by the sound barrier across the road for us." Jim and Aidan took a handgun each, one shotgun, a crossbow, Aidan's bow and some tools including a small bolt cutter and pry bar. They might have to break in, or out.

Riding bikes, they moved quickly but they were traveling blind, going on the description Marc had offered.

They had to travel past the place where the helicopter that auto-rotated down without exploding had landed. Watchers had seen a number of the troops jump when it looked like the chopper was going to land hard, it had come down on the nearby golf course. "Hey Jim, let's check it out," Aidan whispered. Dismounting from their bikes they left them with Arya, while Jim and Aidan crawled up the embankments at the roadside. Seeing the chopper it was apparent it had been a hard landing, a scene of bent and tangled metal and cracked plexiglass greeted them it, but only onlookers were present. "I don't see any grunts," Aidan whispered. Jim nodded.

Fingering his shotgun, Jim wished he had brought something longer. He had loaded up #2 shot, a good load for taking down people at close range, less than 40 metres; the chopper was at least 100 yards away. "Let's go in, see what's goin' on," Aidan said, seeing people coming toward the chopper, looking cautiously at the downed bird.

"Someone help, this man is hurt!" A woman who had moved up to the helicopter, called out. Most of the onlookers were still holding back. Approaching and handing Aidan the shotgun, Jim said, "Hang back a bit, in case I need cover."

The woman was talking to a moaning soldier who lay with his leg and knee at an impossible angle for a functioning human, the injury must be intensely painful. The woman looking back over her shoulder called out, "Do any of you know First Aid, he's hurt bad?" she pleaded.

"Yeah, I do," Alderson said, moving in and kneeling down. The soldier had no gun, his buddies must have taken it. He did as he had been trained, and surveyed the area first looking for hazards. The only issue was the smell of fuel from the helicopter. The soldier was about five metres from the chopper, Alderson decided he could do some treatment before moving. "Yeah I know some First Aid, but I need some supplies, do you live close?"

She just nodded.

"I need you to get me some sticks, pieces of wood or metal about one metre long and some bed sheets that I can tear up, and bring them back here, quickly please!" He felt like he should be telling her to call 911, obviously that was pointless. "Hey Aidan, give me a hand," he called out.

Aidan came over, Jim spoke quietly, "Try and get these others doing something. Get them to get some long poles and a tarp to make a stretcher, that will keep them out of my hair. I may need you because I think I am going to need to straighten his leg and the poor bastard will hurt even more." At that point Alderson kneeled down and spoke to the soldier, "Hi my name is Jim and I am going to give you some first aid if that is okay with you." The soldier just nodded through gritted teeth and streaming tears, he was a kid not much more than 20 years old, a very large youth, probably of South Asian decent. "What's your name?" Alderson asked as he did a survey, looking for secondary injuries.

"Darth, Darth Maqbool," he replied between gasps of pain.

"Well Darth, do you know what happened to the others

that were with you?" Jim asked wanting to know if they were still on their mission.

"I, I, I don't know. I must have passed out, I just remember the chopper coming down quick and the sergeant yelling jump," Darth said through clenched teeth. " Then I woke up and started yelling."

"Darth what unit are you with? You've been here at least an hour." Jim said, making sure to use his name to build trust and command attention.

"I just completed basic, like two months ago, with the Calgary Highlanders," the suffering soldier said hoarsely, with intense effort.

"Darth, I'm no doctor but I am sure you are going to live. Are you allergic to anything you know of?" Jim questioned.

"No, don't think so, ugh."

"Just hold on an minute Darth," Jim said as he went to the chopper. He looked inside, the windscreen was shattered and the legs were bent but it did look like it was survivable. Inside he found what he was looking for, a good quality First Aid kit. He took it back to Darth and opened it up and looked to see if there were any pain killers but no such luck. It did have an air splint but that was for an arm not a leg. There were a dozen triangular bandages. Jim was not sure they were any better than a bed sheet. "Darth when that nice lady gets back I am going to have to move your leg and it'll hurt a lot. To make sure we do less damage I am going to have people hold you so you don't move when it hurts, okay?"

"Man, if it's going to hurt more than it does, please just leave it. I am sure they will send another chopper," Darth pleaded.

Alderson mulled it over for a minute deciding a dose

truth was in order. "Darth, I don't think there will be another chopper, I am pretty sure there was a second EMP," Alderson said somberly. "If you want me to leave it, I will." At this point the woman came back with sheets and blankets and some brooms. Alderson looked up at the crowd and yelled, "Does anyone here have any strong pain killers at home such as Oxycontin, Percocet, Tylenol 3 or anything like that? This man is in great pain. Please if you have anything like that please go get them." Alderson looked back down at the injured soldier and said, "It's up to you if you want me to do anything."

"Okay, I think I can hack it," Darth said gritting his teeth even harder.

Alderson proceeded to lay out the bandages and splints. "Okay," he addressed the crowd, "I need three people to hold Darth while I try to align his leg." Two men and a woman came forward from the crowd. While she was holding Darth, the woman smiled at him and said soothing things which seemed to calm him. He proceeded to cut the pant leg off the soldier so he could get a better look at the misaligned leg. The break and dislocation was right at the knee. It was massively swollen and he did not have any ice. Anti-inflammatories would not touch this problem.

First he had to fix the position. That would mean pulling, and turning the foot to a vertical position and swinging it into place. He looked up to see Darth watching him, then he tapped one of the holders on the shoulder and whispered in the woman's ear, "Block his line of sight."

She adjusted herself and Darth stiffened.

"Don't worry Darth I will let you know when I am ready, try to relax for a few seconds." Darth took a deep breath and tried to forcibly relax, Jim was in position and acted immediately. Darth screamed in pain, everyone present winced in sympathy. Jim carefully moved the leg into position and as soon as he released it a little the soldier breathed a slight sigh of relief. Darth was sweating profusely and moaning but seemed in less agony than he was before. Alderson had one of the holders keep the broken leg in position while he bandaged the splints in place. By the time Alderson had completed the first aid some people had returned with some pain killers. Two people proffered Tylenol 3s, one Percocet. Explaining the difference, Alderson offered the wounded soldier his choice, Darth chose Percocet, the stronger drug. Alderson was certain that within a half hour Darth would be unconscious.

As he stood up, Alderson saw some people coming with blankets and poles that might be able to be used as a stretcher. "Hey everyone, I have a friend I believe is in great trouble and I have to go find him. This soldier needs to get to the hospital at Foothills, it is a long walk but about 12 people working in shifts or maybe getting some volunteers on the way should be able to do it in a couple of hours. Wheelbarrows or wagons could make the work easier. Can someone organize this and get him over there? But maybe wait till the drugs take effect. I really must go."

As he was finishing, the sound of small, loud engines coming up the road sent numbers of the crowd running to investigate. Alderson guessed it was likely Marc and Rosie. Some of the crowd called out, but the riders, on the other side of the fence and moving fast with loud engines, likely didn't even hear. Alderson looked at Darth. With the temperature in the mid-twenties, he realized the soldier would broil in the the heavy body armour. "We need to get him out of this body armour, he is going to roast before he gets to the hospital," Jim said to the woman who had brought the bed sheets. Together they moved him around and took the MOLLE vest off then the body armour. Walking to the broken chopper, Alderson tossed the vest in it. If he could, he would come back for it, but it would not do to let the citizens see him looting a soldier who wasn't even dead. A number of the locals conferred with each other and arranged for six of them to carry the makeshift stretcher. Others went to find wheelbarrows. People followed and helped, Jim nodded at Aidan and they made off, back to Arya and the bikes.

Hopping the fence, they came upon Arya arguing with two young guys trying to take the bikes. "Hey, hands off the bikes!" Aidan yelled pulling the bow off his back. He didn't even have to knock an arrow and they just dropped the bikes and ran. "This nasty world is going to suck, isn't it?" he said resignedly.

"Yeah, and the real suckage hasn't even started," Jim responded, ruminating on the bleak potential for the future. He had often imagined the apocalypse, but now he had to live it, it wasn't as fun in reality as it was as a thought experiment.

"I am really too old for this shit, but a second EMP can only mean someone is planning some bad shit," Aidan said as they mounted up. "Do you imagine there is an invasion coming?"

"Maybe somewhere, but I don't think we will see it here. Well, not for a long time anyway," Alderson responded.

Riding across the highway they worked their way carefully toward the burning sites where the other two choppers had gone down. One site had more smoke and flame suggesting it had hit a house or caused some other burning. They arrived at the still-burning wreckage of a house and the chopper to see people standing around. Clearly people had tried to use a garden hose to no avail, as it had run out of pressure, the house was mostly consumed and another house had caught. There were a couple of soldiers that people had pulled out of the wreckage laying on the ground, it didn't look good for them. There were maybe a hundred people standing around, some wailing, some talking, all looking dumbstruck and frustrated not being able to do anything. It was a good thing that this was a calm day, any wind at all and the whole neighbourhood would be at risk. As it was, there still could be an uncontrollable conflagration. The houses were too close together and this wasn't even the worst-designed neighbourhood.

The trio progressed looking for the next site. They found the still-smoldering hulk of the last chopper in a park that was green enough not to burn, again with people near but not too near, the acrid scent of burned plastics still hung in the air, overpowering the smell of burnt flesh. The pall of smoke shrouded much of the surrounding area in an eerie haze. "Let's have a closer look," Aidan said. As they got closer Jim realized this fit the description of the park where Kareem was taken. When they could see into the burned hulk they saw the burned bodies of the pilot and at least three others in the back. They still had gear, charred and scorched, faces with their lips burned off leaving a macabre smile. Alderson stared in shock, freaked at seeing more burned bodies, it gave him a shiver of his skin crawling. He stood frozen in place. "Let's go Jim," Aidan said quietly. "We will have to look around to figure out what house it is."

- - - - -

Marc and Rosie headed out with no more than empty packs, crowbars, one shotgun and the biker's .45 with some extra rounds in the two moon clips the biker had. They were driving two of the ATVs. The nice thing about no moving traffic was that you really didn't need to follow traffic laws, you could drive wherever the road was the most clear. Alderson's description of the future was running through Rosie's mind as they drove. Mass deaths and disease that would follow this disaster. These were incomprehensible to her, she could not fathom a world with virtually no people. Big cities like this, empty, with only starving, sick, and dangerous people. Even greater horrors, starving people turning to eating pets, or each other, it made her her shiver. Living without the internet is bad enough, it must still be there somewhere and someone just needs to turn the power back on. But who and when? She wondered what Alderson was like when he was her age, she really could not imagine the world he grew up in, no internet, no cell phones, no computers really, three channels of TV. She wondered if he was nerdy, he seemed really smart to her and always had an answer for everything, mind you, she had discovered most of his friends were smart people too. She wondered why he had taken her with him on *the* day.

"What were things like before the apocalypse for you Rosie?" Marc queried, breaking her idle daydreaming,

"Weed, music, food, kitties," she answered.

"Oh yeah, what kind of music?"

"Mmm I don't know, it seems like I might never hear it again," Rosie said, half-yelling to be heard over the engines and now thinking how horrible that would be. "Stuff like Arcade Fire, Led Zeppelin, Pink Floyd, all kinds of music. I liked a lot of stuff on vinyl."

"Oh well we may well get to hear vinyl again. The sound on vinyl is produced by the bumps and crevices on the record, when the needle goes over the bumps it makes a sound and that is converted to an electrical impulse that moves to the speakers. So if a player was not exposed you could hand crank the record and still get sound. That's how the original record players, the gramophones worked. They didn't even need speakers they just had a bell shape to amplify the sound," Marc answered with his typical style of exposition. "The first Gramophone was invented..."

"Hey Marc, what's that up there?" Rosie urgently interrupted, pointing up the road. There were three or four young guys prowling cars, looking like they were looting.

"They're doing what we're doing, just on a small scale," Marc replied. "Let's pick up the pace anyway." Those guys had definitely marked the passage of working vehicles, but they could not keep up with the ATVs, nonetheless distance would be more comfortable.

Marc continued with attempts at chatter but Rosie was

focussed on driving the ATV. Marc did seem to smile at her a lot, which was nice he probably liked her, she knew Alderson had known Marc a long time so it was good to have other people in the group that liked her. She was not sure the female teachers liked her much, she had been a pain in the ass at school.

They arrived at the Canadian Tire amidst stares and yells from onlooking people.

In the store they heard people laughing and saw others grabbing things.

"Just wait here a bit Rosie, stay safe," Marc said as he went in. He came back a short time later cutting open a package of two way radios. "Hopefully the batteries have some charge and the EMP didn't get them." He said while working at inserting the battery packs and handing one to Rosie. He keyed the mic, "testing , testing." He smiled, "Good stuff, it works. Stay with the ATVs, radio me if anyone gives you a hassle. I'll bring the stuff out."

At the front of the store he found two trailers that could be attached to the ATVs, this would make loading easier. He brought back camp fuel, ammunition, camping gear, back packs, another 10 two-way radios, more solar panels, water purification tablets, tie-down straps and other sundry items. The racks on the back of the ATVs were completely full. The generators were loaded onto the trailers.

At the Co-Op store it looked like someone was trying to control the crowd and take information, possibly a store manager who happened to live near by. "Let's just forget that and go to Safeway," Marc said, pointing at the guy. "Before this apocalypse did you have a boyfriend?" he asked Rosie.

"Mmmmm not a boyfriend, a girlfriend. How about you, did you have a boyfriend, Grandpa?" she said, joking.

"Oh no, I am not gay" Marc said evenly, "and I am not

capable of being a Grandpa, I had a vasectomy years ago. I am only 58 years old." he answered looking perplexed at her question, missing the joking tone in her voice. '*Of course*', he thought, '*she might have a Electra complex fixated on a grandfather figure, that could work out for me.*'

"Okay then *Grandpa*," she exaggerated, "did you have a girlfriend or wife?"

"I have had a couple of wives in the past," he answered without elaboration.

"So were you a polygamist, or a serial killer?"

"Oh my, why would you think I'm a serial killer, do I look like one?" he said, concerned he had given off some really negative vibe.

She laughed a little, "Well you don't have wives anymore. What could have happened to them?"

"Just got divorced, nothing sinister." Marc answered. He ruminated on this *She might have read something about him on the internet, but she didn't seem to recognize him when they first met. In fact she seemed a little flirtatious. Now he seemed to be getting a different signal. This young 16 year-old was claiming to be a lesbian but yet she wore her clothes to show herself in a way that would definitely attract men. He was a bit confused about her interests.* He continued his inner dialogue on their way to the grocery store.

There was a mob of people at the Safeway, pushing in and grabbing stuff. There were carts everywhere in the lot with all the dead cars. They pulled up to the entrance to stares and pointing from the crowd. "Keep the radio on," Marc said, handing Rosie a radio. He went to take a shopping cart to find them chained, requiring a coin. He was able to use the Loonie he still had in his pocket to get a shopping cart, it had no other value now.

It was pandemonium inside, people getting pushed and

pushing, bumping into him. Order and mutual respect were quickly disappearing. The smell of human sweat and meat beginning to rot permeated the hot store. Some people were still getting meats, particularly from the freezer section. Marc loaded his cart with rice, canned goods, dried goods, and and vegetables that didn't need refrigeration.

"Grandpa! Help!" The radio crackled as he was moving to get out of the store. "Some assholes are threatening me!" Rosie's voice screamed.

- - - - - -

Jenna and Carrie spent time talking with Ivy and Di, but the trauma they were experiencing was bigger than just what happened to them. It was coupled with the anxiety and apprehension everyone felt now that they would never be safe again, that the world was a lawless place. This wasn't going to change and everyone suffered from it. Carrie hugged Ivy, there wasn't much to be said, human bonding was more valuable than talk right now; there were no good words.

Ivy kept repeating that she wanted to go home, then asked, "Why didn't Mr. Alderson kill him, kill that Papa Bear, he would have raped me," she cried.

"I don't think Alderson wants to kill anyone Ivy," Carrie said. "He may talk tough like that, but he doesn't want to do that. I don't want him to do that."

"If we start killing at will then we have jungle law, and life will be nasty, brutish, and short, particularly heavy on the nasty and brutish parts," Jenna added. "He might be able to kill someone if had no choice but he wouldn't if he had other choices. Once you were safe he would not want to kill someone." Jenna could see both sides, the biker would certainly abuse someone again, left alive.

Ivy suddenly stood up. "Moses!" she yelled, running out the front door. Jenna and Carrie looked and saw a group of four teens walking across the parking lot toward Alderson's condo unit, looking a little lost. They looked very tired, but that whole group hadn't slept well since the first night. Ivy hugged Moses. He carefully put the shotgun down and held Ivy tight. She brought the group back to the house and introduced them to Carrie, Di, and Jenna.

"You guys should come in and get some real food and maybe rest," Jenna said, looking at the bedraggled, weary lot.

"We were lost and we tried the radio but no one answered," Moses said accusingly to Jenna.

"Did you see the flash of light?" Carrie asked.

"Yeah it was kind of creepy. What was it?" Adam asked, the others nodded indicating they had seen it.

"Well Alderson and Marc think it is another EMP, it caused some helicopters to fall out of the sky and it killed all of our radios." Carrie added, "So if you used it after that then the radios were dead."

"Hey, where is that crazy dude Mr. Alderson and the other teacher Jolene?" Daman asked. "That Mr. Alderson is a scary dude, he took down three bikers, snapped one guy's arm. Is he like some Black Ops guy?"

Jenna, Carrie, and Di all laughed, "Did he tell you that? He is just a teacher," Jenna answered.

"Yup he was like, my Junior High counsellor," Carrie added.

"Wow, he told us he was a teacher but after the way he ninja'd that biker I was sure he was something more special," Daman said in awe. "Man if I was in his class I would totally be good." They all laughed a little.

Jenna and Carrie were busy getting some food and water out for the kids. It took about fifteen minutes and the kids were eating and feeling a lot better. As they sat eating in the backyard, White Eagle came over. "Hi Jenna, how are things going?" he asked over the fence.

"Well other than surviving the end of the world and living like cavemen, I guess it is going okay," she answered

"We heard from neighbours across the street they saw some helicopters crashing. Do you know anything?" he asked.

"Jim and some of the others watched it, they were on the roof at the time. At least four helicopters went down. Two of them at least burst into flames," Jenna said sadly, she didn't like to think of those innocent people being killed. She hated the fact that the world was always full of death and weal.

Jenna stared at a hare hopping by. It was unaware of how the world had changed and how much more risk it was at. She was very worried that now the world would turn to savagery people would try to hunt her bunnies, her friends that she always fed. She would not allow it if she saw it. She would rather starve than eat them, and she would shoot anyone who tried to hurt the innocent bunnies.

"Do you know what happened? Was it some kind of accident or something?" White Eagle continued.

Jenna was lost in a moment of sad thought and didn't hear him.

Carrie spoke up, "Alderson and the others sure seemed to think it was a second EMP attack."

White Eagle's wife gasped and put her hand over her mouth. "Oh shit! Excuse my language," White Eagle said, "that sounds very bad. Is Jim thinking of bugging out now?"

"Yeah, he is out gathering stuff to bug out with right now," Jenna answered.

"He offered before for us to join him and I am thinking

we want to do that now," White Eagle answered, "I still know some of the traditional ways, they might be useful. Is there anything we can do right now to help?" he added

"Well the biggest need is transportation, we have some bikes, backpacks, and the four ATVs which still work. If you have any access to any transport it could be useful. Do you have guns or know how to use a gun?" Jenna asked.

"Of course I know how to use a rifle, I'm an Injun!" he answered with a wink and a big grin, "I also have a couple of horses stabled at a friends place up past Rocky Ridge, it would be several hours of hike though. And I have my motorcycle, but I assumed it would be like cars and not work," he finished.

"Some motorcycles still work, Alderson took one from some Hades Animals," Daman piped up.

"He took it from HAs? That is a little crazy and dangerous," Mrs. White Eagle said with a look of horror.

"Alderson is a bad-ass dude," Daman said smugly.

"Well I guess I should start by trying my bike," White Eagle said and then started walking around to the front to where it was parked. It wouldn't start.

His wife snorted, "That thing only works occasionally at the best of times."

White Eagle got some tools and started tinkering, after about fifteen minutes he actually got it running. It was an older street bike, old enough that it had a kick start.

He came back with a big smile. "If it will help we will go get the horses but we need someone to take care of our two kids, we will be gone several hours," he said.

"Walter we barely know these people," his wife said gently chiding, "we can't impose like that."

"No problem, how old are they, I love kids," Carrie spoke up. She kind of looked forward to it as little kids were more oblivious to the problems and they would be a fun diversion. If she kept thinking about the end of the world she would be sad and depressed too, it was better to occupy yourself with something positive.

"Six and eight," White Eagle answered. "They are playing out front of our place, I'll get them over here. I will also be able to pick up my rifle there, ammo for it might be tough."

It took them about twenty minutes and they had changed into bike leather pants and buckskin pullover tops. They introduced the children to Carrie as 'Donald' and 'Destiny'. Just as they were about to leave Jenna came to them. "Hey I think things are getting rough, take this with you just in case." She handed White Eagle the .357 Jim had taken from the bikers and the box of ammo. White Eagle handed it to his wife.

"Thanks," he said, "I hope things aren't that bad yet.

"I don't like guns," his wife said, but she tucked it in the bike saddle bags anyway.

"I know, but if we need it, you can hand it to me," he said. They waved and started riding away.

- - - - -

Knowing only that they were going for a walk, Jolene's dogs excitedly led her, Alex, and Angela down the hill. For the people, it was the beginning of another task that moved them to accept the new reality. Like so many of their actions it was a surreal juxtaposition of a pleasant activity in the backdrop of a world already roiling in chaos. Carefully spying the way forward, the group made slow progress, proceeding only where they knew what was coming.

Trying to learn more about her new reality, looking for

understanding of the people she was now bound to, Jolene asked Alex, "Why do you guys, Jim's friends, seem to be so ready for this, at least mentally ready?"

"Yeah, do you guys belong to some kind of survival·club or something?" Angela added.

"I wouldn't call us ready. I had some weapons I collected as a hobby. We talked about the collapse a lot, but we didn't have things stockpiled or a piece of land outside of the city," Alex replied. "It might have been years of playing role-playing games, you tend to think preparation through in those kinds of games."

"I would be so lost, so alone, if Jim hadn't convinced us to go with him, but it has been just awful, seeing Di's parents dead, the fight with the cop, Jim's story about the bikers." Pausing for a moment, Angela added, "What will we do if we see the bikers?"

"If we see them at long range and they're a problem, that's what rifles are for," Alex smugly patted his old military rifle.

Moving down the steep slope, toward the small bridge that lead to Bowness park, Alex carefully scanned the area. The threat of the bikers made him leery of the park side, but he saw the area near some group homes on the near side. There was a good park area, less developed, with less traffic, that would provide what they needed. The bridge provided a defensible choke point and the fence stopped access to the railway and would provide access control. There were a couple of vehicles on the bridge that could be turned to create roadblock, it would make vehicle traffic difficult, but still passable for pedestrians and maybe motorcycles.

A suitable camp location, slightly covered, close to the water, somewhat defensible, was finally identified. The group homes, housing mentally-challenged clients with professional caregivers, would likely be approaching a state of near panic.

Workers like that were often poorly paid, but dedicated to their clients; they would feel they had to stay. Most likely they would have been there for days already.

On the path, people jogged, walked their dogs, enjoying the spring day on the pathway through the natural area. The scene bespoke no evidence of a disaster, no apparent crisis, no foreboding of what would surely come. They were just waiting for authorities to "fix" everything. There was no productive, survival-oriented activity, it was almost certain these people believed things would improve, they waiting for the cavalry to ride over the hill. But this was no movie.

Things had looked hopeful, the government had got some things operating, but then then came the second punch. Preparing to leave, Alex spotted activity on the other side of the river. He watched, then handed the binoculars to Jolene.

She looked carefully, "Bikers I think. I don't like it. "

"Yes, I believe you are correct. We had best head back. This location may be temporarily convenient but I suspect the neighbours will become a problem. We may have to run them out of town, possibly on those rails." he said pointing at the nearby railroad track. Continuing uphill, occasionally looking back to check for pursuit, Alex suggested they take the steep hillside and go through the natural area, not difficult for a dirt bike, but not something you want to drive a chopped Harley on. It was a hard climb but they felt safer for it.

Alex looked back and surveilled the park again, only increasing his concern. He could see one biker wildly gesticulating and pointing. "I hope that is not because of Jim," he said out loud. "He should have used the sensible advice of Machiavelli," he finished cryptically.

"What does that mean? I always had the impression that Machiavelli was an evil or bad guy but never I studied him," Jolene asked while she pet her dogs.

"Well Machiavelli did not recommend you leave enemies alive, especially defeated enemies because they will come back to haunt you," Alex replied. "Jim left those bikers alive and now they are going to prove problematic for us."

"I imagine he did not want to become a cold-blooded killer," Angela said.

"Yes, but they most certainly will fit that description and their target will be him and those associated with him," Alex said. "Forewarned is forearmed. So armed we had better be."

FIFTEEN

Keying the mic, Marc yelled "On my way!" hoping the response would make the attackers think twice. He let the cart go and started moving quickly, unslinging the tactical shotgun, pumping a round in the chamber. He could see from eighty yards they were about to steal an ATV. He fired a shot in the air, and yelled, "Move away now or I will shoot." He had to get forty metres closer before a shotgun would be effective, worse yet if he fired the shotgun he would hit Rosie. The shotgun got their attention. As it turned out just, long enough for Rosie to deliver an undefended kick in the groin to the one who was trying to get her off the ATV. He doubled up and stepped back. The other guy dithered while Marc gained another ten metres. The uninjured one got his wits back and realized it was a shotgun and Marc could not shoot without hitting the girl. He came up behind Rosie and grabbed her around the neck. In that time Marc gained another ten metres.

"Stay back or I will hurt the girl, we are taking the quads and the girl." Marc slung the shotgun, which the assailant mistook as a sign of acquiescence and climbed on the ATV behind Rosie with his arm still around her neck. Marc kept moving forward. The other attacker was recovering a bit now. Rosie continued to fight the guy, trying to get out of his grasp.

Marc worked the distance down to twenty metres. The wounded assailant was trying to get on the other ATV. Marc drew the handgun and aimed at the guy with the sore balls. "Get away from my bike or I will blow your brains out," Marc said still walking closer.

"Stay back or I will break this bitch's neck!" the other one yelled. Marc fired a shot at the other one. Marc was walking and hadn't had any recent practice with a handgun, The shot missed but scared the guy enough that he hopped off the ATV and ran. The one with Rosie also got off the bike and pulled her with him, he put her between Marc and himself. "I swear, I'm gonna kill her," he repeated.

Rosie was half gagging as he pulled her off the ATV. Panicking as she choked, she dug her nails into his arm trying to get some air. Releasing her a little allowed her to draw in air, breathing again she remembered one thing Alderson had taught her about self-defence. The top of the foot was fragile. She stomped once, then raised her foot and stomped again, her foot followed his shin down to the soft bones on the top of the foot. There was a crunching sound as the bones gave way.

Howling in pain, he let go completely, and tried to hobble away. Rosie turned and drove her foot into his groin, then punched him square in the nose. He dropped to the pavement like a sack of howling, mewling rice. Marc was there now, he winced seeing the attacker crumple, empathizing with the groin pain. Completely enraged, Rosie continued attacking, driving a foot into his face as he rolled over.

"Ow! fuck, I hurt my foot on his face!" she yelled, grabbing a shovel a they had obtained at the other store, raising it over her head, ready to kill him.

Marc holstered his gun as he ran to her, grabbing the

handle of the shovel before Rosie splattered this guys brains everywhere with twenty people watching. "You don't need to kill him, he probably will never fuck again if infection doesn't kill him." Marc said looking at the unconscious assailant's bleeding face.

Letting go of the shovel, Rosie turned toward Marc and hugged him. Holding the big man tightly, she started to cry.

"I thought I was going to die," she whimpered, "he was going to kill me."

"It's okay now," Marc said, "it's okay". He smiled to himself, but he did not push his luck at this point. He just hugged her and felt the warmth of her embrace. He even felt fatherly at this point, not sexual.

She wiped the tears away, disengaging from Marc and moving toward the ATVs. "Clearly, we are going to have to teach you to shoot to keep you safe. You are just too sexy for a lawless world," he said as they mounted the ATVs.

Rosie looked at him oddly thinking, the guys didn't want her they wanted the ATVs. "Let's get that cart of food and get going," Rosie said, "you can teach me to shoot later, Grandpa."

"I can indeed," said Marc, that would allow him to get close to her as she learned. He was becoming more sexually attracted to her as they spent more time together, he just needed her to feel the same.

People were poking around in the cart Marc had filled but as the ATVs roared toward the doors, the re-looters ran. People had heard or seen the gunshots and did not want to offend the armed guy. Twenty minutes of repacking to make everything fit and they were on their way, wending through the community, making only one stop, to deliver the radio to the stash point Jim had requested. Marc explained in excruciating detail about various aspects of survival and the effects of the EMP. Rosie, lost in her own thoughts, responded only robotically to Marc.

- - - - -

In the heavily wooded park, Jim, Aidan, and Arya found cover for their observation to search for the likely house. Staying close to Aidan, Arya was whispering to herself, fidgeting and half sobbing, becoming more distraught.

Aidan, pointing toward an immaculate two-storey house on the far side of the park, whispered "That house over there, lots of activity, I saw a guy in the upper window with some sort of long gun. Some younger guys going in and out. It seems different."

Observing a while longer they could see someone sitting just inside the partially-open garage. Scouting and observing the back would prove more difficult as there were no alleyways. Waiting for dark was an option but Arya was already quite antsy and ready to go.

Unsure if this was the correct park, or the correct house, they were flying blind, making decisions based on deduction from limited information.

"Look no one knows me, I can go take a walk and get closer," Arya suggested. "Maybe I can ask some questions."

"Try to keep in a position so that we can watch you in case anything goes wrong," Aidan recommended. "We don't want to have to rescue two people."

Getting up, she left the wooded area on the opposite side walking around to the roadway, so she would appear from a distance as just another person walking on the road. She chatted with people at another house then moved on toward the target house. As she approached, a large young man wearing a football jersey came out of the house. Going behind some trees, he started pissing, half hidden behind a hedge but people watching could tell what he was doing. The outdoors was quickly becoming everyone's toilet.

Arya got closer. The football player finished then swaggered over to her and started talking. The body language Jim and Aidan saw bespoke a young, macho guy on the make, and one who was used to getting attention. They watched Arya, tossing her long hair, lean in and touch him on the arm, flirting with him to keep his interest. She glanced in the direction of the park, nodding her head as if to signal "This is the one, come now." Looking at each other, Aidan asked, "Does she mean for us to go?"

"I think so," Jim answered. It was over a hundred metres with only a few trees in between, movement would be in the open and visible to the house. Maneuvering herself toward the house, Arya held the boy's attention and put his back to the park, taking at least one potential watcher out of the way.

Getting up and moving from the bushes, Jim and Aidan strolled forward casually, each turning toward the other in conversation, but with the purpose of seeing if their passage was being watched. Aidan had his bow in hand, Jim had a crossbow but they were not leveling either of these weapons, they just made their way forward.

Moving deeper into the garage, Arya drew the football player, reaching her hand to him, his actions became more determined. They were both laughing and sounded relaxed. Jim and Aidan could see into the garage, it was devoid of vehicles, just the usual assortment of lawn tools, pop bottles, and garbage bins.

Arya continued drawing the boy inside. She took the three stairs at the back that led into the house.

Moving quickly, Jim and Aidan followed into the garage, looking back outside to ensure their entrance wasn't marked. Since they would be of little use in the house, they propped the bow and crossbow against a wall, and drew their handguns. Aidan, who was smaller and stealthier, took the lead moving to the stairs, listening first, then looking incrementally around the corner – "slicing the pie". Then, looking inside the door, he carefully moved forward. He stepped forward into a hall. Jim followed with his Sig out and cocked for a lighter trigger pull, covering the other direction and behind them.

Hearing Arya's voice chiding and giggling, leading the boy on, they crept forward on each side of the hall until they could see into the family room. They were sitting close to each other on a couch, facing a defunct fifty-inch TV, with with their backs mostly to Jim and Aidan. The room was dim, with the only light being filtered around corners from outside. Jim carefully holstered his gun, hoping the slight noise would not draw attention, then drawing his knife, looking toward Aidan and nodding to keep the gun on the kid, Jim crept forward.

Pawing Arya, slipping a hand into her pants, the other hand grabbing her breast, the football boy pressed his case for sex. Arya gently refused him, pushing his hands away, but she kept giggling to lead him on and hold his attention.

This boy was used to getting what he wanted, but today he was getting interrupted. It was two steps to the back of the couch.

Jim had to enter the line of fire, but he trusted Aidan. There was a creak in the floor as Jim took a step. Grabbing the boys face, Arya kissed him, holding him until his head jerked back with Jim's arm around his neck.

"Make a noise and I will cut your throat," Jim hissed in his ear. "My friend has you in his sights, you need to be silent or die."

Arya whispered to Jim as Aidan moved in, "They have Kareem but I don't know where. He said they shot one guy and the other they are holding till the police get here. His dad is a big shot lawyer for the city. Dad and another guy are upstairs, mom was out of town when the shit happened. He has a whole football team of friends that are out on patrol."

Aidan aimed the pistol straight at the kid's forehead. Jim grabbed a table lamp and yanked the cord from it. He tied the kid's hands with the cord. He found a t-shirt and stuffed it in the kid's mouth, making a gag around it. Aidan kept a steely glare and his sights on the kid. Unslinging the shotgun and handing it to Arya, Jim took out his handgun. Arya took over covering the kid, positioning herself in a corner so she could not be surprised by someone entering the room. Jim proceeded up the stairs, slicing the pie on each corner. Voices coming from upstairs seemed to be talking earnestly, discussing some point of a plan Jim could not make out; he continued carefully up the carpeted stairs. On the last stair, looking into the room, Jim could see a guy at a table with a scoped hunting rifle leaning against a back wall. As Jim stepped up the last stair, the guy turned and looked directly down Jim's muzzle.

"Do not move or I will shoot," Alderson said in a firm, conversational tone. The guy glanced at the other guy in the room. "If your buddy appears I will shoot you, now lay on the ground face down. Do it now!" Alderson edged forward enough to see the edge of the other guy. Uniform! Serious problem. The first guy was moving too slowly. "Tell your buddy to throw his weapon out. Now!"

"Throw your gun! Alan, throw your gun!", the first guy said. No movement. No response.

"I have back up, throw it now!" Alderson changed aim to point through the door frame approximately where the person was and fired. The report made the guys in the room jump. The bullet tore through the frame, sending a spray of splinters and plaster into the room.

The next sound was a gun being tossed in the doorway. "Okay now put your hands on your head and walk to where I can see you or I keep shooting, and my buddy shoots your friend," Alderson said.

The cop walked into view, a very senior cop, but still wearing a gun holster and cuffs. "Put a cuff on your right wrist and then get on your knees and face the window," Alderson said, his voice quavering. The cop slowly complied like he was hoping there would be backup soon. "Cross your ankles," at which point Alderson stepped in, putting his foot between the crossed ankles to prevent getting up, and pulled the cuffed hand down with his left. "Bring your other hand down."

"Hey son, it doesn't have to be this way, you could work with us. We're shorthanded right now," the cop started talking.

"I'm not your son, and you don't need to speak again," Alderson snarled, he always hated when people called you 'son'. "Bring your cuffed hand down!" he barked at the cop. "Cover me," to the room, reinforcing that there was another gun.

Holstering his gun, Alderson finished cuffing the cop, squeezing the cuffs tight so it would hurt, then stepping back, he hauled the cop up to his feet by the cuff. Pushing the cop forward, Jim grabbed the rifle and slung it. Aidan picked up the Glock the cop had thrown down. "Can you get his extra ammo while you are at it?" Alderson asked.

"I'll cover the stairs after I check the other room," Aidan said.

"Good," Alderson said. "Okay gentlemen there is a boy downstairs being held at the barrel of a shotgun with double-ought buckshot by a girl who is missing her boyfriend. I really hope you can tell us where the boyfriend is."

"The dark guy, big, Kareem?" The guy laying on the floor answered.

"Good, you know what I am talking about and I didn't handcuff a cop for no reason," Jim said.

"Well he has chosen to join with the authorities and work with us," the guy continued.

"Really. Well I guess he should tell his girlfriend that to her face, don't you think that would be a good idea? Where is he?" Alderson said, not buying it.

"He's not here, he went with our official patrol, working."

Alderson walked over to where the guy was lying and put his foot on the guys head. Turning it to one side he started to put pressure on the guys head. "Try not feeding me bullshit. I'm not hungry right now. One more time where is he? Don't act like I'm stupid, your kid already geeked, told us you have him. I'll make you a deal, we are going to search the house and if we find evidence he has been tortured or if he is here, I will cut off one of your balls and feed it to your kid."

"Okay, okay, he's downstairs in the basement locked up," the guy said.

"Well then let's get moving down there, copper first, pops next," Alderson ordered. "All clear?" he asked as Aidan came back into view. Aidan just nodded.

"We're going to the basement. Junior will lead dad who will hold the boy's waistband, that should keep it nice and tight. Buddy, follow me at the ready," Alderson directed. He used the rifle as a prod.

"You are going to serve a lot of time for this," the cop said.

"Yup, could be true, but you were harbouring a kidnapper and doing nothing about it. So go fuck yourself," Alderson replied. He could see the cop getting irate, the effect he was looking for, keep him from thinking too much. "Bring Junior over here," he called to Arya as they entered the family room area. She motioned with the shotgun at the bound and gagged boy, he got up and came forward. "In front of dad, behind the cop. Hold the cop's waist band," Jim ordered. They shuffled into position, "Now take us downstairs."

As the train hit the landing, turning to go down the second flight, the older guy let go his kids pants turned and punched at Alderson hitting him on the cheek. Alderson fought back instinctively, bringing the rifle butt stock up into the guys face, he felt the crunch as teeth were knocked out, he immediately followed up driving forward with a thrusting front kick just in that soft area above the groin. This drove the old guy back three feet, but the kid was in the way, creating a chain of falling bodies going down the stairs. At the bottom the handcuffed cop was screaming "Ah my fucking shoulder.", the old guy was unconscious, the kid, still bound, had somehow rolled out on top and was fine.

"Some people are stupid," Aidan quipped. "You should have let me shoot him.

"The fucker punched me!" Alderson said angrily. The cop continued moaning in pain. "Hey kid, take us to where the guy is locked up." Looking terrified, the kid complied, leading to another room in the basement. There was a cage made of chain-linked fence, made for people, not a pet. Inside was Kareem, passed out on the sleeping pad, looking like he had been beaten. Alderson wondered why that cage was there. Examining the room he saw that this place was incredibly well stocked – at least twenty five-gallon bottles of water, food, and a large gun safe, interestingly closed but not locked. Cutting the cage lock with bolt cutters, Alderson went to the prostrate Kareem, checking quickly to see if he was alive. Alderson had to shake Kareem to wake him.

Kareem woke up, very groggy.

"Kareem, it's Jim we are getting you out of here." He noticed Kareem had many bruises, he was not wearing a shirt. They had beaten information out of him. Looking at the kid, raising the rifle for effect, Alderson ordered, "Go drag your dumbass dad in here." He then called to Aidan, "Buddy, bring that cop in here too."

The cop came in moaning, "I need a doctor."

"Good luck with that," Aidan snorted.

Dragging the unconscious father, the kid with his still-bound hands was huffing and puffing through the gag. When all were inside Aidan found a screwdriver and pushed it through the locking hasp, then bent it. They would get out but it would hold a while.

Kareem used the wall for support."Fuck man, my head aches, I might puke," Kareem said shakily. Alderson put an arm under him to help him get moving.

Aidan opened the safe. He pulled out an AR-15 type gun, slung it, grabbed another scoped hunting rifle, then loaded ammo into his pack.

"How many guns in there?" Alderson asked as he moved Kareem forward.

"That's it, others are out right now I think," Aidan replied as he loaded the AR-15. Aidan went up the stairs first, this time using the rifle.

As they were climbing out, Alderson called back, "If I see your face kid, I will shoot you in the balls, no questions, no quarter. Pass the message on."

"Hey I think I remember this punk from the raid at Canuck Tire," Aidan said.

Arya ran to Kareem and took over helping him as he slowly regained his feet. They hurried out of the garage, picking up the bow and crossbow. Aidan handed the Glock to Arya, Kareem took the shotgun, and they started moving out. Aidan and Jim covered off with rifles when they came out. There were people starting to gather around after hearing the shot.

"These fuckers took this guy and beat him and had him locked up!" Aidan yelled as people stared. "He was only walking home. Do not trust the police or the government, you are expendable to them," he added.

"Stay out of our way!" Alderson commanded. "There are injured people in the house, minor injuries, no gunshot wounds!" Alderson yelled. One person went in the house others retreated to their homes.

Kareem was walking like he was drunk, stumbling and staggering. They went through a couple of yards, some people were trying to follow. Alderson yelled back, "If you follow us outside the sound barrier I will shoot you!" He fired a shot into the dirt in front of them to make the point. People scrambled. Coming out of the sound barrier Aidan looked for a radio and found one. Turning it on he radioed, "Viewpoint this is Ferrari, we are coming home. Have some watchers ready to provide cover."

"Roger that, Sarge here, WILCO."

On the overpass Aidan said, "I have the AR, keep going. I will provide cover, just to make sure no one is following."

"Thanks, on your way back you'll want to check the chopper for that body armour, could be useful," Alderson replied.

"We think alike," Aidan said.

People at the two different condo complexes nearby watched the heavily armed group aiding the struggling Kareem. No one approached, just pointed and chattered.

Kareem, still unstable on his feet, but faculties improving, started to sob, "I'm sorry, I'm sorry. They beat the location out of me, but I didn't know the address. That guy was a big-wig with the city. They were making some plans I heard when they thought I was unconscious. The guy was telling them what 'emergency' by-laws they had to pass to make it legal. Guys, they said most of the city is likely to die! They said they needed to intern anyone who resisted the authority and didn't work with them. But the lawyer guy said they should take undesirables out of the city and leave them because otherwise they would legally have to feed them," Kareem said shakily. "I was worried they were coming your way, they said they were sending choppers to take you out."

"The choppers never made it. There was a second EMP that took the choppers out," Arya told him. "We are even more screwed, but we have you back and we're together." She held him close and kissed him.

- - - - -

Getting back to the top of the hill without incident, Alex, Angela, and Jolene saw more people out walking their dogs, just a regular day in the off-leash area. People did stop and talk, asking each other what they thought was going to happen, or how long this would last, or how to get food in the short term, or what to do with shit buckets. But most, ashamed of answers that would tell of their criminal activity, only shrugged their shoulders in response.

Experimentally Jolene said to one group of three that stopped to talk, "I don't think things will get better for a long, long time, at least months. There is likely going to be mass starvation and death. What do you think?"

"That's ridiculous, this is Canada, not the third world," one person replied while the others murmured assent. "Why would you think such a thing?" he added.

"There is no transportation, that means no food, no food

222

means death," she explained.

The guy shook his head, muttered something about a "doomsayer: and walked away with his group chatting intensely.

Another group that happened by chimed in. "Look, there are all kinds of signs of control coming back, I saw helicopters and vehicles," a woman said.

"You didn't see them crash did you? Look, there is tonnes of food wasting away in stores that people should get before it goes bad."

"If we start looting, it *will* be the downfall of our city," the woman retorted.

Alex interjected. "What will you do when your food runs out?" The woman looked appalled, didn't answer and just marched away, her dog in tow.

Jolene felt that way too, but the more she thought, the more she got scared, knowing that Jim and those with him were most likely right. The problem was simply too big to fix quickly.

Alex, who had watched her little social experiment, was impressed. People reacted as he thought they would at this stage. But she showed cleverness with her questioning of the groups and without a doubt they went away re-evaluating their stance.

Alex added his thoughts, "I see you are evaluating our situation and what you might or might not expect to happen. Have Jim and I infected you with a degree of suspicion about what is going to happen in the coming months? I think you are questioning either the wisdom or insanity of our current path."

"I find I really hate to believe that Jim with his 'End of

the World' view is right, but I have met no one who seems to look for, or accept, the real implications of what we are seeing, nor is there good evidence he is wrong. This scares the shit out of me. The first two days I was just stunned and did not know what to do, but now when I was hoping things were changing. I am starting to believe and it creates a horrible knot in my stomach. I am starting to imagine all the people we know dying in such mean, and primitive ways. I, I..." Jolene started crying uncontrollably at that point.

Already sobbing, Angela, who had been quietly listening, turned and took Alex by the hand and pulled Jolene in together and hugged them both, sobbing even more. Even Alex, who was normally stolid and not easily moved to emotion like this, felt the raw horror of the emerging world. Imagining this kind of world in the abstract many times had always been an academic exercise, this he realized, was real, too real. These were scared, real people, whose lives would never return to any vision of normal they had ever had. People he knew were going to die, the suffering would be enormous, no one he knew would be untouched. It was unlikely he would see his family again, at that moment he knew. The two women knew it as well. All had family in other cities, this group was the only family they were likely to ever know again. He joined that hug like no hug he had joined in the past and cried with them.

They stayed that way for some time, even the dogs were whimpering in commiseration. When they finally pulled apart, they just trudged along, no one speaking. Finally Alex broke the silence, "We have to try to get those kids reconnected to their families or bring their families with us. I'm getting that truck today. We are all any of us really has, for the foreseeable future. We are family now." This had the effect of bringing more tears.

Back at Jim's place there were about a dozen other people hanging around the backyard including Yolanda White Eagle who had just returned on motorcycle. She explained that Walt would be a couple of hours but he would have four horses and saddles and a rifle with him. Other neighbours were here and while most did not take the pessimistic view, some were clearly considering that their view might be wrong.

When water pressure failed again, they went quiet. Concerned murmurs moved through the group. The group included a mix of backgrounds; there was a community health nurse, an accountant, a handyman, people who had some training in various things, but many of them adhered to their optimistic view point. Jenna, too nice by nature, did not argue with people she did not know well, but when Jim got back he would not pull punches about the grim reality they faced. He sometimes scared people when he gave his vision of reality. Sometimes people had to be scared out of their complacency. Jenna saw the returning group, all masked in a pall of sadness. Jolene sat on the step just cuddling her dogs, Angela looked as if she had been crying and Alex, normally impassive, looked depressed.

"What happened out there Jolene?" she asked softly, "All three of you look really down, what did you see?"

Jolene started sobbing again. "I just opened my eyes I think, I feel so bad I brought Alex and Angela down too. The worst thing is that I am beginning to believe in Jim's future and it, it, it hurts so bad. I, I don't know what to do, I feel so lost."

"I know, I understand, we are going to help each other and stick together and do what we can. We have to believe that no matter how bad things get, we will survive with each other. We have some great people in this group and we will get more. I understand how you feel, I have cried myself to sleep since the first night. Knowing Jim is likely right has not made it one bit easier. He's always right about the wrong things."

SIXTEEN

The separate groups arrived back at Jim's place within an hour of each other. There was a gathering of people from around the condo and around the neighbourhood. The group that Jim had collected, plus. There was a lot of talk, stories and chatter going on, lots of tales of the day. Jim retreated to his own thoughts for a while as did some of those that had been out on various missions. In the middle of the crowd, getting to know everyone, Carrie and Rosie related their stories. Jim just felt the need to decompress, a part of him worried about the crimes he had committed. Questioning his own view of the future and his actions made him queasy.

Arya looked after Kareem's wounds, he was still dizzy and nauseated. Aidan and Marc were setting up the generator so they could have refrigeration. Noise of generator engines would attract attention, but the need for refrigeration was greater.

The effect of having to threaten people, assault police, commit gun crimes and theft, was dehumanizing and hardening to the psyche of everyone. Some would not be able to endure this fracture from all they had known, but for now people were holding together. It was not a good feeling, that feeling of suppressed panic, maybe this was all just temporary and jail would be their future, or maybe it wasn't.

Jim forcibly set aside the thoughts of self-doubt, knowing he was as deep as he could go. His thoughts turned to the logistics of moving so many people and how to obtain transportation. The horses that White Eagle was bringing were going to be key to routine transportation. Horses were great but they could not keep up with any motorized transport, this meant they had to be utilized differently at this point. The group needed to move soon, sewage would not hold up long and water was already down. He needed to sound out all these new people. He took Aidan with him and he went to see the crowd that had gathered. "Aidan, you're good with people, we need to find out what this lot is thinking," Jim said.

"What do we need to do, I'm no speechifier. I'm okay at talking with people, not crowds," Aidan warned.

"Well just press the flesh and find out why they are here, what they are thinking about doing, what they think will happen and what they intend to do," Jim suggested.

Rosie came up to him and asked, "So Alderson, what is with Marc, he is a bit weird?"

Alderson chuckled, "You noticed that, did he say anything offensive to you?"

"Not really, but a bit creepy."

"Well that's par for the course, if he worries you let me know, I will talk with him, but I am also sure you are capable of telling him to fuck off, god knows you have told me that enough times," Alderson said.

"Hey are you going to help those kids get home?" she asked.

"We are, but how and when I don't know. It needs to be

soon. We have another mission that needs to be run tonight, after that, tomorrow we will try to arrange something," he replied. "Rosie, my girl, you are a social person can you find out about how these people are thinking and why they are here? Then meet with me in 20 minutes."

"Okay... sure, if you want," she said tentatively.

"Thanks, Rosie." Jim walked over to Alex and Marc. "Hey guys, I hate to say it but we need to do another mission."

"Ahh you are talking about liberation of one antique mode of conveyance aren't you," Alex answered. He had had it on his mind since the walk. He also desperately wanted to get to his place and get the rest of his useful gear. "I propose we move undercover of the blackest of night. I would like to make the run home after that."

"Sounds good gentlemen, just after full dark then?" Marc suggested.

"That works for me," Jim said distractedly. He stood watching the crowd, somewhat bewildered that there was not a more serious tone. Again it had the deceptive tone of a party, there were people even sharing some booze. Watching first, he started talking to the people, he needed to take the pulse too. The general demeanour of the crowd he got was hopeful that things would improve soon, but worried that it would not. It was almost incomprehensible, the contradictory views and beliefs. Many people were not really aware of the second EMP attack or even of what an EMP meant.

He met with Aidan, Rosie, and Carrie who had been working the crowd for him. Their impressions were the same. Most people were here because they heard that Jim and this collection of people were more organized and had some information about the events. Almost no one was certain about what they could or should do. Rosie and Carrie identified one individual that Rosie referred to as a "sneaky piggy", she was certain he was some kind of cop. After pointing him out to Jim, Jim had immediate concerns.

The young man with ill-fitting clothes had told Rosie that he thought this might be a group of anarchists or terrorists from what he had heard. He asked her a lot of questions about how Jim and the collective got their goods. Looking at the young guy, Jim noticed he was uncomfortable in the crowd and trying too hard, the kid was very STRAC (Skilled, Tough, and Ready Around the Clock), lean, military haircut, and no facial hair after almost 4 days after the disaster. His clothes also fit poorly like they were not his — pant legs too long, sleeves too long, back too tight, and he did not seem to have any connection to anyone here.

Jim went to Aidan and Alex, "Hey guys be prepared to back me up," he whispered. He walked over, and chatting to others he put himself between the gate and Mr. STRAC, Aidan and Alex moved up on the guy's front quarters. Jim slapped him on the back and kept his hand there a second. The guy was 5' 10" about 80 kg of wired muscle, young but not that confident seeming. When he turned to face Jim, Jim held out his hand, "Hi how'ya doing, I'm Jim. You are...."

"I-I'm Sammy, Sam Jones," Mr. STRAC said. "I'm good, how are you doing sir?"

"Sir": a dead give-away that he was working above his pay grade, maybe doing this on his own initiative, Jim thought. "Aw shit did the queen knight me and I missed the call. Damn it!" Jim joked. He was still holding Sam's hand, Jim moved so that he could see under the light jacket Sam was wearing, no gun. Sam smiled and snickered.

"Just call me Jim or Alderson, everyone else does," Jim added. "I think you and I should take a little walk Sam, it's a bit noisy here," Jim continued as he led him out the gate to the common area while signaling Aidan and Alex to stay close.

"Sh-sure Jim," Sam said. They walked ten metres to be behind a giant pine tree. Jim had a good look around for other lurkers.

"Sam Jones, you are not a neighbour, you are way out of place, are you with the unit that went down with the helicopter?" Jim asked, giving Sam a steely glare. Jim had been told that his glare was extremely disconcerting to most people, Jim of course, just thought of himself as a cuddly kind of guy.

Sam swallowed and looked at Aidan and Alex, they were not armed with firearms but did have knives on, as did Jim. Sam's head swiveled around as if looking for an escape.

"Ahhh yeah, but our chopper went down and I am kind of lost and useless with a map. I ditched my uniform because I was afraid of scaring people." Sam quavered as he spoke.

"You know that if this were a war being caught by the enemy out of uniform makes you a spy and that can be punished by execution. In a war that is," Alex piped up from behind Sam. Sam's face went pale and he quavered.

"I-I'm sorry, I was just following orders, we're not at war with you." Sam was shaking as he spoke.

"That's good. Look Sam we are not executing anyone, I have never killed anyone and don't intend to start now. That being said I will protect myself. You're from the Highlanders, I believe? How come you didn't return to base?" Jim asked.

"W-We have orders, the government is worried about people like you. They are worried groups like this will increase disorder and terrorism," Sam blurted out

"I have a survival strategy. The government is in over their heads," Jim started. "Look, in a week I will be out of the government's hair, I will be moving on, the city is going to get very dangerous and there are not enough of you guys to change that. Besides are you people really going to tell starving and desperate people they cannot loot the grocery stores? You won't be able to stop them."

"Well, we have to do our duty, we have orders and people like you are going to cause more problems," Sam said with his voice breaking.

"Ahhh someone who has drunk the Kool-Aid. But I guess in the military you have to. At some point you are going to have to learn something. Your unit likely has no more than a couple of hundred to secure a city with a 1000 square kilometres and over 1.2 million people. Give your head a shake," Jim said. "However, you now represent a security threat to us. So we have to decide how to deal with that. While I will not hurt you, I am not so sanguine about what your buddies might have in-store for us. I just can't let you report so soon."

"But, but that is like kidnapping, you can't hold me," Sam said trying to sound defiant.

"I have no problem with that. I'm not keeping you, but I will choose when and where you get to be let go." Jim watched carefully, this was the point where Sam was likely to get desperate. Sure enough, Sam got into a defensive stance and started trying to maneuver for an escape route. He kept looking one direction which told Jim he was likely trying to run that way. Aidan saw the cue and blocked, he had his hand on his knife, just in case.

"Sam, if you try to run I will hurt you, let's try to be civilized," Jim said calmly. "Here is the proposal: you will take us to where you stashed your weapons and gear. We will make those safe. I will provide you with some food and water and you will ride a motorcycle with me to a location about ten kilometres from here. I will drop your ammo and gun a couple of hundred metres from where I drop you then I'll leave. You can take this plan or I can design something less comfortable."

Sam looked around and saw three guys ready to take him down, he thought for a bit, mulling the likelihood of escaping without injury. He made the decision to play for a different chance. "Okay but how do I know you won't just keep the gun and gear?" he said, probing for information.

"Well if I really wanted your C7 I would take you and torture you until you begged me to take it. All I would have to do is break one of your teeth and dig away at the root and nerve with a dental probe. Are you game for that?" Jim asked.

"No, no can we go in the morning I don't want to be lost at night?" Sam asked.

All three of the guys laughed. "Wow, they don't train you very well in the military these days if surviving a spring evening is going to be a challenge. No, sorry this is not a negotiation, take it now or we choose another path," Jim said very sternly.

"I guess I have no choice," Sam said, resigned.

"Okay lets go this way." He led Sam through the house with Alex and Aidan following closely, so Sam could watch as he armed up with a pistol. "Let's go find that gun," Jim added as they went out the front door.

He led them only a short way to the berm and uncovered a pack, body armour, and the rifle in a thicket of caragana hedges. As he uncovered the rifle Jim motioned him back. Jim took the rifle and unloaded it and cleared it He put the magazines, all five of them, in his vest and slung the rifle in front of him. Jim talked privately to Aidan for a few minutes explaining where he would drop him off. Then he walked over to the motorcycle. Jim turned to Sam and said, "Arms up, I need to do a search to make sure you have nothing dangerous to me." He found only a small folding knife and took that too. He let Sam put the pack and armour on. "Mount up. If I am not back in thiry, come loaded for bear," Jim told his friends as he accelerated away.

As they rode Jim spent time explaining to Sam how he thought things would happen. He had to yell to be heard over the Harley, Sam tried a little to argue but really didn't know about the real events so found it hard to argue against Jim's conspiracy theory, as Sam called it. It was a quick ride with no traffic and a bike that could fairly nimbly dodge the dead cars. Jim took Sam near the landfill site for this side of the city. He did not know how well Sam might know the city but this was far enough out that it was a fair hike back. He tossed the ammo out intermittently about 200 metres from where he was going to let Sam off then tossed the rifle as far as he could into the landfill area. When he finally stopped the bike he swept his arm behind him as he dismounted. This knocked Sam half off and kept him from trying anything.

"Ow! Why did you do that?" Sam asked incredulously.

"Just being proactive. Sam if you're smart you won't even report about us. We are no threat to the attempt to re-establish government, unless provoked. I wish all you guys the best of luck, but I think we are in bigger shit than we have ever been in, and so far no one has proven me wrong. So good luck. If you decide to desert, well, we might not turn you away," Jim said and then roared away.

Jim returned to a large congregation of people who had migrated to the front of the condo. He rolled up and everybody was asking where he got the bike. He would only say that many bikes were likely to work and some other simple types engines would also continue to run. Everyone gathered around him with a weird sense of expectancy. He looked at them for a few moments when Aidan walked up and said, "I think most people are wondering what your ideas and plans are, a lot of the people here have come because of you, so give them the speech."

"Pfft who died and left me in charge? That is likely to be a bad idea anyway," Alderson snorted.

"Alderson, we followed you here because you seem to

know more than just about anyone on what to do, besides that you kick ass," Carrie said coming up and hugging him. That started a chatter about the encounter with the bikers, the cop, the guys at Bass Pro. In a few moments there was quite a buzz going up. Then one of the crowd that Jim did not know by name spoke out, "Hey man, a lot of people think you know something and right now that is the best bet going around. If you aren't an end-of-the-world religious fanatic, I am ready to throw my lot in with you based on just the stories I hear about you, and some have said you have no religion. So tell us what do you think is happening, when things will get to some degree of normal, and what should we do next."

Alderson didn't like the idea of being in charge of this group's survival. However, who would lead them? Marc had knowledge and experience but lots would have trouble following him because of his personality, Alex the same — smart, articulate, but both of them were prone to going off on tangents. Jim knew the most people here, he had the respect of many of those. He worried about someone leading who did not understand the scope of the catastrophe. Alderson felt wholly inadequate to the task, but someone had to deliver this fellowship to Mount Doom and it looked like it would fall to this unlikely, reluctant leader. '*Who would feel up to this Sisyphean task?*' Alderson mused to himself. If someone believed they were capable, they almost certainly were not.

Alderson put his hands up to quell the chatter, the general murmur stopped and the crowd watched Jim. He was uncomfortable with being the centre of attention. Alex called out, "All hail T. Lobsang Gnosis of the Church of the Blue Sky," as he raised both hands and waved in a "hallelujah" wave.

"Gee thanks Alex," Jim said. People who did not know Jim or Alex looked around to see what the reaction of the crowd was going to be, a few people followed Alex's lead some were in the process of raising their hands. Marc in his usual not-quite getting the joke joined Alex with a smile and a laugh, Rosie snorted and laughed uproariously, Carrie and Jenna chortled. Everyone who knew Jim had a bit of a laugh.

"As you can see from my friends, I am clearly not regarded as a nearly mythical deity incarnate. However, if you are strong believer, or any type of a believer in any divinity, let alone mine, you probably won't like me or what I have to say," Jim said wryly, starting his speech. "First, as to what happened let me be clear I think everyone who knows anything will tell you we have suffered two EMP attacks. This is not likely an attack by bug-eyed-monsters, not a natural disaster, just likely something we humans have done to ourselves. This is no retribution from an angry god, just plain old humans fucking humans, with relish. While all kinds of the other shit we did to ourselves was stupid and self-destructive, this one takes the cake. Someone took the most technologically dependent culture on earth and took away the technology. So here we are." Jim stopped and looked around.

"How long will this one last?" one young woman asked nervously.

"I will continue with my rant by making it a diatribe, but I am sure if I am incorrect in my speculations or understandings Marc or Alex or someone will correct the error of my ways. This will last indefinitely, things are broken and because there is no effective transport we cannot expect parts to come in to fix things," Jim explained.

The same woman asked "Won't help be coming from like Edmonton or the US? Someone must know we are in trouble." This was a followed by a murmur of agreement from some of those people who were new.

"Oh, I hope I am wrong about this but if this is an EMP attack, Canada was not likely even the target of the attack, it probably was detonated high over Idaho or Kansas and we are just collateral damage. What that means is that damage similar to ours is spread over most of the Continental US. Alaska, Hawaii, Nunavut, they might be okay, but they are not going to offer a lot of help with parts and repairs, they're not exactly the centers of industry. I don't want to get too much more into the effects.

Jim paced as he continued. "People have asked what I intend to do or what they should do. I won't tell anyone what to do at this juncture. If anyone here wants to join myself and the group I am part of, that's great, you just have to know each person must work together in what I am proposing.

My plan is to move. This city, and any affected city, will soon be unlivable. First move will be to the river, we have already scouted a spot. There we will gather goods and transport. In the long term the city is not viable, there will be disease, death, and violence. Missing from our lives will be sewage, security, or civility. We are already in rapid decline. The violence has already begun, as soon as people become desperate and as soon as they realize there is no effective legal system, things will get nasty and for many, brutish and short. Let me add that even the authorities are moving toward totalitarian control."

"Why will law fall apart Jim? They had law in the middle ages and they did not have even the transport or communications we still have," a young man asked.

"Those people had evolved a system that worked in that world. It was predicated on slow communication and decentralized authority. The king might have been supreme but without knights and barons he could not have governed.

The difference between the fighting ability of those in charge and the lower echelons was enormous, but most importantly those people were not as desperate for survival, they had a system that produced adequate food for the population for the most part. The population of the US at the beginning of the industrial revolution was five million, sixty years later it was thirty million and 150 years after that, 350 million. There is no way to support the population we have without modern industrial and logistical systems. All that was skewered through the gut four days ago and was completely decapitated today," Jim orated. With that the crowd grew quieter and more sombre.

"What will I do? Well it is my intent to gather supplies and then get out of the city and find a place where we can establish a community. It needs a couple of things, first and foremost it has to have access to water. That will likely mean sticking near a river at first. It must have land capable of growing food on, and I am no soil or farming expert. It would have to be suitable for for mixed farming. It has to be somewhat accessible to the city because that will be our supply for some time to come. Ideally it would be somewhat defensible too. If the government cannot reassert control in a couple of months there will be complete lawlessness; people will become extremely desperate. The next six months have the potential to be as dangerous, or more dangerous, than living in Somalia when its government disintegrated.

If there is no water flowing in the morning, we move to the river. Water is the key, but we will also need transport. We are not our forebears, we do not have the skills to go and survive with nothing, and why should we try to when there are lots of goods to be had, for now," Jim ranted, becoming more adamant and forceful as he went on.

Another person in the crowd piped up, "Hey man, how will we get transport, nothing much works?"

"I saw a bus working yesterday, some things are working, How do you know what is working though?" another added.

"We will need some people with the knowledge of how to steal a car, some cars that were in some garages when the EMP happened may work, cars in underground garages or steel buildings may survive. We have to send out teams to find and collect. My team has already collected some ATVs that are not affected because of their simplicity. Many basic motorcycles will mostly still work. Small engines that do not have micro-electronics will still work," Jim went on. "That is my simple plan, but it is essential to begin early or you will be fighting with other masses of people for every item, every morsel, and every drop of water. The initial desperation will begin hitting within three days, people will run out of water and critical medications. I will move fast," he finished.

He looked around the crowd which started murmuring amongst themselves. Some even started arguments with each other. Jim started to speak again.

"Look people, for now, tonight, I need you to go home and think about things. I have a collection of people that I have with me and some have already made their intentions known, but each person needs to think for themselves and make the best decision about what *they* want to do, or what they have to do. Some people would say I'm a crackpot and the government will help. Maybe I am wrong, it is a possibility. Some will think my plan cockamamie, that's okay too. This is a time for thinking first, then decisive action. If you want to follow with my plan, then we won't be going till the morning and then only a little ways." Noticing nods of agreement, he continued. "Just understand this, this is not a time for a high degree of democracy, as long as I have the support of those near me I will do what I think is best, I won't be entertaining an "election" – he used air quotes -- in the short term. If my team thinks I am full of shit, they will let me know, but for people joining, until I know and trust your capabilities, don't expect me to give extra credit to what you say regardless of who you might have been. If you don't like the way things are done, vote with your feet."

"Yay Alderson, you rock, we're behind you!" Carrie cheered and clapped, Rosie joined her, a few other people in the crowd clapped, others mumbled and murmured quietly then began to disperse. There were a few hangers-on who waited to ask questions. The most common question was 'How long they would have to live like that?' to which Alderson suggested between two months and the day they died. Alderson was privately betting on the latter. Or until they made a better life. Others wanted to know what their special skills would garner them. Alderson refused to discuss those and said go home and sleep on it. He was thinking about the truck and other transportation.

SEVENTEEN

After all the extras left, Alex came to Jim, "I think we should get that truck before someone else figures it out. We are pretty certain that no one is home and in this world they are not likely to be coming home. After that I want to get the rest of my gear," he added.

"Let's do it then. We should make it a full collection mission, if you are going out you might as well stop and grab what you can," Jim suggested.

"I want to get some wood and make high sides for the box then we can carry more too," Alex said. "And maybe scout for some more working vehicles. I should take 3 people with me. Who would like to go with me?" he asked.

"What will we doing?" Carrie asked.

"We will steal a truck that might be working, then we will go collect more things we need from various places and we will scout for other vehicles. Can you drive?" Alex asked.

"I have a learner's license, but there isn't much traffic is there?"

"No, only obstacles. I don't like the idea of doing this,

but this is a matter of survival. We have to think in the long term now," Alex said.

Eventually Alex, Aidan, Angela, and Arya decided to make the trip, this was dubbed the "A" team. They headed to the ravine for a few lessons in shooting a shotgun, and each of them was armed with the same. Alex took a cross bow and Aidan took his bow. Jim made sure they had a mechanic's tool kit with them, he knew Aidan had skills with basic car repair, especially older cars so he could help if the truck needed some work to get it going.

Jim needed sleep but first he had to set up a watch set. He tried to pair one adult with one of the younger types. Jenna would head the first watch. Their night scopes were working because they had been in the gun safe when the EMP hit. They would last until the batteries ran out.

"Jenna!" a hoarse insistent whisper came from Janet. "There's a guy on horseback and three extra horses." She pointed.

"Must be White Eagle," Jenna replied, holding a scope to her eye just to be sure. "He looks exhausted, he can barely stay in the saddle." He would arrive in ten minutes. "There's the future for all of us, horseback riding," she mused as she watched him ride. '*How long before people could rebuild the infrastructure and bring everything at least to the 20th century rather than the 18th or 19th? It was so hard to even guess when no one even knew the reason for the EMP who did it and why? Would there be an invasion after the dying? So far inland and communications were in such disarray, it would be ages before anyone here knew anything.*' She climbed down and walked over to where White Eagle was riding up. He had been gone for some time and might have some news.

Grimm and Jagger started to bark when they smelled and heard the horses. They were well-behaved dogs and Jolene was able to calm them quickly.

"Hey Walter," Jenna called quietly over the fence. "How was it?"

"Ohhh Jenna, my friends were not there, they are sometimes away at shows. So I took the horses, the farm hands might not get there, I don't know how far away the farm hands live."

She noticed he had loaded saddlebags and a rifle boot on one horse. "Did you have any trouble coming in?" she asked.

"No, no trouble but I did talk with some people. But I will tell you about it tomorrow, I am wiped out and need to catch shut-eye or I will fall over right here."

"Goodnight, Walter," she said with a wave as she climbed back up.

Jim woke with a start. There were dogs barking, then he remembered Jolene's dogs were here. No one came to wake him, so he went back to sleep, he assumed it wasn't important. He needed to sleep and to trust those doing the watch. He knew Jenna would have no problem waking him if she was concerned.

- - - - -

The A Team had to walk and hunt to find the location of the truck. Alex surveyed the cars on the road. They were moved and pushed in odd ways. "Someone must have a working vehicle or there would be no reason to move these cars," he said to the group. He hoped the truck was not gone. They found the house, everything was pitch dark. There was a small waning crescent moon but its light could not fight through the canopy of the mature trees on this block. The house with the truck was undisturbed. Alex made hand gestures indicating they would circle around to look for an entry point. Alex didn't want to make a lot of noise by kicking a door or breaking a window.

Aidan pulled up a lawn chair and climbed up to the window. He tried it and found it unlocked. He cut the screen and crawled in, his nose quickly assaulted by the smell coming from the defunct refrigerator. No one had been here since the EMP. He went to the door and let everyone in.

"Arya, take the kitchen and main floor, Angela take the bedrooms and top, Aidan you check out the vehicle, I'll do the basement. Search everything but take only the most useful things," Alex directed, getting everyone moving. They started a systematic search of the house.

Just moments into the search Arya called out in a hushed tone, "Hey guys, I found something interesting."

Alex and Aidan came to the home office by the kitchen. She had been searching the files, not exactly survival oriented scavenging, but just from curiosity. "Look at these papers in this file." She shone her crank flashlight on the pages on the desk.

Aidan looked his eyes got wider, "Wow this is great, this is the best score in this house!" Aidan said excitedly, he turned and hugged her. "Calgary Classic Car and Truck Club membership list, with addresses and the types of vehicles!" Alex let out a "Whoop"-- a rare show of emotion for him. And hanging on the wall, the key to the classic truck. This find could lead them to other vehicles and people who might have mechanical knowledge. They gathered some canned foods and some camping gear that looked like it hadn't been used in years, including a canvas tent, and some repair manuals on old trucks. The truck was still there and there was a set of good tools. When Alex tried to start the motor there was no effect, the key did nothing. The was a shiver of disappointment through the group.

"Wait a minute, let's have a look under the hood." Aidan said. Seeming undaunted by the failure, he opened the large heavy hood. Inside he quickly noticed there was no battery. "People sometimes take the battery out of cars they don't drive often to keep it charged." He looked around and found a charger and batteries under the work bench. He hauled the battery out and started hooking it up, hoping it was fully charged. He also checked the oil and radiator just to make sure it was in running order. He gave a thumbs up signal to Alex.

Alex turned it over, but it didn't want to start. "Choke it a bit," Aidan said, having had experience with older cars and their starting habits. Alex played with the choke knob and tried again. After a few turns it started. The team shared a quiet 'Yes!'. "We'll have to unlatch that," Aidan said pointing to the automatic garage door opener. He pulled down a step-ladder and got to work. They loaded up the truck and drove out, Alex and Angela in the front and Aidan and Arya riding shotgun, literally, in the box.

A person came running obliquely toward the vehicle, "Hey thieves, stop, I'm calling the cops!" Alex ignored them and drove on. He felt queasy violating his own sense of morals, but those people were not likely going to be home for a long time and this truck could be used to save people now. Besides, judging by the appointments of their house, these people were rich, they could afford to lose the truck, he rationalized.

Alex mulled the route to his place. Traveling the major routes meant more room to maneuver, but higher risk of exposure to authorities; it was late at night and the second EMP had made that less of concern so he decided to risk it. Aidan rode in the box with a pair of binoculars, but he relied on Arya's night vision to help pick out issues ahead. As he was watching, using the headlights to see, he called, "Hold up Alex, the road is blocked ahead, cars are turned sideways. Someone has set up some sort of road block." Alex brought the truck to a stop and turned off the headlights. Aidan and Arya watched carefully, the cars were blocking the road at an overpass. Aidan could not identify any movement but it was dark and this was done for a reason.

"I was going to take that road." Alex said from inside the cab, "Do you think the overpass is blocked too?"

"Can't tell from here but if they are blocking the road they are forcing you to travel on the overpass, I don't like it so I would avoid it." Arya said.

"Hold on, I'm going to turn around." Alex started the truck with a bit of a jump and turned a sharp U turn. He found another ramp proceeded along it. It was littered with dead cars at the bottom but he just drove over the sidewalk avoiding them, giving Aidan and Arya a rock and roll experience in the back. The next road was so blocked he had to drive down the sidewalk. There were many tents on front lawns. People must not be feeling safe inside for some reason.

"Hey guys there is some light ahead," Arya called. "A fire I think."

Alex drove back to the road where they saw the flickering light of a fire, there was a house ablaze and a number of people standing around but nothing much they could do since there was no available water. As they drove closer a group of people came out into the street waving wildly at them. The people blocked the street waving for help. Alex stopped. Aidan warily fingered the shotgun's safety but kept the gun low out of sight.

Angela tensed up, "What are they doing? What do they want?" she asked Alex. She had a tactical shotgun but no thought to using it. The people did not look hostile, just desperate.

"Hey, you have a working truck, we really need your help!" one guy in the crowd yelled out, waving and walking to the driver's window of the truck.

Aidan in the back was motioning to Arya to have the shotgun ready, cuing her to take the safety off. He was highly suspicious of this guy. He leaned close to her and whispered, "Be ready to cover the right side."

"How can we help?" Alex asked warily.

"You could take someone to get help. Or help us put out the fire," the guy said.

Alex didn't like the sound of what the guy was saying, it was like he wanted them out of the truck. "Where would you get help from? You have twenty people here, if you can't put out the fire with that many, it's likely out of control," Alex said. "We have our own worries to deal with."

"We're worried about the fire spreading to other houses," the guy said with exasperation. "Sorry man, we need your truck." He started reaching behind his back.

Aidan brought the shotgun to bear, "I wouldn't," he said. The guy had seen the motion in his peripheral vision and stopped short, putting his hands up. Arya saw what was happening and brought her shotgun up and panned across the group in front to the right of the truck. "Take it out with two fingers and hand it inside," Aidan said forcefully. He snapped the safety off and to make the point he said, "That was the safety coming off."

The guy looked up at him with his hands in the air, others nearby were wondering what to do. "Now!" Aidan yelled at him. The guy reached down and pulled the gun as directed and handed it to Alex, who handed it immediately to Angela, who wasn't sure what to do with the gun so she held the Beretta 9mm and pointed it out the window with no idea if there was a bullet in the chamber or the safety was on.

Alex let out the clutch and drove straight at the line of people. Aidan and Arya covered the mob. As soon as they passed the line of scrambling people, Aidan spun around, covering behind them.

"Hey Alex I think we should take the alleys," Aidan yelled in, "less likely to be blockages." Without answering Alex turned the truck into an alleyway and proceeded down several blocks. This was definitely more clear than the roadways. They spotted a few more fires but they were not on their path and a couple were at transformers or electrical substations. These were set far enough away that they did not set any houses aflame.

They arrived at Alex's and he and Angela went inside the small apartment building. "It looks like some zipperhead, gangsta wannabe has ransacked my place," Alex said surveying damage. Food was gone the fridge was emptied, which was good. He patted the shotgun. "Maybe they will return for seconds, I'll bet it was one of my neighbours, the guy above always looked like he was surviving marginally." Alex went to his gun safe. It was still there and locked, he unlocked it and started handing people ammunition. He still had three rifles and one shotgun that he had not brought the first time. He looked around, his boar spear, armour and helmet were still there but the cavalry sword was gone. He was happier that the viking seax was still there. The ransackers had focussed on food and one sword. They had tried to pry the gun safe open but failed.

Alex suddenly put his finger to his lips, looking at Angela. He was nearest the hall leading out and went to take a look. Catching a quick movement toward his head Alex leapt back a pace, feeling the air as a baseball bat whizzed by his face. It was a weak swing, the hall was too small for a full swing. He reached for the Seax on his belt. The person coming in tried to swing again. Alex remembered with this type of swing Jim had taught him out-and-in, block the recovery. He found he could easily block the bat from recovering, he took an upward swing, not very powerful, but enough with he seax, cutting the attackers arm deeply.

The attacker let go of the bat and howled in pain. Alex punched three times rapidly, just light left jabs, but didn't make any solid hits. The attacker was blocking the way so he stepped in and delivered an elbow to the midsection, the guy immediately doubled over, at which time another elbow under the chin sealed the attacker's fate, he fell over, unconscious before he hit the floor.

Aidan and Angela came in behind him. "Alex! What happened?"

Alex sucked in air, "My greasy neighbour." Alex chuckled, "I guess the elbows do work, just like Lofty Wiseman said they would." Alex quickly searched the downed neighbour and found one of his hunting knives which he recovered. "Good thing he wasn't smart enough to use the knife in close quarters, it could have been worse." He rolled the guy over and tied him up. "We need to plan where to go next."

They sat at the kitchen table examining the membership list by candle and flashlight. They decided that there was only one vehicle in this part of town. It was in Rosedale, a wealthy community, most of the vehicles were in other well-off parts of the city. "I think we should hit the Home Depot up on 16th," suggested Angela. "We could get the wood and make the box for the back."

"The store on 16th is in a too highly populated area, I would say the Beacon Hill one," Alex said, "but we should check out the Rosedale residence for the car. Just in case."

"Okay but I'll drive this time," Aidan said.

"Shotgun," Arya said, with a big grin holding her shotgun in one hand.

They all gave a chuckle, "Guess we're all 'shotgun'," Angela said.

They took off and Alex actually wore his armour while he rode in the back, it might not do anything against a bullet but it would fend off most other things should they get into a scrap. Even though it was only a five minute drive, it took them almost twenty to find the place, having to avoid blocking vehicles and not having a map with them. When they got there the house looked deserted, but without power most did in the dark. They cased the place, saw the car in the garage, and decided to break into the house like before to see if they could find the keys.

Inside there was the now-familiar smell of putrefying food in the fridge. They were quickly greeted by a black cat that immediately began meowing. It seemed desperate, probably for food or water. Aidan stopped to give it some water from his bottle, it lapped a little but then meowed some more, moved away and looked back at him. It did this a couple of times like it was trying to lead them. Aidan followed it. Maybe the cat knew where its food was. It went down the stairs. Aidan shone his flashlight into the finished basement and found what it was meowing about. There was a woman lying akimbo at the foot of the stairs.

"Hey everyone, there is someone here and she's hurt." He went down and checked her out. She was feverish and woke when he touched her. She appeared to be quite elderly.

"Johnny," she croaked in a raspy dry voice. "Help me, those Fall Alert people never came, I fell."

Aidan held her head and gave her some water. "My name is Aidan, we'll try to help you." Angela came down the stairs next and gasped as she saw the woman. "She must have fallen and broken her hip, I think she might have been here for four days now. We will need to make some sort of stretcher to get her out," Aidan said.

"Bedsheets, we could carry her out on bedsheets," Angela suggested hastily. The woman was moaning loudly as Angela ran back to get the sheets, calling Alex on her way. They got a duvet, it would be stronger, and went down the stairs to help Aidan. The woman had passed out of consciousness again. They set up the blanket then rolled her on to it. She screamed as they rolled her, then passed out again. They hauled the motionless body up the stairs, setting her down in the kitchen.

Arya continued searching until she found some keys. "Got 'em!" she called out. She immediately went to the garage and opened it, went to the car and noticed there was another spot for another car that was not present. The car, a 1967 Pontiac Parisienne, started easily. This would not be quite as useful as the truck but it had a very large trunk and could easily be mounted with a roof rack. She had to call Aidan to disengage the automatic garage door. She pulled the car out so that getting the woman in would be easier.

She went back in, "Okay the car's ready, I'll drive her to the hospital, hopefully they are still working. Aidan will you go with me?" They worked to load the unconscious woman into the car. As they got her in, the cat came running and jumped in beside her.

"Sure, but I think we should have backup, they might try to seize the car," Aidan answered. Arya's face clouded. She had not thought about that.

"Let's scope out what to do first and we'll cover you from a distance," Alex suggested. "You can put your radio on when you are talking to them and hopefully we will hear you".

Arya got in the car with Aidan in the passenger seat, and started to drive. The experience of handling a car that big was new to her, she was used to driving modern vehicles which were much more nimble. She used the alleys for easier access. They got to a point where they would have to cross Crowchild when their radio crackled. "Let's check this out on foot," Alex radioed. The truck stopped and Alex and Angela got out and walked ahead. They could see there were cars that blocked the road at points near the stadium and there was activity there. But they could avoid it, although they might still be seen. They did not know if there were any communications at this point.

Alex came back, "You can go but you might be seen. If you are going to go, I would suggest going through the university, it might not be blocked." He went back to the truck and got in to follow. Arya started driving in the Parisienne, the truck following behind to see if there was a reaction. They were both running lights off and very slow to avoid drawing attention.

The old woman had awakened and began moaning in anguish as they approached the hospital. Aidan crawled over the seat into the back. "Shit, she's starting to convulse, she is on fire!" he said urgently. He noticed swelling in her abdomen was growing.

"Aidan there is some sort of military checkpoint ahead at the hospital," Arya said.

"Drive up to it and see if they will take her in," he answered, then keyed the mic on the radio: "Alex we have a military checkpoint ahead, will proceed, take your position and let us know." As they approached they noticed how the military had the main highway blocked as well as the road that accessed the hospital. The checkpoint consisted of a hastily-built shack with an armed man on top and a guard below who was visible. However the shack was large enough to house others they could not see. They turned on their lights and approached.

The guard at the shack was shocked. He called inside, "Car approaching with headlights!" Another guard and the triage nurse hurried outside to see. The nurse was here to determine what cases would be allowed into the hospital, it had been a grisly job for her, people who were elderly were sometimes just given a pain killer and sent away, when a week ago they would have be easily helped and could look forward to years more of life. But the world had changed, now only those under 50 got serious help. The job was making her sick even only with two shifts out here, but there would be no more supplies coming in so they had to be careful. A car incoming was exciting news, but if it was coming here it probably meant a casualty. The only vehicles she had seen in four days were military, a few buses, some heavy equipment, and some cars which the city authority was commandeering.

Alex took up a nice prone position and took aim on the guard tower. The guards were armed with nothing more than C7 rifles, the equivalent of an M-16, but they were not much good past 400 metres, Alex was not sure he was good at this range but at least the rifle he was using was good to that range. It was a scoped 7mm magnum Parker Hale. The guard on top had sandbags, the building below was only plywood and aluminum siding, no protection from a bullet.

Arya drove slowly to the checkpoint where the guard walked out and held up his left hand with his right hand on the C7. "Hi there Ma'am. What brings you here?" he asked politely.

"We have an elderly woman with an injured hip, she seems to be feverish and in lots of pain. She needs help now," Arya said urgently.

The guard turned and waved toward the guard house, "Jasmine, we have one for you," he called.

The nurse grabbed a medical kit with a stethoscope, an old school thermometer, and sphygmomanometer then walked quickly to the car. Aidan opened the back door. "In here, we found her at the bottom of some stairs, she is delirious and feverish and in pain, please help her." He didn't like the look of the guard, so he kept the mic cued behind his back as he spoke.

"Do you know her? How old is she? And how long has she been like this?" the nurse asked.

"We don't know her, we just found her half, maybe an hour ago," Aidan answered.

The old lady stirred to consciousness saw the nurse and focussed. "Oh thank god, please help me, I hurt so much, please help me." The nurse did the vitals on her but didn't even take her temperature with the thermometer.

She drew out of the car and motioned for Aidan to come out, he cautiously followed. "She will not make it, we cannot help her, we do not have the resources to help someone this far gone. I'm really sorry," the nurse said sympathetically.

"That's it, you won't even see what can be done? Can you at least give her something for the pain?" Aidan asked in anger.

"Please just one shot, one needle," Arya pleaded from inside the vehicle. "Let her go out peacefully. Please"

"I'm sorry, I am not allowed to use the morphine on someone who won't make it." The nurse looked depressed. She sighed. "Let me have another look." She crawled into the car, and took out a morphine syringe. Out loud she said, "I could get in big trouble for this," but only loud enough for Aidan and Arya to hear. She administered the drug, shuddering at what she was doing. She wept.

"Ma'am I will have to ask you to turn off the engine and step out of the car. Under the authority of the Local State of Emergency all working vehicles are to be impounded for government use," the guard said a bit fearfully, but bringing his C7 to bear on Arya

"Okay now!" Aidan yelled as he tossed the radio in the car and drew his pistol and spun toward the guard behind the car door. Alex had been expecting that message and was on his target, the guard on top of the hut. He squeezed off immediately. It was a bit of a mistake, he pulled the shot down and hit the sandbags. The hunting round he was using blew a good amount of sand up, but did not penetrate the sandbags.

Aidan heard the shot ring out just as he cleared his pistol. The guard facing him flinched and pulled the trigger, shooting over the car with a three-round burst. He heard a yell from on top of the hut and thought Alex must have hit the guard. Aidan ducked and dove into the car. "Go Arya! Go!"

The nurse, who was still in the back seat with the door open, screamed as Arya stomped the gas. She had kept the car in drive as Aidan had instructed, the tires screeched and she turned the wheels toward the guard.

He dove to the side in a panic. Arya turned hard to try to make a U turn and as she did she mounted the opposite curb bouncing everyone in the car violently.

Alex re-acquired his target but the guard was gone, must have dropped below the sandbags. Alex fired again anyway, just to keep his head down. The shot tore into the top of the sandbag again spraying sand. The car was speeding back toward them, Alex hoped they would swerve enough for him to get a shot at the other guard. As they got closer a firing opportunity opened up. He spotted the guard kneeling taking aim on the car. Again Alex fired a bit hastily, his shot was low and he could see sparks where he hit the pavement in front of the guard. He saw the guard fall back. Time to get in the truck and exit. Angela had it running. He ran for the truck twenty metres away, and jumped in. Angela, dumping the clutch, jack-rabbited it out of the parking lot. They were rolling, the Parisienne would catch up. Angela took them through the university, hoping it was clear.

"Where are you taking me, please don't hurt me?" The nurse begged.

"We'll let you out once we're clear lady," Aidan said.

"Aidan, she should stay with us. We need a nurse, everyone needs a nurse," Arya suggested.

"No way, I'm not keeping anyone against their will, that's for the government fuckers to do," Aidan said.

"Okay, how did you get this car?" the nurse, Jasmine, said, sitting on the floor of the back facing Aidan.

"It is the old lady's but that is another story. How is she doing? Thanks for giving her the morphine," Aidan said gratefully.

The nurse put the stethoscope to her, and listened, she knew if she was not gone she soon would be. She listened but had trouble hearing over the car. It took a few minutes, she checked for a pulse. "I'm sorry, I think she's gone," Jasmine said, sobbing a little, thinking what she had done.

Aidan cocked an eyebrow at her. "So quickly, I thought she might last longer without the pain."

"Some people cannot handle the morphine, we knew nothing of her medical history, at least she passed without pain," Jasmine said still sobbing.

"This is hard for you," Aidan said compassionately, "how are you going to handle it when the deaths start piling up?"

"What do you mean?" Jasmine asked.

"This is nothing. You know there are no supplies coming in, you know the power even the hospital has won't last, things haven't got bad yet," Aidan said, having a hard time believing that this nurse didn't know.

"They kept telling us things would be getting better and the government had a plan, then there was the second attack, even the big-wigs seemed worried then. But it has to get better?" she said with pleading optimism.

"Sure, but first it will get a whole lot worse," Aidan said. "That's why we have a plan to get the fuck out of this city before the dying really starts."

"Really, fuck, I never wanted to believe that, is it just the two of you?" she asked.

"Hmmm I don't think I will feed information to you, you work for *them* after all. Where would you like us to let you out?"

The nurse popped her head up and looked around. "Ummm, if you would agree to get my son, I would join you, I don't want to be there when the shit really starts if you are right." Aidan thought a bit.

"Where is your son?" he asked wary of a potential trap.

"Just on the other side of the university, in Varsity. He's very smart, he's sixteen and graduated high school this year," she added.

Aidan fished around for the radio. "Alex, er Comrade, this is Ferrari, we are going to detour in Varsity. Let us catch you and take the lead. Over."

"Roger that, Ferrari, Wilco." Aidan saw them stop at the entrance of the university and wait. They caught up and passed the truck. The nurse gave them directions to her place.

EIGHTEEN

The mood of the A Team was very sombre as they gathered items from Jasmine's place. Jasmine and her son, Sharif, were very quiet. Jasmine sobbed a lot and Sharif just comforted her. After some discussion the team decided there was no point in trying to get the old lady's body to the morgue, they decided to bury her in a park across the street. They marked the grave with a cross stating her address and that she died "Because our system was not ready." They were startled to hear mewing from the car – the cat must have hidden under the front seats, but now was looking for its owner. "Poor thing," Aidan said, going to the cat and picking it up. "We'll take you back to Jim's, don't worry, it won't be the same as your owner, I know, but we'll take care of you."

Alex handed Angela a gas can, a screwdriver and a funnel and they began draining a few cars. "You guys are just going to damage cars and steal gas!" Jasmine complained.

"At best cars will need repairs and that is all months away ... at least." Aidan said, "and the gas will degrade before these cars get fixed. We need to use what we can find." He shrugged his shoulders.

"We also need to collect items from Home Depot and Canuck Tire," Alex told her. "Is it theft or survival? Besides, has what the rich have been doing to us for years been theft?"

They had to use the truck to push a few cars out of the way just to get past on the road. When they got to the store they set about collecting important gear. They found some working rechargeable tools which had been inside of a mostly steel building and not plugged in. Aidan made sure they got some critical gear: a bolt on trailer hitch for the truck, a portable welder, another larger generator. They constructed sides for the box of the truck and filled it up. They filled trunk of the car. It took several hours to complete the looting. They left some room to get foods in bulk from the Costco, however that one was going to be much harder to break into, it had roll-shuttered front doors.

"Hey everyone, those warehouse stores are going to be good for long-term food supplies, but we need an oxy-acetylene torch,"Aidan said. "Any muffler shop would have one, but I vote we go back for now and sleep. Maybe some others can do it in the day."

Leaving the shopping complex, a group of people walking toward tried to wave them down, but they kept going. They could not collect everyone.

- - - - - -

"We better wake up Mr. Alderson," Di said insistently. "I see two cars coming down the big road. It could be dangerous"

"You're right Di, but hopefully it's friends returning, best wake somebody who knows what to do," Jolene agreed. "Daman, climb down and tell Jim there are two vehicles with headlights coming." Daman went quickly and went upstairs into the bedroom. Grabbing Jim he shook him, "Jim, get up!" Daman said in a loud whisper, "There are vehicles coming, two, with headlights."

Jim woke, startled. Looking around it took him a few seconds to figure out who the strange kid in his bedroom was. "There's vehicles? With lights on?" he asked trying to gain composure.

"Yes, yes, we don't know who they are," Daman said with concern.

"Use the radio." Jim said, wanting to fall down again. The noise had woken Jenna too and she was cursing about her life and how everything conspired to prevent her from sleep. Jim decided he should stay awake at least for a while, just to see if there was an issue. Daman bolted out and started scrambling back up the ladder to the roof. As he got close he called out "He says use the radio!"

"Ohh! Yeah, I forgot," Jolene said, grabbing the radio, but by that point it was too late and the vehicles were only seconds away. They were heading straight into the parking lot, she hoped that meant it was their friends. "Hey guys," Jolene said into the cued radio mike, "is that you driving up on us?"

"Gee how should I answer that," Aidan quipped back over the radio. "Is it who and where?" He had recognized Jolene's voice but was just tweaking her, it was his way.

"Great, glad you guys are back, I was worried," she replied. At that point they pulled up out front. There were some brief reunions and chat about what they had encountered and then inside to get some rest. The rest of the collection would be awake in a few hours.

Some people were up and at it early in the morning, others needed to catch up on sleep. Alderson woke and called all those awake together for a meeting. Some of the neighbours that had been there the night before returned, some did not. It was a grey-overcast day, with on and off drizzle, day five since the first attack. The cool weather would make some things easier, others more difficult, he thought.

This would be a day of difficult organization and moving but it was time to start things in motion. Conditions were not getting better. They still needed good reliable transportation, the motorcycles; the truck, the car, and the ATVs were a good start but they need more trucks. Aidan had left him a note with the membership list, this could be the ticket. But first they needed to be re-located, to prepare more. The membership list would wait. Water, that was the choke point. They could scavenge bottled water for a while but it was not an efficient use of resources.

The group assembled slowly. Jim stood on a picnic table to address them. "Today, if you are with me, we must start to move. We will run out of saved water within very short order. Things are starting to get difficult out there, our people run into desperate people with every excursion. We have improved our transport situation, but we will need more, we will need a truckload for every couple of people. My count right now says we have 24 people here and sleeping. I propose that we set up our tent city by the river today. When we do, we will need guards, latrines, and organization. We need to conserve rare resources like fuel for stoves and use open fires where we can. The spot that has been scouted for us has some trees and likely deadfall. The city is full of wood we can burn, just remember we cannot cook open food over treated or painted wood. We will need information on everyone's skills and capabilities. We will need volunteers to organize camp life details, and people with anything related to security experience to help with security and scavenging details.

I must leave some of this in the hands of others today as I promised some of the young people here I would try to unite them with their parents, so I must do that. I intend to take a motorcycle and one of them with me. White Eagle, I would really appreciate your company on that ride. I ask because motorcycles will be the fastest and most maneuverable, and it is a long way, and they are also the least valuable to the collective." Jim stopped and looked at the more subdued crowd, wondering how many would be reliable and how many would walk away.

"No problem man I will go with you, but who will organize without you, Wise White Father?" White Eagle joked.

"Marc, I would like you to organize security arrangements. Jolene I know you can organize. I would ask that you take that job on for now. I look out there and I know there are people with good skills, you must help where you can and stand by those who are willing to help. I know that many here do not know each other well but you must, must, work together. This is one of many critical junctures to come," Alderson implored the crowd. When he stopped a few strangers started to applaud, then everyone. "Any questions?"

"Does anyone have an inventory of supplies? Or a list of what we need?" one young, yuppie-looking guy with a very pretty girlfriend asked.

"No, and it would be an excellent idea as we re-deploy to do that, it will make further missions more targeted and make future moves smoother." Alderson was impressed and made a mental note of the guy, someone who had an organized rather than panicked mind. It was difficult to do that in a situation where your entire world expectancy had been wiped out in a flash of microseconds.

The guy added, "Strangely my iPad still works, it was in a metal travel case as I was getting ready to leave the city. I could use it for doing things like that. But power will become an issue."

"Power we will get back, we have solar and generators, and even small wind turbines. What is your name, may I ask?" Jim inquired.

"I'm Jason Smythe-Jones, or Jay."

"Okay Jay, we will talk later but you can be in charge of the inventory and please create a personnel file as well, this will help us plan. Work with Marc and Jolene to find what information needs to be collected," Jim added, nodding toward the two of them. Marc was grinning at the possibility of working closely with Jolene, although she hadn't seemed to notice him today ... so far.

"I suggest everyone do what they need to breakfast-wise and meet back in about an hour to start the work. White Eagle and I will be off before then," Jim finished.

Jim went first to the group of teens he had helped in the park. "Hey guys, I know things are crazy and we wanted to help you all get back home. Here is my plan, White Eagle and I will take one of you back with us and you will help us find your parents. When we find them we will determine if they want all of you to come back or they want to try to join with us," Jim said. "We need one of you to come that is most likely to find all of your parents."

The kids started talking and it was clear that of the four families only Moses and Adam's family had both parents. The others were either single mothers or one single father because the mother was currently in Vietnam. "Mr. Alderson?" Moses said.

"Jim, please," Alderson corrected.

"Okay Jim, our dad is a mechanic, he may be able to help you with some cars and things," Moses continued. He must have noticed Jim's eyes go wide with delight because he smiled in return.

"Skilled people like that are just what we need, we just have to convince him we are not crazy," Alderson said.

"But our mother is not very well, she takes many medications," Adam added.

'*Oh shit*' Jim thought, '*Even they are starting to realize the implications of this EMP event.*' Out loud he said "Well I guess we will just have to collect medications for her. Which of you will go with us?"

"Moses wants to stay with Ivy so I will go with you. I know the other parents too," Daman piped up.

"White Eagle, Walter, is it okay if Daman rides with you? Your bike is better designed for a passenger and you are a way more experienced rider than I am," Alderson asked. He was always uneasy riding any motorcycle, it was that much worse with a chopped Harley.

"As long as he wears a helmet, not like you outlaw white man," Walter added with a grin.

He was going to like White Eagle's humour, Jim thought. They mounted up taking radios, binoculars, one shotgun, a handgun each, and Jim's old Lee Enfield, just in case. A just-in-case gun was getting to be like taking a coat or umbrella with you.

They set out, it was thirty kilometres through the city. The bikes would allow them to dodge some dead vehicles but they decided to travel so as to avoid any really big blockages that happen on major roads. As they went they saw a few other bikes and many people out in their yards, some talking, lots waved at them trying to get them to stop, but they didn't. They had to cross some major roads, Jim felt it would be easiest to use the pedestrian bridges as they were less likely to be blocked. By the time they got to the east side of the city they had seen at least five fires burning, fire was becoming a major hazard. Luckily today was damp and chilly. Come August a lightning strike in this city could set a whole neighbourhood ablaze without fire protection. Another incentive to get out early.

As they started the more southward part of the trek, they heard gunshots. They immediately took cover and observed.

They heard some yelling but they never saw where the shots came from. They made a wide circle around where they thought the shots might have been from.

As they turned down a residential street as directed by Daman, a group of people was standing around yelling and screaming at each other. They had knives, machetes, and clubs. As they approached, the guys in one group moved to the roadway brandishing weapons.

"Hey, you fuckers, give us your bikes," one was yelling, clearly getting ready to throw a club at Jim. Jim cranked the throttle, and White Eagle followed suit. The thrown club missed but once again it highlighted the imminent danger presented by desperate people.

White Eagle stopped up ahead, "Hey Jim, if I am going to have the boy, give him the shotgun so he can shoot while I drive if needed."

"That sounds like a plan," Jim replied unslinging the shotgun and handing it to Daman. "Just don't shoot me or White Eagle."

"I can't believe I just told you to arm another white man," White Eagle said with a grin.

"Hey, I'm no whiter than you are!" Daman said to White Eagle who was grinning from ear to ear.

"Hey guys, the 'hood I live in is not so nice, there are lots of people with guns. We should be careful," Daman said.

"Do you know anyone or any family that has guns?" Jim asked, yelling over the Harley.

"Some," Daman yelled back. "Some are not good people."

As they finally approached the south-east neighbourhood Alderson stopped his bike. The noise of the bike had drawn some curious looks. The bikes could be targets. The good thing was that Alderson looked enough like a biker that it would deter all but the most dangerous.

"Daman, how far from here to where you live? And what is the nearest school?" Alderson asked.

"It is only about five or six blocks. The nearest school is Edward Murrow. Why?" Daman asked quizzically.

"I have a bit of a plan, follow me," Alderson said. He knew where the school was and drove quickly to it. He then drove on the field around the back. The back windows were covered in a metal screen to prevent vandalism, but Alderson knew that these had to come off, they were only screwed in. He took out some of the tools he brought and began working to get one screen off.

White Eagle came to help saying "Hey, you keep guard," to Daman, when he saw Daman watching what they were doing. It took about ten minutes. They pulled a screen off, smashed a window and went in and opened the main door and took the motorbikes inside. They exited through the front doors and started walking for Daman's place after taking a careful look around to see how much they had been observed. It appeared clear.

They walked for fifteen minutes and came to the block that Daman lived on. It was a multi-ethnic neighbourhood, Vietnamese, Black, Hispanic, and some Filipino. They were watched, but people kept their distance.

"Daman, what does your father do?" Alderson asked.

"Uh well he had done lots of jobs, worked construction, driving cabs, worked at a scrap yard for a while, recently he has been unemployed. That's why mom was in Vietnam, she was looking to see if it was better to move back there." He was slightly embarrassed that his father had been unemployed.

"Well, we are all unemployed now aren't we," White Eagle said.

Jim was making a habit of watching all directions, he did not want to spend long here. He figured that he and White Eagle looked dangerous enough that someone would have to plan to take them out. They got to Daman's house. The boy opened the door with a key.

"Dad? Where are you Dad?" Daman yelled in Vietnamese. No answer. He went around the house and finally came back. "I don't know where he is. Maybe he went to my aunt's place up in Marlborough".

"Okay, we go to Adam's place, then the girls'," Alderson said.

"Jim, the last house on this side, they have some guns. It is also a meth or crack house," Daman added.

Alderson looked at White Eagle, White Eagle said, "Hey man, I know it would be doing a service and all but I have kids I want to see again and this hood looks worse than a bad Res. I can't go there with you."

"You're right, bad idea," Jim said.

They exited the back door and through the alleyway, more privacy that way. As they went there were a number of yards with evidence of backyard mechanics doing their work. Some even had vehicles that might function given the right work. They found Moses' and Adam's parents' house, and their father working on a motorcycle in the garage. "Hey Mr. Senador," Daman called out.

A short, middle-aged but powerfully built Filipino man whirled around. "Daman! You are okay! Do you know where my boys are? Please tell me they are okay. We have been worried sick about all of you."

266

"They are fine, a bit scared. I'm good, this guy, Mr. Alderson, has been helping us. They are far on the other side of the city. It is a long story," Daman said.

The older man wiped his greasy hands and ran and hugged, almost crushed, Daman. "Thank you, thank you so much," he shook Alderson's and White Eagle's hands.

"How did you get here? How can I get to them? Are those two girls with them, their parents are worried too. Pansy said you were all together when it happened," the man sputtered.

Alderson looked around and noticed some good supplies of food and water in the garage. Senador noticed him looking at those and said, "I will give you all if you bring my children back."

"Mr. Senador, I would not take that from you. I have promised to help your children get back, this was all I could manage today, but I think we should talk first," Alderson said.

"Of course, of course, come in meet my wife and we will share some food," Senador insisted.

They went inside and Alderson briefly relayed that the boys were fine but he was traveling here by motorcycle so they did not have room to bring them all. He also said he wanted to be sure the parents were okay before everyone came.

Alderson began to make his pitch for moving out. "I believe things are going to get very bad in the city, very dangerous and violent. Food will become scarce, there is no water flowing, no sewage, this city will become very dangerous."

"But back in Philippines it was always dangerous like this," Senador said. "People will survive, I will survive, already people bring me food and water to get their motorcycles working."

"It is true there are many places in the world that people live in equally bad conditions, but they have ways of getting water to the people, there is nothing here. They have regular food delivery to the city, I don't think that will happen here. They have evolved in that condition and the system can handle it. Here, nobody is equipped to live this way right now. I am leading a group of people out of the city and we will find a place that we can live and grow food and wait for some recovery. A big difference is here almost none of the cars work," Alderson said. "What will become of sewage for a million people? There is no sea to dump it into here. What I was hoping was that you would join this group."

"Oh Mr. Jim, I am sure people will survive and things will get better. Canada is a very rich place, how long can it be before things are fixed?" he asked.

"Mr. Senador have you got a map, a map of North America? I would like to show you something," Alderson asked.

"I think we have something I can get for you." Senador went out of the room and brought back a very old atlas of the world and handed it to Alderson. Alderson looked around for a pencil and other objects. He flipped to a standard Mercator's projection of North America, not the best view but it would have to do. He spotted a pill bottle or two and grabbed then. Using the scale he did some finger measurements.

"I believe we have had an attack called an EMP, this happens when a nuclear device is set off high up in space." Using his fingers and the pill bottle he estimated 300 km above the map. "Probably about this high. When this is done it sets off an electrical impulse that destroys electronics. The area of greatest damage from the EMP is maybe about this big (he used the cap of a pill bottle). This nuke did not go off over Calgary but maybe somewhere over the USA, I saw the second one and it was almost due South. According to people I talked to the first was South East and maybe farther away. I don't know for sure." He stopped for a moment.

"Why would someone do such a thing?" the mechanic asked, befuddled by the enormity of the event.

"Only one reason, they wanted to destroy the power of America, that is all I can think of. But let me explain some more. Back in the 1960's the US, Russia, and probably China all had plans to use this as the opening attack in a nuclear war. The Americans estimated the area affected by one weapon over Kansas would affect and area this big, (he drew a large circle with his fingers). They believed there would be damage to electronics in all of this area. Military stuff was then improved to handle this, but since the 1990's the militaries of both the US and Canada have been buying lots of commercial stuff, they still harden some things, but not all." He looked at Mr. Senador to gauge his reaction before continuing.

"Do you think it is the Chinese? Or Russians?" he asked.

"I really don't know and right now that is not important. What is important is that circle could include all of the coasts and manufacturing centres of the US. It could have wiped out their ability to produce things, so there might be enough spare parts stored up to repair some of the damage, but even if there were some those parts are all in the East and transportation is largely not working at all. This means it will be a very very long time before goods flow, then the will flow to the easiest places first and the biggest. California has more people than Canada, we will be far down the list. I hate to be the doomsayer, but it does not look good," Alderson finished.

"I don't know, it is very hard to believe," Senador said rubbing his chin thoughtfully. "What about sick people? Will the hospitals work?"

Alderson replied, "Well they have some limited power, but that appears to be generator run and the gennies will run out of gas fairly soon. But some friends took an old lady with a broken hip there and they were told, 'she won't make it, take her away!' They know the resources are very limited and they are rationing already."

"What about the druggists, will they have more medication for my wife?" Senador asked, extremely concerned at this point. Panic was running through his head, he knew her prescription only had one week or so and then she would risk heart failure, she needed blood pressure pills and blood thinners.

"I would be willing to go with you and get the medication she needs, as much as we can," Jim said.

"But no stores are open right now, how will we get it?"

"If you go you will find that the doors of the stores are likely already broken and people are taking things. I know it is wrong to steal, but is it more wrong to let people die when the goods are right there and not even the owners can sell them for profit. If you do not get things from the store, others will get them illegally and trade them to you, so you will end up with stolen goods one way or the other," Alderson added, shrugging his shoulders.

Senador looked at him suspiciously for a few moments, the panic inside growing greater. This man wanted him to commit crimes and he was saying if he did not his wife would die because there would be no medication. Or if he traded with other people for the medication they would have stolen it. This was as bad as the gang extortions that took place in the Philippines.

His wife, who had been silent until now, spoke up. "Johnny, if you do not do this I understand. You are an honourable man, that is why I love you and would never ask that you do anything dishonourable for me. I am concerned about our boys but it seems Mr. Jim here is smart and perhaps they are okay with him. But going with him to move out of the city might give you a chance to be honourable as you are, without having to do work for the gangs. I think if we take the drugs now we can pay them back later. Lots of people will have to do that," Mrs. Senador said with tears in her eyes. Her heart was broken just thinking how hard her husband worked to make a better life for her and the boys, only to have it threatened by this insane event.

"That decides it, I must do as you say but how will we get there? I understand only motorcycles work and I do not have one," he said sadly.

"Ahhh not just motorcycles, very old cars, pre-1979 cars will still work and some later ones probably can be repaired," Alderson said watching the man's eyes grow wide with excitement.

"Really you know this, these old cars they will work?" Johnny asked excitedly.

"Yes, we have obtained two such vehicles. White Eagle, Daman, and I rode here on motorcycles but every truck we can get will make our future work that much easier.

Mr. Senador, a man with your skills will be a very, very important person if you can make some of these cars go," Alderson said.

"I know just where to make some cars and trucks to work, but it will take some hours for some. But I can get maybe three trucks running, for some the body is not so good, is being restored," he said. "Maybe eight hours if you can drive me there, it is several miles away."

"I will take you if White Eagle, Walter, and Daman can find and talk to the girls' parents. Do you have any guns?" Alderson asked.

"No! I do not keep such, I left the Philippines to get away from the violence and guns, that is why I did not go to the USA!" he said emphatically.

"Unfortunately they have become a necessary survival tool," Alderson said.

"Very well, when we go I have some friends who have many guns, we can stop at their places, if they can come with us?" he asked.

"Of course. If you will say they are good people, I will accept that," Alderson agreed, wondering if he was making a mistake and inviting some kind of gang member to the collective. But even gang members can be useful, and if not they *do* have to sleep.

"Daman, how far to the girls' places?" White Eagle asked.

"Only one block, one bad block," he replied. Alderson looked at him and handed him the shotgun.

"What are the laws of gun safety?" Alderson asked.

"Always point the gun in a safe direction. Keep your finger off the trigger. Every gun is loaded ... " Daman searched his memory.

"Not bad, Always be sure of your target and beyond," White Eagle said, then showed the boy where the safety was on the tactical shotgun. "Then we're going to be off. We will come back here and if time permits and it is safe enough we will go to the drug store and at least scope it out," White Eagle finished.

"Okay then Mr. Senador, do you need to grab some tools? I have a pack to carry some," Alderson suggested.

"No, everything I need will be there, but I guess hoists will not work, we might have to use the chain lift if I have to get underneath," he said thoughtfully as he got up, then leaned over and kissed his quietly sobbing wife. He knew that she was thinking this would be worse than living in the Philippines. Alderson and he headed for the doors. Alderson kept the rifle slung on his back but his hand rested on the holster holding his Sig 226.

They got to the school. Senador marveled that they had hidden the bikes inside, he was somewhat dismayed that they had broken in to do so. "Hey Mr. Jim, you should have Mr. White Eagle take his motorcycle to my place, safer there."

"You're right, good thinking." Jim pulled out the radio, "White Eagle, this is Jim do you copy?"

A few moments later, "We copy Juju this is Daman. We are at Ivy's place."

"Right, tell White Eagle to take his bike to Senador's place. It is safer and we will be gone a while. Over."

"A big 10-4 on that Rubber Duckie." It was White Eagle, putting on his best trucker voice.

Alderson and Senador rode off avoiding any crowds of people they saw, speeding up when they got close to any group that could be a threat. They went first to a friend's place – he was not home. Senador was scratching his head but then finally remembered that his friend Antonio was going to a major shooting competition in Idaho and had flown out the day of the disaster. Senador had lost track of the time since the event, it was easy to lose track of time with none of the usual references of daily life.

"We should break in, Antonio is a very good friend, he would rather me than some thug," he said. "He would understand completely in the circumstances. I do not know how long his flight was..." he said, trailing off with a sudden sadness.

They broke in to find the guns were secured in a very high-security gun-safe. They could not collect much of anything as they were only riding the motorcycle and had only a few tools at the time.

"We will come back with a torch, when I have a truck working," Senador said as they left. When they came out, there were some neighbours watching. "Hey Johnny, is Antonio here?" one asked.

"No, but I know where he is," Senador said. Eyeing the person suspiciously he added, "We are going to get him now." Alderson did not react. It is what he would have done. He did however let the handgun at his waist show so they knew he was armed with more than just a cumbersome rifle.

They mounted the motorcycle, which widened the eyes of some of the neighbours' eyes as they understood it to be a biker's bike. It did have HA markings on it, but the guy driving it was not wearing colours. Most people in this 'hood knew 'you do not fuck with a biker's bike'.

They got to the shop. "Small Guys Vintage Vehicle Restoration" the nondescript sign said. They had to manually open the bay doors, after detaching the electric opener. There was a small wrecking yard behind the shop with about thirty old vehicles in it in various stages of dilapidation. They were mostly used for parts. Inside the steel Quonset there were three hoists with vehicles being restored and three more vehicles on the ground also obviously having work done. There was one flatbed tow truck of newer design. They searched through the building, finding some working radios. "Johnny, give the flatbed a try," Alderson called out, tossing Johnny some keys he pulled off the key hooks on the wall.

Senador hopped in and started it as if everything were normal. Popping his head out he yelled " Why did this work, Mr. Jim?"

Speculating, Alderson suggested, "I would guess that is because it is inside a metal container with no contact to the walls. The walls of the quonset would have grounded the

EMP."

The truck had a crane on the back used for lifting heavy dead cars that could not be pulled on. This was a stupendous find. There was also a VHF base radio in the shop and a mobile in the truck, which both worked because the shop one had been unplugged when they switched to cell phones.

"We have to take this truck, it is very, very valuable," Jim said.

"We can," Senador replied thoughtfully, "The owner is very sick in hospital, he was 80 years old and he was going to sell me the business next year, but his son was trying to stop him. I think many shops could have working vehicles," Senador added.

"You're right, but one would have to know where to look," Alderson said.

"Yes, that will be for other days. We will have to get to work here while there is some light. You will have to be my apprentice, Mr. Jim," Senador said almost apologetically.

"No problem, but let me set some security." He looked around till he found fishing line type material which he strung across the open bay doors and then attached some precariously perched items to the line. Anyone crossing the line should make some noise. Senador began working on one of the trucks at the hoist line.

White Eagle and Daman were only able to talk to Ivy's mother. There was no answer at the other girl's place. Ivy's mother spoke poor English so Walter could not do much of the talking. Daman was able to translate. The other problem was that she was drunk. Partway through their discussion there was a knock on the door. She answered it, putting on her best sweet voice. The middle aged white man looked askance at White Eagle and Daman. While Ivy's mother and the man got very cuddly, he put down a bag of goods and started holding and touching her. Daman was staring gape-mouthed when White Eagle stood up, cleared his throat and said, "Daman I think we should go." They walked out.

Daman asked as they walked back to the school, "Do you think she's a ho?"

White Eagle looked at him angrily and snapped, "People do what they must to survive, some things are less harmful to others than others. Do not presume to judge. I think we will all have to do something we find distasteful."

"Sorry," Daman said, admonished. "It is just kind of sad."

They got to the bike and drove to Daman's aunt's place only to find no one there either. The house had been ransacked. "I don't like this," Daman said, "I don't know where else they could be. I don't know what to do." His voice cracked with tears, the stress on everyone was intense.

"Daman, the best we can do is leave him a note at home for now," White Eagle said putting his hand on Daman's shoulder.

- - - - - -

The collective worked moving gear and people down to the river park. Marc was very specific about security arrangements at the camp site. They made some trips to the Canadian Tire store, got hunting blinds, tents, camping gear in general, so they had an excess of basics. Everyone expected the group to grow and it did. By the time they had set up camp and moved all the gear, it was early evening and they had obtained at least ten more serious people and twenty curious onlookers asking questions.

Once the A Team had woken up and joined in the work, Aidan took over as the nominal spokesperson. While Marc was knowledgeable, he often drove people nuts by saying too much and not picking up on the cues to stop. Aidan was very personable and was a fairly good judge of character. Kareem, Angela, and Arya also set to collecting information and helping to feed it to the new 'bean-counter poobah', as Aidan had dubbed Jason. Jolene, with Marc's input, organized the camp layout and directed people as they came in. Everyone worked, even those who normally avoided work like Rosie, Di, and Adam.

The atmosphere was strangely lightened by the focused continuous work. The work was not arduous, but it was taxing because of the scope of the job and all the requirements. Finally Aidan took a group on a run to a new grocery store. They opted for one farther out that might not be as looted. He aimed for the frozen meat section and the big freezers in the back of the store. He was on track, there were still some meats that were partly frozen just because of where they were. They took all they could collect. On the way back they stopped at Alderson's and picked up his small chest freezer, they would use the generators to freeze as much as they could.

"Now we make the most important stop," he told his crew – the teens, Carrie, Rosie, and Moses. He drove to a liquor store, it had already been fairly looted but there was still a lot of good wines left, some vodka and a few other hard drinks, but absolutely no beer. The kids went nuts at the thought of adults getting them some alcohol. They loaded up cases of booze. Aidan knew this had lots of portable value.

When they got back and Marc saw the booze he called together twelve people he had selected. "Sorry to be the downer here but you people cannot get drunk tonight, no more than one drink each. You are on watch tonight, but I promise you won't be tomorrow so you will be free then." Rosie was in that group and she had been looking forward to getting hosed, it made her a bit wild and she always had lots of fun.

"Oh please, can't I be on tomorrow instead of tonight?"

She begged Marc, smiling sweetly at him and batting her eyelashes. She also made sure he could see inside her relatively low-cut top.

"Well, we would need someone else tonight," he said, thinking he could leverage this favour for others in the future, that he could do guard with her tomorrow, show her the ropes. "If you can convince Angela or Jolene to go out tonight instead of you, it's okay with me." Jolene would be an excellent choice for him to be on guard duty with as well he thought.

"Hey Ms. Klemper, I was wondering if we could switch guard duty, Marc has me on tonight and I kind of wanted to hang with Carrie tonight. I think Jason is on tonight and he is kind of cute," she said, hoping to bring Angela in.

"Hahahaha, well I agree he is kind of cute, but I wasn't thinking I was trying to get close to him. I will switch with you but just remember you will owe me one," Angela bargained. She didn't really care but it always helped to build allies and friends. This kid could be snotty but she also knew the girl would need an ally and would likely help her in the future.

"Thanks, but if I were you I would totally check him out," Rosie added.

After the guard duties were set people started having dinner and chatting, some drinking and smoking weed, but no one, not even Rosie was getting totally wasted. The atmosphere was surrealistically like a barbecue party. There was some idle chatter about what happened to Jim and White Eagle, they had no communications that would carry across the city.

People started to retire to bed in tents. Jenna would not go to sleep until she knew where Jim was, but she had no way of knowing what happened or why he was away this long. She didn't want to think about worst-case scenarios, but they infiltrated her mind anyway. Beyond her loss who would lead this bunch of people? Who could keep them together? What would it mean to those kids if Jim didn't return after looking for their parents? It seemed that only Jim had a vision for this coming darkness. He was the driving force behind this group. It would also be bad for White Eagle's kids and wife. She sat up just petting the cat, hoping for Jim's return. She had a sense of foreboding that this feeling was going to be all too common in the coming years.

NINETEEN

Alderson and Senador worked on two trucks until late in the evening when the shadows grew too long to make working effective. They got both trucks running. Senador had chosen two that did not have much body restoration done because most of the trucks were being restored in a low rider style, not very useful if you had to go off road. There was a fair bit of rust and damage on the outside but they were able to bolt in new seats from some of the other trucks that were closer to completion. There were hardly any passers-by as the shop was in a industrial area.

Once finished they loaded one of the trucks on the flatbed with the motorcycle as well. They strapped the bike down as best they could. They loaded on tools, a compressor for air tools, an oxyacetylene torch and as much hose as they could find. They also got some spray paint. Once loaded up they drove out. Senador led in the flatbed, he could push most cars out of the way if needed. Jim followed in the other truck.

They went back to Antonio's. When they got there, they found the door they had locked opened. Jim drew his gun as he went in. Senador called, "Antonio, are you here? Then said something in Tagalog. They heard sounds from the basement, but no reply. "Whoever you are, you had better get out of here!" Senador yelled. Two sets of footsteps clamoured up the stairs at high speed.

Alderson took a half-cover position behind a door frame. Two young guys came up wielding crowbars. "Whoa there guys, I have a gun. Drop the crowbars!" Alderson said loudly. It didn't look like they were going to stop and he was worried he would have to shoot them. He fired a into the wall beside them. They dropped the crowbars.

"Hey man don't shoot, were sorry," the leading one said.

Alderson backed away from the frame, "You can get out now!" he ordered. He took a position behind a table that would be hard to rush, and Senador behind him had picked up a garden shovel from the yard.

The two guys started speaking what seemed like Arabic as they came up the stairs, they saw Alderson and ran out the door. Alderson worried they were coming back with friends, particularly when they saw the trucks outside on the lawn. Senador unwound the hose for the torch and dragged it downstairs to the safe. It took him a few minutes to cut the lock out of the door and then figure out how to disengage the locking bolts. In the end he had to cut through some of those too. Alderson stood outside watching from the bed of the flatbed truck, rifle in hand, moving to make less of a target. Fifteen minutes later he saw a group of five males, some with hand guns, appear about 100 metres away. He leveled his rifle on the roof of truck, aimed at the pavement in front of them, and fired. The shot was deafeningly loud without hearing protection. The bullet ricocheted, causing the group to scatter. Alderson worked the bolt to put another round in. "Stay back!" he yelled. "Next person I see getting closer gets killed!" he threatened.

Senador would be another fifteen minutes. The group was not retreating but not obviously getting closer. Alderson was worried they were going to work their way into the alleyway where he could not see them.

"Hey why did you shoot at my boys?" one guy asked in a thick Arabic accent. "We want to talk with you."

They were working a plan for sure, Alderson thought. He could not just shoot them at this point, but he kept checking behind. "Your boys were trying to rob a friend's house. I didn't shoot at them or one would be dead. I shot to give a warning, just as I did now," Alderson answered. Talking was better than shooting at this point but he could not become distracted and let them sneak in.

They hadn't raised a gun yet. But he knew there was at least a shotgun in the bunch. As he was looking behind him and ducking behind the cab of the truck his radio crackled, "Hey Jim, it's White Eagle, where are you?" He was momentarily startled, then he grabbed the radio out of his pocket.

"White Eagle, good to hear from you, we are just west of Father Lacombe school on 36th. I am having a problem right now," he replied.

"Roger that. We will provide backup if I can find you," White Eagle said.

Popping up to see if they were moving, Alderson yelled out, "Hey guys, no one got hurt, you should just go home before something bad happens."

He took careful aim at a rock one guy was behind and fired. The he could hear the thrumming whistle of the ricochetting bullet. There was still no movement and no reply from the Arabs. Then he heard the crunching of gravel in the alleyway. He could not see, but he took cover behind the truck loaded on the flatbed. It would not stop a bullet like in the movies but it would prevent him from being seen.

He heard the crunching again and knew the steps were

closer, he took his handgun and aimed at the corner of the fence and fired two quick shots, just hoping they would not hit some innocent person.

"Fuck! Dirty pig!"

Alderson heard more swearing from behind the fence, he hadn't hit anyone but he scared him. He heard footsteps quickly move away, two sets. He popped up again looking down the street. One of the Arabs was making a dash to get closer. Jim popped off two shots with his Sig, at this range almost no chance of hitting, but it was a scare tactic. One shot tore into a wooden fence just in front of the running man. If he had shot a quarter second later he would have hit the guy, the thought made Jim queasy. Alderson heard him yell something and dive – the desired reaction.

Alderson waited and watched all directions for another two minutes. No movement. "Hey Jim!" Senador yelled, "I have the goods. Is it safe to come out?"

"Right now, yes!" Alderson called back in a lower voice. "Did you get a shotgun?"

Senador didn't answer but came out carrying an armload of firearms, including a scoped carbine in .223, the only issue was the 5-round magazines in Canada. Alderson helped load the guns into the box of the truck and then was going to snatch up the carbine but it was trigger-locked. The shotgun was not, but no shells yet. He had to just stick with his guns for now. Senador ran back in and brought out some ammunition including shotgun shells with buckshot and some slugs. Alderson just watched down the road, this was the vulnerable time. Johnny came back again huffing and puffing from running up and down the stairs. Alderson loaded up the shotgun and kept it nearby. "How many more loads?" Alderson asked.

"Many. Should I just leave it and go now?" Johnny asked.

"And leave this stuff for them, no way. White Eagle is coming," Alderson said. "We need the reloading stuff too."

"That will take a while, maybe an hour."

"I will call if we need to bolt. Keep yourself armed just in case," Alderson cautioned.

"I will keep the short shotgun," Johnny said, taking a tactical shotgun from the box of the truck. He then rolled up the torch hoses and went back inside the house. Alderson loaded up some other weapons and carefully placed them in easy reach. He heard some kind of noise in the alley and just fired the shotgun at the fence blowing a board out of it. He heard scurrying away but no voices, it was probably just a small animal, but better to make the noise and be safe.

Alderson turned back to see a another guy sprint across the roadway. They were now all on the near side where he would have a more difficult sighting angle. They could be advancing through yards which would be tough to see. He had to move. He slung the rifle, reloaded the Sig, and carried the shotgun, then got down from the flatbed. He advanced to the next yard and looked around the corner, slicing the pie, he didn't see anything. He went to the back yard, carefully slicing the pie around the corner very slowly, keeping the barrel of the gun back. As he leaned out he saw a jacket behind a garden shed.

"Guys, I know where you are and double-ought buckshot will shoot right through that shed. Come out hands high, backing up," he called out. The one guy he could see complied, Alderson put himself behind the guy so the guy was cover from that corner. "On the ground, on your knees and tell your buddy to come out. In English. Now!" he snarled.

Alderson knelt on one knee behind the guy and rested the muzzle of the shotgun on the guy's shoulder right by his ear. If Jim shot, the guy would likely be deaf in that ear.

Before the guy said anything, his friend stepped out with a Glock handgun in one hand. "DROP IT!" Jim ordered.

Looking straight down the bore of a 12-gauge at three metres, the guy dropped the gun.

"In the shed, both of you!" Jim ordered. Once they were in the garden shed, Jim found a piece of wire and stuck it through the lock holes and tied it shut. Wouldn't hold anyone long, but it would do for now. Alderson unloaded the Glock and stuck it in his waistband and put the magazine in his pocket, then ran back to the next yard. He picked up a few rocks and went back up onto the truck for a view. He could not see any of the Arabs.

This was both good and bad, mostly bad he figured. After 5 minutes he heard the guys in the shed banging. He threw some rocks at it and yelled, "Shut up or I will shoot into it."

Then he heard the sweet sound of a motorcycle approaching. He took a step out of cover off the truck to see if he could see White Eagle. White Eagle was cruising slowly then suddenly sped up and roared down the street and drove up where he could see the flatbed.

"Hey Jim, what's up," White Eagle said casually.

"Did you see a group of about six or seven Arabic types on the road as you came in?" Jim asked.

"That's why I sped up. I saw five behind a that blue house maybe 200 yards down. One had a shotgun, they were doing that wild talking with their hands thing but when they saw me I goosed it here," White Eagle explained.

"We are just working at getting the reloading equipment, then we are out of here. I'll go help Johnny. Keep watch and yell if there is a problem. There are two guys in that shed next door. Throw rocks to keep them quiet," suggested Jim.

White Eagle agreed, "Sure can do, just hurry up before everyone gets here. I saw too many people milling about."

Jim sprinted down the stairs. When he got down there he saw Johnny had it almost complete, he looked for boxes and started loading. He found some camping equipment and took that, he used a cooler to load some primer, powder and bullets into and started hauling up the stairs. It took another ten minutes. "Hey guys, I see about twenty people gathering down the street, let's move!" White Eagle called out.

Throwing what they had into the truck, they each started their vehicles. Jim and Johnny each had a shotgun out the window. They started with the tow truck going first. They rolled down the street. There was a gathering of people that were armed with clubs, knives, machetes, and a couple of shotguns. As they approached Senador stepped on the gas and got the truck going about 60 kph. One guy in the crowd leveled his shot gun at the tow truck. Johnny ducked down but kept the truck going. The guy lost his nerve and moved, stupidly to the left side where Jim had a shotgun out the window. Jim fired into the wall of a house behind the guy, he hoped that would keep heads down. It did, long enough for them to get out of range and turn a corner.

It was a quick drive back to Senador's. "I think we should stay the night and go in the morning," White Eagle suggested. They set watches over the vehicles by putting someone by turn on Johnny's roof. They had to trust Daman with the first watch, they could not afford two on a watch.

- - - - - -

Morning came early to the encampment. It was a grey rainy day but the early light woke most people before what would be 8:00 am, but virtually no one knew what time it was because most people did not have a working watch. Even Jenna, who hated the mornings, was up early. She was growing more concerned as she waited; even if something happened to one of the motorcycles at least the other one should have come back for help. She was constantly asking who ever was on watch if there was news on the walkie-talkie but now they were at a low point it was less likely they would get a signal.

People were bustling about the camp getting water from the river, but that had to be filtered with coffee filters then boiled. Jenna was pleased to see both Aidan and Marc were up ahead of her, that meant they had probably made some coffee – they all had that addiction, which would become an issue when no more was available. Marc continued watches during the day by putting stationary spotters in locations where they could watch the major access points, the road and two bridges. Jolene was organizing people to making breakfast, the grocery run crews had obtained lots of eggs because they were easy to keep cool for a while by putting a cooler in the river. They had the generator going to charge radios and keep the freezer going. All was going amazingly smoothly.

Later when things were getting cleaned up, one of the spotters called out about people coming their way. "I'll go meet them," Aidan offered.

"Take a firing position and aim," Marc ordered the spotter, unfortunately this spotter had no combat or even firearms experience. Aidan approached the people, he was openly wearing a handgun.

"Hey, how are you doing?" Aidan said, greeting the group of five young males approaching the camp. They were in their early twenties, several days unshaven, looking like they might be hung over.

"Hey man we heard there's a party going down here," said one of the guys, clearly trying to get a look around at who was here. They did not appear to be armed other than a couple of belt knives.

"Sorry, no party here. Just people surviving. What did

you want?" Aidan asked, he could see these guys were likely here to mooch food or worse scope out the site. He looked them over carefully, noted the ripped jeans, grease covered clothes, rough worn hands on young guys and a few with low-quality tattoos on their forearms. Some of them were quite muscular like they spent too much time in the gym. They had come down the escarpment but he did not know what else they were doing.

"Well could ya give us some food, we're kind'a starving?" the obvious leader said. He had a tattoo on his upper arm that Aidan could not make out and a single piercing in his left ear.

"It is not that far of a walk to the nearest grocery store, I suggest you go get some there. We don't have extra, sorry," Aidan said firmly. If he believed they were lost souls truly suffering he would at least offer some food.

"Well the stores aren't open, come on, we'll pay you for it, we have cash," the guy said quite earnestly.

Aidan chortled, "Hahahaha, what would I do with cash, it has no value here. If you had something worth trading we would consider it, but I can see you have nothing we might want. Unless you want to give up your belt knives." He looked at them and raised his eyebrows. "Yeah, I didn't think you were that starving."

They looked around, all eyes rested on the holstered gun and Aidan's stance before they decided to move on. They did not go up the way they had come but instead proceeded to the bridge. Aidan did not trust them, they could easily have been sent to scope things out, they might be working for the bikers.

"Marc, I am not sure about that crew, they didn't ask us much, they asked for some food, said they heard there was a party here. They were really trying to get a look inside the camp. They made clear note of the gun I was wearing and then took off without argument but they were clearly pissed. They were a rough looking lot, not intellectual types at all. I was even hospitable and offered to trade food for their knives, if they were truly starving they would have at least made some counter offer. They didn't even ask to join the group," Aidan reported.

"We could follow them and see where they are going, but there is risk to that," Marc mused, "I think we just have to watch more vigilantly. We will keep the spotters, I think we will start seeing more people soon."

As the day wore on toward mid-afternoon they had seen several groups of wanderers. Aidan had recruited one family to stay with them, a man, woman and ten year-old boy. Dad was an engineer of some kind, woman was a psychologist, maybe Jim would know her. They were on route to a family member's place in a neighbourhood on the edge of the city. They had left their home because a fire had destroyed a bunch of houses and a gang of local thugs seemed to be robbing everyone. The family figured they would stay the night. Aidan hoped Jim would convince them to stay. But where was Jim and company?

Two groups of people came across the river. They reported that HAs were gaining control of Bowness and there was a reward for a really big guy, bald headed, long goatee, special forces or police training who had injured an unarmed biker and stolen his bike. Aidan laughed when he heard that, but said he did not know any such person. Most of the people who came by seemed to have a destination in mind.

- - - - -

White Eagle woke Jim up about an hour before full light. "Hey Jim, you best come here and see this." Jim climbed the roof and took the binocular and looked where White Eagle was pointing. A huge pall of black smoke and flames were erupting just south of their location. Jim knew that was not the industrial area but a commercial strip, could be a gas station. All fire was bad news with no fire protection.

"Let's get everyone up and packed, time to bug out," Jim said. He continued to scan the city and saw numerous fires burning. This was not good. Time to hit a scavenge centre and get the fuck out of Dodge. They were doing well now. The take of goods from Antonio's was impressive. Three excellent hunting rifles with scopes, ten different handguns ranging from the exotic, single-shot 410 gauge to a collectable Walther P38. Most were good quality revolvers and semi-autos, as well as four shotguns – two tactical (one in pink camo!), a couple of over-under skeet and trap guns, and three military-style tactical rifles. There were also some modern black powder type weapons and a couple of cowboy action handguns.

Daman would ride with him and have a shotgun. The Senadors would ride together and White Eagle would scout a route on his bike and have the radio. First he figured they would hit the shopping centre and loot like crazy, starting with a Walmart. It would have everything from drugs to ammo. They got there and found the Walmart being ransacked -- no problem, they just joined in. They worked with people to get the pharmacy open, it just took some heavy tools. It was only Jim and Daman looting, the others were on guard. They loaded a shopping cart with necessary items beyond the drugs. They got some more ammo and lots of canned food. All the water was gone; they took some cases of pop instead. They also found some more radios, likely left because no one believed they would work, these kind used regular batteries so they took a cart of assorted batteries. They had just finished loading when the the radio sparked to life.

"Yo Jimbo, we are gathering an audience and I don't like the looks of it," White Eagle was saying.

"Copy that, on the way," he replied. "Let's run, Daman." They pushed as fast as they could. The good thing about an apocalypse is when you move fast with a loaded cart or two, everyone moved and there were no people with children in strollers blocking your way.

The vehicles, which were parked at the opposite end of the lot where it was mostly empty, had a crowd of people gathering. White Eagle was asking questions, but others were in the back of the crowd who looked far more dangerous. When Jim and Daman arrived, there was some pointing. Jim unslung his shotgun and told Daman to be ready with his.

"Hey Jimbo some of these people are asking for rides or to join us, lots of questions about working vehicles," White Eagle said over his shoulder. Jim walked up and called over his shoulder, "Daman, load up the truck."

"Hello all. We all have to survive in our own way, if you go looking there will be more working vehicles, ones in metal buildings or underground may work and ones older than 1979 might work. We did our homework. Now you know what we know," Jim announced.

A professional looking man came up to him, "Hey I would give a lot for a ride to the west side of the city, my practice is here but I live in West Hills, I'm a doctor and my office nurse is with me, we need to get home or to one of the hospitals. We waited here as long as we could but I want to know if my wife is okay," the man pleaded.

Alderson walked to him and spoke quietly. "I will take you toward the Foothills but I won't go there. I will explain as we go. You ride with me. Your nurse can ride on the mounted truck. Daman you will ride up top for now."

"You got it Juju man," Daman replied.

"And keep that shotty primed."

He looked at the doctor and the nurse and said, "When we are loaded, we go." They took the hint and helped Daman load the truck.

"Let's roll!" he called to Senador. The convoy moved out with many disgruntled people looking back at them. The first intersection was tricky and Senador had to push some cars out of the way but after that they were clear for a stretch. They took residential streets to avoid the big intersections and the possible ambushes at bottlenecks. Jim spent the time telling Dr. Grosvenor what he knew about the EMP and how the hospital and government were operating. He gave no information about his group. The doctor was likely to become part of the establishment.

"Look, I really need to get to my wife and the cats, I have no idea what is happening at home and I am sick with worry. I will consider working with you if you can help us. Linda has a husband she hopes is at home too. Help us and I will try to help you," Grosvenor begged.

"I will make you a deal, I am sending the big truck and one truck and the guys home, I will take you two home in the other truck." Jim replied after some thought. "I can't risk the big resources."

"Fair enough."

Jim felt the best way through was actually to go home first and then take the main highways to that southwest area. It would also give him an opportunity to report back and find out what was going on.

They had no serious issues getting back due to good point work by White Eagle.

When they arrived back in the early afternoon, White Eagle got off the bike and walked over to Jim as everyone gathered around. "I hope White Eagle, Faithful Injun Guide did good," he grinned, in a good, awful movie Indian accent.

Everyone gathered around and unloaded and shared reports. Again everyone's mood was boosted. Marc took charge of the weaponry and started talking to everyone about firearms training. Alex was also going to be part of that training team, they both had lots of gun experience.

It was decided that the best vehicle to make the trip to the southwest would be the Pontiac. It was the least valuable and held the most people comfortably. Jim took Rosie with him this time, she asked to go, he hoped they would be back before dark.

TWENTY

"I think paranoia can be instructive in the right doses. Paranoia is a skill."

- John Shirley

Before they headed out Jim went over gun safety and handling a shotgun with Rosie. He put a rifle, a siphon hose, food and water in the truck. "Hey Doc, we're ready to roll," Jim called out.

The trip was going suspiciously well, cars had been pushed aside so a single vehicle could easily get through. He had Rosie in the front watching with wide field-of-view binoculars, just to see if there was anything amiss ahead. Nothing, no problems. They cruised right on to the main highway.

"Hey Jim, if this route gets blocked there is a back way using the old Banff Coach Road," Grosvenor offered.

"Okay but only if needed, this is wider so less chance of complete blockage," Jim said.

They cruised up the high road that gave a great view of

the city. "I want to stop and observe the city for a few minutes," Jim said. He stopped the car and got out.

"Base this is Juju, do you copy? Over," Jim said into the walkie talkie. He scanned looking for activities. Foothills Hospital had some action but nowhere was there a single chopper in the sky.

"Here Doc, take a look at Foothills, you might know more about what is going on there than me." Jim noted numerous palls of smoke over the city, it was not a good sign, he also noticed some motorcycles moving in a few places, too far to make out any details but clearly some people were getting around.

"Juju we copy you," an unfamiliar voice replied.

"Give me Aidan, Alex or Marc please."

"Marc is sleeping, prepping for watch duty tonight. I can find Alex, I think," the male voice replied. A moment later: "Alex here, what do you have? Over."

"I'm on Sarcee overlooking the city, many fires including some downtown, no chopper activity but I have seen motorcycles, too distant to determine provenance. The road here was cleared. Mostly easy access, don't know who or why. I'm staying wary," Jim reported.

"Paranoia is a survival trait," Alex replied.

"We will motor on and hopefully all will go smoothly. Should be back in a couple of hours. Over and out." Jim ended the transmission quickly, just in case the government was listening again.

They got back in and drove, for a large part of the drive they were able to go 80 kph, making it a quick journey. Linda provided directions to her place which was nearest. They pulled up into the driveway. Seeing no activity, she went in to find no husband, no notes, nothing disturbed, garage empty.

While she searched, Jim unhooked the electric garage door, opened the garage and moved the car inside. Out of sight, out of mind.

She sat down and sobbed a bit, muttering to herself, "Where could he be, he should have walked back by now."

"Linda may I ask, where did he work?" Jim questioned gently, sitting down beside her.

"He works -- worked – for En-Encana," she sobbed out a reply. She must have noticed the pained look on Jim's face. "What, what has happened?" she cried.

"I don't know anything Linda, I only know there was a helicopter crash the first day on the Bow building and there was a fire, I know most people made it out and I ran into streams of people leaving the downtown. He probably stayed with a friend hoping power would return," Jim said, trying to sound optimistic. "Cars in underground garages might still be working, too," he added without thinking.

"Maybe he is with Alan, Alan lives in a condo downtown and would have put him up there," she mused.

"Perhaps, high-rise elevators would not be working in most cases so it would be a climb back down. What would you like to do?" Jim asked.

"I would like to go find him but I don't know where to look, you say the Bow building was burning so they likely left. He worked on the 17th floor, so not at the top. But they still wouldn't stay there, would they?"

Other thoughts had been going through her head, she would like to think he was with a friend but she was not naïve. She had been wondering for months if he had been having an affair. She didn't want to believe it but all the tell-tales were there. She wondered if it were the pretty manager in the department he supervised. He looked after a team of geologists looking for gas in northern BC, she managed all the support for the exploration. She was very young and very hot. Linda could not imagine the girl would be interested in Fred, he was a balding, slightly podgy 50 year-old, nothing special except being her boss. Still she did not know what to do next.

"Theo," she said addressing Grosvenor, "I don't know what I should do, are you going to work at the Foothills during the crisis? I guess I could just go there."

"Well Linda, I don't know what to do, part of me says that's the right thing, but if I were to believe all that Jim has been telling me, the right thing would be to take Salma and get out of Dodge. Things are going to be horrific here if he is right, it will be incomprehensible, I am seriously wrestling with the enormity of the problem and I don't know where to start." He shook his head as he thought. "If Jim is even half-right, doctors will be needed but you would be swimming in a marsh of death. I would rather go and be a doctor to a small community like what Jim is trying to create. I just don't know."

Jim jumped in, "Look, what we know is that your husband is not here. I won't tell you what to decide. I will say that my group will be moving from our present location soon, going to a more rural location where we can grow some food and create a community. It will be rough, very, very rough to start. But the way I see it, it's our only good choice. The other choice I see is staying here and fighting with others for resources that will get less and less each day. Not a pretty choice either," Jim explained. "If you want to go looking for him, I wish you luck. If you come with us, we will run you back here when we make forays into the city."

"Can I think for a bit?" she asked.

"Of course but I think we should take the Doc home

and see what his situation is. We will come back here for you if you like?" Jim offered.

"Hey guys, we have visitors," Rosie called from the front room. "A man and a woman, normal looking old people, no weapons."

She is learning how to report important info Jim thought, and we didn't even teach her, she must be paying attention. Linda and Grosvenor went to the front door and opened it, Jim would have been more cautious but he was professionally paranoid these days.

There was a happy reunion and chatting, it was obviously neighbours, What Rosie had meant by old people was in that over-forty range, professional types. There was some chat and then they introduced the Wilsons to Jim and Rosie. Graeme Wilson asked some questions about finding working cars, Jim told him what to look for.

About fifteen minutes later Jim interrupted the story exchange, "I think we should be moving along, doctor. We will come back, but my people are expecting me back this evening."

"No problem, I'm ready, Linda we will be back for you, if you go somewhere just leave a note in the mailbox for us," Grosvenor said. They loaded up and drove out. It was a fair ways winding through some dead vehicles but many had been already moved aside, only intersections posed a problem. The nice thing about the Pontiac was that it was heavy enough to forcibly move most other vehicles, they hadn't made them like this one for a long time.

They were soon opening another garage while Dr. Grosvenor had a happy reunion with his wife. They were both in tears, two beautiful cats swirled around and meowed at their feet until Theo picked each up in turn and pet them. He brought his wife, Salma, over and introduced her to Jim and Rosie.

"Come into our home," she invited, "I'm sorry I cannot offer much, a drink perhaps, but warm only."

"Thanks, but I want my wits fully about me when we travel home," Jim said.

"I'll take one," Rosie blurted out. Jim looked at her, Theo looked at her, and at Jim.

"I'm not her father and I don't hold that there are any rules left, your decision," he said looking at Grosvenor. "But Rosie you have have watch duty tonight and do not let Marc catch you sleeping on watch," Jim said.

"Watch duty?" both Theo and his wife said in unison. The doctor asked, "Is your camp run like the military?"

"Mmmm, in necessary ways, a watch is prudent for anyone, too many risks associated with surprise. We do have some military-like features, simply put, those are necessary evils right now. We are living in a world where rules are optional so we have to impose order on our lives. Even those who are philosophically anarchists agree with me on that point, for now," Jim stated.

"How did you become the leader? Do you have a military background? You certainly seem to know what you are doing," Theo questioned.

Jim laughed and commented. "Hardy har, har, me military, not a chance. I became the *de facto* leader of the collective by chance and by simply doing it. Then when we started accepting people whom I did not know, I simply set it as condition, for the short term. You can't function effectively in a crisis with a lot of democracy. I listen, I take advice, I will even listen if someone tells me I am full of shit, but I make decisions based on my best judgment, those who disagree don't need to be with us."

"It sounds autocratic, if you have no background, how

can you feel qualified to take control? It seems an awesome responsibility," Theo said, curious.

"It is autocratic and I don't feel qualified, but to qualify that, I feel right now I am likely doing at least as good a job as anyone else who is with me could do under the circumstances." Jim looked at Rosie to gauge her reaction. "I do have a friend with military knowledge and experience, but no one would follow him for long. Let's just say he is not such a people person. There will be time for democracy later, in the right doses."

"Alderson is kick-ass, if you saw what he can do you would do what he says, but I'm not afraid to tell him to fuck off either," Rosie commented.

Alderson blushed, "Err sure, but if the people close to me think I am a fuck-up, many have known me long enough they would let me know in plain English."

Theo looked at his wife, then back to Jim. "So your plan is to move out of the city and find some land, but most good land close to the city is owned and a farmer will not take kindly to someone trying to take it."

Jim outlined his first solution. "You're right, I have two plans to consider. First, no modern farmer can work his land without equipment or labour. If we can find one who understands the predicament they will let us join their community. Those who work as a community will fare the best. For example, Hutterites will do just fine." He waited a moment.

"What if you find no willing farmer, will you be nomads?" Salma asked.

"No, we will need to persuade, or find empty or crown land. These are not preferable because the land is not as good for farming. I am fairly certain we can persuade," Jim added more darkly.

"Persuade, how, farmers are known for being intractable," Theo added.

"Can't say I know how it will go at this point, I will work it out on the fly like I have done everything else," Jim said. "It is not a bulletproof plan, just barely any kind of plan, I need more smart people to give advice, but right now it is the best I have."

There was a moment of quiet. Theo and Salma looked at each other. "Jim, I'll be frank with you, I am not convinced you are right about how dire things will become. I am not convinced your plan is the best course of action, I believe it should be possible to stay in the city for weeks at least. Have you considered taking longer to take such drastic action?"

"Hell Theo, I am not convinced I am right or that my plan is the best, but here is what I firmly believe. You *are* right you could stay for weeks even months. But if I am right or even fifty percent right, it will be far better to leave now than a month from now when things are critical. When people become desperate, things will get much nastier. Also it is spring, if we want to grow or plant anything we need to move quickly. We have heard rumours the Hades Animals are taking over Bowness. We know they are becoming bolder and less civil just based on our own experience. If that is true, they believe the same as I do, organize and prepare now while things are sort of easy. If many people start believing like I do, things will get very bad very quickly. For now I am sticking to this unless someone can show me sure signs of things getting better," Alderson expounded.

"The city is a crowded place and sewage concerns me a great deal, poor sewage will breed disease." Theo ruminated on the obvious health risks. "Jim, if things start getting better will you disband?"

"I won't have to, people will go back to their twenty-first century life in a heartbeat, so would I but if I have to live in the pre-industrial world I am going to start now while I can loot the good stuff," Jim said sounding light, but being serious.

"What would you say if I said we need to sleep on it Jim?"

"You should just trust Alderson, he is a smart guy," Rosie said impatiently.

"I would say I would try to send someone back for you, no guarantees, I won't lie -- you are a valuable person, but we can only risk so much. I would make an effort to come back for you if I knew there was a chance you were with us."

"What about our cats?" Salma asked with tears in her eyes, holding one of them while the other cat was actually rubbing around Rosie's leg and she was absent-mindedly petting him. "Would you allow someone to have pets that take up resources?"

Jim smiled and looked at her, "Salma I view pets as a resource in many ways, not the least of which is they have proven good effect on people's mental state. We could all use an improved mental state right now. There is going to be a lot of psychological trauma out of this world and anything that helps should be used. If anyone in my group were to question that, I would question them. Pets are good, not a waste of resources. I would be far more concerned if you left them behind. We already have people with dogs and cats in the group."

"Give us some time Jim, just a few moments," Salma asked and she tugged on Theo's arm and led him out of the room. Rosie picked up the cat who was purring and pet him a while.

"Hey Alderson, I don't think they will come with us. Are we going back soon?" she asked.

"A little while won't hurt us, having a doctor would be

very useful," Jim said.

They could hear pleading and imploring and even some crying in another room. Then fifteen minutes later Theo and Salma came back. "Jim, it seems your tales of the end of civilization have sufficiently traumatized my wife that she would like to take up with you. I have never been able to refuse her. We shall join you if we can have time now to gather things. Jim do you think it possible to attach a Thule carrier to that car, we have one in the garage?" Theo capitulated to his wife.

"We will find a way, being a show piece is no longer a concern, being functional is. Do you have a cordless drill?" Jim asked.

"I do, but will it work?" he answered, leading them to the garage workbench. Salma got busy getting cat carriers and things the humans would need too.

"There's a chance, depends on a lot of factors. but the electrics of the drill is simple and robust so it may have survived." The doctor had a metal workbench, which was impeccably clean. The drill was in one of the storage areas; though not completely enclosed, it might have been protected enough. Jim tried it and got a satisfying whir of the chuck turning. He even found some silicone caulking so when he drilled the holes in the roof he was able to seal them tight against water, just a comfort thing. It took them about two hours to get everything together and loaded and they headed back to Linda's place.

"Jim, I think Linda told me her husband was an occasional hunter. He might have some guns."

Jim kept that in mind as they drove up her driveway. If she came with them it was going to be crowded drive back, it was a good thing they were driving a 1960's car with comfy bench seats.

Linda was out front talking with a different neighbour. They pulled up and attracted attention again, a working vehicle was the cynosure of all eyes.

"Hey Jim this is Ismail and Luanda," Linda introduced, "You know Dr. Grosvenor, that's his wife Salma, and the young one is Rosie."

They talked for a while about how people were coping. No one was very aware of the cause. Linda talked about what Jim's theories, and he got a lot of questions about it.

"To tell you the truth, I am not sure, it could be alien space lizards for all I know, I only know that it is causing a disaster here and now. In the last five days there have be virtually no vehicles coming into the city from the west, I can see the highway from my place. All we ever see are a few motorcycles, once in a while a vehicle going out," Jim explained.

"So when do you think help will arrive?" Luanda asked.

"If nothing of note came in for the last five days, that tells me it is a huge area of effect, probably covering well into BC, Saskatchewan and the US. So my best guess is a long time, months minimum. Which to me means, we are royally fucked, pardon my French," Jim said emphatically.

"Well after Linda explained this to us we kind of thought we should get out too, but we can see you have a full vehicle now," Luanda said.

Ismail added, "Fred and I used to hunt together, I have some rifles. I can see you are going about armed, is it that bad out there? I have not been out of the neighbourhood since the event."

"You know we can get cozy on the way back, you could ride or we could try to come back for you. To answer your question, it is bad in some places, we have had weapons brought to bear on us when we were in Forest Lawn," Alderson said.

"Alderson even had to take down a crazy cop with a gun, you should have seen him!" Rosie added making Jim cringe, he didn't really need that story being broadcast when he was trying to seem like a good guy.

The others looked at him. "Yeah, it's a long story for another day. If you want to come with us we will make a way. Linda, do you want to get your husbands weapons? Or will you leave them here for him?" Jim asked changing the subject.

"Ummm I am not sure how to get into the safe, I could try to look and see what he has." She answered tentatively, leading them to the safe. Jim noticed on the way down she had a backpack packed and ready to go. The safe was an expensive combination lock type, large which boded well.

"I think he keeps the combo in the tool box, he once told me." She went to a work bench where he did some minor work and looked through drawers until she found a note book. Nicely labeled inside were the numbers of the combination, but no instructions. So turning left or right was trial and error. It took fifteen minutes to finally get the turns right. Inside was a rich man's treasure trove of guns.

There was a beautifully scoped 300 Winchester magnum, a Benelli over-under shotgun, and several rifles in .308, and the prize of prizes if you were just a thief, a 500 nitro Holland and Holland big game rifle. "That is an expensive rifle and very fine, but not practical unless you mean to shoot a cape buffalo. We should leave that and the shotgun then if he comes home he has something," Jim suggested. They took three rifles and the ammo for those rifles, and cases. Ismail had his hunting rifle and trap gun, they were more than well armed. Now they had to fit everyone in, seven people and two cats in cages in one car, it reminded Jim of being in high school.

They squeezed and squished, Rosie was the smallest so she sat on Ismail's lap and they went off slowly so as to not throw anyone into the roof. They had almost no trouble going down the road. Jim did stop to call back and say they were on their way home. Marc answered the radio and indicated they were being observed from across the river but didn't know more at that time.

When he came to the highway, Jim stopped again and took a look into Bowness. There was activity, bonfires and motorcycles, too many motorcycles. Jim thought it probably would have been less problem for him to have shot the bikers, easy to consider in the abstract, hard to do in reality. There were going to be problems if they didn't leave soon.

Jim drove home to the camp as quickly as he could, leaving the headlights off even though the light was dim, he wanted to avoid attention. At the base the mood was quieter than other nights, everyone had the sense that the watching and the stopped flow of people from across the river meant there was going to be a big problem. The only question was whether it could be avoided by getting out, and if they could do that soon enough.

TWENTY ONE

The next morning brought a meeting of key people. Jim led the discussion saying that it appeared from what little intel they had that the bikers were in control of Bowness. This would mean that they would soon want to push across the river, the Hades Animals were not known for their tolerance of rivals, or for their tolerance period. "We need to move out of the city regardless, this is perhaps sooner that I would have chosen. Does anyone have an inkling of what we need to start the move?" Jim asked. He had around the table his original team plus White Eagle, Jason, and Dr. Grosvenor.

"I don't pretend to know how many days of supplies we need for the now thirty-six people with us, but I think what we have is insufficient," Jason started.

"My thoughts on supplies would be that we need as many days as we are going to be moving." Jim suggested. "We need to remain in short striking distance of the city so that we can come in to scavenge."

"What about somewhere around Jumping Pound Creek?" Dr. Grosvenor suggested. "We are close to a water supply, close to the city, and close to an RV lot that we might be able to get some easy housing out of."

"Right now we have too many people to ride in the

vehicles we have unless we are loading the flat bed which we need to load with supplies," Jason added.

"We will have to move people in shifts; a scout team will go out and establish a location and negotiate with a landowner. Most will stay here and gather and prepare to move. Then we will move in stages, maybe three groups," Alex suggested.

Marc joined in, "We will be most vulnerable when we reduce our numbers below ten or fifteen. If the bikers are going to attack they might wait till that point."

"Then two groups maximum, we will just have to run a Cuban bus, put some benches and sides on the flatbed," Jim suggested.

"We also need to scout around the city and set out some eyes and see if we can get any visual intel and maybe talk to some people. People are going to start getting more desperate now," Aidan said. "I would say put some eyes on hills, Nose Hill by Brentwood, Broadcast Hill by Sarcee, Nose Hill again at Country Hills and Stoney, Cougar Ridge or C.O.P. looking at the highway. Just so there are no surprises."

"So let me recap. One team will be a scout and negotiation team to find a spot, they will need at least one vehicle. Five people looking out over the city, plan to make contact only if we know we need the people. The main group to gather and prepare to move," Jim said making a few notes.

Several people murmured assent, there were no detractors. White Eagle spoke up, "Jim, I would like to lead the scout group. I will ride my bike on point, not very threatening but the car should follow, the trucks are needed here. I would suggest the doctor go in the car, it is a great selling point to tell someone your group is coming with a doctor."

"Great thinking Walter, pick another to go with you, and

make sure you are adequately armed too," Jim agreed. White Eagle said he would take Ismail as he had some hunting experience so could shoot. "Time to tell everyone the plan," Jim concluded.

When announcing the plans to the group, Jim asked for volunteers to do the scouting missions. Jolene offered to go back to the ski jump house, Jim let her know she had to take the long way, Bowness could not be considered safe. Most of his original team volunteered but few others did. Jim did not want to leave the camp devoid of strength so he insisted that Marc, Aidan, Angela, Rosie and Carrie stay. Alex would be a good choice to go.

He asked again and when they saw that Jolene was going Kareem and another young guy, whose name Jim could not even remember, volunteered. Jim himself decided to go to the furthest location on Nose Hill. Time alone would allow him to think on his own without distraction or stress. Alex chose the Stoney Trail location, Kareem the Sarcee location, and the other guy, Ivan, was the relay point at the highway looking west where the scout team would travel. There was a cell tower that was visible many kilometres away and would provide good radio reception, one day the house there might even make a good outpost for radio relay. Everyone who could shoot armed up and rode.

It was a long while before everyone was in position. One of the big surprises as reports were issued was the number of people roaming the roads. Kareem reported he avoided making contact most of the time because of the dangerous look of the small crowds and presence of weapons. Most carried only melee weapons, although several groups sporting rifles were also seen.

The camp itself became a beehive of activity. One truck was sent out to loot a grocery store, they choose one that was near others, hoping it might not be empty yet. As it turned out there were still plenty of canned and dried goods. They loaded the truck with what they could. Wooden sides had been added again to increase the capacity.

Aidan led this group. He took four people, two to load and two to stand guard. He himself stood in the truck bed behind the cab with a shotgun and his bow. They had several people who marveled at the truck and asked questions, but no threats. They spent about one hour loading the truck. At one point a girl drove up on a motorcycle, dirt bike type. "Hey," she called, "My family would like to join with another group, can we join you guys?"

Aidan replied suspiciously, "Why would you want to join us, you don't know anything about us? We could be a group of white slavers."

"My dad says it will get very tough to live alone soon, when all the food you are taking runs out. We could help you too you know," the young girl added as she took off her bike helmet to reveal flowing dirty-blonde hair. She had a bright smile and looked to be between fourteen and nineteen years old.

"How would your family help us?" Aidan queried.

"Well my mom knows how to do canning and smoke meats and my dad can build stuff," the girl replied. "We just need to get with a group and get out of the city, we each have our own dirt bike and they still work."

"Hmmm where is your family? I would like to talk to your dad," Aidan said.

"If you wait fifteen minutes, I will go get him," she said and then rode off on her bike.

Aidan and his crew kept loading the truck. He would wait the fifteen minutes but not much more. There were a lot of people looting and lots who looked and pointed and commented to each other about the working truck. Having a commodity everyone wanted made you a target, it made

Aidan antsy.

Within ten minutes two bikes roared up, dirt bikes of an old vintage. "Hi, I'm George and this is my daughter Willow, you look organized and equipped. I know we have to get out of the city soon and we know we would be better off as a larger group, do you need and carpenter, welder and handyman?" he asked, wasting no time.

"Well I don't know. We are planning our exit now we have a large group, but we may also have issues with the HA's in Bowness." Aidan tested the waters. Most people would not want to buy into that kind of trouble.

"What are HA's?"

Aidan smiled, "Hades Animals."

"Oh, that's not so good, How big a trouble? Is your group armed better than you are?" George asked, plainly a bit squeamish about crossing the bikers.

"We haven't had trouble yet, we are just expecting it, we know they are in control of Bowness and they are watching us. Sooner or later they won't be content to watch. We hope to leave before they do something," Aidan finished the warning.

"Are you guys well-armed?"

Cognizant of operational security Aidan shrugged his shoulders, "Sorry, no comment."

George looked at him questioningly then thought for a moment, "Ahh I see, security, you don't know me so no info is the best policy. Okay, I get it. Can you tell me how your group is run?"

"Well right now we have a leader, he listens to people he wants to listen too, if you are looking to vote on everything it ain't going to happen at this point," Aidan replied, knowing lots of people didn't understand the need for that, but better to know up front.

George asked shrewdly, "I am assuming people can leave if they want though?"

"Mmmm, guess it depends on what they are going to do, I don't think he would take well to someone walking over to the HA's," Aidan said.

"Can I meet your leader?"

"Not right now, but you can join our group if you are going to commit to us, we are not a cult or religion but we have people who know how to survive," Aidan said.

"Do you have the authority to let us join or will your leader come along and tell us to leave?"

"He will listen if I say it's okay, but if he tells you to leave it would be for a reason I would have done the same," Aidan responded, knowing that he and Jim were often of like mind on such things.

"We will get our packs and gear, should we meet you here or elsewhere?" George had made up his mind that this would work.

"We will send someone to meet you at Nose Hill Drive and Crowchild on the overpass in about one hour, is that good?" Aidan suggested.

"Perfect, I figure they will know us correct?"

"They will," Aidan said, then he pounded on the roof of the truck and said, "roll out." George and Willow rode away popping a slight wheelie. Aidan's team went straight back.

Riding outside the truck cab, Aidan heard bells -- like church bells -- as they went through the area. He wondered what might be happening but he was not going to investigate.

When they returned he organized people to meet this family up the hill on bike, no sense in wasting fuel. He also talked with Marc and Jason about the new people coming in, he believed they would be useful but he needed them to be checked out.

- - - - - -

Alex biked north to find a suitable lookout station. He was only able to reach Ivan, who could relay information back. The only info Alex had on first report was some fires, some groups of people wandering and most likely heading to get supplies. There didn't seem to be any organization or threats that he had seen. He was there about an hour when he heard church bells ringing. These sounded authentic, not like the recorded types many churches used. They seemed to keep ringing in the mostly silent city. He decided he should scout out the church bells. Though it seemed ludicrous to him, he could understand lots of people would turn to religion in a crisis like this. He was curious about what message would be peddled by the purveyors of their own self-created truth.

Luckily the bells rang a good while and the lack of traffic in the city made hearing much easier. He zeroed in on the sound as he rode, eventually coming to the church. It was an Evangelical mega-church and there were streams of people moving toward it. They clearly had given a long lead time before the indoctrination was to begin, they knew they had to allow time to let people on foot find them. He switched course and found an alleyway, he needed to find a place to ditch his rifle – they were likely to want to hold that for him when he entered. The handgun he concealed behind his back. He found a pile of grass clippings, made sure he was not being observed and tucked the gun under the clippings, then made the pile look uniform. He then rode his bike just as if he were one of the parishioners. The likelihood was than most people did not belong to the church but were looking for information or solace. They had a place for the bikes and someone standing watch over them.

The church would hold thousands and it was filling up. People were taking seats and chatting with each other. Finally a tall man with piercing blue eyes and close-cropped hair, and military bearing stood at the front. "Everyone please be seated and we will begin," he intoned loudly with a tone of authority. At that point ushers closed all the doors and stood like guards, yet they showed no evidence of being armed.

A tall thin man with a thick black beard and wild hair came to the pulpit. He began speaking in a deep baritone voice that carried on its own, but it was clear that they had some amplification, it would be hard for anyone to be heard in a gathering this large without it.

"Let me begin, children of the Lord, by saying I *know* why you are here. I *know* some of you have little experience with faith, I *know* some of you were even hitherto unbelievers. But still the Lord has brought you here for a reason. I *know* that some of you are even denying that in your heads right now. But *I implore you* to **listen!** to me and hear me out. *Listen* to the words God has commanded me to offer to you." People sat respectfully and listened, none left.

"*I know* you are here for answers; We *all* want answers brothers and sisters, and answers we shall have. The Lord provides. Even if you have not found Jesus to be your personal saviour, You Will! I come to tell you **First** why, why this has happened." He waved his hands in a sweeping motion toward the sky. "The Lord knows all and commands all. He has commanded his servants to do this horrible thing! But *How* would a loving and compassionate God command such evil because surely it shall cause suffering? Let me tell you." He paused while people processed the idea and asked the question.

"The suffering will be great, but suffering is not evil to the Lord, suffering builds strength, suffering is a test. The Lord loves the strong; he loves most dearly those who are strong enough to show him great devotion. The meek shall inherit the earth only once the strong build that earth for them. The Lord loves *all* of his children, but those who show him greatness shall show the image of the Lord himself, in this he knows you love and revere and honour him," the preacher orated with great skill.

"The Lord has commanded this event to make his faithful grow stronger! I for one will never call the Lord's work a disaster, but it is a most ingenious plan! He has commanded this event because *He* needed to cleanse the decadence and wickedness from the world. The wickedness is the work of Satan himself. Our society has forgotten the love of the Lord. We have forgotten that which he taught us, ages upon eons past. *Look!* to the bible and nothing else for evidence that we have become wicked. **Know** that your Lord is loving for he has NOT done to us what he did to the wicked in those doomed dens of despair and decadence, those wretched souls of times past who inhabited the cities of Sodom and Gomorrah. In his great wisdom and undying love *He* has spared us. He spared those who can pass his test. For Jesus came and sacrificed himself for our sins, yet still we sin.

We sin, we condone evil, we let the unborn children of God be ripped untimely from the womb and slaughtered like sacrificial sheep, yet we cry when animals are harmed. We consider the life of the sinner, of the mother, to be above that of the innocent, the unborn child.

Our wickedness is rooted in false tolerance. We allow the Jew, and the Mohammedan, and the heretic, to walk freely amongst us, even when we know their beliefs are wicked and hateful to God. We take no action and we claim they must be free. We are **Not** building a righteous society. We are **Not** righteous people when we allow evil in the name of tolerance. Jesus did not tolerate the moneylenders, even though he himself was born a Jew. Jesus knew that the Jew had lost his way and was despised of God. Jesus Knew! Jesus changed that."

A chorus of applause and "Hallelujah' started, but when Alex looked around he realized these were started by a few people and backed up by the audio system. But the chorus was picked up by a a good number of others.

"We have grown wicked. We ask that women, whom God loves so much he allows to carry his children, become his priests. God does not wish this, he needs men, men of power, men of force and fortitude to bring his word. He does not want his word to be taken gently as women would tell it. Yes God does love, but God is also a vengeful God and he demands action when people deny his word, follow false gods, or become wicked. He does not want the kind gentleness of women to be burdened with the awful weight of bringing his word to the people.

Wickedness is in our laws, laws that we are all responsible for. We say it is okay that man lay with man and we even allow the sanctity of God to be sullied and shamed by calling what they do marriage. The bible forbids this behaviour, we *must* follow the word of God if we are to survive, if we are to become a great society again. **ONLY** God's word can bring us there.

These are just the tip of the wickedness we allow. We must return to a pious and holy life or God will set us aside as he did with the wicked of the past. God has had *Enough* of our arrogance, our hubris, and our *disdain* for his word. I ask you, do wish to disdain His Word?"

Cries of "No!" and tears erupted in the audience, again there was some excellent stage management. Shills started, electronics reinforced it, and members of the audience picked it up.

"We need to *Praise the Lord!*" Arms rose, people cried out in support. "We need to sing his praises," at which point a choir of twelve started singing a vibrant gospel song about "Praising the Lord".

"Let me continue for this is very serious. God, He loves that you sing his praises, but is it enough?"

More orchestrated screams of "No!"

"You are right, it is **Not** enough. Why? Because there is still wickedness around us, we must end wickedness and sin. We *must* have productivity and work *for God*, not for our own gain alone, for our gain and for God's *Glory*.

The Lord knows that we *must* come together to survive this test and he has gathered his flock. He did this to us to force us to gather for His glory. Those who do not see this *Will* be extirpated. God will see to it. God will love us more when we do God's work and sometimes God's work is difficult work. God knows, God tests, and God rewards. He will reward you here, but the real reward lies beyond. The Mohammedans believe you shall have virgins for doing God's work, but that is their wickedness speaking, Only God knows what your reward shall be and it shall be that which you cannot ever hope to understand without God's grace. His grace is earned, not given. To earn that grace you *must* obey. You must follow those anointed by God himself to lead you."

The members of the church continued with calls of "Love us God, Love us Jesus," encouraging others to pick it up. The preacher waited smiling.

"You must always be on the lookout for the tricksters, the false prophets, the cheats and the charlatans. They are all around you. But God, and God through his servants, will deal with those. God will heal us, when you prove your FAITH! Are YOU With Me, With God, With Jesus!"

More well-managed screams and cheers for God. Alex watched the show but was beginning to get worried that this fanatic was turning people to his cause. A few people had been let out and Alex was about to escape when the preacher started talking again catching his attention.

"The faithful shall rise. He has said it shall be so! We at this church *know* what it takes to survive. We *are* prepared to survive because Jesus has told us to be ready for this. We will help the faithful. If you are *not* one of the *faithful* we can help you come to Jesus. But you must know in your *Hearts* that you will be faithful. Jesus does not keep the faithless, God *Punishes* the false. God commands us to help you, but God will also judge you. Are there people here today ready to be tested by God, ready to put your faith in Jesus, ready to let Jesus Save you?"

A few stepped forward. The preacher had them give their names and their experience with Jesus, then he had them do a full body baptism and held them under. Some came up gasping and sputtering for air. The preacher smiled and told them God had accepted their faith. Then one young man did not come up but seemed to expire, without missing a beat the Preacher turned serious.

"You must not ever approach God with falsehood in your heart. You cannot hide from the mind of God and He *will* punish you for mockery of his sacraments. It seems a sad thing, but wickedness and falseness *must be eliminated at any cost.*

God understands if you are not yet ready, you do not have to be tested until your heart is true. But you can gain favour and grow in your faith by doing God's work. We have need of workers and Soldiers for God. If you are ready to start your journey to salvation and the everlasting happiness of love then join us in our cause!" he bellowed, pumping his fist into the air, the speech at an intense fervour. "The good Christians of this church will guide you and help you grow your love for Jesus, our saviour, and for his holy father, God.

I will not speak of the scriptures today, for today we need to work for God. Those looking to find salvation, respite, food and shelter, see my friends after this service." There was a series of 'Praise the Lords' and 'Hallelujahs' till some people were crying.

Alex quietly slipped out, noting that his leaving was duly noted by the ushers at the door. He smiled at one and said

"Praise Jesus" as he left, he didn't think the usher bought his sincerity.

Alex circled around the church for a while trying to see what he could. He picked up that they had watchers, they did not appear to be armed. He started to ride away when a working school-type bus drove up with "Evangelical Church of Jesus" stencilled on the side. Beside that was written in less professional stenciling, 'The Army For God Almighty'. It looked to have been added quite recently. As he watched the bus was loaded with cheering people. Alex was not sure how many were newly recruited or how many were already 'of the faith'. What would be more interesting is to know where the bus was going. He decided he would follow and report as far as he could, these people had huge potential to be very dangerous and the collective would need to know what resources this church had and where they were locating their people, it was obviously not here.

It took only a few minutes for them to load the bus, at the same time some people were walking away talking amongst themselves. Alex rode to the main road, quite certain they would have to go by there and if they went down hill so he could follow easily for a while. He rode out ahead and then made a report.

"Base this is Comrade, do you copy?" No answer. He waited and tried again. This time he made contact. "Comrade this is Ivan, I can relay your report, I have contact with Base but they could not hear you. I hear you fine."

"Roger that Ivan, I have a bus load of religious fanatics rolling out of the Ranchlands area. The church is preaching extreme intolerance. They claim to have facilities and material to help people survive, people who believe. I will attempt to follow as far as possible. Over, Comrade out."

At that moment the bus turned the corner and started heading down the hill, this was good for Alex as he was able to keep up for a while. If they went along the main roads they might have to move some vehicles which would slow them down enough for him to keep them in sight.

As it turned out the road had had enough clearing done in this part that they went too quickly. He could not keep up to their speed which was probably only 50 kph, but up a slight grade at first. He rode for thirty minutes after losing sight but did not gain any idea where they had gone in that time so he turned back.

- - - - - -

Jolene had little difficulty getting to her watch post. She had ridden with Kareem, he continued on to another watch point. After observing for a couple of hours she reported in: "Base, I have what is likely armed people stationed at two access points I can see, Bowfort Road and Shouldice bridges. There are streams of people leaving on the highway. Some just leave, some are changing route into Bowness. Can't really tell which ones are leaving or staying, too far to tell. Jolene Over"

"Copy that Green, any other activity?" A voice she did not recognize on the other end answered. She realized they used her code name as she should have, so it must be the base.

"Yes there is intense activity at the high school. They are building structures in the corners of the field. looks like wooden towers.

"Base, Abdul, multiple groups, three to ten in each, traveling, some scrounging, others look like they are aiming for the shopping centre."

"Roger that Abdul, Arms, gear, threat?" Base responded seeking detail.

"Backpacks loaded in most groups, sticks and knives or machetes, a couple of rifles," he responded. He pondered that people had come to the stage where they had to get out to resupply themselves, what people didn't realize was that things were going to get much worse before they got better. "I'm beginning to think like Jim," he mused to himself.

Reporting much later in the day, Ivan, the furthest out, also had the best view in both directions. "Base, I note limited vehicular activity, some off-road west of the city, mostly bikes and old cars a couple of school buses. Have made contact with some groups leaving the city. Base, the bikers are recruiting but some they are just taking, young girls in particular, that is the intel I get from some groups."

"King, come again, you said the 81's are *taking* some people by force?"

"Yup, Roger that, it was only young girls or people with particular skills. Note there are also Native groups going to the reserves to return to a traditional lifestyle, like anyone has a choice about that now! Most people are just looking for a safer place to live with better chance of growing food," Ivan responded, adding to his report.

"Equipment and readiness levels?" base queried.

"Most have a .22 rifle or more and camping gear", '*well equipped for camping, but not the long-term survival of a community*' Ivan thought to himself.

Jim found a spot on the top of Nose Hill. There were far more bushes here than he remembered from his childhood. That suited him as he was able to find a fairly well-hidden location to watch from. He noted that there were a couple of places where he saw smoke on the hill indicating a number of people were camping up here.

He saw some groups, not as many as others, but he was closer to the action than any of the others. With the optics he could make out the depressed looks, bedraggled appearances, and the beginning of suffering on some of the people he saw.

He saw some groups of younger punks, he saw fights and robbery.

He lay there for a couple of hours, nodding off occasionally. This was the first chance he had to just stop and think and watch since the Nail Day. Nail Day was bad, but little did he know this day would test him like no other.

TWENTY TWO

"If you must break the law, do it to seize
power: in all other cases observe it."

- Julius Caesar

A group of survivors stumbled along looking a little
bedraggled. They were a large group, about twelve people --
three children, three women, six men. They were dressed for
the hot summer day, but they did not look prepared for the
cool Calgary summer nights. They approached a clump of
dead cars, an all too common scene after the event. It looked
like there might be more than one group that had coalesced.
That was positive, it meant they were seeing the value in
working together. Two men were on mountain bikes, five of
the adults seemed to hang together quite a bit. Two were
older men, moving in a laboured, painful way. Alderson
winced, the old ones didn't have long in this new world of
harsh survival. Most had backpacks, another good sign, some
survival thinking going on. Alderson had not seen much
survival thinking in the first days after the event. Six days
after, he was beginning to see people change. Good people
take time to change, the nasty adapt faster.

When Alderson noticed the second group he thought
they might be avoiding contact, but no, they were too well

laid out . Unbeknownst to the first group, they were approaching an ambush. Maybe this would be resolved positively, result in cooperation, but Alderson doubted it. The survivors ambled into the ambush. The deadly dance began.

Alderson lay on the ground watching the trouble grow, not knowing if there would be death, but here would be either a fight or someone would run. The first group he had seen wasn't in shape to make a run for it. He could tell by their slow, staggering movements some were exhausted. The youngest of the children were likely tired and cranky and not understanding. Watching this, Alderson thought back to the decisions he made on Nail Day and he was glad for what he did. The people with him were scared but surviving. Laying on a small knoll covered in brush, fetid with sweat with ants crawling over him, his bald pate caked in muck and leaves to be less visible, he wondered, How did we come to such a low place? By "we" he meant the human race. So many disasters, but worse yet the human screw-ups, and the most civilized culture ever falls apart in days. "Humans are pathetic," he answered himself.

Coming back to the present Alderson focussed on the second group, popping up from behind some vehicles. All males, 20-something, looking unfriendly. They came up swaggering with aggressive attitude. Alderson labeled them The Thugs. The one doing all the talking was 6-foot, dirty blonde or just dirty, unshaven for several days like most every male. No packs, no gear, but weapons, knives and clubs. In Canada guns were uncommon, particularly in the city. The government estimated there were 7 million firearms across the country, owned by no more than two million individuals. Most shooters he knew owned more than 7 guns, himself included. That meant one in 30 households had firearms, but far more rural ones had guns and far fewer urban.

The Thug group advanced, the leader making greetings. Jim couldn't hear due to the distance but clearly the others saw a potential problem and stopped. It was the two older people, two of the women, and two of the children. Too sexy,

Alderson thought, seeing the one woman turning around, she will be a target. Emptying his pack, one of the older men started handing things to the Thug leader, trying to appease him. In his gut, Alderson knew this shakedown was not going to be enough for the Thugs, they wanted more.

The negotiation continued, the subgroup that had hung together -- the two women and one man on foot -- started taking their packs off , advancing to the parley. Something was wrong, the man was holding something else behind the pack, Alderson thought it was a knife. This would get ugly. Riding in from 50 yards, weaving among the motionless cars, the two on mountain bikes were going to act, it might make the others scatter. Drawing together, the Thugs bought their weapons to the ready, the leader swinging, dropping one of the older men. The one hiding the knife dropped his pack, lashing out at the Thug, skewering a thug under the ribs it seemed, the Thug went down. The knifeman stood there stunned, a different Thug took a swing at him, cracking him in the head. The bike outriders, dismounting on the fly, came at the other Thugs with clubs. No one in either group was skilled with violence. The Thug leader had confidence, but no particular skill, swinging his club wildly, but staying on the attack. It was game of tag, both groups trying to score a tag but not get close enough to the other to get tagged.

Taking an escape opportunity, realizing the cost was too great, the Thugs retreated when they had an opening. They left the injured one behind, abandoned to the hands of the enemy, no honour among these lowlifes.

Watching the women, Alderson saw their desperate attempt to give the old man First Aid. They were shouting, crying. The knifeman reached down, grabbing the Thug by the hair, slamming him against the ground. The Thug didn't move again. They tried CPR on the man for ten minutes, then one outrider helped the young beauty up and just held her. The old man was another victim of the EMP.

"How quickly our humanity dies," Alderson thought,

"but then how far would I have gone with Kareem had he not seen sense? Would I have pushed the limits of civility? How far did I go with those I assaulted?" His thoughts brought him back to the first day of the brave new world – or just the shitty old world with a new pile of crap.

Alderson, watched the three Thugs move away. They started coming his way, up the hill into a copse of trees, less than 200 yards to one side. Checking out what they have going on would be prudent, he thought. The other group moved on, the one woman wailing with the one adult male consoling her and a young teen and maybe ten year-old girl also consoling her. The older woman on foot had a hand of each of two younger children and they trudged along the roadway. The outriders on bikes now ranged wider and farther ahead, aware this was not a social walk. They needed to be wary of hidden dangers. Alderson wanted to make contact with that group, but the Thugs were his immediate concern, scouting their camp was a priority. It was a fair walk to the river where the collective was, but he had communications.

"Collective, this is Juju, do you read me?" He whispered into the mic. They should have the radio on, drawing power from the solar cell.

"Roger that Alder... Juju," a female voice on the other end answered. It sounded like Rosie, he had taught her to answer using code names because it would make tracking them less easy, he was after all, most likely a wanted criminal now.

"I have a group moving along John Laurie, I will try to send them along. There's also a group of Thugs ..." he stopped suddenly as he heard a foot step behind him. He rolled over to his left to get an upward view, to find a large garden fork pointed at him.

"Well, well, what do we have here, an armed intruder with a working radio," the Thug said. "LARRY get over here!" he yelled. The Thug looked about five eight, maybe 160 pounds, long greasy hair, young -- barely started shaving. Alderson could see the remnants of face paint and thought it was just camo paint that had not all come off, then noticed the jacket had an evil clown insignia on it. This guy was a Juggalo, a wannabe gang-banger. They acted tough but were for the most part just punks. Alderson had known a few at the school, the school always worked to get rid of those types or disconnect them from the gang. But now one was standing over him with a pitchfork. He had to give it to the punk, he hadn't tried to grab the rifle off the ground which would have put him close to Alderson, close enough to act.

"LARRY!" the Juggalo punk called over his shoulder again. "You, get up!" he ordered Alderson.

Alderson complied, first moving to his knees bringing him closer to the weapon. As he did the punk noticed Alderson's handgun under his vest. The kids eyes went wide and he squeaked, voice breaking, "Keep your hands up!"

Making a big mistake, the kid put the tines of the fork on Alderson's chest right underneath his neck, "*Too close kid,*" Alderson thought. Alderson's hands were up in the surrender position. He had practiced taking away a knife in this position many times, a long-handled weapon made it a bit more complicated, but he could do it. It meant he would have to take the weapon rather than the arm, but he out-massed the kid by a good fifty kilos so it shouldn't be too much of a fight. Then he heard footsteps coming from behind the kid, he had to act now.

Leaning back a bit, Alderson snapped his hips sideways, letting his forearms follow his shoulders. Deflecting the fork away from himself with his right arm, his left came up inside to follow and grab the fork. As soon as his left hand covered the handle of the fork, he made a fist with his right and drove a backhanded hammer-fist into the punk's nose. The kid immediately let go of the fork, leaving it in Alderson's hand. "Ow!" the kid yelled, grabbing his nose as it gushed blood.

Alderson quickly drove the handle back into the young punk, causing the kid to double over.

Then Alderson saw Larry, the blonde Thug from before, club at the ready. Larry was still about seven metres away. Alderson took one step back, dropping the fork, drawing his pistol with his right. "Larry, put your weapons down, do it now," Alderson said firmly. Larry hesitated. Alderson heard more footsteps, he fired his weapon, aiming to miss Larry, not wanting to kill anyone. Larry dropped his club. "Get on the ground, both of you, face down!" Alderson ordered. They complied slowly. Alderson took a few side steps to put them between him and the new footsteps. The blonde punk on the ground whimpered, "I'm not L-Larry, he is . . ."

"Oh shit!" Alderson exclaimed as he saw Officer Mancha come around the trees, still wearing his uniform, complete with body armour and a pistol in his hand.

Mancha said in a sneering voice, "YOU, Alderson! I see you left Smiley alive. You might as well drop your gun, you won't shoot me, you don't have the guts to kill anyone," he sneered, raising his pistol.

'Wrong,' thought Alderson as he squeezed the trigger twice. The Sig P226 was in single-action mode after firing it once, the trigger pull was short, making a more accurate first shot. Mancha made a whooshing sound, struck twice in the chest, as he went down. 'Okay, right' Alderson thought, 'I don't want to kill anyone.' He was hoping the vest had done its job well enough.

The punk with the smashed nose started sniveling, "He killed Larry, man. He killed Larry!"

Alderson, de-cocking and holstering his gun, walked over to Mancha who was groaning on the ground. He reached down and grabbed Mancha's gun. A shiny Kimber 1911, Alderson wondered where he had found it. After carefully letting the hammer down, Alderson tucked the gun in his waistband at the back. A 1911 was a nice gun of tried and true design, but it had no built in mechanism for de-cocking like the Sig.

Alderson said out loud, "Now if any of you move I will kill you." He got para-cord from his small pack and began tying them up, Mancha first, then collected his rifle and slung it. He got the three of them up and started marching toward their camp using the fork as incentive. He kept Mancha in the middle, that way he had to get around his followers to do anything.

Alderson jabbed his gun into the back of Smiley's neck and demanded the whereabouts of their camp.

"Up the hill, up there," Smiley whined, nodding his head toward a paved path.

Mancha snorted "Stupid punk!" in derision.

This would be a bit of a hike. "*How have things gone so ugly, so quickly?*" Alderson was thinking, even on Nail Day there had been some hopeful signs, "*but a cop gone completely rogue, what was next?*"

Remonstrating himself for choosing to do this scout alone, Alderson walked behind the trio of vermin. Working in pairs was always the rule, but he had felt things were not so bad, he thought he should have been able to avoid trouble. Fewer people meant more locations covered, but now the social fabric was degrading faster than he had dreamt was likely. On further reflection he had been part of that degradation, he had broken so many laws he would get life in front of the firing squad, if there was anyone running this shit-show. He had assaulted people, including a couple of police, he had even committed attempted murder on that same officer it could be argued, he had committed theft, been part of a conspiracy. This was the new world order.

Approaching what was the camp area, Mancha started

trying to talk to him, much louder than he needed to. "Hey, you know we could work together," Mancha offered. "You seem to have some skills, I need people like you."

Alderson wasn't buying it. "Shut up or I'll crack your skull," he snarled between clenched teeth. Alderson thought Mancha was likely trying to make enough noise to alert someone else. Alderson stopped and looked around warily. There were still the other two from the encounter on the road. "All of you take a seat against a tree out of reach of each other." he ordered. The two punks complied, Mancha started looking around trying to find a tree in a forest. Alderson pointed and said, "That one over there", not sure what kind of plan Mancha was hatching. Once they were seated he duct-taped each of their mouths and retied their hands behind their back around the trees. He searched each one thoroughly, as he had been taught to do when he was a correctional officer at the Young Offenders Centre, a one-time summer job. Finding a boot knife and another magazine on Mancha, he ordered the cop to sit cross-legged and used his last length of para-cord to tie Mancha's ankle to his neck with a slip knot, making it difficult for Mancha to move his legs without strangling himself.

Proceeding up the path, Alderson looked for traps, manmade or natural. Re-cocking the 1911, he carried it in a ready position. He scanned the trees looking for others, looking for signs of the camp. He could smell a latrine, and stale smoke, he couldn't be far now. Crouching by a bush, looking and listening, thinking "*I'm way too old for this shit*", he heard a whimpering sound then the smack of a person being hit. A hushed voice in an angry tone said something he could not quite hear. Crunching sounds of shoes on the forest litter indicated someone moving a short distance away. Alderson questioned himself again, "*I'm no, hero, no master spy, and no special ops soldier, what the fuck am I doing. I should fuck off and get out of here, let them work it out.*" But he didn't leave, he listened some more. Nothing. They were expecting something.

Advancing a little through the bush off the trail, stopping

again, listening in silence, hearing birds but no people, he picked up a small stick and tossed it into a clearing. A harsh whisper "Over there," some quick footsteps. Breaking the quiet and silencing the birds, the boom of a gun – likely a shotgun. "You fucking idiot," he heard another voice. "Now they know where we are, they must have Larry, I know I heard him."

Alderson would have belly-crawled but the underbrush was too thick, crawling would be noisier than walking. Forward a step, searching more, finally a glimpse of a person. One guy with a shotgun, partly behind a lean-to, scanning the path. Shooting him would have to be a head shot, twenty-five metre head shot, too difficult with a handgun. He did not want to take that step to murdering someone in cold blood either. Ducking down and creeping a little further, then popping up, he could see more of the camp from a better angle. Three more guys with clubs and knives, hiding beside two other lean-tos. He could see a garbage pile, empty water bottles, and empty cans. Then he heard the whimpering again, drawing his attention to the nearest lean-to.

Someone was inside the lean-to. Shotgun boy yelled out, "LARRY ARE YOU OUT THERE?". No response. Then in a whisper the same guy said, "Rick, you go look."

"Fuck you, you have the shotgun. If someone took out Larry they're dangerous, he was a cop you know," the other Thug replied. He was one of the group that had assaulted the people on the road.

"But I heard shots, then later Larry's voice. I think he did the shooting," Mr. Shotgun said. "You go or I will shoot your ass, punk."

"Smiley and Jiggles aren't back either, this is bad," Rick said in a near-panicked, whining voice. He deferred to the other, getting up, moving forward, holding his knife out front, looking afraid and unsure of himself. Alderson assessed him, noting the position of the knife indicated a guy who did not know knife fighting. Alderson had two choices, run, or act now. It would not take long before Rick found Larry, Moe, and Curly Joe and let them go, and that would not be good for Alderson. He unslung the .223, he did not want to kill the guy, He wondered if he could make the shot on his hand. It was close range and he had a scope. Bracing in the Y of a tree branch, aiming carefully, he held his breath and squeezed. No squeeze. He had forgotten to take the safety off. He disengaged the the safety, aimed again, held his breath and squeezed again. The shot rang out, the shotgun wheeling out of the guy's hand, Alderson didn't think he hit him. Alderson ran in, drawing the 1911 again, leaving the rifle.

Coming in at an angle Alderson had a side view of Mr. Shogun. Mr. Shotgun was still stunned, looking around, holding his hand, staring as Alderson approached.

Alderson ordered, "IF YOU BREATHE WRONG I WILL KILL YOU!" Aiming the Kimber at the guys chest, he yelled, "All of you on the ground face down. NOW! If I wanted you dead you would be," he added for effect. Mr. Shotgun fell face down. The guy nearest looked at the shotgun, then looked back at Alderson. Alderson said, switching his aim, "Go ahead punk, make my day." The punk didn't, instead he did a dutiful face plant.

The third guy was more problematic. He stood up with a club in hand, hands raised. Alderson was thinking he might throw the club. He was half-covered by the lean-to. Alderson aimed toward him but aiming for the lean-to, and shot. The .45 calibre bullet tore of a big chuck of the wood from the lean-to, launching it toward guy with the club who jerked violently trying to avoid being hit. The bullet deflected into the trees. "That was a warning not a miss, make a choice," Alderson barked, trying not to reveal his own visceral gut-clenching fear. Dropping the club, Clubber joined the others on the ground. Taking a moment to scan the camp, Alderson was horrified by the tableau before him. Now he was thinking what a cake-walk Nail Day was, today this scene showed humanity was fucked in the ass with a hot poker.

Alderson looked inside the lean-to where he thought he heard the whimpering from. There were two young girls chained to one of the trees that supported the lean-to, they looked between eleven and fourteen years old. What clothes they had were a mess, they were bruised and cut, but it wasn't their condition that horrified him. It was the dead, mutilated, and rotting body that lay between them. The stench of blood and beginning rot was in the air. It was an older male, dark-skinned like the girls. His body was nude, and it looked like he had his throat cut and had bled out right there. Even the girls had dried caked blood on them.

Alderson's fury rose. He stormed toward Mr. Shotgun and said in a cold vicious voice, "Spread your legs wide."

The punk started sniveling, "I didn't do anything dude, it was all Larry and Smiley, don't kill me please."

"Did any of you fuck these girls?" Alderson said coldly.

Both of the other two guys pointed at Mr. Shotgun and said simultaneously, "He did."

Alderson booted him in the ribs and said again, "Spread your legs. Now, or I will kill you." The Thug complied meekly. With red hatred and volcanic anger, Alderson wound up and kicked the Thug with all of his power in the groin. One of the girls shrieked in fear, the Thug howled, gasped, rolled over, grabbed his balls, and then passed out.

Alderson thought he might have killed the guy and he didn't care, at that point he knew he was losing his humanity. The dead city, the dead world, was stealing it from him piece by piece. He knew he would have to get out soon, but he had a more immediate problem -- approaching footsteps.

One of the Thugs on the ground took the opportunity to try to get up and run but Alderson was able to catch him just as he got off the ground and drilled him in the back of the head with an elbow. The guy dropped like a ton of bricks, again this might have killed the guy. The last one just covered his head and cried. Then he saw Larry and Rick coming but he didn't see Smiley and Jiggles, that was a problem. Alderson could have shot both Larry and Rick right then but he hesitated, still squeamish about killing. It was a mistake.

Reacting instinctively to a grunt behind him, Alderson brought his hands up to cover and ducked. Something meant for his head cracked into his forearm, spinning the 1911 out of his grip. Keeping his hands high, spinning to his right Alderson found a Thug loading up a baseball bat for another swing. Using his momentum to close the gap, crashing into the Thug, blocking the next attack with his already throbbing left arm, his right hand pistoned down, then up. Alderson drove a palm heel into his attacker's chin, separating the Thug from his tenuous connection to the ground. Alderson pumped his leg into action, sweeping the Thug's leg, continuing to drive the attacker's head toward the ground. The Thug's head met the ground while his feet were still splayed in the air. Training taking over, Alderson dropped a knee on the Thug's ribs, simultaneously stripping the baseball bat away from the thug, gripping it, ready to strike with it.

Holding the bat with his right hand he looked around, checking over both shoulders. Alderson's eyes snapped to a movement, a second Thug lunged for the dislodged gun. Desperately attempting to stop his enemy from getting to the gun, in a single fluid action Alderson launched the bat at the second attacker. Even missing the target, the bat made the Thug dodge. Alderson stepped and drew his Sig, putting real fear in the would-be attacker, forcing him to take a hasty retreat into the bushes. In the melee Alderson had lost track of the the cop, Larry. A yelp and scream from a girl and Alderson snapped around. As he turned a sudden impact from the side lifted him off his feet, careening Alderson to the ground. Fighting to maintain his grip on the gun, Alderson held on, but impact with a tree knocked the gun free. Feeling weight on him he looked up into the enraged face of Rick.

Rick had height on Alderson but gave up probably thirty kilos of mass. On the ground mass was king if you had equal skill. Alderson doubted Rick had the skill.

Sitting up, Rick began to rain punches downward, aiming to turn Alderson's face into pulp. Grinning at Rick, Alderson covered up then expertly trapped Rick's second punch, pulling Rick's body down, at the same time driving up to the corner and over to roll Rick off. From between Rick's legs, Alderson grabbed the collar of Rick's jean jacket, driving, rolling Rick up, scooping a leg and twisting out to the side. Once on the side Alderson applied his body weight to control Rick and, using the collar of the jacket, applied a choke, driving his knee into Rick's temple twice in succession. Rick flailed once, then went limp. Alderson pressed up and looked for his gun.

There it was!

Alderson looked right down the muzzle. Looking down the gun sights he saw the livid and gleeful face of Larry Mancha.

"Now I get to hurt you, I get to take everything from you. Just as you did to me when you took my gun," Officer Mancha growled menacingly, "I'm just protecting citizens from a murderer, you killed Jiggles." Alderson glanced around and saw the Thug with the bat with a pool of thick blood around his head, it looked like his head hit a rock. Mancha looked around and said, "Smiley get that damned gun over there," using the Sig to point to where the 1911 was.

"Smiley, put this rope around his neck with a slip knot." he said throwing Smiley a long piece of rope. Once it was tied Mancha made a wide circle around Alderson, came behind him and took the cord. "We are going to march him up to the rock and hang him there for everyone to see. Bring that pole Smiley," he said, pointing to a long pole. "You keep your hands up," he commanded Alderson.

As they was walked Alderson replayed everything in his mind. His first thoughts were that if he lived, Mancha had to die, no options. He thought more about the preceding days and how he wanted to avoid the complete disintegration of society, that seemed moot at this point.

Mancha was careful to not get too close, he did not make contact with Alderson. Smiley followed behind Mancha. Alderson even tried changing his pace to get Mancha closer, but it didn't work. As they climbed the hill Alderson stumbled a bit, Mancha pulled the cord on his neck and started snarling something, however when he pulled the cord Alderson back-stepped making the gun come into contact with his back. Spinning sideways, deflecting the aim of the gun just for a second, Mancha fired.

Hearing the sound first, next feeling a searing pain across his back, Alderson was already facing Mancha, his right hand looping around the Mancha's gun hand. Driving back, bending Mancha's arm using his mass and shoulder, Alderson covered the gun with his left, forcing it toward Mancha as Alderson leveraged Mancha's balance, driving to the ground. The gun went off again before Alderson had control of it. Startled, Alderson jerked back, sprayed with blood and bone, some getting in his mouth. Alderson had done this take-away a thousand times but never with a live gun. Mancha flopped the rest of the way to the ground.

Standing there stunned, Smiley gaped at the gruesome scene, Mancha missing half his face and head, Alderson covered in gore, now looking at him. Smiley had the 1911 in his right hand and the pole on his left shoulder.

Alderson, looked up at Smiley. Smiley, no longer smiling, dropped everything. He turned and ran. Alderson was stunned, he started shaking. "Oh god, oh fuck, what have I done?" He turned, saw the corpse of Mancha, and then vomited, falling to the side still shaking.

Alderson lay there, trying to believe this was some

nightmare. He could not believe he had just blown someone's brains out, worse yet, a cop. He had to think. He rose, deciding the best thing would be to strip the body to let the coyotes and crows scavenge it. He shook and felt faint as he went about the grizzly task, he jerked away with a shudder several times, his revulsion of dead things too intense. Only necessity made him continue. What should have taken five minutes took fifteen.

Taking the cop's clothing, he found a wallet with Mancha's police ID and a picture of a pretty young woman and the cop together. Feeling worse for what he had done, knowing he had taken Mancha away from someone, Alderson cried. He kept the driver's license with the address.

He then followed the trail back, carrying the soiled and bloody clothes. He stumbled into the camp to find Smiley still there talking to the two girls. Smiley heard him and raised the shotgun and squeezed the trigger. Alderson was so stunned he didn't even move. Smiley tried to pump the shotgun but it would not cycle. Smiley frantically tried to find a way to shoot the gun, fumbled with the mechanism, but did not understand shotguns.

Alderson finally came to his senses and walked up to Smiley. Grabbing the barrel with one hand and the forestock with the other, pushing the barrel down and pulling the stock, he stripped the gun from the gobsmacked Smiley. In the process he smacked the barrel into Smiley's groin, causing Smiley to groan and grab himself. It wasn't a hard hit but it made Smiley double up, then hobble off, shocked that Alderson hadn't shot him.

Surveying the camp, the other Thugs were missing, except Jiggles -- the one whose skull he had broken on the rock. Alderson found the fire pit and started a fire. He threw Mancha's clothes into the flames, getting whiffs of the acrid smoke of the burning synthetic material. Coming out of his stupor from the horror, he looked around.

Remembering the two captives, he walked over to the chained-up, skinny, bruised and half-naked girls, bent down and started to talk. He did not know what kind of trauma they had endured but he suspected. "Hey there, it's okay, I am going to help you. I'll get you out of here." He said bending lower to be on their level when one started screaming. The girls tried to retreat further into the lean-to. He found the keys he had taken from Mancha's body then reached for the lock on the chains around their necks. Unlocking the first one, both of them screaming, he saw something fast moving in his peripheral vision, making him duck slightly. His move, the slope of the hill, and the impact, all caused him to roll away from the girls.

Lying there stunned, noticing movement in his direction, reorienting himself, Alderson saw it was one of the girls, who could not reach him because of the chain. He had dropped the keys to the locks but he could not tell if she had found them. Another couple of moments shaking his head, Alderson realized it had been one of the girls who had cracked him with a rock. He rolled away from them.

Hearing them scrabbling for the keys while he lay there with his head spinning, he hoped they would just escape. He was developing one hell of a headache, probably a concussion, he needed to rest. Of course he could just die right here, brained with a rock by a tiny, mostly naked, East Asian girl. No, he decided, he would not have that happen right now. Rolling again, getting to his hands and knees, staggering up, using a tree for support Alderson righted himself. His head was swimming. The rough bark of the tree on his hand, the smell of fire and blood in his nose, and a pounding in his head, all made him turn and puke again. The one unlocked girl eyed him warily.

"Why did you hit me? I was going to free you," he asked, confused.

The one with the keys looked at him, "Then you point your gun at us and tell us you wanted to .... fuck us or we have to suck your dirty cock or else you make us ... f, f, fuck

338

our dad!" she yelled, then broke into tears looking at the dead man beside her.

The other twin whispered in a chant. Alderson, finally understanding, heard the rhythmic "Kill him Arlene. Kill him for me please!" insistently repeating. The more functional twin looked at the dead Thug in the camp area and went over to him, quickly searched the body and found a knife.

Watching this, Alderson thought to himself, "*You didn't secure the weapons you idiot.*"

She came back to her sister holding the knife out front of herself. "If you come near us I will cut your thing off. I will!"

Her sister rocking, repeating, "Kill him Arlene, kill him for me please!"

"My sister says to kill you, she knows you're bad, she warned me about him," Arlene said, pointing at the Thug. She slowly came toward Alderson, the knife held out front, looking for an opportunity to gut him. Alderson drew his gun pointing it at her, so groggy he thought he would not be able to hit the skinny twelve year-old, but he needed her to stop.

The threat failed, with a gleam in her eye, she kept stalking him. Unable to actually shoot the waif, Alderson holstered the gun, hoping he had enough faculties to deal with the crazed child. She moved into the danger zone, only two steps away.

"Look Arlene, do you like chocolate bars? I have some," he said, reaching into a pocket taking out a bar. He looked down as he put it down. In an exquisite bit of timing, she attacked.

Alderson caught the sudden movement of the waif in his peripheral vision, his sluggish body and dulled responses conspired to make him slow enough that he was unable to avoid the girl completely.

She stabbed forward. She lunged, he tried to follow his training and side-step toward her while redirecting the knife hand, but he was slow enough that he felt the blade rend a gash in his side. He was shocked, he had never been stabbed by a person before. The training again, 'When you fight a knife you will get cut, be ready.' He reacted slowly and instead of catching her arm and controlling it, she spun to face him.

"Die, Die, Die!" she said emboldened by her success. Knife forward, she came at him again.   This time he was a bit quicker and avoided getting cut, but still failed to catch her arm. The next attack was a wide slashing attack which he stepped and leaned back to avoid, then thrust himself forward to block the backswing of the knife. This time he was able to block the arm, then reach over and control it. Then he was able to roll her wrist upward and create pressure on her elbow effecting an arm lock. He used his position near her to apply pressure by squatting down in a horse stance, forcing the girl face down on the ground. Removing the knife from her hand, he stowed it in his waistband.

He waited there, controlling the now sobbing, yelling, frustrated girl; he had to catch his breath. "Okay I am going to let you up but I am going to hold your wrist because I don't want you to try to hurt me again, okay?" She nodded. He stood up holding her wrist. Getting up, she lunged and tried to claw and bite the hand holding her wrist.

Alderson was ready for her, he spun her around and grabbed her from behind. Pulling her close to him, he could feel the mostly naked girl tense and fight harder. He knew holding like this was creating more trauma, but he had no backup, there was just no other choice. Her kicking and squirming made holding her like trying to put a cat in a bathtub.

Alderson went to his knees, forcing her to sit in front of him. He pressed his head against her back; just in time, as she attempted to head-butt him. Screaming, yelling, squirming for a full minute, Alderson just held the wildcat, letting her rage at the cruelty of life, watching her sister crying hidden in the lean-to. He knew restraining this child was bad psychologically, but he could not free her yet. This seemed to be just one of a myriad of ugly choices that were in the future.

He knelt there feeling increasing pain in his side and in his knees. He needed to do something. "Arlene, will you be calm for me?" he said quietly to her. She nodded. "If you try to hurt me again I will have to sit on you, please be good for me. Do you promise to be good?" She sobbed harder, but nodded.

"I'll be good, I'll do whatever you want, please don't sit on me and f-fuck me, it hurts so bad," she whimpered.

"I'm not ever going to do that to you. The bad men are dead," Alderson said very quietly to her.

This time he released her completely, stood up, and stepped back, watching to see what would happen next.

Arlene stared blankly at him for a few moments then she got up and ran back to her sister still chained to the lean-to and hugged her. Then she fumbled around looking for the keys. Finding them she unlocked her sister. Alderson, dead tired and worried, moved around the other side of the lean-to, watching flies buzzing around the dead body of the girls' father. He wondered how these girls could ever survive; rape, kidnapping, murder, torture, their psychological trauma was immense, no counsellor, no trauma centre, no justice.

How many people were going to die because they could not get to the doctor or hospital he thought, even if all the technology in the hospital worked, people could not get to it. Mobility was going to be a great commodity in this new world.

Alderson was becoming aware of a pain in his side. Remembering he had been stabbed, he watched the girls.

Whispering in soothing tones to her sister, Arlene unlocked the other girl. They started to move around the camp looking for things. Finding some stale pita breads and cans of food, but no opener, they chewed on the bread. This jolted Jim out of his fugue. He went to find his backpack and took out some granola bars and chocolate bars. He held them out, "Girls you can have these if you like."

Arlene came forward and took them meekly. She and her sister shared them silently. Taking out his small first aid kit, he started to work on himself as best he could, just cleaning and covering the wound. Preventing infection was the key. He knew he needed to finish the job and get back to the collective. He had left his radio back on the look-out spot, but he did not want to leave the girls.

Searching the camp he quickly found a shovel, he should at least bury the girls' father, even if he left the other scum to rot or be scavenged by coyotes.

After an hour of digging with the two girls just watching him and eating what they could find in the camp, he turned to them. "Girls, I know it has been very bad for you, but we need to bury your daddy. Do you want to say anything? Do you want me to say anything?"

Arlene just started to sob quietly. The other girl who had not spoken to Alderson at all said, "You can say something." She was beginning to lose the crazed fearful look. Alderson shuddered touching the dead man. He found the experience of touching and dragging a lifeless body horrifyingly surreal. He dragged the body through the dry grass and dirt to the hole in the ground. The two girls came holding hands, looking apprehensively over the edge at their father. There was no dignity in death. The girls wept.

Alderson started to speak. "Here lies a decent and good man who died trying to save his two daughters. He lived for them in life, providing for them, raising them to be good and decent people. They were robbed of his love. He was a kind-hearted and honourable man who only wanted the best for his children. He was taken from them by evil far too early in life. May he rest knowing he did a good job in life, knowing his beautiful young daughters will carry his memory forward." Alderson ended there, shedding a tear not for the man he did not know, but for the damaged young girls, for the damaged world that killed this man and created orphans. He shed more tears knowing they were not the last or only girls who would be orphaned, knowing that the world was not going to be kind to orphans. Having nothing more to to say, he stayed silent for a moment.

Arlene went to Alderson and took his hand and said through a flood of tears, "I'm sorry I hurt you, I didn't know you knew my dad."

"Arlene, I didn't know your dad, I just know he must have been a good man because he raised such lovely young ladies," Alderson said trying to make the girl feel good.

She responded with a wan smile, her eyes desperately sad. Alderson mechanically began to lob dirt on the body, Arlene helped with her hands, her sister joined her, then they stopped and the girls hugged each other. The other girl kept her distance from Alderson, still wearing fear and apprehension. Alderson finished the grizzly task and turned to the girls. For the first time noticing that the clothing they had was not really attached, but shredded clothes just thrown over them. He noticed red welts on them and bite marks on the one girls breasts, he winced and turned away. He had to find something for them to wear.

There were the clothes of the dead Thug. He stripped the clothes off the one who had died here. The shirt and t-shirt were big enough to act like night dresses on the thin girls. He found some water, soap, and paper towels in the campsite and offered it and the shirts to the girls.

They were very tentative at first but then hid behind the lean-to and cleaned themselves. In the meantime he collected any useful items he could find. He was about to leave to get the walkie-talkie back when Arlene called out, "Please don't leave us here, mister." He stopped and turned. "We don't know where we are and how to get home, please help us," she implored.

He realized that even walking the couple hundred metres to where he had been observing from would seem like abandonment to these girls. "Okay girls just come with me. You can call me Jim," he croaked out. They followed, a good five metres back from him. He started trudging toward his lookout spot. When they were fifty metres from the camp he heard an ear-piercing shriek from one of the girls, he spun only to see the blurry image of a fist as it crunched into his face.

Jim reeled, feeling tears welling in his eyes, pain in his nose, he reacted with his training and brought both hands high to cover. The second blow was a big haymaker punch, he was still staggering but he was able to catch it mostly on his arms using a deep covering block. He was feeling wobbly but he knew he had to regain composure. Another left, then right, but he was catching these on his arms, back-pedaling as he went. 'Not good to give ground' his training told him, there were no effective attacks while retreating. The attacker swung again. After blocking again, Alderson returned with three quick punches, jab, cross, left hook, all three made contact. The attacker reeled, they weren't hard punches, he hadn't been quite ready. A big haymaker came again, Alderson blocked it, scooping in under his arm, then stepping in to sweep the leg. As he stepped in his foot slipped on a root and he went down practically pulling the attacker on him. Alderson now recognized Rick, who was as surprised as he was but quickly exploited the advantage chance had given him. He slipped his arm out and wrapped it around Alderson's neck in a scarf hold, getting ready to punch him. Alderson quickly turned in, locked on to Rick's waist, and did a very fast 'bridge and roll' throwing Rick over and off of him.

Because of the slope of the hill Rick rolled out of Alderson's control and came back to his feet. There was enough distance between them that Alderson was able to get up. As he did he was suddenly grabbed under the arms in a bear hug by a second person.

Alderson locked the guy's arms and immediately launched himself twisting forward, reaping outside the guy's leg behind him. This caused the attacker to be thrown over and land underneath Alderson as they went to the ground. There was an audible whoosh of air and a crack as the attacker's ribs cracked. Alderson quickly held the attacker's arm and drove two hard elbows into the side of the guy's head. The unknown attacker went limp as Alderson saw Rick launching a kick at his face. His hand came to block but he only caught part of it, knocking his blocking arm into his own face. Alderson was thrown back. He rolled with it, rolling over the unconscious attacker and getting up on the other side using the body for a block.

Rick sidled around his dormant friend and rushed Jim. Jim was stunned and slow enough that he could only just stop from being bowled over. Rick managed to grab him under the arms and was trying to lift and squeeze him, likely to throw him to the ground. Jim immediately boxed Rick's ears twice in rapid succession. Alderson felt Rick slacken and drop him. Jim spun inside Rick's loosened grip, locked his neck, drove forward and executed a sweeping hip, *harai goshi*, throw. Rick landed at Jim's feet, Jim holding Rick's right arm. Alderson swung his foot over Rick's head and smashed his heel into Rick's nose the using the position to lock the arm back. In an act of spite and anger Alderson violently pushed the arm back snapping it at the elbow. Rick screamed.

"*Unlucky bastard was still conscious,*" Alderson thought. Alderson stepped back and looked around for other attackers. He felt his nose streaming blood. He took out his gun aimed at Rick. Out of the corner of his eye he saw the two girls standing fifty feet away, looking terrified, mouths agape. He stopped and holstered his gun.

"Come on girls," he croaked, "let's get out of here." They walked tentatively forward, then ran in a wide circle past Rick and his now awakening friend. Alderson wiped the blood from his nose as he left. Rick would have to do the same, but with his left hand, the right wasn't going to work for a while.

Jim started walking again, feeling more like he had been run over by a truck after being taken out of a tumble dryer. He had to finish the trek to pick up the radio and other items he had left behind. That meant going up the hill. The girls followed but would not get closer than about ten metres. He forced himself to make the climb, moving his leaden legs, just thinking 'one more step'. Just as he got to his lookout spot he heard "Juju, this is the Collective do you read us? Over." The sound startled him. He yelled a muffled yell, the girls who were now closer screamed. He whirled. Areen screamed again.

"Shhh it's okay girls, these are friends of mine," he said showing them the radio. He keyed the mic getting a little more strength from the sound of the voice. "Collective, this is Juju I copy you. Over."

"Are you okay Juju, your last transmit was stopped, we were worried." The voice was Rosie, he was impressed how she was maturing in the crisis. He was always wanting to know where she was going in life, now he would be a part of that. It was the people in his life like Jenna, Rosie, Alex, Aidan, and Marc that made him want to pull this collective together, they were worth it, but he really felt touched by all the people that were following his lead at the end of the world. It was a crazy awesome responsibility he had barely thought of before.

"I'm okay... ish," he replied with tears in his eyes.

"Ohhh my god what do you mean 'ish' Alderson?" Rosie sounded almost panicked. "Jim, what's happened, tell me what has happened?" Another slightly panicked voice, this time Jenna.

"I'll be fine, if my heart holds out," he joked in his usual way.

"Jim that wasn't nice," Jenna replied, "you just scared poor Rosie again."

"Oh sorry, I will report now. There are several large marauding groups of people out there, one has just decided to disband. None with our organization or transport capabilities. Bigger problem, more fires. I will be a couple of hours coming back, I have two young ladies with me who will need medical and support. I might need some medical. Over."

"What do you mean, you need medical Jim?" Jenna asked sternly.

"Minor, I assure you. Trust me."

"Should we send Aidan and Jasmine to get you in the car?" Jenna asked getting worried, she knew Jim would underplay injuries to himself.

"Negative, too much risk. I have to walk the bike back because of the girls," he replied.

"Then give us your location just in case," Jenna insisted.

"Negative this is an open air transmission," Jim responded, remembering how the city government had previously listened to and honed in on transmissions. "Coming back now. Juju out."

Jim and the girls then headed down the hill. He was not very alert to anything at this time, exhausted from the adrenaline rushes, getting punched, stabbed, and shot. He snorted to himself, the only thing that that hadn't happened was he hadn't been pissed on yet. He wandered, leading the girls to a residential neighbourhood and started slogging through. It was probably not the wisest choice, but he was not sure about going on the big roads. That is where people waited in ambush, he didn't think he had another fight in him today.

He was wrong.

Jim could see a haze of smoke and smell the acrid scent of burned plastics, wood and maybe even burned hair. He did not want to think about it. The girls walked behind him a pace, hand in hand; he looked back every now and then to get make sure they were safe. They were scared shitless, who wasn't, he thought. They were wide-eyed and fearful of every sound. He rounded a corner on a sidewalk, suddenly experiencing a pain in his stomach and finding himself doubling over. It took a second for him to recognize a bat retreating from his gut. He heard his own air whooshing out in some bizarre movie slow-motion image. He felt himself being propelled forward. It took every ounce of willpower to force his arms up to slap down on the sidewalk to prevent a face-plant. He instinctively twisted to his side after he had hit. He saw one guy advancing on him with a bat and another at his feet. He saw the bat raised and he reached for the gun on his hip only to take a numbing shot to the arm with the bat.

The gun clattered out of his hand to the cement block, the rifle slipped off the other side.

At this point he became aware of intense screaming from the girls, then a crack and only one was screaming. The bat was raised again, he rolled quickly toward the guy's legs and grabbed on, this locked the legs and took the guy to the ground with a satisfying thump. He rolled up the body and delivered an elbow to the face of the guy under him.

As he was able to look around he saw the other guy bring a bat to threaten one of the girls. He knew the implication, give up or she gets hit. He raised his hands and heard the guy under him yelling "The fucker broke my fuckin' nose!" He repeated it three times.

Jim kept his hands high and went to kneeling then standing. He could now see Areen's bleeding nose. He seethed inside, he just needed the asshole to get close enough.

As he got up the complainer under him got up as well and scooped his arms to pin them behind his back. "Pound this fuck, Abe, he broke my fuckin' nose!"

Abe moved in a poked him in the gut with the bat hard, but not so hard when he was ready for it. Jim doubled up for effect and to bring the guy closer. The guy dropped the bat and started doing close punches to the stomach. After two Jim snapped his head up and caught Abe under the chin. Using the grip the other guy had on him to balance, he drove a kick into Abe's groin. Then when he returned his leg he stepped wide and fired his hand to the other guy's groin, not just hitting, but grabbing and squeezing as he stepped one leg behind and lifted. Mr. Busted Nose let him go and started slapping ineffectually.

Jim lifted high and drove to the ground where his elbow drove into the stomach. He rolled over the guy and delivered an elbow straight down on the guys broken nose with the head just lifted off the concrete. That was a double smack to the head. The guy was instantly limp. He pulled himself up just in time to see Arlene retrieving the Sig and pointing it at the other guy who was holding his groin.

"No!" Alderson screamed, but her finger was already squeezing the long trigger pull. As if in a movie, the time dilated and he saw the puff of smoke and heard the crack of the gun. He saw the recoil take the gun over her head, her tiny hands barely holding on. His gaze followed to Abe whose face was contorting in anguish as he moved a bloody hand away from his groin and started crumpling to the ground. She had shot his groin through his hand.

Abe started howling, Jim could now see him bleeding from the groin and the hand. Arlene looked at the gun and dropped it before Jim could get there. He got up, collected the gun, his rifle that had come off, and his pack that had been pulled off. He took the girls by the hands and started to move to the middle of the street. Abe would likely die, he didn't know about the other guy. He didn't care.

No words were spoken till they got away. Then he took out the radio and tried the mic: "This is Jim, I'm at Churchill, I could use rescue now." He waited and tried again. No reply.

It was going to be a long walk home and he felt weak. Too much adrenaline will kill you, he thought.

"Okay girls, I guess we are on our own, we need to start walking. We'll see if there is some food and water over at the mall." It was clear that the mall had been looted but it was quite likely there was something left. They went first to the drug store and there they found some candy and pop. He gave some to the girls. They ate and drank in silence. They moved to the Walmart, where Jim found some clothes for the girls. He found some packs for them and loaded some bottles of water and food into them and additional changes of clothes. In kitchen wares he found some knives for them, just in case. Sporting goods was already looted of knives.

The girls began to talk to each other after walking a while. When they crossed the main road on the overpass Alderson stopped to look around with binoculars. Looking west, at a couple of kilometres, he saw some moving motorcycles, one had what was likely an HA patch. They were moving quite slowly his direction.

People were giving up on being rescued by the authorities. The exodus and the violence would only increase, it was time to get out. "Girls, we have to go quickly now," Jim said. He double-checked all of his firearms, making sure they were fully loaded and safe.

"Where are you taking us? Will you take care of us?" Areen's sister asked. She then whispered something to her sister.

"I am taking you to a whole group of people who will help you and keep you safe, you can be with me and this whole bunch of people. They will be nice to you," Jim said.

"Arlene wants to know if we are sluts like those other guys said, and if we will have to do slut things." Areen said. "Will that man die? Was it bad when she shot him?"

Jim stopped, put a hand on each girls shoulder and looked them in the eyes in turn. "No, you do not have to do anything like those 'slut' things. I want you to live with our group, but if anyone ever hurts you or tells you to do something like that you have to tell me right away. Arlene, you had to shoot that man, he was very bad. You did the right thing." He hated telling the girl that shooting someone was the right thing to do, but it was. The world was different now, not so nice, you could not just call the police for protection.

"Will we have TV or computers?" Areen asked.

"I am sorry girls I cannot explain right now, but there is no TV, no internet, and no computers anymore," Jim answered. The world they knew was gone, it must be so much more foreign to them, at least older people knew what it was to live in a world with out those trappings.

They marched on. He was approached by a couple of groups but his demeanor usually ended their inquiries. He answered tersely and nobody pushed him, he was likely a grim and grizzly sight with blood on his naturally stern face, carrying a rifle at the ready, bearing two side-arms and a shotgun sticking out of his pack. Still he was cautious and gave a wide berth to blind corners.

They arrived first at his place, that was now abandoned. He went inside out of some sense of nostalgia and just to rest for a while before they made the trek down the hill to the river.

TWENTY THREE

"Do you live here Mr. Jim?" Arlene asked, "is it okay if I use the washroom?"

"Just a moment, then you can use the washroom," Alderson said as he went upstairs and scooped some water from the bathtub into the toilet tank. "Okay Arlene, you can use it now but there is no water for the taps."

She went in and used the toilet. Then flushed. She seemed thrilled with the idea that the plumbing worked, even though Jim knew that somewhere a sewer back up was going to be increased with each flush. They rested on the couch a while. First Areen, then Arlene, fell asleep. Jim didn't have the heart to wake them so he let them sleep. He thought he should call for help but Areen was resting her head on him so he would wake her if he did. He just sat and dozed too. His snoring must have woken Areen, she awoke with a start that awakened Alderson. When she woke she gave a little yelp and that woke Arlene as well.

"We don't have much farther to go, but we should go before dark," Alderson said.

"But it is comfortable, it feels good," Areen pleaded.

"Yes I know, but we will have to make a new home somewhere else and we will make it feel good too," Alderson said, hoping he was right.

They collected all the gear and started down the hill following the pathway. Jim had the girls go out front and he carried his rifle like he meant to use it. They proceeded westward looking at a beautiful sunset, the sun painting the light cloud cover crimson, with the purple and white caps of the Rockies in the background. Alderson thought, 'such beauty in such impending doom, mother earth she goes on, doesn't care about our petty problems.'

People they met were looking somewhat haggard, some carrying bags or packs of goods and probably returning to their homes. They all looked at Alderson like he was a monster crawled out of the black lagoon. He knew he must have been a sight, dried blood and dirt on his face, his shirt torn and bloody, blood streaming down his back and side. The girls were wearing new clothes but their beautiful thick black hair was a matted rat's nest, Jim did not want to imagine what might be in their hair after the unspeakable horrors they had been part of. For now all was good. He gave a half a thought to how it might look with the two girls walking in front of him, with him carrying the rifle, but he really didn't care what others were thinking. That was all solved when part-way back Arlene came back to him and held his left hand, making him hold the rifle with only his right, using the sling to keep it on.

As they approached the camp Jim could see that it was working like an ant colony. He noticed that there was likely an increased state of readiness. He saw the watcher posts seemed to be doubled. He hoped there hadn't been any trouble. He walked down the road to see that the post there had Rosie, Marc, and Jenna at it.

"Jim! Oh my god! Oh god, someone get help!" Jenna cried out.

Simultaneously Rosie yelled out, "Alderson, what the fuck happened to you! You look like shit." They both ran toward him when they saw him, both hugging him.

"I'm fine, never better, but we need to look after these girls. Get the psychologist woman and if Dr. Grosvenor is back get him, or the nurse," Jim said. Within a minute the nurse was coming with another person and a bag of supplies. Jim took her aside and told her quietly what he knew of what happened with the girls.

"Marc, how many of the scouts are back? Has something happened that you doubled the guards? Let's get key people together." Jim started giving orders as if he was an officer.

"Yeah we got a note from across the river. You need to see it," Marc said, pulling the note out of his pocket. "All the scouts except Ivan are back, and the doctor's team found a place with the agreement of the local farmer. Ivan said he would stay and be our exit scout, we can pick him up on the way."

The note was in poor handwriting but it was clear enough.

"We believe you have a criminal who stole from us and attacked our members with no cause. His name is Alderson, short, fat, stupid, bald, with a long goatee. Give him to us and live in peace. Tomorrow by midday.

Kevin O'Reilly

President

Hades Animals Calgary Chapter

PS You must also return the stolen bike we KNOW you have."

"Well he got the stupid part right, I should have shot the fuck," Jim said. "Have they tested defenses or anything? What do you think, if they have me they won't try anything?" Jim asked.

"Well let's get everyone in and you can hear all the reports, then we can plan. We have a good twelve hours if they are good to their word," Marc said.

Aidan, who had just walked up and heard the conversation, raised an eyebrow and looked at Marc like he had two heads. "I don't think they are in the business of keeping their word unless there is some benefit for them. Be ready tonight."

The group gathered around a campfire and all the scouts reported on what they had seen. Jim found Alex's report very interesting: that could be a problem if they crossed paths with the fanatics, they would be more intractable than the bikers -- well except maybe where he himself was concerned. The reporting from the scouts took an hour, the reporting of camp readiness to move was more positive and looked good to start moving. Some of the people expressed concern about moving while the bikers were planning to attack, they felt they would be more at risk if they were caught on the open road with the material. Some advocated attacking the bikers first. Some asked why Jim wasn't going to give himself to the bikers for the good of the group.

At the end when everyone was quiet Jim stood and talked. "I could give myself too them," he began. There were shocked expressions, and calls from some saying 'fuck that'. "Or I could try to leave, but I am sure that would not placate them. Or we can see what they will do, but I am most concerned they will hurt someone here, and no one needs to be hurt." There were murmurings of what to do, Alderson allowed it to continue for a few moments. Then he raised his hands.

"I think there is risk of a big conflict regardless of our path. I am going to try a risky path, I am going to try to talk with them, see if this Papa Bear will consider some other options. I have had a very, very bad day, and the one thing I know for sure is that this city is going to shit much faster than I imagined. So for now, keep a close watch and get those night optics out and see what we can see. I need some bandages and rest, and then we will see," Jim said. "There is a way out and we are not powerless."

He went with Jasmine who looked at his cuts, bruises, and various wounds. She carefully cleaned, stitched, and bandaged the knife wound. "Mr. Alderson, I know you have shown incredible foresight and perseverance in delivering people this far, but I have heard the story about what you did to Papa Bear, I think you won't be able to walk away unless you run tonight. Do you need some pain killers?" she asked sympathetically.

"No, it doesn't hurt that much, Polysporin should do the trick. Keep infection at bay," Alderson replied. "Even if I showed up dead the HA's are still going to be a threat to this group. The problem we have is we don't know how many they are and what weapons they have. I have to sleep to think of a way of dealing with the threat."

He went to his tent but before he could go to sleep he had a stream of people come, Carrie and Rosie were in tears telling him he could not give himself up, most of his close friends and people he had brought here came to say the same. Finally he went to bed, Jenna joined him. "Tell me what's wrong Jim, I know there is more going on with you right now. Tell me the story of what happened today," she questioned.

"I, well I killed two people and one was that same cop from before, that was an accident, but he is dead just the same. Jenna, he had a girlfriend or a wife somewhere," he took out the picture and showed her. He started sobbing, "I never in my life thought I would take someone's life."

"Was he with the two girls?" she asked, Jim just nodded.

"Then you saved two lives too, sometimes such things are necessary, you know that. You could not help what happened. He could have." Jenna held him for a while.

"I know, but it frightens me to my core, thinking about what I have become. I worry because I am also thinking of how to kill that Papa Bear. I just don't know how to handle that," Jim sobbed. Her being with him helped him eventually fall asleep, but his mind did not rest.

Alderson dreamt of a fight with Papa Bear where they traded blows and Jim had no effect; Papa Bear repeatedly hurt Jim, beating him at every turn. They were fighting amongst some houses in a cul-de-sac. Jim would run, but always be caught, he would fight and lose and Officer Mancha was there with a rope that he would tie around Jim's neck and pull him down whenever he tried to fight. Then Mancha and Papa Bear took Rosie and Jenna and Carrie and Jolene and repeatedly raped them while Jim watched but could do nothing because his neck was tied.

He woke several times is a fitful sweat. He knew the next day could be his undoing, he woke and decided he needed something to change his sleep. He went and found some booze and had a couple of shots. Hopefully the soporific effects of the booze would quell the dreams of doom and failure.

Eventually he slept with dreams no more. He awoke to daylight, based on this time of the year probably before seven a.m.. He was very stiff and sore and his nose hurt.

The camp was slowly arising. Within the hour there had been breakfast cooked and people were eating and people were asking what to do. He needed to talk to the watchers. He brought in all who had been on watch and asked what they had seen. The indications were that the bikers only kept people on the two bridges, two people on each. Armed but not threatening.

Jim asked the whole camp to join him. Even Rosie came and being up this early was unheard of for her. "We must make this camp ready to move out. We have a place to start, our scout team has found a farmer who needs hands and has a place we can build a village. We will be in a place where we can move in RV's, given some time. We have not shown the HA's what strength we have, but they may know. We have no less than eight scoped rifles and ten other rifles, plus shotguns and handguns, but going up against them will mean pain, suffering and probably death. I do not want that. We must prepare the camp to move but not do so until the bikers are distracted. I realize we cannot move everyone and the gear at once so in the first load I will ask the women to go with what gear can be taken, then the others will leave in a later run. I ask this because the women are without a doubt a target for the bikers." He paused a moment.

"I will seek to talk with Papa Bear and see what we can come to. I do not want to engage him but such a meeting might provide the distraction we need, his club will want to watch and know what to do. They won't likely move without his okay. My problem right now is to find a suitable place to meet," Jim finished, looking for suggestions. There were none forthcoming.

Jim told Marc to arm everyone he could and sit and be ready. The tactical problem was that the enemy could come from two or even three places, and to watch and defend all three would mean splitting forces, yet the enemy could concentrate forces in one spot. Marc set up a sniper on either side of the main bridge to get a good view of anything coming across.

Jim armed himself and got a white flag. By the time he walked to the bridge the bikers had a dump truck on the other side ready to start pushing the dead cars. Alderson waved the flag, hoping there would be a positive response. Then the hauler started to back up and Alderson thought they were calling back the offensive. But it was a ruse, the truck roared and came crashing forward, pushing the cars along in a cascade of screaming steel; sparks flew from the pavement where the car groaned and dragged against it. A moment after the impact there were people popping up in the box of the truck and shooting. Jim ran for cover as another shot rang out and the truck stopped, someone had managed a shot on the driver. Shots spanged off the sides of the box, hunting rounds were deforming and stopping on the steel sides. Even full-metal jacket rounds went only through the first layer then rattled around in the second, but it kept heads down. Jim estimated five guys in the truck box.

Other shots rang out from across the river, then from the collective's side. More popped up shots, then a shot and a spray of blood and bone from the truck, a sniper had killed one in the truck. At that, some guys hiding inside started leaping over and ran back to the biker's side of the river. Jim took the opportunity to move back to the camp area where most unarmed people were cowering and hiding. The armed ones were doing not much better. Fire continued across the river, ineffectual on both sides.

Jim found Marc, "What do you think?" Jim asked.

"I think they are pinning us and doing something else, I don't know what it is," Marc said. No sooner had he said that than they heard a scream from by the foot bridge.

They both ran, others were running too. They got there to seen Angela being held by Papa Bear with a knife to her neck. He had five of his gang with him armed with automatic rifles. Jim stepped out, several of the Collective had shown up with rifles and were taking positions. No one felt confident they could make a shot like that.

"You know it is me you want, you don't want to hurt a pretty girl like that Papa Bear," Jim said. "You want me don't you, not her. If you are any kind of a man you will let her go," Jim badgered.

"Fuck you, I am going to see you die slowly asshole, but

I might just fuck your friends first," Papa Bear threatened.

"Look if anything goes wrong here there is going to be a lot of lead in the air and that won't be good for anyone, will it? We have more weapons than you see," Alderson countered. "If it is me you want you will have to give her up, or you might have to give up your goal of watching me die slowly. I thought bikers were tough. Take me on!" Jim hollered, "What's wrong, you pull your balls off with a string?"

That infuriated Papa Bear remembering the humiliation that Alderson had caused him. He grabbed Angela by the hair and yanked her to Pinky who stood with him saying, "If anything goes wrong, kill her first." Angela shrieked and cried. Pinky held her close with a hand on her hair and one feeling her breast, just to humiliate her.

Papa Bear, purple with rage, came at Alderson, covering the distance in just a few bounding steps. As Alderson saw the livid rage in his opponent, he began calming down. He had a gun but he knew to go for it would mean being shot by the others. Papa Bear was not going for his either, nor his knife. This was going to start unarmed, just the way Alderson preferred it.

Alderson got his hand up in a defensive posture and Papa Bear came at him wildly. Papa Bear was a match for him, equal in size, but Papa Bear had likely seen many more real and more brutal fights. Alderson's experience was mostly practice.

The first two punches were wild haymakers, Alderson just ducked under them, an energy-taxing strategy but one that was harder for the opponent to recover from. After two punch attempts Papa Bear was going to grab and punch. Alderson blocked the punch and used the grip to step in and deliver a return blow to the side of the head. He moved to attempt a throw but Papa Bear was not off-balance enough and Alderson had to retreat from the attempt.

Papa Bear pulled in and went for a head butt but Alderson ducked in, presenting the top of his head. O'Reilly howled in pain on making contact – he let go and backed off.

They circled for what seemed minutes, but was in reality seconds. Alderson waited, O'Reilly provided. This time a straight jab, Jim caught it on his hands and side stepped, not quite enough to get in.

"Come on dick, are you too much a pussy to punch me, not so easy now is it," O'Reilly taunted.

Jim just circled, he would play his game. The adrenaline rush was exhausting, O'Reilly was likely more comfortable and likely had his adrenaline under control. O'Reilly stepped in and faked a punch, gauging Jim's reaction. Jim attempted the block but missed, so he pressed in and drove a hard elbow, making contact with O'Reilly's chest. Not ideal, but a solid hit. O'Reilly stumbled back a bit, air whooshing out of his lungs.

Jim pressed the attack on a slim advantage, O'Reilly had opened his guard. Jim threw a jab-cross-hook combo with a right-hand lead. This southpaw stance caught O'Reilly off-guard and he took the jab and the light hook. This enraged O'Reilly. He began punching furiously, driving Alderson back on defence.

Alderson tried to cover up, but took a few to the body. The ones in the stomach didn't bother him much; he pulled down after the first rib shot. O'Reilly pulled him in and drove a knee up, the knee hit in Jim's chest and driving the wind out of him, O'Reilly tried again to knee Jim in the face, but Alderson was able to block using the point of his elbow, causing some pain to O'Reilly.

O'Reilly wrapped his arm around Jim's neck from the top side in the guillotine choke and started to apply pressure, jerking upward. The choke was inexpertly done, Jim stepped in and drove his arm and hand into his opponent's groin, repeating the action and the second time attempting to grab and squeeze O'Reilly's balls.

O'Reilly made the sound of a bear in pain but he loosened his grip. Jim stepped deep inside and scooped both legs, dropping O'Reilly hard on the packed gravel surface. Then he quickly drove a knee toward the groin, but as he did it he slipped on the gravel. Papa Bear, moaning in pain, turned to the side, kicking Alderson over onto the gravel and giving Alderson mild road rash.

O'Reilly proved his resilience as he quickly rolled with his falling opponent, landing on top of Jim. He immediately started raining down punches, with some connecting, as Jim moved to protect himself. Jim tried to scoop and control some of the strikes but was not very successful, so he planted his feet and bucked O'Reilly forward. Papa Bear put out his hand and stopped the fall and was ready to go back to pounding, but he did not realize Alderson had slipped one hand under his leg and was able to lift and turn out, turning O'Reilly over, coming up between his legs.

This was a fighting position Alderson knew very well. He drove forward, bending O'Reilly's leg and applying pressure. As he spun to the side, he reached up and grabbed the collar of O'Reilly's colours to apply a choke. As he turned, he tried to drive a knee up, catching his opponent only lightly on the side of the head.

Jim immediately popped up, putting a knee on O'Reilly's solar plexus. Holding the biker's lapel, he delivered punches to O'Reilly's face. Unfortunately Jim had never trained on the slippery rolling gravel that was underfoot, so when Papa Bear jerked toward him he slipped off. Jim immediately backed up.

With a second to breathe, he looked around and saw Pinky had transferred Angela to another biker. People were engrossed in the fight, and did not notice what Pinky was doing.

O'Reilly got up, nose bleeding, head and face scraped, Jim imagined he didn't look any better. They circled again, Jim worked the fight to the grassier area hoping it would provide more purchase. Papa Bear came at him enraged, swinging with a wild left haymaker, which Jim blocked easily. At the same time he stepped in and struck with his elbow, catching Papa Bear on the chin, again it was a lighter shot but it stunned O'Reilly who staggered back; Alderson was not quick enough to capitalize on that success.

O'Reilly screamed in rage and came in drawing his knife and thrusting in, it was all Jim could do to avoid and parry the thrust, he had no chance of controlling the knife at that point. As O'Reilly withdrew the knife it cut Alderson's arm. O'Reilly missed his mark, but recovered with a vicious backswing. This was easy for Jim to block and immediately he slid down the arm, gaining control of the hand and the eight inch Kabar. O'Reilly felt this and tried to jerk the knife forward and away. Jim did not resist but followed, added his push, and guided the knife hand toward Papa Bear's midsection.

By the time Papa Bear realized what happened the knife slipped just past the leather vest and embedded itself an inch under the ribcage. Alderson gave it an additional push with all his mass, driving it in to the hilt as the shocked Papa Bear let go completely. Alderson backed up, shocked. He had not expected an end to the fight like that.

The knife had punctured a lung. Papa Bear looked down at it, looked up, coughed once with a gout of his blood spraying Alderson's face, then staggered three steps backward and fell coughing three more times before expiring. Jim watched in stunned silence.

Alderson felt a pain in his face, his ribs, his hip where he had landed on his gun, which was amazingly still there. He looked up at the faces of the bikers, they were stunned, confused and enraged.

The one holding Angela acted. He took his knife out

with his right hand while holding her with his left, Jim started to yell "NO!" as the biker drove the knife in her back and under her ribs as he pushed her away. Insane fury took Jim as he drew the gun and fired two shots to the body and one to the head of the biker, just as he had practiced so many times in IDPA competition. All were hits and the biker died long before he hit the ground.

Other bikers started to raise their guns, Jim fired one round at each of the three other bikers, hitting one in the arm, the others scattering. Jim ran forward holstering his gun. Marc showed up right behind him as they caught Angela staggering forward. They hauled her behind the nearest trees as a hail of gunfire erupted around them. Jim heard the sounds of agony as others got hit. He did not know on which side.

"Hold on girl, we have a doctor, coming," Jim said, pressing a hand against the wound in her back. It was bleeding way too much; she was losing colour fast, getting weaker by the second. Jim kept cradling her and holding his hand on the wound. Marc was yelling for the doctor.

The doctor came running a moment later. Alderson was crying. "I'm so sorry I got you into this," he kept repeating to Angela, holding her. She was already unconscious when the doctor got there, Jim didn't even notice the sounds of gunfire had ceased. The doctor looked at Angela, checked her pulse, looked at the pool of blood Jim was sitting in and tried to look at the wound. He just shook his head sadly to Jim, but Jim already knew she would not make it, even if they had a trauma ward minutes away, she would have bled out. The knife had cut a major artery going to the liver. Alderson sat crying and holding her for a good twenty minutes. People came by putting their hands on him compassionately. But when Di, Carrie, and Jolene came, the scene was heart-wrenching to the extreme. They all knew her, liked her, and cared about her. They lost all thought of the larger situation around them.

The doctor was called to two others, one died shortly after as well, this was a person who had taken a shot to the chest – a person who had only been with the group for a day or two. The third wound was Arya who had been shooting back at the bikers across the river, she had taken a .223 bullet in the forearm and then fallen out of the blind she was in, breaking the same arm. The doctor was able to set the arm and patch the wound. She should recover fully.

Alex, who had been the sniper responsible for stopping the truck and taking out one of the people in the box, came back after an hour. He was completely unaware of what had happened, his post had been away from the camp with the view of the main bridge, everyone had forgotten he was out there. The camp was still in disarray. He came back and directed some people to continue the watch. He could see that Jim was of no use, Marc was with him.

Eventually a walker with a white flag approached across the bridge. Alex greeted them, but only from cover, he did not trust the bikers.

When Alex asked what she wanted, the young girl announced: "Pinky Finnegan, President of the Hades Animals of Calgary, grants you 6 hours to leave, then there will be all out war."

Alex laughed out loud. "Tell your 'Pinky' we will go only if and when we want to." The girl's reaction shocked Alex, she started to cry, "Please don't make me go back please let me stay."

Alex could not think of what to do so he called to her, "Run, Run over here quick!"

She did and as she did a shot rang out behind her, but it missed her. Alex thought, 'As I suspected they were covering her, but didn't want her to leave.' He was wary of the girl, she could be a plant to gather intel, but he would let others worry about that at a later date. For now the organizing of the move was falling to him. Jason, Aidan, and White Eagle would lead the team out.

It took another two hours to load the camp, someone had recovered the guns of the bikers and there was talk of retrieving the dump truck. Alex suggested they try that only after everything else was ready to go. He was surprised the bikers hadn't tried already, in fact he found that suspicious.

The people seemed to be moving slowly, there was an air of fear, anger, and trepidation about moving to a rural place away from the imagined security of the city. Everyone had accepted that they would have to move, very few wanted to do it yet.

TWENTY FOUR

"To live is to suffer, to survive is to find some meaning in the suffering."

- Friedrich Nietzsche

"Before we leave I want us to honour our fallen." Jim addressed the group that was near him, consoling those who knew those who had died. Jim hated death, he hated the world. He was a wreck, incapable of speaking for Angela. That fell to Jolene as the person who knew her best.

It was a very difficult event burying two people. Jolene started a tearful eulogy. "This crazy world, the events of six days ago just happened to leave Angela and I at work with our friend and colleague, Jim, and that was our good luck. Angela had no family here, I had only my dogs. Jim asked us to go with him, he had knowledge and foresight about what was coming. At first we were shocked at the things he engaged in to survive, because surviving did not seem so difficult at first. He never told us that things would be easy or that he had all the answers. Angela knew it was risky, she also knew that alone it would be a riskier, far more difficult time.

Angela loved people, she loved the kids we worked with. But she was smart and she knew deep down, as I did, that Jim was right – we had to go with him.

Some may think that Angela's untimely death was brought on by Jim's actions, but he angered the gang because he stood up for what was right, Angela knew this. She said to me even just yesterday that we were so lucky to have someone who stepped in front of the inhumanity that was going to develop as the crisis deepened. Yes he could have killed that biker the first time they met, but that was the important difference. Angela agreed with his choice not to. She knew there were risks but she also knew Jim was doing what was right, what was necessary. I didn't get to see her at the end ..." at this point she stopped and cried, many joined her.

"I'm sorry, it is too raw right now. I did not get to see her at the end, but I know she did not blame Jim or anyone else here. She would want people to live, to survive and most of all work together. It bothered her that those people across the river were being controlled by a gang of thugs, but she did not think violence was the answer. She remarked just this morning that if she could get to talk with their leader perhaps something could be worked out so everyone would be happy. That was her, she always had the positive outlook, she always knew there was a better way. But she was wise enough to know that sometimes others would not choose the better path. Let us lay her to rest knowing that she was whole-heartedly behind this enterprise, that she wanted everyone to survive and live life. She was the one person looking somewhat forward to an outdoor way of life. She loved the outdoors, she loved nature. She was sad to see the suffering the EMP created but she was never sad to be leaving the city. I know that she cared passionately about all of this group. Those she did not know personally, she cared for as part of her adopted community. Even though she had no experience with 'taking watch' or shooting a gun, or any of the tactical things people talked about, she volunteered to be part of it because she new it was important for the group. I know she will live on as an example to the rest of us. Angela, I love you." She turned away, crying.

There were no dry eyes in the audience. They then listened to the farewell for Simon, a guy who had only joined the group a couple of days ago with his girlfriend when they travelled by and knew this group had a plan and they could contribute to it. His girlfriend gave a quiet but loving send off. She did not cry but spoke so softly it was as if the crowd did not even breathe so they could hear it, again people cried.

Aidan stood there remembering Alice and how he did not even get to grieve her properly. His grief was his and he could not share it. He stood there with his arm around young Di, the person who most understood his loss as she had suffered loss as well. So few days and yet so much death and loss. He was not sure he wanted to continue to see everything get worse. He knew it would. He thought about Di, this was devastating for her, a week ago she had two parents and Angela was teaching her phys. ed, now those people were ripped from her life in most unnatural ways. She would need a lot of support in the future, he was old, and tough, he would survive. He worried about the little girl, he thought back to the woman and the younger girl he met that first day and he wondered how they were doing.

Jim watched the proceedings and cried. He sat there between Jenna, Rosie and Carrie and stared blankly, wondering why he was in charge, why had this happened? He should have just taken off with Jenna and his close friends and found a place to quietly live out his life. Then he looked around and thought, most of these people still had no concept of the horrors that awaited. It was going to get worse; he didn't know if he could bear that.

The first run took two more hours to get to location and unload. People met first with the farmer who directed them to a chunk of land somewhat near the creek, but far enough back that latrines would not pollute the water. This chunk of land had several copses of trees and would make a good community. It did not easily meet the requirement of defensibility but that was secondary, some defences could be built over time.

The farmstead itself had a metal Quonset with farm vehicles in it so this farm could still operate, but it was not a cereal grain farm, it was mixed. They did not have a big combine, but the farmer had some equipment and the Quonset would hold more. Isaiah was a very young farmer, with a wife, Sandra, and child of just three. He was eager to be part of the community and learn what had gone on. Like most farmers he had a few firearms, but he wasn't a hunter and not very skilled with the guns. He had a well but his pump had stopped working when the EMP happened. Luckily he had a generator inside his Quonset and that was operating, but he was draining diesel to keep it running. He had gas, and diesel tanks for the farm, but these were not topped up being that it was early in the year. He would run out of diesel for the generator within a few days.

Isaiah and his wife came out to meet everyone and help with the tent city. The camp was set up with two camp circles of tents arranged around two fire pits. Wood for cooking would become an issue but Isaiah noted there were woods around where quite a bit of dead wood could be found. That was a concern for later, today was just get set up.

- - - - -

Back in the camp the tension was high and the mood was dour, sombre, and touchy. At one point, one of the watchers fired a shot at the bridge when he saw a lone person approach, nobody was in any mood to give quarter or leeway to anyone from across the river. Ten armed people covered the camp as people packed and prepared to leave. The biggest thing left to move was supplies. Jim and Aidan sat watch without speaking, both in a grim and destructive mood. As the last load was being readied, the unmistakable rumbling of Harleys came from across the river. They saw bikes approaching the bridge. Everyone started to take aim, calling

370

out their shots.

One of the bikers stopped his bike and dismounted. He started waving a white flag, and proceeded across the bridge on foot. He was yelling something but no one could quite hear him at first. As he got closer he could be heard saying he was unarmed and he wanted someone to come talk with him. "I wouldn't send anyone there, make him come here," Aidan said. Jim nodded agreement.

Jim called out, "You can come over here behind these trees." Jim moved deeper in cover and drew his handgun, he was in not mood to take chances.

The biker who came forward wasn't even a prospect, he was a nobody or in disguise, Jim assumed a nobody.

The biker started talking, "I come here to speak for the Calgary Hades Animals." Jim listened. "Pinky Finnegan is now in charge by selection of his peers, he demands you release the bodies of the dead, and the colours and bike belonging to the late President Papa Bear O'Reilly. These remain property of the Hades Animals Motorcycle Club." The biker wanna-be finished and waited.

"Why is it that he sends un-patched people to negotiate? You have no say in club business. You cannot negotiate, you are completely expendable, all you can do is deliver demands," Jim scoffed at him. "You can deliver my counter-demands. First, he should free those who do not wish to be part of his rule. Second, he can have the bodies, when we are gone. Third, the colours and bike are spoils of war and will remain with us. Fourth, any attempt to set foot on either bridge before four hours is up will result in us opening fire without warning. Did you get all that? Oh and one more thing. If he has anything more he wishes to say, he needs to send a patched member. I hate pussies who hide behind underlings, anyone else coming across the bridge will result in us opening fire. Please feel free to quote me."

The guy gulped and then forced himself to look defiant. "Well you are fucking with the wrong people, he will find you if you fuck him," the messenger said.

"Yup, Papa Bear found me too," Jim said as he whipped the pistol up and poked it at the biker's forehead with a little force. "I won't shoot the errand boy … this time. But if you want to come looking for us, you don't have much time. Go home now!"

The messenger squeaked out, "I'm unarmed, I'm unarmed," shaking adrenaline. Jim lowered the gun and stepped back. The messenger turned and walked very quickly. Jim thought 'at least he didn't piss himself'.

They continued packing the last of their goods. Ninety minutes later they were running one of the ATVs up on the flatbed when Aidan came and said, "Do we want to do anything about the dump truck? We could attempt to get it."

"Mmm it would be nice but I think the risk is too high, we don't know what kind of snipers they have set up. I think we should destroy it, shoot the gas tank then Molotov it. What do you think?" Jim suggested.

Marc was standing nearby, "You really want to make enemies with this gang don't you?" he said smiling.

"That ship has already sailed," Jim said. "I am sure we can find other haulers. We have a mechanic and a fair cache of goods. Get a bottle and a rag. I will throw the Molotov." They proceeded to make a Molotov cocktail. Alderson grabbed a lighter and laid in wait undercover, he hoped he could make the throw. Alex aimed and took a couple of shots, puncturing two holes in the truck's fuel tanks and watching the diesel drain onto the pavement. One of the shots was perfectly placed near the bottom of the tank. Mark took a shot at the pavement hoping to create a spark, he did but it was not sufficient to ignite the diesel. Jim took the half-filled pasta jar, lit the rag, and heaved it onto the bridge.

Unfortunately he hit higher on the truck, the gas on the truck ignited but the rag stuck in the step on the truck's side.

Just at that moment gunfire came from behind Alderson. He dropped on the ground and looked, it was his guys firing. He crawled back to the tree cover and got up and looked. The bikers were trying to advance on the bridge. It looked like two were down, others were dropping to the ground and crawling, covered by the sides of the bridge. They were advancing on the dumper, they probably had intention of rescuing it. They waited, it seemed a while, then Jim heard a whoosh of big flames erupting and saw the diesel on the ground light. The tanks in the truck would likely go up soon. Four Bikers got up and ran, Jim's guys kept firing, hitting at least one.

"Okay guys, let's fly outta here," Jim said as he ran for the motorcycle. Aidan jumped in a truck with a bunch of the other guys, Marc took the flatbed with people in the box at the back, everyone kept their guns at the ready and they sped out. Just as they hit the bridge the radio crackled, it was Ivan on lookout: "Guys you have four bikes heading for Stoney moving quick".

"Copy that Lookout," Jason replied. He was riding in the cab of the flatbed with Marc. Jim was riding out front. Marc blew the air horn, Jim looked back and slowed. "Bikers coming down!" Jason yelled.

Alderson waved the flatbed forward. "Take the lead. Start shooting well before you get there!" he yelled as the truck passed him. In the back was one guy with a .223 carbine type semi auto, one bolt-action, and one lever-action, three rifles might be able to drive them off. Chances of making a hit were slim in a moving vehicle, but it could be scary. Jim readied the pistol-grip shotgun and then pulled in behind the trucks, last in line. Just to infuriate the bikers, he wore Papa Bear's colours.

The flatbed geared up and jumped forward as Marc gave

it all he could. This road was clear enough. There were a couple of bikers with bikes to one side, guns out and aiming. The guys in the flatbed started shooting. The bikers shot one bullet that passed through the wooden box on the flatbed. Mark aimed the truck straight at the bikers, but he was still 400 metres away. One of the bikers broke and ran to the other side. Aidan in the truck behind aimed for him. The guys in the truck now had a line of fire, and shot. Marc started swerving to avoid an easy shot, however that also meant his guys could not get a clean shot. At 150 metres the bikers became nervous and only one kept shooting, he hit the truck in the cab and winged Jason in the arm.

Jason screamed, Marc jerked his head toward Jason and veered the truck sharply, glancing off the wall, jolting everyone in the truck. They now careened straight toward two big-eyed bikers, the fourth biker had got up on the wall to avoid being hit.

Guys in each vehicle dropped their rifles and picked up shotguns. Shooting as they closed distance, one biker was hit but with bird shot at thirty yards, not enough to kill him – but enough to stop him from continuing right now. The biker who had got on the wall shot at them with a rifle, but the recoil pushed him back, he rocked but had nowhere to put a foot down. The rifle twirled up almost like the beginning of a gun drill, he went backward off the wall, it was a long way to scream before hitting the river.

The convoy roared past, one biker was taking aim on the last truck as it passed when Jim rode up on the bike and, taking the shotgun in his left hand, fired a wild shot. He was shooting buckshot, some pellets hit the guys bike, but one at least hit him in the leg and he folded like a paper doll. The convoy sped away.

They approached Ivan on lookout at the cell tower, the flatbed pulled in, the others followed. There were two injuries, Jason's did not seem serious but he had passed out, the bullet left a fragment in his arm. Aidan and another guy worked quickly to bandage him before moving on. The other guy had fallen when they swerved and been knocked unconscious by hitting his head on the lifting gear.

They just laid him down and did what they could. "Guys, time to move, but we need a rear guard to make sure it is not easy for them to follow us," Aidan said. "Jim I would suggest you double someone and use the bike, easiest to hide.

"Aidan can you do it? I'm hurting, can you take that duty?" Jim asked, he would love the comfort of a truck cab. He had taken a beating in the last couple of days and he was not as young as he once was, he needed rest.

"Yeah sure, I'll take Eric with me and a radio. We'll set up on the overpass," Aidan answered as they armed up with the semi auto carbine, a scoped rifle, and two shotguns with buckshot. They rode out fast, ahead of the rest of the team.

The group drove out. This required more time as they had to dodge some dead vehicles but there was plenty of space with the wide shoulders and the fact that many people had rolled over to the side when their cars died. The total trip only took them thirty minutes.

Aidan reported that in that thirty minutes they did not see any bikers, but they would hold on until early evening as they had seen a bike crest one hill then turn back; they could be using watchers to determine where the convoy turned.

The remainder of the team roared into the farm. Isaiah was waiting. He had not yet met Alderson or the most key people of the group. Seeing a guy jump off the bike wearing biker colours threw him for a loop. He had heard the stories, but it was still jarring. "You must be Jim, I hope?" Isaiah asked nervously, holding out his hand.

"Guilty," Alderson answered, shaking Isaiah's hand.

"I'm Isaiah, this is my land. I understand you are the

leader of this community. But why, may I ask, are you wearing that?" he said pointing to the colours.

"Umm thats a long story, but thank you for having us. I am not a biker though," Jim replied.

"I want to invite you to the house so we can talk," Isaiah said, looking more relieved as Alderson stripped the colours off and draped them over the Harley.

They chatted as they walked toward the house. "Even though this is my land, I am willing to live with the group by the groups rules, I know I cannot run or defend this without the strength of community. I see you have the support of a diverse group and I hope you have a system that will allow the development of a functional society, at least on a small scale. I only reserve the right to keep my home for myself and my family, although I feel we should be able to build a good clinic for the doctor there as well."

"We are very happy to be here Isaiah. I would hope that you will join our leadership team as you have the knowledge of producing food that will be critical for survival. I pledge that while I act as the *de facto* leader of this group you will always have control of your home and we will work to protect this land and what is yours, as if it were ours. We will work together in all things," Jim said, it was almost like a statement of fealty. It was meant to convey to everyone that they were in it together and anyone accepted to the group would be accorded the protections of the group.

Aidan had been checking in regularly and had indicated no activity until they were getting ready to leave, at that point they noticed two bikes going to the lookout point the collective had used. The bikes stopped there and surveyed. Aidan looked with the optics and saw the bikers scanning with binoculars. He and Eric remained very hidden, Aidan occasionally popping up for a look. The bikes were coming their way, one was a Harley, the other some other crotch-rocket type road bike. The bikers were driving into the lowering sun making their vision more difficult.

"Eric here is how we will do this. We will get to the far side of the overpass. When they pass under we will pop up and hit them with the shotguns, if we miss and they move away we use the rifles," Aidan said.

Eric nodded. "Okay, I sure don't like the idea of killing these guys, but I guess we have to."

"Eric, they did not have to follow us, they could leave well enough alone, but they won't do that. Even this is not likely to be the last time we deal with them as a group. For now it is just these two. I hope," Aidan added in a resigned tone.

The bikes came along, the only noise on the highway, their slowing was obvious. Aidan knew they were going to take this overpass, they had not seen where the group had gone. That was good news. "Eric! They're coming up here!" Aidan whispered loudly. "Get ready." As the bikes slowed to make the cloverleaf turn. Aidan popped up. The first one had passed but he took the other with a shotgun blast almost to the top of the skull. Curious, he thought, just because there were no rules bikers must have thought helmets were no value – this guy had no helmet and the shotgun blast coming down from above caused his skull to vapourize gruesomely leaving a headless rider to wipe the bike out, sliding and spinning down the highway. Aidan noticed the full patch, the ranks of the 81s were thinning.

Eric shot at the other rider but missed. The guy must have caught the action out of the corner of his eye; he swerved off the embankment and came to a stop out of sight behind the ramp. Aidan immediately started advancing in a crouch with the shotgun ready. The biker popped up with a handgun in hand. Aidan shot but the guy had seen him and ducked again. Then a gun clattered out, "I surrender, I give up! Don't shoot!"

"Come up with fingers laced on top of your head then," Aidan yelled as he jacked in another round. The biker complied. This was no Patch member but just some hang-around, no partial patch even. "Face down on the pavement. Eric, if he moves shoot him in the head," Aidan said harshly.

Aidan went down the road to see the other biker, when he saw the body up close he shivered and vomited. It was completely unnerving to see what happens with a close range shotgun blast to the top of the head. Aidan looted the guy, removed the patch, and moved the bike to the ditch, it had not taken that much damage and they could send the flatbed for it. It would also not do to leave it where the bikers could find what happened to it. They now had two more handguns, and another set of binoculars and some other incidentals including some weed.

"Search that guy," Aidan instructed Eric. After vomiting from what he had seen, he could not just shoot this guy. He made a blindfold, and used shoe laces to secure his hands. "Eric can you ride a motorbike?" Aidan asked.

"Sure, nothing quite like a Harley," he replied.

Aidan called in. "Base, this is Aidan I have one of their scouts, the other is not a problem anymore. We will be bringing one man in."

"Do you need transport?" someone at the base asked, it sounded like Kareem.

"Negative, he provided."

"Hold for Okay on bringing him back," Kareem responded.

"He will be blindfolded. Over and out," Aidan returned.

"Eric, prisoner number one here is going to ride with you. I am riding behind and if anything goes wrong I am going to kill him," Aidan said. They mounted up and left.

They returned to the camp where Marc and White Eagle took charge of the prisoner. They cuffed him and chained him to a tree. They would question him and find out what he knew. They were not sure what to do, no one in the group had real experience extracting information from people, well at least not 'enemies'. There were no 'tough guys', no soldiers, no cops in the group. The closest was Marc and he was not the type; he knew how to use the information but not how to collect it.

Jim thought about the scariest torture he had ever seen in a movie and thought he would try the idea, he would never lower himself to the torture, but he might let the prisoner think he would.

Jim and Aidan sat around with the prisoner while they talked about various tortures, at one point Aidan quipping, "If he doesn't cooperate and he were to die he won't even make much soap, not enough fat on him." Jim laughed, it was a private in joke from their discussions many years ago when they had mused about disposing of people. The laugh and the comment had enough effect the prisoner.

"Okay look, I'll tell you what you want to know," he whimpered. "Papa Bear, er now Pinky has about ten patch members and some prospects who will now move up. Each Patch is allowed only one prospect."

"They need more people than that," Jim said, glowering at the scared flunky.

"Papa Bear expected each patch to recruit ten soldiers, so far they were only about half that, I think. They are systematically controlling the food in the area, they have the two grocery stores, but have little control of the water because of the river, but if you don't boil it, it will likely kill you."

"How are they keeping people under control?" Aidan asked, fingering his knife blade.

"They have been executing those who show any disrespect or are slightly out of line. They're holed-up in the high school and their bunker which was EMP-proof. I saw about fifty weapons of their own but they were trying to take others in the area by force. They met with some resistance and several recruits got killed. I think they are going to need other food supplies though."

Jim and Aidan looked at the hapless prisoner. "How did you get recruited?" Jim asked.

"Um, when I saw them pushing people out, older people they thought useless, I figured it was the only game in town. Just survival that's all," he answered as he looked back and forth from Jim to Aidan. "And ya' know, I'm sure they are going to come after you again," he added.

"Yeah, so am I." Jim added, "So what is this Pinky like?"

"The guys thought Pinky was good as the Sergeant-at-Arms, but he is fuckin' nuts, doesn't know when to quit, ya know. He is like a rabid dog with a bone. Hey man, I gave up, didn't shoot at you .. like, can I join you guys, I'll work for you and everything," the prisoner begged.

"Well, you will be a prisoner, until we decide to put you on probation, and after that you will only be a member when we decide you have shown loyalty to the Collective in a dire circumstance," Jim replied. "That could be a while."

Aidan arranged for two others to go set up a watch at the highway. It was important to keep tabs on who came and went. There would be a lot of foot traffic going that way and they would need to keep watch on who they were -- some would be useful, some would be dangerous, all would be desperate.

People had set up the camp and prepared food. Everyone sat down to eat, talk, and decompress. It was a sombre place.

Jim thought about how they had come here and how this was only the first step in a very long trek for survival. He wondered what was going on elsewhere, how things were in the USA that had likely been the primary target, how communities that were not affected would be reacting, would they isolate or try to help. The unaffected communities were not the industrial or transport bases, they were at best resource-extracting communities. What would they even do with their resources now? If the unaffected tried to help they would be outnumbered by the affected by hundreds or thousands to one. Before he could sleep there was a duty he had to take care of. After everyone had eaten he invited everyone to meet.

"I wanted everyone to be here. I know we have said this would not be democratic to start, we needed action not much debate. That said a leader must be responsible for his actions. I fucked up."

There were murmurs from the crowd. Some seemed to agree, others cried, some denied.

"I made decisions that got two of ours killed. Primarily due to poor personal decisions. I did not want to get my hands dirty with murder. But I failed on that too and I have killed at least four people. I have now left powerful enemies in our wake. This is not a good record for a leader. I must ask at this point that all of you think on my decisions and know if you want to continue with such a leader."

First stone silence, so quiet coyotes could be heard in the distance. Then a rumbling. Then White Eagle stood. "I will speak my mind. I have heard from others mostly about the things you have done. It speaks to me of incredible determination and foresight. The world leadership has failed us first. If I had been in your place I would have hoped to have made the same decisions you did, but I would not have had the confidence and skill to have survived those harrowing situations. You made good decisions, for good reasons, and there were some bad outcomes. From my perspective I would have had a much more difficult time knowing what to do without your leadership. I stand with you."

Ivan stood next, he did not even know all of the decisions but spoke anyway. "Jim, you have earned the enmity of a powerful, violent gang, I understand you may have earned the enmity of the law. That puts us all at risk. What I don't know is, are we at greater risk because of those things than we would have been floundering on our own? I don't know and cannot know what I would have done differently. We live in hell and some horrors came our way. I am not sure we can hold those to you. I see no one else who has shown the necessary forethought to lead us yet. I stand with you."

After these two Rosie, Jenna, and Carrie just came to Jim and hugged him. Eventually Isaiah stood and said, "I am lucky, I have not experienced the horrors you have, but what I see as an outsider is that Jim has your confidence at this time. I am impressed by such loyalty among strangers and I think this community has a future in a messed up world. I am so glad you were first on my doorstep and not the man who formerly owned that bike," he finished, pointing at Papa Bear's Harley.

"I am not sure I should thank you all for your support," Alderson said. "I am not sure I should be here. But tomorrow will bring more planning and work, but I think we have some safety here. I wish for everyone to get what rest you can," he finished, his eyes welling with tears at being accepted even with his flaws.

As the group dispersed back to their tents, most people stopped to offer Jim their personal support, condolences, and heart-felt friendship. It shocked him in a very emotional way. But soon he had to leave to seek recovery from the emotional drain, to find a moments peace.

Jim could not shut his brain down. On a local scale there were going to be months of daily hard work. This would be an ongoing struggle, but today's battle was won. There was a great cost; battle always involved cost. Jim slumped as he thought, he could not even carry on a conversation. He was numb. He needed to sleep now or he would never be able to lead this group into the future. He was completely overwhelmed with the requirements of what would be needed. There would be months of gathering goods, months of building and planning, getting ready for the winter, people would have to become farmers overnight. Worse yet he knew there would be more fights, more killing, and a lot of dying yet to happen. He hoped being here in the countryside they could avoid the worst of it.

As he crawled into his tent, it was his cat Batty that made the world real. Batty just came to him purring, wanting love, a need grounded in the most basic of instincts. It was the only thing that could make Alderson feel human, to feel he could continue. This was the best thing a person could have in a time of such horror and stress. Not one thing he could think of would be easy, except maybe sleep. He was wrong about that too.

ABOUT THE AUTHOR

All Systems Down is BA Anderson's first novel. He was inspired, or perhaps driven, to write the novel as a result of watching too many post-apocalyptic movies and television shows. What drove him to write was the use of stupidity as a plot device. He felt there were too many characters too stupid to actually survive, he believed he could do better. You be the judge.

By day BA is a teacher. He has a lifelong love of martial arts and in his latter years, being too broken to be good at martial arts, he took up action shooting or as he calls it "old man martial arts". He has an ongoing interest in ideas of survivalism. He also spent many years as a role-playing gamer where he loved to test out survival strategies in the no-risk sandbox of gaming.

You can learn more about him at www.baanderson.ca.

www.ingramcontent.com/pod-product-compliance
Lightning Source LLC
Chambersburg PA
CBHW051551250626
47157CB00001B/260